Hostile Takeover

A Gideon O'Donnell Legal Thriller
Book 1

J. A. Bouma

Prologue

The woman in the plain blue nightgown living out her sunset years in room 527 had lived a simple life, with simple pleasures, in a simple double-wide on a double lot with a bed of peonies and a dog missing a leg.

And then the murders began.

Well, *murder* might be too strong a word. Killings though... definitely *that*. Whether the sin of omission kind or of *co-mission* kind, didn't matter. Not to her. Not when Herb had been one of the victims. Not when the gigolo Joe's had taken her husband from her last year.

And now, with what she found, with her friends dropping like flies...she wondered how much longer she had.

Because she'd been on a mission, for a year now. Ever since uncovering the one thing that led from Herb's thing that had brought her to the quiet comforts of the Dreamscape Manor senior care center. And now, on the other side of the thing she'd come to do—well...nothing was adding up no more. Not to nothing but a hill of beans. And she'd know.

Yessir, two plus two added up to six at Dreamscape Manor, that's for sure!

The Devil's number at the Devil's playground…

Again, she'd know, since she'd been a number cruncher, as they say. Director of a handful of number crunchers, in fact, climbing through the glass ceiling with the sisterhood of the traveling pantsuits from a different sort of era after slaving away for years as an accountant for Mercy General.

Being a star at keeping the books had honed her peepers for spotting the things others didn't peep. Worried her head off the d'mencha would descend and snatch her second love from her after it had snatched her first, but so far…

Now, to be sure, her son would say otherwise, believing the mental bug was about to send her wandering around Happy-Living Estates in the dead of night before ending up in someone else's double-wide!

It's why her son had put her up in the retirement resort.

Resort. *Bah!*

A coffin more like it. A place to go and die.

Oh, her son had sold it to her as a "community of warmth and wonder" where "golden years shine bright" and "dreams and friendships flourish" in a home of "care and connection." Suppose that's how the joint itself had sold the joint to him when he'd gone looking for answers after Herb had passed and she had wandered off the reservation. So he assumed.

A bunch of hooey was what those sappy slogans were!

She knew better. She'd *seen* better. Or worse, given the vibe shift.

Back to the killings. The *murders*, in her book.

Because the books at Dreamscape Manor were adding up right as she expected—or wrong, given the numbers she'd been able to crunch, a stack of spreadsheets smelling to high heaven! To be expected after she had set off to sniff out the carcass that had flared a righteous stench, beginning with her next door neighbor.

Maurine was her name—had *been* her name. Now, the woman in the blue nightgown hadn't never put up no fuss. So she never got the happy pills. Maurine though...hers was a cocktail that could lay an elephant flat on its back for a week, snoring to beat the band.

Until she'd keeled over during the dead of night.

Maurine plus Herb was her starting place. One plus one definitely equaled two.

Two deaths.

The murders, as those stankin' spreadsheets would soon reveal.

It's funny, because all she had wanted was a life filled with biscuits and gravy for breakfast before midmorning tea time with the ladies, followed by soup and sandwiches and euchre in the afternoon with the fellas, on toward meatloaf and reruns of *M.A.S.H.* and *All in the Family* before retiring to bed before a variation on that institutional routine struck back up again the next day.

Wasn't meant to be. Not after Herb.

And this day, the one in question had started in a way that ended in away she wouldn't have expected.

'Twas a bright sunny day, all happy and warm, with cherry blossoms outside her window in full bloom, a nest pregnant with life perched outside her window in some piney hedge that reminded her of home, the fruits of that mama bird's labor making a ruckus that reminded her of her former life, the one with her son and husband and church's ladies Bible study that hadn't seen sight of her in months. The day promised hope, light, revelation! After all, the Good Book itself promised the latter when the right sort of light dawned.

'Nothing is covered up that will not be uncovered,' Jesus

Christ himself declared in Doc Luke's Gospel, '*and nothing secret that will not become known. Therefore whatever you have said in the dark will be heard in the light, and what you have whispered behind closed doors will be proclaimed from the housetops.*'

She was that light, and soon she would belt her proclamation from the rooftops of Dreamscape Manor itself!

First things first...

She shuffled to snatch the last piece of the puzzle—so she could get the whole kit and kaboodle of pieces she'd assembled to her son. But one thing remained. One piece to the puzzle. She had to take it before she was taken down.

Or out...

Darkness had settled inside the dormant office she had been volunteering in for months. The soft glow of a monitor reflected in her wide eyes trained on the invoices and spreadsheets and numbers that added up to exactly what she had suspected.

She had to find a way to get it to her son.

She *would* find a way.

Because if she didn't...

Things could get ugly for a whole lot of people she cared about. Mill Creek Junction people.

Most of all, her son.

Neglected hinges threw up a sudden, unexpected mournful cry behind her—flooding her with a coldness that rivaled her drafty double-wide in the dead of a Mill Creek winter.

She gasped, then turned, her eyes wide with a searching glance that turned up nothing but nothing.

Just a breeze. From an open door leading out into the courtyard, perhaps, or that blasted air conditioner that had frozen her nose.

She was no boo boo the fool, taking a step, then another to scope out the intrusion. But it looked like nothing but nothing, so she returned to the monitor, sending her fingers twinkle-toesing across the keyboard in a mad-dash search for—

Another gasp. Then a grin.

That's it. There it was.

Knew it as plain as the nose on her kisser. Knew it was her.

Them...

A wide grin of satisfaction spread across the woman in the blue nightgown. Couldn't help it. Couldn't help herself. It's what she was trained for. Trained to do, to look for.

Another cranky cry flared from behind.

Followed by a rush of footfalls.

What the—

A hand clenched around her nose and mouth, firm yet soft.

No, not soft. Cottony. Like a wad of cotton balls or a balled-up cloth.

Stars instantly danced across her eyes a beat after she inhaled a startled breath.

And what was that at her—

Ouch!

A stinger to her neck, it was!

Before everything started fading to black.

In the sudden, confusing haze of fading consciousness, her lizard brain took over. Fighting, not fleeing (definitely not!). She activated to put up her dukes like the spitfire she was back in her Baltimore days.

But a tightening grip and the flaring scent of alcohol sieved away any resolve—confirming what she knew to be true. What she feared.

She'd been found out. Followed.

And—

And...

Taken care of. For good.

Supposed she shouldn't have expected anything different, anything less. When you go poking your nose in someone's pile of bulldookie, you're bound to get your nose chopped off.

Or head, in her case.

Which quickly bloomed with a thick, threatening fog.

And blackness.

Blankness.

Then—

Then...

It all faded. It all went south.

For good.

Chapter One

"Madam Foreperson," Judge Joey Heller said, "have you reached a verdict?"

I eased in a measured breath and straightened, clenching the thick, glossy Montblanc pen and massaging its rounded white star representing a snow-capped peak. Waiting, discerning, intuiting whether my record batting a thousand would be tarnished by my client fidgeting at my left.

Or strengthened.

I slid my right hand clenching the classic Meisterstück LeGrand fountain pen Dad had gifted me after graduating law school into my pocket, then rested my left on my yellow legal pad, palm flat. A ritual I had carried over from high school mock trial competitions and into law school, then into my law practice. Something to center me, the soft paper beneath my left hand and that smooth, heavy expense cradled in my right that my janitor father could hardly afford grounding me when my senses were firing on all cylinders.

And boy, were those senses firing, my brain homing in on the sights and sounds and smells of the courtroom moment.

The lemon polish rubbed into the fine oak table from over a century of care nearly overpowered by my client's fancy cologne, the cardamom and touch of vanilla dancing with delight. The sunlight flooding into the vast, stately chamber through stained glass windows casting a prismatic nimbus of secular holiness throughout the mahogany-paneled temple dedicated to Lady Justice, her bronze statue tarnished by a century of green-brown perched behind the bench. The shifting bodies on creaking pews, the stiff shoes on veined marble floors, the sniffs and coughs of a public awaiting what that foreperson held in the manila envelope I hadn't let out of my sight since the twelve women had returned—every last one of them I had been eyeing for the sort of anger that might sink my client.

Knew it was the fight-flight response tuning my nose and eyes and ears to precise calibration from the epinephrine skating through my veins, the hormone dilating my air passages to flood my body with oxygen to prep my muscles for action, and my pupils with light to spot threats, and the little hairs in my ears with blood to snatch aural indications of those same threats.

"We—" A hitch in the elder woman's throat yanked my attention back to the moment and interrupted her reply, the answer to her officiation over the fate of my client dying to nothing but nothing.

"What do you think, Gideon," my client whispered, breath stale and sour.

I ignored him and clenched the pen tighter, at first sensing that answer from the foreperson had died in a hitch, perhaps an emotional one at justice having slipped through her fingers.

Or a relieved one that justice had been served...

She coughed then reached for water, loosening my grip.

Some.

My client tried again: "O'Donnell, did you nail it or what?"

I shushed him as the woman recovered, then went back at it.

"We have, your honor," she continued, Juror Number 23, as she had been before becoming foreperson of the jury, a wildcard that managed to slip through jury selection.

There was the scuffing of a chair against the wood floor to my right, then a shuffling of feet.

Judge Heller motioned for my client to stand, a protocol that wasn't standard but a tradition the old coot had carried forward from the start of Mill Creek Junction's founding. Didn't get it. Didn't care. All I did care about was that verdict.

I stood, as did my law partner, Reggie Wilson, and my client, Gerald Peterson, who had been seated between us in a fresh suit, the faint smell of soft wool and laundry solvent thrown up as he stood, along with the Italian pomade that slicked back his long-well manicured black hair streaked silver.

I threw a quick glance over at the opposing counsel, who had scooted to the edge of her seat, a ritual I knew she'd performed since joining the prosecuting attorney's office a few years ago after moving to Mill Creek Junction from Knoxville, Tennessee. Annabelle Kirkland, who also happened to be my girlfriend.

And prosecuting my client for murdering his adulterous spouse.

Waiting, along with me, for the verdict to a homicide case that I had worked my magic to bring to a resolution.

Signed, sealed, and delivered on a silver platter.

Or, as was the case, in a manila envelope clenched tight by the foreperson shifting with glassy care. The elderly woman who had been a wildcard from the start toddled from side to side on wide scuffed pumps beneath a plump body stuffed in a plainspoken black dress. Looked ready for a funeral more than the reading of a jury verdict.

Perhaps the ill-fitting dress meant there was no chance in hell the accused was getting acquitted. A sort of reverse Johnny Cochrane aphorism at the coda of a case he would just as soon be through with. No *'If the dress don't fit you must acquit!'* in this hall of justice.

To be honest, I was surprised it had been this easy. There had been issues. Missteps. Which Annabelle wasn't in the habit of transgressing under normal circumstances. She had been a worthy opponent for a few years since moving to the Junction. It was one of the reasons I'd fallen for her, figuring if I couldn't find my equal, I sure as heck could find my better.

Took some doing, but I could admit Annabelle was her, in spades.

Privately admit, of course.

This case, though...it nearly broke us in two.

She'd accused me of "defending Junction lowlifes" before, but something about this case had set her off. On me. I had tried to pry it loose from those luscious lips of hers, but she sure as heck had kept them suckers closed through the trial. In more ways than one. I had hoped after Juror Number 23 had read the verdict we could return to our normal dating rhythm. Now...I wasn't so sure.

Annabelle's boss leaned in from behind against the wooden rail at her back in a rushed whisper. Dean Lawlor, the Junction's lead prosecuting attorney, and the biggest prick in the Mitten State. Mostly because he was the biggest prig in the Mitten State—the self-righteous, moralistic bozo who dared lecture me on legal ethics knowing how he would work the system to suit his own legal-scoring ends. I had even sued the city, too, because of those shady antics. And won.

I'd do it again today if necessary.

Had been bowled over that the man hadn't taken first chair, or even second, given the highly publicized nature of the crime—not to mention the highly *politicized* nature of it all. Probably got advice from some pair of suits suggesting the trial would roll better for the prosecution if a woman ran point, given the grizzly nature of what the councilman had been accused of.

And who the victim was.

Penelope Peterson.

The councilman's wife.

I wondered what Lawlor was telling her, what sort of last-minute order the bozo was barking in her ear after his hands had been all over the case from the start. Suppose there were good reasons, given the nature of the case.

When one of the Junction's councilmen is found skunk-drunk passed out on Main Street by one of Mill Creek's finest, and mumbles something about his wife being gone—

Allegedly, of course.

Well, brows were liable to be raised. Especially when they're part of Mayor Goodall's cast of political cronies, and the opposition aligned with the suspect has a gold Rolodex with dirt on every last one of the boys in blue patrolling Main Street and that city council, along with all the rest of Mill Creek Junctions ruling class.

Damn small-town politics.

Doubly so when the attending officer brought my drunk client home with his front door wide open and looking like he had been robbed blind.

And triply so after discovering the body of my client's wife after inspecting the premises thanks to that alarming front door.

Annabelle had called it a true Shakespearian tragedy with what was found inside. I had just called it a payday.

She didn't like that.

I didn't like it when her number had been drawn from a

fish bowl of other assistant prosecuting attorney grunts. And when the press got involved—and not the local kind, mind you, but the *Detroit Free Press* and *USA Today*, even *The New York Times* ran a piece—well, again, the whole blasted thing nearly broke us in two.

That was a month ago. And now Annabelle was sitting at the edge of her seat, I was shifting on a new pair of English tan oxfords I had bought special for the trial, the rancid smell of fried onions and kielbasa wafting from Lawlor's kisser still flapping a mile a minute.

Everyone was waiting for the jury foreperson to get to it already.

Except—

Except I had doubts. And I wondered if I should beat Juror Number 23 to the punch, intercept the reading of the verdict, and make a deal with the PA's office. Plead guilty to a lesser charge and hope for the best. Voluntary manslaughter, even murder two. Something that copped to a heat-of-passion break with reality, leading to the—well, to the slaughterhouse that had been my client's bathroom.

Had tried to coax the man into trying for the deal. Reggie had turned the screws something fierce, laying out in his own special Reggie way what happens in the "J-Max" on the outskirts of town, the state's maximum security joint as it's known. No budging and no-go on that front.

So we had rolled the dice and played the cards we'd been dealt—and hoped the odds were in our favor as they had ever been.

As the elderly woman finished another cough and sip of water, I eyed the jury. Every one of those eleven women still seated, which had been a cruel irony, to be sure. A fluke, really. Had never seen anything like it before, the way the jury pool had turned up the XYs in spades. Worst roll and worst hand possible.

And not a one of them looked our way. My way, me and my client's.

Not good Gideon Paul...

Hadn't had a good feeling about this one from the start. Not in the slightest. I'd had serious doubts whether a jury would move for a dismissal after the evidence Annabelle and her team had presented, even after pulling out all the objection and stall-tactic stops. Which wasn't so much about the evidence itself as it was the nature of the crime itself.

That's where I'd had my work cut out for me.

Again, as Annabelle had framed the whole blasted thing: a true Shakespearean tragedy.

Which was why I had also pressed Gerald Peterson to make a deal for a lesser sentence. I'd won with worse hands, but not when the rest of someone's life was on the line. And with the way things had gone down—with that bathroom!—I didn't want to chance my client's future.

Or my impeccable winning streak. Not spotless but near there. I wouldn't let this urchin sully my reputation.

The man hadn't budged an inch, even after everything that had come out at trial, on top of what had gone down the moment that blasted front door had been opened, then entered.

Which had gone down like this.

Chapter Two

The first indication all had not been right at the Peterson residence was the door itself. Which was unlocked and cracked open. With no sign of forced entry, no splintered jamb or broken glass. As if the person who had been standing on the other side of the front door had known who had rung the bell. Or worse—for both the vic and for me: the vic's killer had come from inside the house itself, only to later flee and binge-drink his life away down Main Street.

Which was exactly what Annabelle had argued, and I had countered.

But that wasn't all of it, and not the most damning. Not in the slightest.

The bloody handprint had sent the Junction cop sailing inside. Or rather, *prints*. And four-pronged streaks, racing up and down the pale walls in curving arcs following a staircase to the second floor. Like some ankle biter had plunged their hand down into a can of grape jelly and went to town. I'd seen my share of violent crime scenes, given the nature of my job as a defense attorney, but that—my client's house...

Alarmed, and understandably so with visible evidence of violence in the house, the officer had instructed the councilman to remain in the police car for his own safety before heading up for a look-see inside.

Someone cleared their throat, yanking my attention back to the prosecutor's wing of the bar table. A hissing sigh joined by an insistent *"Well?"* was followed by another wafting whiff of kielbasa-covered onion breath.

Annabelle looked like she was going to answer her boss when the clompy shoes of an old woman thudded against the scuffed courthouse wood floor. The pinched face woman with her silver hair spun up into a wicked bun stepping back to the mic.

Juror Number 23. Ready to deliver.

"We have, your honor," Madam Foreperson announced in a shrilly tone that set my teeth on edge.

"Well?" I heard Dean again in a whispered rush. Then some mumbling, beneath the breath.

That caught me by surprise.

A word, actually.

Deal.

Which sent a ping of adrenaline coursing through my veins, sending my heart lurching, a coldness spreading through my chest, and drying my mouth with the trace taste of pennies.

"No!" Annabelle said with conviction, matching Lawlor's same whispered rush, but adding a pinched brow and down-turned mouth that told her boss to back off.

He did, slinking back into the walnut wood bench that had been his perch for the last few weeks of trial that had seriously made me question my professional pursuits.

And my sanity for taking on this case.

Because after clearing the main floor of any threat, and finding no victim, the attending officer had proceeded up the stairs to the second floor, following the crimson-streaked wall toward destiny. Clearing the other rooms, he opened the door to the master bedroom.

And found nothing.

Not a drop of blood on the carpet. Not a misplaced pillow or rumpled sheet on the bed, which was still made. No broken glass or torn curtains or toppled nightstand.

Nothing.

Except for a ribbon of light cutting through the cracked bathroom door.

Which he'd proceeded toward. Then opened.

Finding a white-marbled toilet room covered in blood. Painted. Like that toddler who'd gotten into the fridge and smeared Welch's finest with giddy glee.

And a body.

Floating in grape juice.

The kind of water left over from the same kiddo who had spent a morning painting with jelly. Penelope's throat was slashed open. Not once, not twice. But three times.

Hence the bathroom doused in blood, then those streaks down the stairwell wall to the main floor. It was everywhere!

With one exception, which had played into my defense.

Because not a drop of that grape jelly had been found on the councilman.

Those two competing details—lots of blood; no blood—had played beautifully into my strategy, something I had hammered from the start.

Bloody house. Bloodless suspect.

I made sure not to reference the victim. It was the "house," *his* house, even.

Now the drunk part was tricky. So much so that he had

been passed out on Main Street. Odd part about it was that when Reggie had checked in with my best bud Max Blade as part of his recon, he claimed the councilman had never been to his bar that evening. My other associate, Elizabeth Seward, had interviewed Burt and Sheila, two of Max's employees. They confirmed the same: Councilman Peterson hadn't gotten drunk at Max's Place on their watch.

The other tricky part of the case was the fact the vic had been—shall we say, *involved* with someone else. The owner of a regional chain of auto parts stores. Which certainly gave the prosecution at least one leg of the three-legged legal stool to work with.

Motive.

Sort of had opportunity, too, given the councilman had keys to the house, and the front door was wide open, without any forced entry, and given the pair were husband and wife, so he had access to the victim. Only problem—for the prosecution, not for me—was the means part.

Again: bloody house; bloodless suspect. Best part? No knife had been recovered.

That wasn't even the biggest problem—again for the prosecution, not me, which I had hammered Annabelle on, without mercy. Felt a little bad about that. But a defense attorney needs to hammer all the nails in sight to find the one that will be the final one in the prosecution's coffin.

Between the Junction police officer keeping Gerald in the back of his cruiser and him scoping the premises—for his safety, of course—the councilman had passed out in the back seat, and Annabelle had instructed Chief Roller to take him back to the Junction police department for questioning. Which he did, and she did.

Again, big mistake.

The replay of the video from that night showed Gerald

sitting in an interrogation room of dim white fluorescent light and mint green tiles, a steel table and chair bolted to the floor. The crime scene detective, Jamie Ramos, got to work after handing him a large cup of coffee. And without Mirandizing him. Probably feared he would lawyer up, which anyone in their right mind should the minute they're hauled into a small room of white light and green tiles, a steel table and chair bolted to the floor! Regardless, not Mirandizing Gerald—

It was a big mistake.

Had been surprised by the misstep, actually, knowing Annabelle to be an uber by-the-books APA. But her misstep was my opportunity.

Ramos was a different sort. Skirted and blurred the lines of the law more than I did, which I had used to my advantage a time or two in court getting evidence submitted by Junction PD she'd collected thrown out.

Annabelle wasn't in the room, instead behind mirrored plexiglass as the woman stepped up to the plate and began slowly edging the councilman toward a confession.

Ramos began leaning into his reason for drinking, his reason for hanging around Main Street. Gerald had said he'd "had a bad day and needed to blow off steam."

Safe, as far as I was concerned.

She'd pressed him about leaving the house—when and why he left the door open. He didn't know when, and thought he'd shut the door on his way out.

Then she'd moved to questions about his wife: What was she doing when he left; he didn't know. Was she upstairs in the bathtub; he didn't know. What was her demeanor like before he left; seemed fine, but they didn't speak much. Any known associates who might want to harm her, or unknown ones who would want to harm her, enemies and such; he didn't know. Was she alive when he left the house?

None of it mattered. Only one thing did.

Which wasn't in that room. Didn't even happen in that room or at the station. It's what had happened before Gerald had been carted off to the Junction PD station drunk as a skunk on a steamy West Michigan August evening.

And had made my day. Not to mention my case!

Because while Gerald was passed out in the back of the arresting officer's patrol car, the genius had taken it upon himself to swab the underside of Gerald's fingernails for DNA when he took his blood alcohol level reading.

Major Fourth Amendment no-nos.

It was obvious to any first year law student—shoot, any freshman criminal justice major!—that the man hadn't voluntarily offered the evidence. There hadn't even been a warrant issued for the evidence. And, lucky for Gerald and me, and every other American citizen, judges tend to be sticklers about people having the right to secure their person, even the undersides of their fingernails.

Where sodium hypochlorite was hiding.

Also known as bleach.

Which does a bang-up job of getting rid of grape jelly and dissolving DNA.

And apparently had ticked Annabelle off to high heaven when she'd received a report on the matter. She'd dismounted from her perch behind the glass and marched into the interrogation room herself. Leading to Gerald sobbing before lunging for her with a red face and raised fist and raging cry.

Then confessing. Sort of.

Not his proudest moment. Especially the confessing part.

"That no good, cheating wife," Gerald had raged, "had it coming with what she'd done to me. Embarrassing me like that, making me the talk of town. With an auto parts store owner— on top of her ultimate betrayal!"

Eyes had bugged out and face had turned purple, his silvering black hair standing on edge and a corkscrew vein popping at his temple from his display of vengeance in a way no jury should ever see!

Wasn't quite a confession, but his admission could be played many ways.

One of which was probable cause.

Annabelle had held it together, stepping back toward the man. Then she read him his rights, he was cuffed, and that was that. He went limp, probably from resigned understanding, and was hauled out to spend the night in lock up.

Then the real work began—for both Annabelle and me.

Because a man raging after discovering his wife had cheated on him was one thing. But a man raging after discovering his dead and slaughtered wife had cheated on him, even drinking himself into a stupor before stumbling down Main Street and passing out in a way that smacked of remorse—

Between the DNA and the circumstantial evidence, compounded by the near-confession admission, it was definitely enough for Annabelle Kirkland to work with.

Giving me a run for my defense attorney money.

No surprise, she had charged the councilman with first degree murder, then attached second degree as a lesser included offense, given the nature of the crime. I had to give it to her, suggesting the killing of his wife had been premeditated. Definitely dicey. When I had challenged her on it she'd gotten super feisty, saying there was plenty of solid evidence to get him on it. She'd also pushed for no bail, given the nature of the crime.

Which I had obviously objected to.

"Your Honor," I'd said, "my client is an upstanding member of the community, a councilman for god's sake, who poses little risk to the Junction and carries little flight risk."

"I'm sorry," Annabelle had retorted, "but since when does nearly decapitating one's wife and draining her blood in a bathtub of hot water not pose a danger to the community?"

"Objection, Your Honor!"

"And since when do we allow murderers of any sort to roam freely up and down Main Street, even and especially politically well-connected ones?"

"Oh, come on! Should we just convict the man now without even a jury—"

"Alright, alright, you two," the judge had interrupted, jutting out his hand to us both. "Two counts of murder are rendered, bail set at one million dollars."

He dropped his gavel before I could interject, and Peterson was hauled away. But not before I stepped back up to the plate for the next swing at the ball.

"Your honor, at this time we move for a hearing to suppress as evidence any confession or admission given by the defendant while in custody."

"On what ground?" Annabelle scoffed.

"On the ground that it was involuntary."

"Are you high—"

"Alright, alright, you two," the judge interjected again. "The judge assigned to the case is Heller, so you may submit your motion with him. Until then, the suspect is remanded to Mill Creek Junction police pending bail."

Then he gaveled us again, and we were dismissed.

Not a bad start, as far as I'd figured it.

Round one went to me, which wasn't the biggest gain. But I knew as well as any attorney, defense or not, that you want the Big Mo on your side from the get-go. There's a sort of energy to a trial that begins straight away. From the time a suspect is fingered and booked and arraigned clear through the trial itself, with its witnesses and objections and cross examinations, all the way up until the verdict is read. Gave me a high greater than my days dinking around as a Junction teenager and then some more in undergrad and law school.

So winning bail, as outlandishly high as it was, was a fine way to start. The real work would come the next day with the suppression hearing.

Along with the fireworks.

Chapter Three

I hadn't wanted to take the case when I had gotten the phone call from Councilman Peterson. Had been the first call he'd made, actually, his wife having—well, "died unexpectedly," as he had explained over the phone. The couple hadn't had children, and the man didn't have anyone else to contact using his one jailhouse phone-a-friend. So I was it.

Gerald had said he knew of my reputation as a street fighter. Said my winning streak was proof positive I was someone who could "get down and dirty and do what had to be done to win." Said I was a winner, and he needed a winner—needed me, and only me, to spring him from jail, try his case, and keep him from life in prison.

"Because there's no way I'm going down for this—not after what she'd done to me!" he'd barked before bawling.

I had told him to sit tight, keep his mouth shut, and tell Annabelle that his attorney was on the way. Then off he went.

Which was odd timing. Because just that day, my associates, Reggie and Lizzy, and I had had a powwow about jettisoning our work defending people that involved blood or other bodily fluids. The work had paid well, and had been a consistent cash stream. Stephen King was right on the money: *'Just when you think you've seen the worst human beings have to offer, you find out you're wrong. There's no end to evil.'* Which meant no end to criminal defense work, especially the sort involving blood or other bodily fluids.

So there were considerations to be made, a real back-and-forth convo about the practicalities of shutting off the spigot that had kept us afloat. But the work was wearing us out, me especially. Didn't admit it to Reggie and Lizzy, but my weariness was born more from the nightmares that had surfaced from my scarred soul, literally keeping me up at night, than any moral dilemma saving the cats that clawed their way into the criminal justice system.

That, and a conversation I'd had with my father before he had passed, one the man had repeated several times over the years. It was sparked by a case brought to me by the National Fraternal Order of Police. One of their officers from Grand Rapids had shot dead a driver after a routine traffic stop went south. Like many of these things nowadays, the officer was white, the dead driver black, launching round-the-clock protests in Rosa Parks Circle in downtown Grand Rapids.

Ma had been tight-lipped about my work. Dad...well, it was understandable he was enraged, since they themselves were both black, and he'd had his own share of run-ins with Mill Creek Junction PD. As their white-boy adoptee, I understood some of their experiences with injustice. Not its depths, but enough. That case was the proverbial straw that had broken the dam that opened up the hydrant of rhetorical heat on me. Mixing metaphors, sure, but Dad had brought the big guns when it came time to say his piece that had struck me to the core, in a way his other complaints hadn't.

"'*It is not right to be partial to the guilty or to subvert the innocent in judgment,*'" he'd shouted, quoting the Good Book, from the Book of Proverbs. Channeling the Puerto Rican side of his family tree, he'd waved his arms around and clenched his fists in a fiery sermon that lived his emotions in the moment.

But he wasn't through, and neither was the Good Book: '*When justice is done, it is a joy to the righteous but dismay to evildoers.*'

He had another ready before I could get a word in edgewise: '*Partiality in judging is not good. Whoever says to the wicked, 'You are innocent,' will be cursed by peoples, abhorred by nations, but those who rebuke the wicked will have delight, and a good blessing will come upon them.*'

Yeah, that was sure convicting!

Before I could offer a well-honed retort—legal mumbo jumbo about protecting the rights of the accused and ensuring the integrity of the legal system, that '*it's easy to defend the innocent, but who is eloquent enough to defend the guilty*' (thank you Publilius Syrus!), and my fave: '*a doctor would never deny a patient because he is too ill and a priest would never turn someone away for being too full of sin, so a lawyers should not deny a client because they are guilty*'—all of which I'd recited to rationalize my work, often (mostly?) to myself. Before I could get to all that, Dad had beat me to the punch with his own retort.

"'*Many seek the favor of a ruler,*'" he'd quoted from Proverbs again, "'*but it is from the Lord that one gets justice.*'" Then he leaned in and explained, "the Lord knows, Gideon. The Lord knows who is guilty and innocent, '*for human ways are under the eyes of the Lord, and he examines all their paths,*' as Proverbs again reminds. Those clients you represent, and your own representin'—the Lord sees all!"

Then the kicker: "'*One who justifies the wicked and one*

who condemns the righteous are both alike an abomination to the Lord.' Why do you want to participate in what God detests as an abomination, Gideon?"

I wasn't all that religious. Hadn't been to church in a long while. But the idea that God was seeing me defending rapists and murderers, corrupt managers and police officers, and that he detested my participation in their acquittal, in justifying their crimes—well, let's just say I was close to having my own come to Jesus moment.

Except—

Except the money was right. So was the price, and I'd worked out a deal with Councilman Peterson to keep him out of prison if he paid up. And boy, did he pay up. Which had reinforced a running dilemma I had tapped to hold off actually walking down the aisle and getting baptized a little while longer.

I had long ago made peace with the Devil's bargain of taking on "defending the lowlifes," as Annabelle had accused, so I could get the large, sure-thing payouts to fund the cases I really cared about, to fight for real justice for the little guys. That's what I told myself, anyway. Most days I bought my bull.

Today wasn't one of them.

Except this case *was* right. Because of the glaring prosecutorial and police procedural misconduct that I had bet would make it a slam-dunk win. For my record, sure. But for my innocent client.

Obviously.

And even if he wasn't innocent, wasn't there something to be said about fighting for the *system,* holding the powers-that-be accountable, and all that jazz, given that glaring prosecutorial and police procedural misconduct?

Again, I wasn't sure I was buying my own bull. Even at the hearing.

"All rise," the court officer had intoned, nine o'clock sharp the next morning. "This court is now in session by the honorable Judge Joseph Heller."

"Yes, yes, yes," Judge Joey Heller chittered before settling his thin frame into his overly large black leather chair, "be seated, and what not."

The judge was a colorful character who was the butt of many jokes among the Junction legal community.

"What business is being brought before me this morning?"

I stood and announced, "Gideon O'Donnell, representing Councilman Gerald Peterson. We have a motion to offer."

Predictably, Annabelle threw me a wry grin from across the aisle before scoffing, eyes locked with a smirk on the judge.

Who asked, "And what motion is it you, well, come offering?"

"To suppress his confession," I replied, eyes similarly locked without a smirk. I was serious, and my locked jaw said so. "At trial it is wholly unreliable and coerced, given it was made by the defendant while so intoxicated by alcohol that he lacked the mental capacity to make it voluntarily."

Annabelle folded her arms and shook her head with a muttered, "That's real rich. Even for you, Gideon."

I didn't blanch, but tightened my jaw. Heller *ahh-hemmed* and glared at her before motioning for me to continue.

I did: "I call the court's attention to the fact that the evidence indicates the defendant was obviously intoxicated during the time the arrest took place and throughout the interview and interrogation. Consequently, the court should find the defendant was not mentally competent to waive his constitutional rights at any point. On top of that, we move to suppress the DNA evidence gathered while my defendant was passed out."

"This is a waste of the court's time, Your Honor!"

Annabelle had complained, jumping to her feet. "Routine DNA swabs are common police procedure and the fact the man was three sheets to the wind isn't a matter of law. The councilman was fully cognizant and aware of his surroundings during the duration of his interrogation and was well aware of what was happening at the time he all but admitted to butchering his wife!"

"Oh, come on! He admitted nothing. And besides, it was basically coerced, given his drunken state. And in no way, shape, or form did my client give consent to have his person searched and his DNA seized, much less have the option to assert his Fifth Amendment right against self-incrimination!"

Heller had done one of his comical chittering sounds behind pursed lips and waved a hand. Then he leaned back and stroked his scrawny bare chin, replying, "I must say, Mr. O'Donnell, I agree somewhat with the prosecution here. What precedent do you have for such a maneuver?"

I had been ready for that one.

"*People v. Knedler*, Colorado 2014, found that a defendant's level of intoxication at the time of the Miranda advisement is relevant to a waiver's validity, and that he may be so intoxicated that he could not have made a knowing and intelligent waiver—"

"But it ultimately concluded," Annabelle interrupted, "that the totality of the circumstances adequately established that Knedler's decision to waive his rights was informed and deliberate."

A surprising defense, catching me off guard and drawing a sideways glance I regretted. She'd smirked and held her head high. Like she knew she'd just scored.

"Yes, Ms. Kirkland, that is true..." Judge Heller replied, leaning back in his chair and casting a long gaze at the ceiling— before tapping his nose and snapping his beady eyes to her behind tiny spectacles clinging to the end of it and bringing home my bacon: "But I don't find the totality of the circumstances adequately establishes Peterson's decision to waive his rights through his self-confession was informed and deliberate."

That smirk had sieved to nothing but nothing before she sucked in an audible breath. "Excuse me?"

"That's right. I'm granting the defendant's motion to suppress."

Tried suppressing my own smirk of success, but one slipped. I quickly recovered and went for the jugular.

"In that case, Your Honor, I move for an immediate dismissal, given the fruit of the poisonous tree doctrine would surely be at play here."

"Is not!" Annabelle objected, actually adding a foot stomp, as if throwing an exclamation point at the end of her exclamation. "We have crime scene evidence and eyewitness testimony that will place the defendant at the victim's residence."

"You mean his own house?"

"We also found secondary trace elements of the victim's DNA on the defendant—"

"Trace elements—they were married, for goodness' sake! Of course you'd find—"

"Can I finish?"

"No!"

"Yes, yes, yes," Judge Heller interjected. "You both have mounted a vigorous rebuttal, but I've heard enough. The motion to dismiss is denied. I find enough cause to proceed. Trial starts in a week."

The gavel fell before Annabelle could object and the race was on to find the crime scene evidence and eyewitness testimony I needed to keep my client from the clink and my record spotless.

But the evidence presented at trial posed a problem.

Footprints left behind from the councilman in the bathroom put him at the scene. At least his shoe size and shoe print. Somehow, the traces of blood under his fingernails, as well as the trace chemical compound of bleach, got admitted. Knew the Supreme Court had ruled such routine non-invasive swabbing didn't violate the Fourth Amendment, though I would use it on appeal, if it came to it.

Then there was the neighbor. Oh, the neighbor!

Who claimed hearing raised voices, then a long string of silence, hours in fact before the councilman came stumbling out of his house drunk as a skunk. Annabelle had even gotten testimony of the affair, putting the lover up on the stand for all to see and hear.

Then there was the arresting officer. Who had not only heard Gerald moaning and groaning in his patrol car. There were those seven words that shouldn't have been admitted, yet were.

Amounting to a confession on top of the one I had suppressed.

'I can't believe my baby is gone.'

Annabelle had replayed and replayed those seven blasted words till they set my teeth on edge! And probably the jury's...

'I can't believe my baby is gone.'

And that's how she ended. With that testimony of the officer who found the councilman passed out on Main Street jibber-jabbering that seven-word near-confession.

Except—

Gerald Peterson's lawyer wasn't just any small-town shingle.

He was Gideon Paul O'Donnell.

I had muscled through my own defense, leveling the DNA evidence with masterful hypotheticals with the medical examiner that pried open a window of reasonable doubt about the double helix. Problem with juries these days is they think they know it all because they've binge-watched umpteen-some seasons of *Law & Order* or *CSI*—the original plus Miami, New York, Cyber, and Vegas! And when they hear "DNA evidence" they think slam dunk.

Except it isn't, especially in one's own house, and with one's own wife. Even if he might have killed her.

Allegedly, of course.

Then I raised all sorts of possibilities with the eyewitness who had heard the alleged arguing all from an open window across the street. Then grilled the arresting officer that the man could have been mourning the loss of his marriage after drinking half a bottle of Courvoisier cognac. What man wouldn't drink himself silly after his wife confessed her undying love for the auto parts manager from across town?

"Very well," Judge Heller said, snapping me from the cinematic run-through. "What say you?"

Time for the verdict.

I slipped a hand back into my right pocket, returning to that smooth, heavy talisman. Hoped it was good for more than marking up legal pads and offering my John Hancock.

Here we go, Gideon Paul...

Time stopped.

Which that blasted jury box leveraged to snag my attention again, my lizard brain that had kept my ancestors alive for millennia taking in those eleven faces again from Mill Creek Junction's finest pool of people less savvy enough to get out of jury duty.

Before darting to Annabelle again for a second read.

She shook her head and muttered something back at Dean Lawlor, who frowned and flared his nostrils.

Looked like the deal was off the table.

The foreperson fumbled with the manila envelope, slipping a chipped navy-painted nail inside the sealed flap and struggling to break it loose.

Opening a window for me to make my final move.

And final shot.

Chapter Four

I leaned over to my client, whispering in a rush, "I think I can get you fifteen years. Ten with good behavior."

Councilman Peterson offered a weak and confused "Huh?"

Another glance toward the jury box told me I was right on the money mark with my Hail Mary. Not a one of those other eleven jurors looked our way as the wheels of justice lurched toward the verdict. The window opening up by the clock's merciful *tick-tick-ticking* gave us a helping hand while the woman struggled.

And the sands of time sieved to nothing but nothing.

Along with my opportunity.

"Time's almost up," I replied lowly. "And this fiddling with the envelope is the sign! The universe has thrown you a bone, Gerald. Pick it up and let me take it to the APA. I'll say you're ready to plead guilty to voluntary manslaughter."

Didn't believe in that hooey for a second, the universe's signs and what not. But I knew the councilman was into that sort of woo-woo nonsense, manifesting his not guilty verdict and all with Tibetan tea rituals and burning lemongrass, probably while smoking the other kind.

"Are you taking crazy pills?" my client hissed, drawing narrowed, scornful eyes from Judge Heller.

"Keep your voice down!"

Juror Number 23 offered an embarrassed laugh as she continued wrestling with the envelope, the top slowly coming apart in papery crumbles and prolonging the agony.

But also the opportunity.

I returned to Councilman Peterson: "Dead serious. I'm not sure we've got this one. With those seven words. Those twelve jurors. Who haven't given us one passing glance."

Now Gerald gave the jury box a glance, and frowned, furrowing his brow and draining of color some.

"I can sell voluntary manslaughter," I rushed.

Had to talk fast and convince even faster. This might actually be the most important rhetorical moment of the entire trial: convincing my client of his guilt! That pleading guilty and going to jail was his best option.

"You acted during the heat of passion, under circumstances that any reasonable person could understand would cause any reasonable person to become emotionally and mentally anguished. To the point you couldn't reasonably control your emotions."

Judge Heller blew an irritated huff through pursed lips and waved the bailiff over to assist the foreperson with that merciful bone tossed into open court by the universe.

Which meant the window was closing. Fast.

"Come on, Gerald! Tick-tock, tick-tock."

A relieved sigh sounded from the front, followed by ruffling paper.

From the jury box.

Where the elderly woman had stuffed her hand down

inside the mangled envelope, then yanked it out, holding a yellow single-sheet and wearing an accomplished grin.

"Just say the word, Gerald."

My client snapped wide, blood-shot eyes to me above a mouth gaping as wide, as if filled with a bazillion questions.

"Say the word and I'll hustle up to the APA and make a deal. Signed, sealed, delivered before the foreperson reads the verdict."

Those eyes narrowed, that mouth snapped shut, and that face drained of color quickly replenished with a raging red that sent an electric charge of confirmation racing up and down my spine.

He'd done it. No question.

And it looked like he'd sever my own head if I didn't back down.

"How about we start over?" Judge Heller said with a chuckle and a wide grin, echoed by the room.

"I'd very much like that!" Juror Number 23 said with a sighing chuckle of her own.

Another chuckle from behind, joined by a warm laugh from the judge's perch. Straightening, he jutted his arms out to let his robe settle around him before setting his hands on the desk and scooting closer.

"Madam Foreperson, members of the jury, have you reached a verdict?"

"We have, Your Honor."

"Very well, what say you?"

I flashed my client wide, searching eyes again. Getting nothing but a hard, scowling stare.

Fine. He'd made his decision.

And his bed.

The crisp crinkling of paper snapped my attention back to the jury box.

Where the foreperson eased chunky black glasses chained to her neck onto her face, adjusted them, and held out the yellow single-sheet for the reading of the verdict.

Here we go, Gideon Paul...

Moment of truth.

I clenched my pen tighter after replaying the crazy from the past few weeks. The money sure was worth it, if not the thrill of the chase and rush of the defense.

None of it would add up to a hill of beans if that slip of paper held by that woman and decided by those women delivered the big NG. Neither the thrill nor the chase, because Gideon Paul O'Donnell played for keeps, and those keeps weren't playing for unless I won.

Certainly the money wouldn't be worth it, given the bulk of my fee was contingent upon me winning. And without that win, which Councilman Peterson was more than happy to pay to avoid J-Max and the horny roommate waiting for him inside —well, without it my practice was toast, not to mention my next case, the real one.

Slumming it as a fly-by-night defense attorney these years had taken a toll. I'd managed to keep my head above water well enough, making sure my associates were paid, and even enough to cover my own salary and pay my mortgage and eat out at Max's Place from time to time. I'd built up a solid reputation as a reliable defense attorney who'd score the big NG, on top of winning enough liability and insurance suits to offer alternative cash streams.

But those streams had begun to sieve away to a trickle, and the sort of defense work that was my bread-and-butter wasn't enough to cover all the bills. They would probably be shut off anyway if Reggie and Lizzy had their way, and my conscience.

Sure, the stupidity of humanity was reliable enough to keep other cases coming at a reliable clip, even the occasional blood and fluids ones I'd been loath to keep taking. Yet springing people from the clink for driving under the influence and reducing simple possession charges, drafting wills and moderating divorce proceedings, even handling neighborly disputes and wrongful terminations—none of it was enough. It was all just one hamster running wheel that gave me a run for my fruitless bolder-pushing money. I was Sisyphus in a suit.

Which was why I was behind on the rent due on my office, and the landlord had sent that final letter threatening to turn off the juice to my lights, and, and, and...

Hence this murder case. Which really wasn't about this case. Definitely wasn't about the jerk shifting at my left in that Old World suit that cost more than my mortgage payment.

No, this one was like the books Big New York Publishing fought tooth-and-nail to acquire. The James Pattersons and Stephen Kings, the Nora Robertses and Janet Ivonoviches—even those trashy celebrity memoirs, the cookbooks by people who'd never cooked a day in their gilded life. Those guaranteed bestsellers, with their six-figure advances and seven-figure sales payouts, were about the other books, the *real* books Big New York Publishing wanted to publish that never earned out the cost to pay the author and print the books. The stories that move people to tears and the deep-dive studies that motivate governments to get their acts together.

This case was that. It was about the next case, the *real* one, which would die before it got started if I didn't win this case.

And I couldn't let that happen.

Not for those class action plaintiffs. Not for Ma, even for Dad, though he had passed. Definitely not for them, that dear couple who had rescued me all those years ago...

A cough, then a clearing of the throat, then a searching grope for water again.

To which I heard another whispered reply that sounded like "Are you sure?" from Dean Lawlor.

There might still be a chance if the Big Kahuna was pestering his underling to fall in line and make a deal with my client.

A slurpy sip, then: "In the matter of the *People versus Gerald Peterson*—"

"Gerald?" I tried again in a hurried hiss.

Which was only outmatched by an almost equally hissing "Shut up!" from my client.

Supposed that settled it.

"—in the matter of murder in the first degree, we, the jury, find the defendant—"

Moment of truth.

A breath. An agonizing beat.

Then—

"Not guilty."

Had I heard her right?

Not guilty?

The air fled the room in a gigantic gasp of disbelief, the vast hall of mahogany and marble not computing what had just happened. Signaling I'd for sure heard right.

She continued, "In the matter of murder in the second degree, we, the jury, find the defendant—"

Juror Number 23 interrupted herself, swinging her gaze from the yellow single-sheet over to me and my client. A penetrating, hard, misty-eyed stare that signaled resigned regret.

Then again: "Not guilty."

Time and sound hung in the vacuum of the chamber's collectively held breath at the dual not guilty verdicts.

Then the floodgates opened, gasps and commotion, shuffling and actual motion rushing into the maw of disbelief.

My eyes snapped to Judge Heller, who looked as surprised as I was. While my ears heard the faint sounds of whimpering and groaning with the same disbelief.

Right before I glanced at my opponent.

Who just sat, statue-still.

I barely registered what came next. It was all a muffled blur of sound and motion, all around.

"Gerald Peterson," the judge announced, "you have been found not guilty of first and second degree murder. You are free to go."

To which Peterson threw up a victorious *"Huzzah!"* and laugh, clapping his hands together and yessing me on a job well-done.

"Thank you, members of the jury," Judge Heller went on, "for your service today. This court is adjourned."

The loud smack of wood against wood, then a mournful "All rise. Court is adjourned" from the male court clerk, snapped me back to the moment.

I didn't know what to do, how to act—what to feel, even. Supposed I should be grateful for the win. Peterson sure was, clenching a solid, relieved hand on my shoulder, slapping my back and offering a round of I-told-you-sos before spinning dumbly for direction.

Before my client wandered off, the bailiff sauntered over. I explained the man would take him to fill out paperwork, then he was free to go. Gerald left without even a thank you. Good riddance.

"Don't know how you did it, bro," Reggie said, shoving papers in his briefcase and shaking his head, "but you yanked the rabbit outta the hat again."

"Yeah you do," I replied, a wry grin rising at one end of my mouth.

He stopped his paper-gathering and looked at me, cocking his head with a raised brow like Reggie always did when he was confused.

"I am vengeance. I am the night. I am—"

"Yeah yeah yeah. Right right right," Reggie interrupted. "Gideon Paul O'Donnell."

"You know it."

He sputtered his lips like he always did when I used that line, my favorite line from my favorite comic-book character.

Batman. The caped crusader's motto.

As a boy, I had fantasized about flying from Mill Creek Junction rooftops and lurking in the night's shadows, leaping to the rescue to run down a purse snatcher or banging some bank robbers' heads together after following them to their warehouse lair.

Now look at me. Defending the very scum I had wanted to string up from a Junction lamppost for Mill Creek's own Harvey Bullock, a very young Chief Roller at the time, to nab and jail. I let my smile fade at the thought.

I stuck my hand in my right pocket and looked around the courtroom, avoiding Penelope Peterson's parents hunched and clenching one another in their rumpled off-the-rack Kohl's special dress clothes. My hand clutched my Montblanc, my gut clenched with a dose of regret. Then my face flushed with embarrassment, taking a beat too long to move on as her father glanced up with wet cheeks and bloodshot eyes, staring me down with a fixed, agonized face.

Swallowing, I spun back toward the front to gather my things, when I caught sight of Annabelle again.

Just sitting, still and unmoving, eyes fixed on Lady Justice.

Didn't know whether to move on and move out, the professional in me figuring it best to take my win and get on with my day. Or walk over and ask how she was doing, the boyfriend in me figuring it best to offer a reassuring word. The latter seemed the way to go, on many levels.

So, clearing my throat, I slipped beside her, letting my Montblanc go before withdrawing my right hand and gently resting it on her shoulder. She didn't move, didn't even blink.

I bent toward her ear and offered, "You win some, you lose some, Annabelle."

That startled her, and I caught an updraft of warmed lavender, joined by her flushing neck. Which jolted her and snapped her eyes from Lady Justice to my own, her face twisted up with anger. Sure hope she didn't think I was sticking my win in her face!

She stood and spun toward me, the chair flying out from underneath her with a sudden scrape before thudding against the back wood railing with an echo that caused me to startle backward.

I took in a sudden breath, even as I took in her face that matched her reddened neck. Looked like she wanted to slap me, she looked so furious! Might, too.

But she didn't. She held steady, held her hands at her side.

Until—before I knew it, my face was wet, and the front of my navy pin-stripe suit coat was soaked as well. And Annabelle was holding an empty water glass and a scowl that meant business.

The room gasped, joined by a few chuckles.

I didn't know what to do, and neither did it seem Annabelle. Her boss, Dean Lawlor, sauntered over with a satisfied grin. Smirking, he gently tugged her toward a retreat.

"Come on, Kirkland," he said. "Not worth it."

Annabelle set the glass on the table, spun from my grip, and strode down the aisle of scuffed wood and through the exit, Lawlor in tow.

"You alright?" Reggie asked from behind.

I brushed away the water from my suit, reminded that I really, really, *really* hadn't wanted to take this case.

"Never better..."

Chapter Five

A guy gets 525,600 minutes a year to make something of himself. To make his mark on the world. All before biology takes over, or the randomness of life events, and you're rotting in a pine box six feet under.

After all, as Saint Paul wrote somewhere in some letter to some church somewhere: *'the days are evil.'* The wise Teacher from Ecclesiastes upstaged him in the nihilism department: *'Utterly meaningless! Everything is meaningless!'*

Word.

Last thing I wanted to spend those meaningless, evil days on was springing drunks from the clink and getting murderers off on technicalities. Most days, that's how I felt. Knew the only way for justice to work for all was if it worked for the lowlife. Equal justice under law, and all that jazz, as the Supreme Court's face declares.

Yet sometimes I had serious doubts about my chosen profession. Beach bum looked mighty appealing many days.

Like today, after that verdict. And yet—

Yet this day wasn't like those days. Not anymore, not with Peterson out of the way.

Those ambulances and drunks and murderers were in the far view of my rearview mirror hustling down Courthouse Road toward Main Street. For this day was payday. The real one that would put Peterson's stack of Benjamins to shame. Or would be soon, once I got to court and nailed those bastards.

I yanked the sleeve back to my suit, a custom-made blue pinstripe I bought from some Main Street-adjacent shop in London last summer. A jaunt with Annabelle, my competition whom I had just bested, the Junction's assistant prosecuting attorney on top of my girlfriend.

Talk about awkward courtroom drama. Especially after what had just gone down.

Hopefully cuddling on the couch over wine and a home-made veggie pizza would more than make up for it later that evening.

I smiled at the thought. Then sucked in an aww-crap breath when I realized the time. Had a deposition with Happy-Living CEO in an hour, the final piece to the payday puzzle. Then there was final prep for the trial of my life, and certainly of Mill Creek Junction's century.

Which didn't leave much time for the breakfast I hadn't gotten before trial thanks to a power outage that ganked my alarm. Even then, I couldn't stomach anything more than an apple until the morning verdict was read and over with.

So I put my new Johnston & Murphy money where my fancy shoes were and hiked it toward destiny.

Starbucks.

Hey, Mill Creek Junction might be small town, but it wasn't backwoods.

I smirked. Mill Creek. Never in a bajillion years would I have thought I'd be making a life for myself here. But after today, after my win, besting Dean Lawlor and Annabelle, which I knew I'd hear about later, but still—well, I was feeling like I'd made the best decision ever moving back home to set up my small-town law practice.

Mill Creek Junction never looked so good.

I hustled the few blocks from the courthouse down to Main Street, hanging a left down toward the Starbucks next to my law office. I much more preferred independently owned joints, something Annabelle and I shared, but it was what we had.

The corporate cafe used to have more of a local vibe, having been owned by Mayor Chet Goodall's wife, Millie, as a second cash stream aside from her Millie's on Main diner. But they ran into trouble when someone sued them after getting scalded by hot coffee. Yeah, a replay of that charade from the '90s and Mickey Ds. I had actually represented the plaintiff, and the parties had come to a settlement, but the whole thing bled the Mayor and Millie dry. She didn't want to have anything more to do with the business, so I helped them sell by acting as a broker between them and Big Coffee Shop. Was happy Millie had made out big, letting her pay off the plaintiff and walk away with some spending money.

A wind whipped from behind, shaking towering hedge maples and American elms lining the main drag slicing through my childhood hometown. It was sort of nice, the breeze chilling the summer air that had roiled to a West Michigan boil. And a steamy boil at that!

Almost as bad as a DC August. My V-neck would stick to me waiting for the Metro bus outside a subdivision in Northern Virginia for my legal internship at a lobbying firm on K Street in the city. Already at 7:00 a.m. my nice white collared shirt would show sweat marks at my chest and pits. No wonder the Founding Fathers had quickly devised the whole August recess scheme for Congress, those suits representing the Fifty Nifty getting out of the marshy hinterland of the nation's capital real quick for safer (and cooler) ground.

There it was again, a clear cold front gaining purchase on the Junction I didn't mind one bit. Except if it screwed up my day, which had suddenly dimmed, the bright orange morning sunlight now a muted, muddy gray.

Continuing my hustle, I glanced behind. And frowned.

Yep. Cold front. The charcoal shelf clouds were still a ways off but gaining a head of steam. Looked like a UFO hovering somewhere between Grand Rapids and Coopersville.

Definitely a storm brewing off Lake Michigan and barreling toward the Junction. Wouldn't be long before it reached Mill Creek.

And ruined the rest of my day!

I scoffed and kept at it, shaking my head at the thought.

Never took much stock in those old sailor idioms. Red sky at night, sailors take delight; red sky in the morning, sailors take warning. Was much more of a captain-of-your-ship kind of guy. Our life is the creation of our mind, as Buddha was reported to have quipped.

Same for our day, the creation of which was a combination of gumption and ingenuity and bootstrap-pulling, which no woo-woo phrase of nautical yore could derail.

Except—

Reaching the heavy wood door anchored to the face of the Siren, I crossed myself anyway before slipping inside. Which was sort of odd, snatching for the childhood religious ritual from a faith I hadn't practiced in years.

With a day like today, and with the road ahead, I could use any help I could get!

A rumble of thunder shuddered through the place of exposed wood and brick. It was a quaint little thing that bespoke its Midwest roots stretching back to the founding of

Mill Creek Junction back in the late 1800s. Was almost sad I'd had a hand in Big Coffee's hostile takeover, swooping in all Joe Fox like to capitalize on my lawsuit that had brought down the little guy—or I supposed gal, according to my Kathleen Kelly metaphor from *You've Got Mail*. Either way, another piece of Small Town, America, had lost its soul thanks to me. Which was a bit ironic since I was the guy who had fought for the little guy or gal!

I was a sucker for Starbucks, like many Americans, but sometimes Corporate America really sucked. Yet a triple-shot americano was calling my name.

"Hey, Cameron," I said to the college kid with large silver gauges working the espresso machine. He was nodding along to AirPods stuck in his ears with a crown of blond hair stuffed under a gray knitted cap.

The kid offered a saluting greeting then got back to slinging drinks. I saddled up to the register and ordered a bagel and my drink of choice. Just espresso and boiling water. None of that sugary, creamy froufrou nonsense for me. I handed the older woman a Jackson and told her to keep the change, which she tried to refuse but I insisted.

I imagined the woman toasting my bagel as my mother. Couldn't imagine her having to work well into retirement. Supposed that was the American way now, late-stage capitalism shackling folks to a lifetime of indentured servitude while Wall Street fat cats retired behind gated communities in Boca Raton and Coral Gables.

Finishing, the woman thanked me again and handed me my raisin bagel, an extra thick layer of cream cheese piled high. I took it and wandered toward the end of the bar, phone in hand to scroll through email, hoping my day hadn't blown up.

Saw some press inquiries from the local Junction rag asking for comment after my win. No thank you! Then some notice from the landlord with double red exclamation marks, a final notice that sent me chomping into my bagel. Double no thank you, not until Peterson's check cleared. I saw a missed call from Ma from yesterday evening. Missed it while I was prepping for court. Probably about the impending trial. Maybe to re-litigate our disastrous convo about it, what she said she wanted to do. And my own boneheaded response...

It would have to wait. All of them would. Because first things first—

My bagel and triple-shot americano.

Waiting for my drink, I spied an abandoned copy of the local newspaper lying lazily on a table by the window and snatched it. Sitting, I chomped into my bagel and turned to the sports section that ratcheted my ticker some before putting a smile on my face.

They won. Against the odds!

My odds. The ones I'd placed on my team the night before.

Minor League Baseball. The West Michigan Whitecaps.

It had been a nice 78 degrees, lounging under a cloudless sky. A Johnsonville brat in one hand, sizzling hot and scarred by black grill lines, a Blue Moon in the other, an orange slice floating on the top and adding a touch of citrus tang to the wheat beer laced with a sweetness and spicy finish. With a game that had stretched into a 10th inning overtime that looked like it was the craziest ending ever!

Now there was a profession worthy of a second chance at life, if there was such a thing.

I had ducked out at the bottom of the seventh with my team up one-to-zero. Because, you know: worst career move ever! Some drunk had blown a point-two on the outskirts of Mill Creek. Over twice the legal limit for alcohol in Michigan. And just my lucky night, I'd been snagged by some judge with no life but the law and assigned the case.

Lucky for me, thanks to my bet, I might be able to retire from my life of legal purgatory earlier than I thought.

Long game short: my West Michigan Whitecaps were tied up at three. With bases loaded, three balls, two strikes, and two outs. And it all came down to a fella with a .106 average.

No pressure or anything!

Lucky for my up-to-bat fella, dude was on the shorter side. The pitcher was on the taller side. And that last throw was about even with the batter's noggin.

So ball four and game over and a win for Grand Rapids.

From the accompanying picture, the crowd had gone wild. Fireworks went even more wild. And I wore a smile that eased the day's burden some.

That's what summers are all about, right there! Baseball and game-winning pitches against the odds. Hanging with family and friends till sunset, a hot dog in one hand and a cold drink in the other.

And sports bets that would pay for this trial.

"Well, well, well..." a familiar voice sounded from across the cafe, snagging My attention from my paper. "If it isn't the Junction's Superman himself."

Didn't even have to look up. Didn't want to. Knew that voice from anywhere. The last voice I wanted to hear.

From the last Junction person I wanted to see.

But I did anyway, glancing toward the voice and frowning. There she was.

Tracy Nolland, editor-in-chief for the Junction's only newspaper, the one I was holding, *Mill Creek Junction Guardian*. My face started to fall, a few awkward memories of our on-again-off-again dating surfacing.

I cleared my throat and smiled, especially at that laughable rag name. Had to be the most pretentious small-town newspaper moniker ever, which she'd inherited from her grandmother. Wasn't there some daily Brit rag across the pond called *The Guardian?* Shooting way above the Junction's pay grade, that's for sure.

A tall ginger in her mid-30s with icy eyes and a refined nose, Tracy wore a tight-fitting navy dress and a chunky gold necklace and those killer legs of hers. A crimson hair clip clung to the back of her head, holding up her normally long, straight hair. She held her head high with confidence like she owned the town. Which she sort of did, being the go-to source for Mill Creek gossip and used to getting her way, given how she could make or break deals and careers, even marriages if she got the right source and you pissed off the right people.

Mainly her.

Which meant I had to tread lightly.

Chomping another bagel bite, I returned to my phone, mumbling, "I am vengeance. I am the night."

"What are you going on about, Gideon?" she said, sidling up to my table, a whiff of rose petals rising above the heavy scent of roasted coffee beans and hazelnut syrup dominating the stuffy air.

Pecking out an email, I replied, "Batman."

"Ahh, yes. The caped crusader, come to set the world right."

"And avenge the wrong, with justice."

Tracy snorted a laugh. "Like the stunt you pulled in court?"

"What stunt?"

"The one where you got a murderer off?"

"Allegedly!"

"Allegedly my—" She let the retort die with an eye-roll.

"Justice was served, alright? You heard the bull MCJPD pulled."

"And Annabelle?"

I returned to my phone. "She didn't have anything to do with it."

"That's not what I heard?"

That got my attention.

"What's that supposed to mean?"

She folded her arms. "You can read about it in my trial coverage in tomorrow's *Guardian* edition."

I laughed. "All the news I need to know from that trial is what I made in that courtroom."

A buzzing vibration snapped me back to my phone.

Dreamscape Manor. Where Mom was staying.

Went to take it, but Tracy intervened, tapping a single, well-filed fuchsia nail on the wood table.

"So, are you ready for trial?"

I set my phone down and leaned back, crossing my arms now.

"No comment."

She frowned. "Oh, come on! We used to date back in the day. So that basically makes us family."

"You wish! And you know why we stopped."

She leaned in, one end of her mouth curling upward. Thought she had some snappy retort ready, but she bypassed the saucy in favor of the juicy.

"There's a rumor."

"What rumor?"

"That HappyLiving is about to settle with a majority of the lot holders. Any truth to that?"

A ping of adrenaline snatched my breath and twisted my gut. That rumor, if there was any truth to it, was news to me. If it was true, it would completely blow apart my case. The whole blasted thing was contingent on the residents of HappyLiving Estates acting as a class, with a majority rendering the lawsuit null and void.

"Triple-shot americano for Giddy?"

I snapped my head toward the bar and frowned.

"*Giddy?*" Tracy said with a snorting laugh.

Saved by the barista. But—

"Cameron!" I said with a huff, snatching my phone from the table and shuffling to the bar to snatch my drink. "It's for me, for crying out loud. You know, your regular customer?"

"I know. Just like it better."

I shoved my phone in my pocket and swallowed back a slurp. The thick, muddy espresso shots were a bit watered down but still held their earthy, caramel goodness.

"The irony of it all, you know? Giddy Gideon. Never the twain shall meet, to quote the good Rudyard Kipling."

"Gee, thanks, pal. See if I ever bail you out again next time you're caught driving while reeking of weed."

The jab was lost on the kiddo who had returned to those AirPods of his.

"He's got you there, caped crusader," Tracy said.

"Whatever."

My pocket buzzed again, and I retrieved my phone.

This time it was the mother ship.

Saved by the office.

I answered it, getting a "Where are you?" in reply.

"Hey to you, too, Lizzy."

"You coming in or what?"

"On my way."

I ended the call and explained I needed to do some prep work, then left.

Didn't tell her then, but it was for the HappyLiving CEO deposition that afternoon.

Just hoped it was still on...

Chapter Six

The breakfast crowd was just winding down when Johnny Pope rolled up in his F-150, the vacant tables and just-finished ones mocking him through the large picture window to Millie's on Main at the heart of Mill Creek Junction. The proprietor of the joint had been something of a mistress going on a decade now, on account he'd come every morning for her tasty breakfast dishes, without fail. Sort of like the postal service, come rain or shine.

Not today, and far later than he could afford with the amount of work on his plate. He was confirming a development in a case for his main client, Gideon O'Donnell. While most guys his age had lived for retirement, golfing and building model cars and whatnot, he still lived to live. Still lived like he had when he was a priest. Helping people, righting their ship when it bent toward hell, working for justice in a world mowed over by the wicked heart of mankind.

Only instead of hearing confessions, he sussed out leads as a private investigator.

And now it was a quarter past ten, the day nearly finished,

as far as he was concerned. Couldn't believe he'd overslept. Must have hit his alarm off instead of snooze, which was unlike him. Blamed it on a wicked headache, compounded by a sinus infection. Hated getting sick, period. Especially in the dead of August. You're already feeling like crap, sweating to beat the band, and then you've got to deal with a Midwest sauna, the consistent 90s marked by 90 percent-plus humidity. Then you've got the chills and don't want to flip the switch for the air conditioner, which his craftsman bungalow didn't have anyhow except for a bedroom wall unit.

Didn't matter how he felt. He had a job to do. And felt guilty for the morning mishap, cursing his old sack of bones for needing more of the Zs than he'd ever needed before. Getting old sucked.

Had prided himself as being one of those guys who was up before six most days. Usually around five, if he could swing it. Nothing like getting a leg up on the day before it went stale. Besides, he couldn't stomach letting the day go to waste on something as silly as sleep. Never understood people who slept in, snoozing their alarms a dozen times until they finally mustered up enough self-worth to drag their sorry rears out from under the covers to tackle the day.

Blamed it on his Catholic guilt, his aversion to sloth courtesy of the seven deadly sins, the clock a constant reminder of our fallen nature. Perhaps that was it. But Johnny Pope had a hunch it was more than that, a dyed-in-the-wool Catholic from birth who had once kissed the ring of Saint Peter as a mini Vicar of Christ, serving the parish of Saint Thomas the Apostle as Father Papadopoulos just up the road from Millie's on Main.

It wasn't just guilt. It was taking seriously the human propensity toward vice at every turn, and how easily our flesh bends toward vice when the lights go dark. *'And do not bring us to the time of trial, but rescue us from the Evil One'* was part of the Lord's Prayer in Matthew's Gospel he prayed with the fervency of a Pentecostal.

Yes, the irony wasn't lost on him.

But still...he knew the Devil roamed the earth. *'Like a roaring lion your adversary the devil prowls around, looking for someone to devour,'* as Saint Peter himself wrote in his first letter. And the morning was the Devil's playground as much as the night.

Sleeping in was gluttony compounded by sloth, pure and simple. And now it was a quarter past ten, and he had visions of Sisters Helga and Hepsiba from grade school dancing in his head, grabbing both ears and bellowing for him to wake up and pay attention.

Where was a priest when he needed one.

Supposed that was him. Or had been him until he'd hung up his cassock and handed in his clerical collar. Sort of like a cop turning in his badge and gun.

A mug of coffee and a hot breakfast would have to do instead.

Johnny hoped it would assuage both the wicked headache and lingering guilt, but something told him not to ask too much of the Most Important Meal of the Day—even from Millie's fine fare, which was the best darn breakfast a guy could get in the Junction.

Putting the old dog in *Park*, he donned his black fedora and climbed out of the Ford's cab. Left the trench coat for another season, but he did take a well-worn paperback he'd picked up at a local used bookstore and his weapon. No, not one of those pedantic Glocks yuppies kept in their bedroom safe for hoodlums and rabble-rousers. A Colt M1911. Yup, they still made them suckers, a single-action, recoil-operated, semi-automatic pistol he got to know personally slinging 45 ACP rounds at commie Charlies for Uncle Sam in Nam.

That was then. Now he just concealed the thing under his trench coat or displayed it at his side. Michigan was both an open carry and concealed carry state, which made it easier to do his job. Didn't have a shiny badge to go along with the gig. But his criminal justice undergraduate degree from Notre Dame came in mighty handy, meeting one of the requirements for licensing in the Mitten State. The other being a US citizen (check) and over 25 (definite check, having started the second career just before his sunset years), along with his employment for *O'Donnell and Associates*.

Speaking of which, he had work to do. But first, some breakfast.

Walking through the front door, a familiar jingle announced his arrival as a pair of working hands headed out. Probably to Warner Farms on the outskirts of town, where the historic windmill still turned amidst a sea of vegetables sitting right alongside Mill Creek, which was more like a river, giving the Junction its namesake.

Taking a deep breath, Johnny felt better about the day now. Couldn't help it, what with the smell of freshly ground and brewed coffee saturating the air, compounded by melted cheese and frying bacon and baked biscuits and flapjacks that could feed the lumberjacks that had roamed these streets over a century ago when the town was founded. Now he was smiling, and his throbbing headache wound down to a dull ache, joined by a rumble in his belly. Food would do wonders for his mood.

Waiting for a hostess to seat him, he eyed a stretch of wood benches near the door that served as a waiting area. And spotted a newspaper, facedown. He picked it up and turned it over, then frowned.

A *USA Today*. It would have to do.

"Johnny Pope!" a familiar voice bellowed from behind. An itty-bitty, high and heady voice attached to an as itty-bitty woman with gray curls and fair skin and killer lips that surely melted the hearts of a few high-school quarterbacks in her day.

Johnny turned around and grinned. Millie on Main herself.

"Hey, Mills," he said before sneezing into his forearm.

"Yikes! You sick Johnny?" she asked before leaning in all conspiratorial like. "It's not the ro, is it?"

He snorted a laugh. "Hope not. Feels more like a cold."

"Sure does bite the big one getting sick in the summer."

"Sure does bite the big one getting *old*."

Millie laughed. "Can't argue with that. Here, I've got just the thing to make you better."

She grabbed a menu and a set of flatware rolled up in a cloth napkin.

Johnny said, "You don't have to throw out the red carpet for me, coming to greet and seat me yourself."

"Aww, I wouldn't have it any other way, seen as how you're my best customer and all. Wouldn't miss catching JP before I headed out for the morning."

"Best be careful, or Chet's gonna get jealous. And then I'd be in some serious doo-doo with the mayor himself."

"Ha! Jealous? You wish, hot stuff." Millie motioned for him to follow. "Your usual spot?"

"You know it."

She led Johnny toward the back across the black-and-white tiled floor through the wide dining room looking like a diner straight outta childhood. Basically preserved what had been here from before he was born when she took over the joint. Complete with chrome seats at a counter near the kitchen, baby blue- and pink-patterned booths along with steel tables and chairs. Which he much more preferred than the booths.

His spot was right near the back at a big picture window along a side street jutting off Main Street back toward a neighborhood with turn-of-the century craftsman homes. In fact, the one where he and his late wife, Lynn, had first bought their own newlywed abode when they got hitched after he'd returned from Nam. Hadn't lived in it since she died and he left for the priesthood. And when he came back and got the gig at Saint Thomas's up the road, a parsonage had been provided on the church grounds that made the home up the road moot anyhow. Sold it and stashed the cash in an IRA that had been paying dividends ever since.

Johnny sat down with the *USA Today*, and Millie asked if he'd like the usual, eggs and bacon and unbuttered wheat toast, but he said he wasn't sure and she handed him the menu before leaving to fetch a cup of joe. Black. None of that hippy cream and syrup nonsense. Definitely no grande this or americano that. Just a good ol' US of A cup of black mud for him.

Johnny set the newspaper on the table and wrenched his wrist up for a look-see at his Benrus watch, a holdover from his days outside Chu Lai. Just a simple thing, the DTU model, with a woven olive green strap perfectly shaped to his wrist now, stained by decades of sweat, and white hands set against a black background. Loved it only because it was a reminder he had survived that crazy-awful war.

It was nearing eleven now, near midnight in his book. A tragic waste of the day it was, sleeping in, the morning nearly over. Threw off his whole ordering scheme. By the time Millie returned with a sufficient cup of joe, black and steaming and smelling of caramel, he decided against a heavy breakfast and went for eggs Benedict.

She scrunched up her face, making a sucking sound through pursed lips. "We ran outta ham, darlin'. Sorry about that."

"Again? I seem to recall this merry-go-round a few months ago. What kind of joint you runnin' here, Mills?"

Johnny threw her a wry grin. She threw him a punch into his left shoulder.

"Got the thin stuff for lunch if you'd like that instead of the Canadian-style bacon we normally use. Or salmon again."

Now she threw him a wry grin. He snorted a "No thank you!"

Recalled the last time this had happened, and he'd opted for the Benedict—*with salmon*. Came with capers and a sprinkle of dill. Not at all to his taste. Didn't tell her, of course. He muscled his way through it and told her it was "a real interesting take" on the classic dish, one of his go-tos he'd discovered on the West Coast before shipping out to Nam, vowing secretly never to touch that sort of thing in whatever years the good Lord above had set.

Johnny said the thin stuff would be fine, but Millie said she'd had an idea, something extra special. Knew he could count on her for a good breakfast, no matter what that might be.

Except for salmon eggs Benedict.

After she trotted off to make his meal, he reached for his *USA Today* and huffed a sigh just thinking about it.

Who the heck ever thought ham should be swapped with salmon should be shot. Probably some commie pinko from back in the East, or some commie pinko wannabe hippie from out West. Them types were always messing with a good thing, trying to progress what history had settled generations ago for some newfangled version that was less regressive, less offensive, less blah-blah-blah.

Now he snorted a laugh and just shook his head at his cranky complaint. Boy, was he an old coot or what? Was far too set in his ways to swap ham for salmon. Even thin-sliced deli-style ham was a stretch for his old tastes.

Whatever. It was food, for the road ahead.

The Gideon O'Donnell road ahead.

Waiting for his food, Johnny scanned the headlines. And frowned.

Taiwan had been run over, apparently. Fully in the mighty claws of the Dragon. Which the stock market didn't like, shedding almost double-digit percentages on all three major indexes yesterday. And now a new bird flu variant was settling in along the unsecured Southern Border.

Nothing but what the King James Bible preached in Matthew's Gospel: *'And ye shall hear of wars and rumors of wars: see that ye be not troubled: for all these things must come to pass, but the end is not yet. For nation shall rise against nation, and kingdom against kingdom: and there shall be famines, and pestilences, and earthquakes, in divers places. All these are the beginning of sorrows.'*

What's the saying? If it bleeds, it leads?

Was pretty much the business model of every cotton-pickin' paper from sea to shining sea.

Johnny had another King Jimmy chestnut, this time from John the Seer's Revelation: *'Come, Lord Jesus, come...'*

He tossed the paper to the table and reached for his paperback. A John Grisham. *The Street Lawyer*. Seemed appropriate for his current profession. Before he could crack it open, two chatty Cathys approached from the rear. Or Kens, as was the case.

Johnny glanced behind, giving the two suits a once-over as they approached and settled in at a table behind him.

And actually, matching suits. Tan three-buttons (were those coming back into style?), with stiff, dry-cleaned white shirts and wide, shiny ties. Looked like the Robert Talbott's Gideon wore. Lavender with light pink flowers. Probably 7-folds, their trademark high-end ties, with their hand-rolled ends and seven folds of silk.

The men clearly weren't from around here. Both Asian,

hair black and skin complementary shades of bronze and porcelain. One was built like a linebacker, the other more like an office worker.

They started gabbing about the weather and how the Holiday Inn up the road was no Ritz-Carlton.

A couple of elitist blowhards, they were.

Any retort on his part was intercepted by his eggs Benedict turning up, care of Millie herself. And—was that?

"Is that corned beef?" Johnny asked, eyes wide and mouth salivating for the salty meat.

"You know it!" Millie said, setting down the dish.

Johnny grinned wide. This was going to hit just the spot! His stomach rumbled in agreement.

"I know it ain't your normal, but you look like you needed to liven things up a bit."

He chuckled. "Sounds about right. Thanks, Mills. Looks like you've outshined yourself again!"

She laughed and demurred, patting him on the shoulder before turning away and calling back, "Enjoy! Let me know if you need anything else, Johnny, you hear?"

"Oh, I will!"

Johnny stabbed his egg, orangey yolk spilling across his pink corned beef. Smelled like heaven, the buttery, lemony hollandaise sauce soaking the homemade English muffin the size of his palm. Cutting a piece of the bread with his fork, he stabbed a piece of poached egg white and scooped up the corned beef smothered in sauce and yolk, then shoved it in his mouth.

He melted at the combination of it all—the salty, spicy, slightly sour meat joined by the bright lemony butter sauce and rich egg yolk. Sent his tastebuds dancing, it did!

"*Privet, rebyata,*" a woman from behind interrupted his Nirvana, voice husky from a few packs a day.

Speaking a language Johnny hadn't heard up close and personal in over five decades.

Russian.

Stiff, patent leather shoes clattered on the tiles as the two men stood to greet the newcomer.

"*Sonyusha,*" one of the men said. "*Kak vy?*"

Sonya. How are you?

Ballsy to speak the language of America's on-again-off-again then-back-on-again enemy in such a public place.

Such a small-town Midwest place.

They quickly sat and got into it. His corned beef was no longer appetizing.

He pretended to eat, picking at his food with his fork. Mostly, he just took sips of coffee and stared outside, hoovering up what those real commie pinkos behind were saying—and translating what he had translated for Uncle Sam in Nam.

And now for Gideon O'Donnell.

None of it sounded good. Could seriously mess up his client's case if things proved true. He kept listening, kept taking mental notes to relay back to the boss and his crew. They were going to want to hear this.

First things first...

Eggs Benedict with corned beef and his Grisham paperback.

Appropriate, given what it sounded like they were up against.

Chapter Seven

The building for my law practice was sweltering by the time I arrived, the dead-of-August heat pressing in like crazy and thickened by those midnight storms that continued to swell.

Did our air conditioner fritz out?

If it did...what a way to start the day at the office after the win. Add to that preparing all night for trial against Annabelle Kirkland later in the week, yet again, and something knocking around under the Audi hood—and, well, it was going to be one of those days.

Wet wood hung heavy in the hallway, the midmorning humidity compounded by the floorboards left over from the 19th century. At least the hallway smelled of coffee. Not the tin-can kind, mind you, but the coffee shop variety, the vents from Starbucks next door working about as well as they usually did, but probably compounded by the heat. Not that I minded. On top of the grande triple-shot americano I was holding, the strong coffee scent alone should do the trick to smack me upside the head and wake me up, the air itself probably laced with caffeine.

And at least my name was on the door to the office.

O'Donnell and Associates.

I stood in front of it holding my white grande cup bearing the green Siren, one end of my mouth curling upward at the sight of that gold ink set inside thick black edges in a sort of old-school banker-like serif typeface that hearkened back to Mill Creek Junction's early days, the text set against frosted glass and arched with just the right amount of curve, a judges gavel set underneath in a sort of exclamation point that emphasized the justice I offered my clients.

Scratch that. *Brought* my clients.

Not so bad of a day after all. Especially after scoring that mega NG verdict!

Credited Dad with the whole thing. And not just the graphic arts job that rivaled the best in the business.

After graduating law school, I'd hemmed and hawed over my next steps. Georgetown Law, where I'd spent three years slaving away in Washington, DC, wasn't the top law school around. But it wasn't the worst either, tying for fifteenth with Cornell and Vanderbilt and University of Texas-Austin. Could have gotten into some decent lobbying firms in the city, even a banking gig up the East Coast. None of it sounded appealing. I'd even caught a dose of Potomac Fever for a spell, putting out a few feelers on Capitol Hill, but politics made my stomach turn. And I thought I was better built for solo work anyhow.

When I had brought up my misgivings and trepidations with Dad, he suggested I start a private practice back in the Junction. I'd literally laughed out loud at the suggestion. Taking the solo-practitioner plunge was attractive, but I'd vowed never to return to West Michigan after fleeing for grad school. Yet there I was, a ring to his suggestion that seemed true. Seemed alright, seemed meant to be.

Wasn't much of a praying man anymore, so I'd spent a weekend along the Appalachian Trail hiking and camping and weighing it all. And when I made it back down the trail to my Honda hatchback, the plan had been hatched, so to speak.

When I finally made the decision to return home to Mill Creek, Dad had put his graphic design know-how to work and fixed me with the shingle anchoring my front door. It had started as a hobby a decade back before it turned into a side hustle after he lost his job at the farm during the Great Recession. Which lasted another few years before they were able to hire him back before laying him off again and he'd picked up a job as a custodian with some large West Michigan outsourcing firm. Thankfully, Ma had her job at Mercy General—not nursing, accounting—but things had been tight for a while, and Dad's graphic-design side gig had made up part of the difference.

And there that difference was, staring me in the face after the morning win, sweat beading down my forehead now grasping the burnished bronze doorknob to my office thanks to the August stuffiness that still hovered in the wake of those rain storms. Where was a polar vortex when you needed—

The door suddenly opened.

And Lizzy screamed in my face something fierce. Which sent me jumping back with a startled yell. And then Reggie joined in the fun behind her.

Then she lunged forward and smacked me in the chest with a manila folder, nearly sending my grande triple-shot americano to the scuffed wood floor below.

"Oh my heck! What are you doing creeping up on us like that!" she said before breaking into a giggle. "Nearly scared the pants off me."

"Creeping up? I own the place!"

"Rent, more like it," Reggie corrected with that deep baritone voice that was so effective in court, but not what I needed coming in hot and frightened myself. "Which apparently don't count for much, since it's hotter than an Easy Bake Oven and we don't got no air!"

I frowned and shoved past the pair, taking my triple-shot americano and memories into the back office, which wasn't saying much.

I shouted back: "Don't worry, I'll call the landlord and straighten things out. Besides, we just won big! Which means a big payday is in store."

My practice was really just four walls and another two for my office slapped together to separate the main area from my own humble work abode. Two windows, blinds drawn, peered into the larger space of carpet the shade of mint Listerine from another century ago, walls white and blank and begging for some love with two dented wooden desks shedding their stain from sometime last century where Reggie and Lizzy slaved away for far less than what I made, which wasn't saying much.

I closed the door behind with a thud and set down my drink on a desk piled high with manila folders spilling bent and misshapen papers. At least it all was shaded by pulled blinds, but what it shaded wasn't much better. The same century-ago wood desk bowed under the weight of too much work, a laptop anchoring a corner from back in college and a few thick hardback books, their old cloth fraying at the edges. The heat hovered with the same menacing molestation as the hallway and outer room—clawing its way into my mouth and esophagus and lungs, it was so bad.

I loosened my tie and unbuttoned the top of my shirt, wishing to the Great Siren I would have sprung for an iced coffee instead. Or at least an iced version of the ten-dollar concoction threatening to pass me out with every sip. I slumped into my well-worn leather chair, a gift from Dad when I had opened up the joint, saying a workin' man needed a good chair. Popping the top to my americano, I closed my eyes and savored the earthy scent, then took a sip. The smooth yet spicy liquid fell heavy on my tongue, making me hotter.

Definitely should have gone for an iced coffee.

There was a knock at the door.

Another sip, then: "Come in."

The door opened, and in walked Reggie and Lizzy. Actually, Lizzy first and then Reggie. She glanced back at him before pushing her long blond hair behind her ears, her mouth closed tight, lips pursed, eyes not making contact. Same for Reggie, his bald head glistening under the pressure of the fritzed-out air conditioner without saying a word.

Uh-oh...

I took a breath, then a beat, then another swig of the espresso and water concoction. Then willed myself to take another, knowing I needed the jolt to get me through whatever was coming next.

I leaned back, the chair creaking in protest. "Hey, guys. What's up? If it's about the air conditioner, I was about to call up Tom right now and get things—"

"It ain't about that," Reggie interrupted, still looking at the floor.

Not good.

Another sip, another breath.

"Then what's this about?"

He stepped forward, not looking back at Lizzy and now fixing me with determined eyes. Guess it was his meeting, then.

"Gideon, we need to talk."

My heart sank, and bowels went with it, a cold dread spreading through my veins. Which were pretty well spent after the adrenaline roller coaster from the morning courthouse events.

Reggie's tone and timbre told me he meant business. And now Lizzy was looking at me too, face whiter than she'd been with lips still pursed.

Definitely not good.

I sat forward and took another sip, the liquid barely cooling under the oppressive heat, but forced down the gulp, my tongue having formed a sort of callous under the amount of coffee I downed each day. Then I motioned for them to take a seat in a pair of crimson velour wood chairs. Before I realized they were piled high with more detritus of my law practice. More folders, more books, a stray brown paper lunch sack stained with grease.

I reddened and offered a sheepish smile, embarrassed at the mess. How had things gotten that bad? Standing, I cleared a path then motioned for them to sit.

They did, and I went back to my desk, mumbling: "It's hot as Hades in here."

"Yeah, that's why we're here, my man," Reggie said, slumping down to my left. Lizzy followed, twisting up her long hair now behind her head and shoving a pencil through the pile to make it stay. She looked at her folded hands in her lap, saying nothing.

The look she wore reminded me of a middle school English teacher I'd had. A shiver ran up my spine at the memory of her shrilly voice and those nails that dug into my arms whenever I misbehaved. Mrs. Byrne still gave me nightmares!

I cleared my throat and swallowed. "What do you mean? What does the heat have anything to do with why you're here?"

Reggie said nothing, glancing at Lizzy, who looked up in time to meet my eyes. She cleared her throat now and offered,

"It's Tom, Gideon. The landlord. He's...well, he's shut off our utilities."

The news thudded in the middle of the room like my shiny bowling league ball. I recalled that double-exclamation email, which I would fix. Which I *could* fix now that the Peterson trial was done and won.

Except—

This is about utilities? And they're shut off?

Felt some relief at the news. Thought they were going to ask for a raise or something. Or worse: get up and walk out of my practice.

But then I glanced around the office, noticing for the first time the place was darker than usual, no lights on. My printer was off, as was the green banker's lamp sitting at the corner of my desk opposite my laptop. Didn't dare reach for the brass string hanging down to check it. Knew exactly what I'd find.

Nothing.

Almost grinned with relief knowing utilities could be fixed. But their still-determined faces made me stuff my relief in a sack for now.

Because whatever was going down felt deeper than a dark, superheated office.

I swallowed and shifted in my chair, not returning to my coffee. Couldn't stomach adding to the adrenaline rush surging through me again after coming off from the morning high.

"I'll call Tom right now and see what's the matter. Surely there's a reasonable explanation—"

"We know what's the matter," Reggie said, interrupting again. I took a breath, drawing back his pursed lips as if mustering up the strength for what came next. "Rent's late. Again. Three months now, in fact. And not just late. Behind. Almost four months now, in fact. Which leaves Lizzy and me wondering what the heck is going on here."

Busted.

Now, any normal person might suck in a startled breath at the revelation. They might offer a tell or a reveal in the movement of their eyes or mouth or nose, a hand reaching for an ear or to rub their forehead or scratch the back of their head, their heart pounding and chest rising for more air and heat clawing up the back of their neck until it bloomed across their face with reddened revelation. Something to show weakness, to show they'd been caught or at least exposed.

Not me. I was Gideon Paul O'Donnell. The best blasted attorney in Michigan. I knew how to hold a face.

And win.

I said nothing, for a few seconds. Then another set until I swallowed and leaned back, mouth sandpapery from dehydration—from the caffeine and confrontation, compounded by the hot-as-Hades heat threatening to keel me over.

The day had started so well, with scoring another win. Now this?

Could the day get any worse?

Chapter Eight

I cleared my throat and said, "Where did you hear that?" About the only thing I could think of saying in response.

"Straight from the horse's mouth. I got off the phone with Tommy after trial."

Tried wetting my lips; it was no use. An unfortunate tell, but one I had to give because my mouth was a parched desert. I seriously needed water.

"And what did he say?" I asked.

"That you've fallen behind rent. After having a spotty payment schedule to begin with."

"Gideon, what's going on?" Lizzy finally said. "Are we going under, or what?"

I shook my head. "No, it's not like that."

"Well, then are you embezzling?" asked Reggie.

An angry heat flashed up my neck and bloomed offense in my cheeks.

"No," I said firmly, insulted the man even went there. "It's not like that, either."

"Then what is it like, Gideon?" he asked, voice rising in a way I usually appreciated, because it meant he was closing the deal in the courtroom.

Now...not so much.

I stood, darting for a black mini fridge left over from college, weighed down by another pile of folders. Buying time but also seeking relief.

I crouched and opened the door, visions of hydrated saturation dancing in my head.

A single Dasani sat alone in the warm, empty fridge. Had to be a metaphor in that somehow for my own lot in life.

I grabbed it and twisted off the top, bringing it to my lips.

Only to realize the other two were probably just as thirsty. I hesitated, glancing their way, but they both nodded for me to have at it.

A twinge of guilt wound its way through me, but not enough to stay my hand. I took the bottle of hydration back to my desk, gulping back the blessed water before slumping back in my chair.

"So?" Reggie said, mouth open now and sweat dribbling down the side of his clean-shaven head he seemed to be ignoring. Was clearly more focused on me and my answers, or lack of them, than his own discomfort.

And for good reason.

I had gone silent because the man was exposing something I'd long known about, but was too ashamed to admit.

I went with: "I've just fallen behind paying, that's all." It was the truth. I had.

"Fallen behind?" Reggie sounded exasperated.

"Three, going on four months' worth?" Lizzy added.

"And several times over?"

I was getting hot under the collar now. And not from the

blasted air conditioner being taken out of commission. Time to come clean.

"There's been a cash flow issue on and off all year."

Reggie twisted up his face in confusion. "All year?"

"And when that blasted virus hit, things became more precarious."

"But that can't be all of it," Lizzy said, "because we've been getting paid just fine. And there have been some decent settlements lately as work has picked back up."

Work had picked up. Which was part of the problem, trying to keep my head above water with some new clients and big cases, on top of getting our names out there to drum up new business, a hamster wheel or rat race or pick the analogy that was running me ragged.

"Hello, Gideon?" Reggie asked, voice laced with annoyance.

I startled and took another swig of water, then snapped back a "What?" he didn't deserve.

He looked at Lizzy. "I said, what's the deal then, if we're getting paid but you can't make rent?"

"Like I said, cash flow."

"But—"

"I'm bad at administration. So sue me!"

"But that's so unlike you, Gideon," Lizzy said. "You're a powerhouse. That's why we came to work for you."

"Yeah, Gideon, what's happened?" Reggie added. "What's the root of it, then?"

"The root? I can't do it all, Reggie!" I finally yelled, exploding under the weight of the interrogation and suffocation of the heat. "That's the root of it!"

I instantly regretted my outburst but didn't know what to do. So I threw back the rest of my Dasani.

"Hey, Gideon," Lizzy said, scooting to the edge of her seat, "no one is asking you to!"

"Yeah, my man," Reggie said, voice low and buttery and apologetic. "That's why we're here. To help."

I took a breath and sighed, leaning back in my chair. "I'm sorry. Sorry for the outburst. And thanks for the support. I'll do better next time."

"Do better?" Lizzy asked.

"I'll catch up on the payments, sending out what we owe. I'll set a schedule and get back on track. Don't worry. I've got this."

Lizzy smiled and looked down at her lap, then back at me. "But that's the thing, Gideon. You don't."

I was stunned. Too stunned for words.

"Other things have been falling through the cracks."

"Such as?" I said quickly, coming to my defense and regretting it.

She took a breath. "Such as...follow-up calls to new clients not happening, follow-up with long-time clients not happening. Some of the—"

"Alright, I get it."

She looked at Reggie and nodded. He nodded back, and he leaned forward.

"And, well, that's part of what we want to talk about." Reggie shifted in his seat, clearly getting ready to go for the kill.

And I was the prey.

"Oh, yeah?" I said. "What's that?"

Reggie didn't even wait a beat. "We want equity."

Just like that. That was their demand. To own a piece of what I had built.

I was stunned. Too stunned for words, for a second time. Literally. I couldn't get anything out.

"Partners?" was the only thing I could manage.

"Not in equal measure," Lizzy added, shifting back into her seat and pushing back a stray lock of hair. "But something. We want skin in the game. And we want to help. Help build the practice, help you manage it all."

I scoffed. "Help? You want to own the game, you mean."

She went silent. So did Reggie.

Humming traffic outside was the only soundtrack for the tragedy. Or comedy, depending on the perspective.

"It's like the Book of Ecclesiastes says, Gideon," Reggie said, finally breaking the silence.

"Please don't quote the Bible to me right now, Reggie..." I moaned, taking a swig of watered-down espresso to dull a pain beginning to needle the middle of my forehead.

"Naw, man, you need to hear this. It's not preachy Scripture, just some wisdom my mama would remind me of from time to time. *'Two are better than one,'* it says, *'because they have a good reward for their toil. For if they fall, one will lift up the other; but woe to one who is alone and falls and does not have another to help. Again, if two lie together, they keep warm; but how can one keep warm alone? And though one might prevail against another, two will withstand one. A threefold cord is not quickly broken.'"*

I paused, glancing at Lizzy, who continued: "That's what this is about, Gideon. Building this unbreakable cord, the three of us. Together. In this fight for justice, for our clients."

She did have a point. As much as I didn't like the idea about giving up control, about no longer going it alone, managing it all had become a burden. The oppressive heat was Exhibit A on that one.

I went to respond when something caught my eye across the room, anchored to a wall struggling under the weight of sagging bookshelves.

A framed one-dollar bill.

The first buck I had made at my practice, before Reggie and Lizzy had joined as associates.

There'd been a lot of sweat and sleepless nights and even some tears since that first buck I'd been paid. Had won a whole heck of a lot of cases, but the field had been tough to hoe too. Clients had walked out and left me high and dry. Others I'd picked up on retainer. Immigrants and their jobs and families had been protected. Wrongfully accused murderers had been spared life sentences—gotten a few questionable ones off on technicalities, too, but it was in the interest of upholding and preserving civil liberties. Then there were the settlements and judgments I'd gotten from hospitals and corporations for negligent disregard and wrongful termination.

The list went on. All thanks to that dollar bill sitting behind that dusty glass in that cheap bronze frame.

Then it hit me, in a way it hadn't before. Because that wasn't the truth of it. The full truth, anyway.

Two are better than one, because they have a good reward for their toil...

All that toil, all those other dollar bills since that first one, was because of the pair sitting across from me. Problem was, I hadn't let them have a share in the praise and honor of it all.

A strand of three cords, huh?

One end of my mouth curled upward, something melting inside at the thought. Maybe it was my hard heart or thick head from being confronted and getting exposed. Probably that, but it was more. Less about embarrassment from exposure, more about possibilities from partnership.

I stood, shirt sticking to my back now and feeling like I was about to pass out. I walked toward my office door then motioned for my associates—for my *partners.*

"Let's take a walk."

The cooler air hit me like a welcomed hug outside. Not as

stifling as my office, but the air was still warm and stale and hanging with a pause. I took in a breath, old carpet and paint combined with roasted coffee and stacks of photocopies all combining to remind me what this was for. More than the smells and feel of the place was what I saw.

Two desks piled high with cases, surrounded by more boxes and file cabinets filled with more cases—wins and a few losses, but mostly wins—the whole place manned by two co-laborers fighting for justice with everything they had.

What more could I ask for?

What more could *Mill Creek Junction* ask for?

"See this place?" I said, motioning around the room with both hands. "After law school, I came back to the Junction on a whim thanks to my old man suggesting I set out on my own and chart my own course and see what happened. Well, this is what happened. But not thanks to me."

I turned toward the pair still standing behind me at my door. "Thanks to you two. So, yeah, you more than deserve an equity stake." Then I smiled. "You both deserve to make partner, as little as that might mean in this modest practice."

There was silence, as if Reggie and Lizzy hadn't heard me right.

Then they also broke out in smiles, their mouths widening into toothy grins of thanksgiving, a cheer rising from them both before they reached out with an embrace.

My throat grew tight with a surprising rise of emotion. I laughed at the display, especially since they were all soaking with sweat now. But it didn't matter.

They were partners, or would be soon enough once they completed the paperwork. But more than that, they were family—a word that hadn't always sat right with me as an adopted white boy, left at a firehouse and raised by two black parents who gave me the world. Had still carried baggage from that piece of me, my soul feeling incomplete in some way from my personal history.

That moment reminded me that I had all the family I'd ever need with the people in my life.

"So, what do we call ourselves?" asked Reggie, leaning back and getting down to business. Always one to cut the bull and get to it, which was why I liked him so much.

"You mean which order should our names go in, right?" I replied, one end of my mouth curling upward.

"Obviously by level of seniority," Lizzy quickly offered, "with Gideon's name at the front."

"Makes sense," Reggie said.

"*O'Donnell, Seward, and Wilson*, then?"

He took a beat, then smiled and nodded. "I like the sound of that."

"Me, too!" Lizzy replied, her grin returning, wider.

"Taking on that knucklehead Prosecuting Attorney Dean Lawlor and whoever else wants a piece of our justice! The three of us together."

I nodded, a grin of my own spreading. "Yes. Together."

Mill Creek Junction wouldn't know what hit them.

"Can I just say," Reggie said, "the time seems as good as any to crack open Gideon's bourbon."

I laughed. "What bourbon?"

He sputtered his lips. "Don't what bourbon me! The bottle of Wild Turkey you've got hidden away in your desk drawer."

Now I sputtered my lips. "Wild Turkey is for HappyLiving Estates."

Lizzy hit my arm. "That's not classist at all!"

I yelped. "Hey, I grew up there!"

"Doesn't make it any less classist! Besides, they're our clients."

"Suppose you're right."

Reggie cleared his throat, wiggling the brow of his wrinkled bald head and nodding toward my back office.

Now I smiled. "Yeah, sure. Right this way."

My office was still dark, but I knew where I kept the good Irish stuff. Kneeling, I snatched the premium bottle of Redbreast whiskey from my bottom desk drawer, almost tasting the lush fruity spice and oaky notes. Reaching for three glass tumblers—

My phone buzzed in my pocket, interrupting the party. Withdrawing it, I saw it was a five-alarm text from my mother.

"*CALL ME!* 911!!!"

My gut plummeted.

Nine-one-one.

Code for emergency.

Except it was dated yesterday. Had I missed the incoming text? More than likely it had been my cell service. Dang thing had been acting up for months.

Either way...

My mind immediately snapped to that conversation with Tracy Nolland. The one about the class action lawsuit I was representing, with my own father as chief plaintiff.

And the rumor.

Surprisingly, standing in that sweltering office, my veins ran cold. A chill at that rumor—*HappyLiving is about to settle with a majority of the lot holders*—sent a shiver ratcheting through my spine.

Swallowing, my mouth chalky, sandpapery, I turned to my new partners.

"Are we still on for today, with the HappyLiving CEO? Th–Th–The deposition," I stammered.

Lizzy crossed her arms, scrunching up her face and jutting her head out like an ostrich, like I was a crazy.

"No...I emailed about that this morning. Didn't you get it?"

"What email?"

"The one about them needing to reschedule."

A sudden thudding knock at the door intercepted the cursing reply that was on the tip of my tongue.

Then another. More insistent.

"Gideon O'Donnell," someone barked, then: "It's the Mill Creek Junction police department. Open the door!"

Chapter Nine

Did I hear that right?

MCJPD, at this office door—*my* door? *The Law Office of O'Donnell and Associates*, soon to be *O'Donnell, Seward, and Wilson, Attorneys at Law?*

Pounding at the door—like they were about to pound it down?

Did not compute. Not in the slightest.

"O'Donnell, open up. MCJPD. We need to talk."

Definitely heard that right that time.

And definitely still did not compute.

"Say *waaa?*" Reggie said, throwing me that raised-brow, cocked-head look of his.

Lizzy just laughed. "You must have hit a real nerved at trial to get Dean Lawlor to sic the boys in blue on—"

A thud, then a crash, followed by shattering wood echoed through the hot, humid hallway.

Sending me leaping to my feet and spilling my americano across my desk.

"What the heck?" I shouted, not paying the mess any mind.

Just as several pairs of feet pounded through that darkened, sultry tunnel.

Our way. *My* way.

Three of those boys in blue Lizzy mentioned were storming through the newly minted law office of *O'Donnell, Seward, and Wilson*—followed by two more in back with a few more suits trailing.

Weapons outstretched and aimed for the lawyers huddled in my office with wide eyes, mouths opened with a bajillion questions.

The quintet yelling for Lizzy and Reggie and me to raise our hands and stay where we were.

We were quite the Three Amigos, hands up and shouting for answers, sweating to beat the band from the assault on top of the heat.

The lead officer barreled inside, bypassing Lizzy and Reggie, storming around the desk for me, clenching a meaty hand on a wrist and wrenching it behind my neck.

Setting off Reggie and Lizzy with shouts and screams to take his hands off from me.

I joined the same demand: "Get your hands off me!"

On instinct, I twisted around to meet my new friend.

Bad idea. Worse move.

Before I knew what was what, I was kissing my desk, right cheek and hair soaked with spilled watered-down espresso. Thankfully cooled, but still.

I struggled under the weight of the rotund officer, one elbow jammed good and tight into my spine holding my one wrist while the other arm wrenched the other back behind. I put up a fight, against my legal instincts and own client counsel. Couldn't help it. Something baked into my lizard brain from ancestors past battling mastodons and outrunning saber-toothed tigers surged through me.

The will to fight, to survive, to live.

To figure out what the heck had just sent Junction PD storming into my office and sitting on my backside!

"What the bleep is going on here!" exclaimed Lizzy, colorful language for her.

"I'll tell you what, *amiga*," a voice echoed, joined by more clomping shoes.

A woman's voice. Latino.

From the trial.

Distracted, cold steel suddenly slapped against my skin. Followed by the full weight of the Junction bozo jammed into my spine now. And the snapping, ratcheting click of handcuffs, tightening then biting into my wrists. Yanked my attention clear from the newcomer and onto my new fate.

A hard yank from behind re-centered it, that rotund officer wrenching me from my desk.

Just in time to see a woman with dark brown hair, long on the top and streaked by blond highlights, close-cropped on the sides, sauntering inside my office on generous hips.

Jamie Ramos, lead detective on the Peterson case.

She wore her middle-age years well. Toned and fit, wearing dark denim and a snug white blouse, with smooth, bronze skin and dark eyes to match her Latin locks. Looked like Catherine Zeta Jones playing that Elena Montero character from *The Mask of Zorro*. Had totally shaped how I imagined a Latina looking before I learned Ms. Jones was actually Welsh. Go figure. Believed they called that appropriation these days. I just called it beautiful.

"Gideon Paul O'Donnell," she said, sauntering over with a smug smirk, "you're under arrest."

The A-word barely registered. Not only because of the ogre on my back. But also because it was the most ridiculous thing I'd ever heard uttered about myself.

Under arrest. Me?

Did not compute.

"Say *waaa?*" Reggie said on a questioning breath.

"You're off your rocker!" Lizzy complained. "For what?"

Ramos inched closer, smacking gum between perfect teeth, the faint trace of spearmint distinct.

I locked my eyes on her, and locked my jaw. "What is this about?"

Another step, then another, a floorboard creaking under her weight before she stood and crossed her arms. A breath, a beat, a smile—an actual smile that showcased brilliant pearly whites eager to drop the hammer.

And detonate a bomb.

"The murder of Florence O'Donnell."

Time stopped. Again. For the second time that day.

No way I'd heard her right.

Reggie tried to confirm what I disbelieved: "Did you just say what I think you said?"

"Murder?" Lizzy said on that same questioning breath.

I panted for breath while Ramos just smiled, smacking that stick of mint gum between her white teeth.

"*Así es,*" she said, still smiling. "You heard me right."

"This is madness!" exclaimed Reggie with a huffing complaint.

Florence O'Donnell.

Dead.

Killed?

My mother?

I went to sit, without thinking. Had to. My legs required it, growing weak. As did my head, growing faint.

I didn't get far.

"Oh, no you don't, partner," someone said from behind.

The officer—no, correction: arresting officer. The one with

the vice grip on my cuffs and now neck, lifting me from the desk and shuffling me out from my stuffy office and down the less-stuffy hallway reeking of roasted coffee and wet wood.

Waiting for me was an unexpected sight.

An unexpected someone.

Annabelle Kirkland.

Face drawn and stricken with tension, having been caught in the middle between the accusation of a crime—the requirement to *prosecute* a crime!—and her boyfriend. And was that grief, fear even?

Couldn't tell, and I couldn't ask. Only one word escaped my mouth when the officer—arresting officer!—manhandled me toward the exit where she was leaning against the open door.

"Annie..." I said on a disbelieving breath, using the pet name I rarely used, and never in public.

My tongue stumbled over itself, throat parched and chalky, tongue thick and heavy.

Swallowing, I managed, "Say it isn't so..."

Annabelle didn't, stiffening, not beating around the bush: "She's dead, Gideon. And—"

This time a beat, then a breath.

Then: "And it's bad."

She dropped her head and turned away, eyes flooding with glistening emotion but not before whispering a final, haunting: "Real bad..."

For whom? My mother, me?

I didn't want to know.

Chapter Ten

Sometimes I wished I had gone into a different line of work. Something with a definite nine-to-five vibe.

Punch in, punch out. No questions asked. Where the only thing left after a long day of work was a large pepperoni pizza waiting for me to pick up at Max's Place, and a six-pack with my name on it waiting for me in the fridge, longnecks begging to be cracked open and slurped dry.

Like working the line on the auto parts stamping plant, for Vick McKnight north of the tracks in the dead of July. No air conditioning to speak of. Shoot, no air to speak of. Just a soaked V-neck stained by elbow grease and actual grease and a pile of hoods towering toward the festering ceiling still hazy from third-shift cigarette smoke idling for a Mack truck to cart them over to Ford or GM or one of those Korean outfits that had set up shop on the east side of the Mitten State. Or picking corn at Warner Farms in late September, when the ears were ripest and after the celery and onion rows had been plucked clean.

My real fantasy, though, was working down south. Not

Deep South. Something more like Key West, or maybe Havana south. Something at some seaside port fixing up some muckety-muck's yacht, or some fisherman's schooner needing a bit of love, its riggings all twisted and hull in need of a good rubdown.

Again, with that six-pack close at hand. Six longnecks shoved in a cooler full of ice, limes shoved down the glass bottles.

Yes, sir. That would be the life. Any of them, really. Spin the bottle. Take your pick. Anything but slinging it as an attorney in small-town, Nowheresville, Michigan, getting by with court-appointed minor offenses and chasing ambulances for a larger cut of the litigation payout, defending hard crimes and hardened criminals.

I shook my head and smiled. Mill Creek. The Junction, as the Midwest town was known. A speck on Google Maps that had actually been a depot titan on the Chicago-Detroit rail line from back in the day. Something about sawmills and flour mills sitting at the crossroads that fed the heartland food and wood.

Never in my wildest imaginations had I pictured myself practicing law back in my small-town hometown. The Junction was for the Sams and Andys and Mikes I'd slung burgers next to at Max's Place before I'd bounced on out of town for college and beyond. That life was for Max, my best bud from high school in a long line of Max Blades.

Not Gideon Paul O'Donnell.

I'd fled West Michigan and vowed never again to return. Had packed up my Chrysler LeBaron convertible and bounced onto the biggers and betters. Which had first been Wayne State University undergrad on the east side before law school at Georgetown University in Washington, DC. And every first-year law student knew hanging up your shingle in some Nowheresville, Midwest Town, wasn't where it was at.

Corporate gigs were. Any first year knew that. And every Georgetown student worth his salt knew they were destined for greatness in one of the big urban centers of law.

DC. LA. NY.

Those top three letter combos had definitely been high on my list. Followed by Atlanta, Houston, and Chicago. Even Detroit, but it was a bit close to home. And their winters were worse than the ones that plagued the Junction.

So practicing law in MCJ? Definitely not!

But that's the way I rolled, nearing a decade now. Fighting for the little guys and gals. Righting wrongs. Landing mega paydays for the left out and left behind—even scoundrels accused of murder who probably did the deed but needed defending anyhow from the wheels of justice and shadiness of law enforcement.

Like that day, and the one after.

The one that was *supposed* to come after.

Now, having been yanked by the arm into a Junction PD cruiser and shuffling now across the baking blacktop radiating heat in the noonday sun, the class action lawsuit seeking an injunction against HappyLiving Estates from raising the costs of rent on a slew of Junction residents—to save my mother's home!—and tanking their real estate equity, their very livelihoods, was the farthest thing from my mind. Everything was far from my brain, a three-pound mess of matter numb to what had been and would be. Couldn't even register half of what was going on around me.

Press had already flocked to the station, that I managed to note. No doubt tipped off by Dean Lawlor or Chief Roller or whoever, maybe both. And not just the *Mill Creek Junction Guardian*, either. Local broadcast affiliates, with their large satellite trucks, dishes raised and ready to go live. Well-make-uped field correspondents in neutral gray suits and cream-color dresses, mics in hand, lined the walkway leading into the back of the beige brick, two-story building as old as Mill Creek itself. Thought I caught Tracy in her navy dress at the head of the pack, shouting questions with her iPhone extended for comment.

Didn't make one. Again, barely registered. Something deep in my subconscious did manage to kick in to keep me from saying anything boneheaded stupid. Probably my professional training, and all the times I'd barked at clients to keep their yappers shut. Supposed a hundred grand in grad school debt counted for something when the chips were down.

Even my booking flashed by in a blur, when I had always told my clients to be on their best and most on-guard behavior. It was a crucial moment as the wheels of justice turned, both for the client and the city.

First, the basics, which I had managed to mutter my way through on autopilot. Name, emergency contact information, and the alleged crime. Gideon Paul O'Donnell. 3325 Springdale Road, Mill Creek Junction, Michigan. Didn't give an emergency contact number. My only family left were Reggie and Lizzy, and I knew they would be on this in a flash.

Then: Murder in an unspecified degree.

Of Florence O'Donnell.

My mother...

My ears began to ring at the wicked notion, and eyes began sparkling with overwhelm. Breath was hard to come by. My chest felt like a horse stomping on my sternum.

Was that what a heart attack felt like?

No. Not a heart attack.

Panic attack.

I'd had barely a moment to process the turn—the accusation!—before I was whisked away by MCJPD and hustled into the station across the street from the courthouse, where I had just mucked up the Junction's wheels of justice.

Irony of ironies.

And now, with the heat of the day, with the people barking orders and pressing in, all around, with the cramped quarters and rising heat and blooming body odor—

I feared I would pass out.

A winking white flash snapped me back to the moment.

From the Nikon snapping my mugshot in front of one of those classic plain backgrounds. At first, front-facing, then from the side. Just like in those made-for WeFlix streaming shows I vegged out to after a long day hoeing my fields of justice after the day went dark, sipping on a mouthy Malbec red wine and popping bits of dark chocolate into my mouth. Who knew when I'd have that luxury again.

Actually, I had a hint, thanks to Jamie Ramos.

The fact of the matter pulsed inside me as I removed my clothes—unbuttoning my white shirt before peeling it off with my T-shirt, stained and soaked by sweat; slipping off my stiff, new Johnston & Murphy's, then my equally soaked navy dress socks; taking off my pants, then underwear, the final act of humiliation before I was given a once-over exam for weapons and other contraband and a brief health assessment.

A murder accusation obviously meant standing trial, probably long and lengthy, given my profile. Which would follow a preliminary examination, the formal process in front of the judge where I would get to make my case challenging Dean Lawlor's show in court that enough probable cause existed to send the case to trial—*my* case. Because I would be damned if I myself didn't put on the best blasted show the Junction had ever seen defending my honor, my innocence!

Which itself would follow my arraignment—all of which could take a while, depending on the circumstances. It could also be a while until I had my day in court in the first place, depending on the court docket. And if I didn't make bail—

Make bail...

The thought seized me at the end of the booking gauntlet, my fingers stained with purple ink from having been finger-printed, my mouth cottony from the DNA swab. It continued to clang around in my head with vague recognition and disbelief at what I was facing—*me,* Gideon Paul O'Donnell!—my flip-flops whispering and the heavy boots of law enforcement thudding through an echoey, stale hallway pierced by dim fluorescent lighting.

Right before a heavy door of steel and glass clanged behind me.

Snapping something inside that lizard brain of mine.

I spun behind, blinking and darting my eyes around the cramped room.

I went numb with disbelief, a coldness flooding me, followed by a pit growing into a clenching ball of dread in my stomach.

That suddenly needed out.

To escape.

Evacuate.

I felt warm all over, and an ache bloomed in my head. Then my mouth began flooding with saliva, my body preparing the chute for what I knew came next.

A steel toilet anchored to one corner was my only saving grace.

I lunged for it.

Just as that ball of dread climbed up and out of my hatch in a sour, chunky explosion of chewed bagel bits and raisins, cream cheese and espresso. Then again, and a third time until I was dry heaving with a clenched stomach and spitting what was left of my breakfast into the bowl.

I moaned and groaned and held my pose a moment, then a few more beats, waiting for round two.

There was nothing left and nothing more. Neither in me nor from me.

All energy had drained in that phantasmic show of bitter bile, all will to go on, all will to fight the nightmare that had literally haunted my nightmares for years.

Throwing up a final moan that returned to me in a solitary, mournful mock, I eased from the toilet and hit the flusher.

Nothing happened.

I yanked it again, then pounded it.

Same nothing, my cell stinking of puke, the expected rush of water coming up empty, dry.

The stuff of nightmares...

And deliberate punishment.

I'd bested Mill Creek Junction law enforcement for years, winning cases I knew set off MCJPD. But this...shutting off the water to my cell, not to mention fingering me for a murder—

My mother's...

Twisting from the malfunctioning toilet, I leaned against the cell wall shedding white paint like a leper. My orange jumpsuit was soaked through, and all I wanted was to go to sleep. To dream away the terrifying, malevolent monster that had found me.

Accusation.

Incarceration.

A similar steel bed was anchored to the opposite wall, a thin, stained mattress and a folded threadbare sheet resting on top. I thought about climbing into it, wrapping myself in the cruel and unusual punishment. Instead, I banged my head against the cinderblock wall.

Knocking a thought loose. No, two.

First: *What am I going to do?*

A second thought quickly followed: *How am I going to avenge Ma's death?*

Then another: *What about the lawsuit meant to save my mother's house, not to mention the others and their future?*

I had to get out of there.

Had to find my mother's killer.

For Ma's sake, as much as my own...

Chapter Eleven

The clang of metal on metal looped a hooking finger around my dreamland consciousness, motioning for me to surface from a sleep that had been hard to come by.

An alarm, muffled but livid with warning in the near distance, finally brought me back to the land of the living. Or, in my case, the walking dead, if the machinations of Mill Creek justice had anything to say about it.

Easing my eyes open, panic pierced me at the sensations of the unfamiliar.

The peeling white paint and the faint light glinting off from the metal toilet bowl from a narrow slice of the world shining through a window anchored to a heavy metal door painted black. The stiff bed under the thin mattress driving my spine mad and gaunt blanket spreading goose flesh across me from a chill blowing from a vent in the ceiling. The sour stench of undigested food and my own piss from a midnight bathroom break.

The sensations of prison.

The stuff of my nightmares.

Ever since I had gone all-in on defense work scooping up Junction clients left and right, even from Grand Rapids on toward the Lake Michigan communities to the west and clear east to Detroit—anything to bolster my street creds and street rep—that's when the dreams had started, coming in hot and heavy.

A shrink I'd seen for a mental-health checkup chalked it up to feelings of being trapped or restricted or limited in some part of my life, even subconscious feelings of guilt or shame for something I had done, my inner self censoring some area in my life that needled for personal recompense. I'd never identified what that might be, though I chalked the feelings of guilt to Baptist guilt, not having gone to church in ages. Perhaps.

More than likely, it was my profession that was eating away at my inner self, my dreams a source of projection for my clients' own guilt, or even surfacing deep-seated feelings of being cornered in a rat race that never ended. Mostly because the depravity of humanity never ended, but it was more like the needs of my own life never ended.

Mortgage and car payments, food and utilities, the occasional bite out at Max's Place, new Johnston & Murphy oxfords and Zegna blazers. You know, the stuff of adulting that trapped forty-somethings get to deal with. And I had to pay for it all defending people I'd rather not have to defend. Which seemed to feed my subconscious aversion to the trap I'd laid for myself with my line of work, compounded by those my clients laid for themselves with the crimes—and the incarceratory consequences of those crimes.

Again: the stuff of my nightmares.

Which seemed to be playing out in living high-definition color—before my very waking eyes!

My mind screamed for an answer as the alarm continued

bleating, joined by the turning of gears in the wall, followed by something heavy sliding from the door, perhaps a key.

The answer wasn't what I wanted.

Prison.

My new lot in life, a confusion about the who-what-why compounded by a bone weariness thanks to that new lot.

I had slept like crap, explaining the snap deep-sleep wake and disorientation. Had finally dozed off maybe an hour before the commotion. And not just because of the thin mattress and even thinner blanket. Not even because the walls felt like they were closing in with the same stifling humidity and heat I'd endured before being arrested following me to my cell before that frigid breath flooded it. The stench of the cramped quarters had actually faded into the background noise of my new lot in life, so that wasn't so much of an issue either.

Still—

It all added up to a major Eighth Amendment violation I was itching to litigate.

Sort of.

For any other client, sure. But the fight to make Junction PD pay for their cruel and unusual punishment was overshadowed by more pressing matters.

Like why I was holed up in that cell to begin with.

The question mark was quickly chased by an exclamation point. Which was really an accusation.

Against me, Gideon Paul O'Donnell—blamed for my mother's death.

Her *murder*.

Which I knew nothing about.

The revelation had consumed me the rest of the day and into the waking hours of the nightmarish night. My thoughts, my emotions, my energy, my very soul. Who wouldn't obsess over how their life had taken such a turn—and toward such a dramatic accusation, such a heinous, totalizing crime.

Perhaps my only solace was that my father wasn't around for the drama. His own soul would have been shattered under the weight of his soulmate's fire being extinguished. Under the weight of his own son being fingered for her—

I couldn't bring myself to voice it, to think it even.

Somehow, at some moment during the night, my body spent of everything I had left in reserve, had given way to slumber.

Which was fast and fleeting thanks to that metal clang of arrival and the klaxon blare of warning—

And now the same steel and glass that had shuddered me inside this six-by-eight nightmare rattled open with sudden interruption.

"Rise and shine, princess," a short, squat, nasally guard cooed as he barreled inside. He stopped short, throwing up a muffled *oof* and inching out.

"Aww Marv, lookie thar," a gruff, oversized ogre said from behind with a deep laugh. "The newb crapped his pants silly."

Nasally Guard chittered his own laugh, a drooping handlebar mustache reminding me of Yosemite Sam, before stepping back up to the plate and yanking me from my bed.

"Wha—" I managed, disoriented and tumbling forward on uncertain feet.

Meeting the hard end of a kneecap.

Cartilage smacked against bone. Pain lanced through my face.

A warm build up, then a slick wetness, oozed.

I fell to the floor, one hand planted on the cool tile, the other reaching for my nose gushing blood. A moan escaped, but I held any further complaint at bay as I sucked in a stabilizing breath, the metallic taste of pennies heavy in my mouth.

Recovering, the sweet smell of cinnamon rolls and coffee wafted from my left side.

"Looks like somebody's got two left feet, right Marv?" Ogre Guard grunted, bent low beside me.

Nasally Guard laughed. "Sure looks that way, Bert."

"Must be overtired, defending bastards like Councilman Peterson, and getting rapists and drug dealers off on *technacalities!*"

"Sure looks that way, Bert."

"Maybe prison is just the thing for this sorry sack of shyster sh—"

"Now, Bert. Mind your tongue around our guest of honor."

"Sorry. Where are my manners? Sorry sack of *crap*. Maybe the extended break will let our frazzled guest put his feet up a bit. Catch up on his shuteye. Too bad something more permanent ain't no longer on the table..."

A chuckle, from the right, then the left. I knew what he meant: The death penalty, the ultimate punishment, had been constitutionally banned in Michigan since 1963.

The back of my head suddenly burned. Hair actually, a tuft of it flaring agony with a fist full of my dark, wavy locks gripped by a strong hand.

Head was jerked back. I was raised to my feet. Then thrown against the wall.

All without uttering a cry.

Wouldn't give the goons the satisfaction, though it was clear the show was intentionally vindictive. Probably for years of revenge after I had scored wins against their shoddy police work, even getting some of their own prosecuted and tossed into the clink.

Good to know...

A stiff baton jammed into my spine from behind by the

guard. At least, I assumed it was a baton. Never could be certain in MCJPD lockup.

"Spread 'em and give me yer wrists," Nasally Guard demanded.

I complied. I wiggled my feet from side to side, mustering enough energy to spread eagle, then jutted my arms out and planted my hands against the cool, rough wall.

"*WRISTS BEHIND YOUR BACK, MORON!*" Ogre Guard barked in my left ear, a returning hot breath of Cinnabon and dark coffee sending that ball of dread threatening for relief again.

Thankfully, I held it together. Now I just wanted some of that hot, sticky, cinnamony, gooey goodness with a hot cup of joe.

I quickly complied, bringing my arms around at my backside.

Cold, hard steel ratcheted around my wrists before I was shoved out into the hallway.

It was brighter and a bit warmer, both a relief from my cold, dark cell.

After a short walk through stale hallways of dim fluorescent lighting, I was ushered into a modest room the size of my garage. A steel table with seats on either side, like my nonfunctioning toilet and bed, was anchored to the floor. It was empty but for two people. Familiar people.

I had met countless clients in this space, lawyer and the accused getting on the same page before appearing in court. Which was what my arrival was about. And the reason for the two people, Reggie and Lizzy.

My lawyers.

They stood as I was brought inside the room, a firm hand from Ogre Guard guiding me forward to a chair anchored to the floor. Both knew well enough not to ask questions until the guards left the room.

Reggie nodded on my approach, offering a reassuring smile. Lizzy didn't look so good, her eyes wider than normal and lips drawn in a thin greeting. Looked like she tried offering the same welcome, but she was struggling to hold it together.

Bert released the first cuff, right hand, then the other. Felt good to get them off. Tingled less, blood seeming to return to my fingers.

Until the man yanked my right arm around to the front, joined by Nasally Guard jerking my left toward a second set of cuffs chained to an anchor at the center of the table. Should have known that was coming, but I thought I would get a few moments of normalcy with my friends.

"Aww, come on, Bert," Reggie complained.

Bert ignored him, cinching the cuff around my wrist with a ratcheting click, tighter than before.

"Really, you gotta cuff the guy?" Lizzy sneered, arms folded.

"Protocol," the guard replied with a grin.

"Yeah, protocol," the other pipsqueak agreed.

Lizzy muttered something under her breath and plopped down in her seat. Reggie just rolled his eyes but did the same.

The pair finished securing me, and I eased down onto my seat. The goons sauntered out, no one making a sound until they left.

The heavy steel door clanged shut, and both of my friends —my *lawyers!*—leaned in.

Time to get down to business.

"What happened to you?" Reggie asked first.

"Tripped," I replied.

Lizzy scoffed. "Did they hurt you?"

"Asked and answered, counsel."

"This isn't funny, mister."

"I know. Look at me."

Reggie sighed, "Seriously, did—"

"Drop it, alright?" I interrupted, louder than I intended, my voice echoing back to me.

Guards weren't too keen on prisoners getting excited with their lawyers. Knew from experience, with a few of my clients being sent back to lockup when they got too mouthy with me, and loud.

Shifting, I glanced at the exit before propping my elbows up on the table. I sniffed, wiping blood from my nostrils, and grimaced. More from the sight of the crimson, orangey smear than the pain. Couldn't worry about that. We had bigger things to worry about.

Which I voiced, lowly, above a whisper: "We've got bigger things to worry about than a friggin' bloody nose. Don't worry about me. Heads in the game, alright? It's go time."

They regarded one another and sighed, probably with resignation.

"What do you have for me?"

Lizzy leaned back, hanging her head. Reggie's shoulders slumped. He was the first to share.

"Annabelle was right. It ain't good."

I had prepared myself for this talk. The one where my two lawyers—or *partners*, rather, my co-counsels. Because no way would nobody but me be trying this one. Regardless, I'd mentally prepped myself for what came next.

Still—

I wasn't sure I was ready...

Swallowing, I let my arms fall to the table, the chains shackling me to it rattling. I folded my hands then nodded for Reggie to get to it.

"It's like Ramos said," my partner continued, "your mama was killed."

"Murdered," I corrected, facing the headwinds of reality.

He just nodded.

"How?"

"In her room at Dreamscape Manor."

I said nothing. I took a breath and leaned back, staring at my folded hands.

Mom had been placed—

I clenched my jaw tight at the passive voice. Been placed.

No, I had *put* her there, in the assisted living center last year after Dad died unexpectedly. It was bad enough dealing with his sudden death. And with everything I was wrapped up with at work, my cases, the class action suit I was building... Dreamscape Manor had been the best option after her primary care person had passed, especially given her condition. At a price.

Such senior-care facilities are remarkably expensive places that drain the living of their livelihood, and their heirs. Uncle Sam didn't start footing the bill until after their assets were drained. You build a life for forty, fifty years, hope to pass along some of it to your children, their children, and it's sold off for parts until there's nothing left. The one thing Ma was entitled to was the piece of property at HappyLiving Estates.

She and Dad had built a life there, for decades. I'd always been ashamed of that life, hiding my trailer-trash background. They were proud of it, for the simple reason they hadn't needed it. Living in their mobile home was a choice built around their Christian conviction to give away most of their money to charity work and Christian missions.

Mine could have been a comfortable middle-class life, with a two-story house and backyard pool, a two-stall garage and closets full of junk. Sort of like my life now. Ma and Dad had made a choice to reject those bourgeois expectations, instead opting for inexpensive housing they cultivated into an abundantly rich home.

And when that was threatened, when *she* was threatened—well, Gideon Paul O'Donnell would be damned to let that happen.

But that was business, and it could wait. Would have to, with me in the clink and tied up with some bogus murder charge.

I returned to the original question: "How?"

A wheezing breath escaped Reggie, the start of his answer dying. He glanced at Lizzy, who straightened and answered for him.

"A bullet. To the back of the head."

The revelation sliced through me, a jail-yard shiv to the gut. I had imagined her being poisoned or something, even suffocated. Not killed in such a violent manner.

I snapped my eyes open, not wanting to let my mind's eye wander to a room soaked in my mother's blood.

I stood. "We've got work to do."

Reggie joined me. "We'll prove your innocence, bro."

"No doubt." Lizzy nodded and rose next to her partner.

Took a moment to register, but when it did, I twisted up my face. With revulsion as much as offense.

"I'm not talking about me, my innocence!" I exclaimed. "I'm talking about my mother."

Reggie put out a staying hand. "One step at a time, bro. First things first."

Lizzy nodded. "That's right. Springing you from this joint and getting you the big NG verdict is the—"

"You're not listening!" I yelled, pounding my fist on the metal table, my chains rattling with an exclamation point.

Which sent the door flying open with a heavy clang.

And both guards pounding just inside, ready to pounce.

"We're alright," Reggie said with a raised hand.

I said nothing, heaving a breath and bowing my head, smacking my hands on the back of my greasy hair.

"One minute, princess," Marv said.

I passed a glance over my shoulder, the goon grinning and running a tongue along the bottom of his upper teeth.

The guards left, closing the door.

Silence settled, for several beats, Reggie and Lizzy at a loss for words.

Not me. I knew exactly what I wanted to say.

"I will prove my innocence," I said lowly, eyes narrowed with resolve, hands balled into fists. "Prove who killed my mother."

And make them pay...

Chapter Twelve

It would be another full day and sleepless night in my six-by-eight until I left the Mill Creek Junction PD holding cell and reappeared at the courthouse across the street. Between my meeting with Reggie and Lizzy and my arraignment the next day, I had managed to muddle through prison life.

That afternoon, I had been served a minuscule lunch of chicken soup in my cell—heavy on the salt and broth, light on the chicken, if the gizzards and veiny white strips were in fact chicken. Dinner was a hard puck of beef that crunched in my mouth. More like charcoal slapped between a dry bun, served with a side of mushy, over-cooked green beans. At least my toilet had gotten fixed, someone deciding to turn on the water, and the sour, rotten stench subsided. The water was exchanged for the air, though, the chill from the ceiling vent gone, and a thick, humid heat flooding the cell instead. Complaints to Marv and Bert went unanswered.

So when morning came, the faint dawn of a new day slicing through the narrow window of my cell door before it shuddered open, and Tweedle Dumb and Tweedle Dumber appeared, I thanked the good Lord above for the wheels of justice continuing to crank away in my absence. It was the day of my arraignment, my initial court appearance as a defendant hearing the charges brought against me, with the opportunity to make my formal plea in response.

An obvious "Not Guilty!" would be entered.

As would a request for no bail, though I wasn't banking on it, given the charges. Although, being the progressive state it is, Michigan began implementing a bail reform agreement that limited cash bail only to cases where a judge determined a defendant was a flight risk or danger to the Junction community. Something about modeling for the rest of the country how bail reform could work. Didn't care for the reasons, only that my clients had benefited. Especially didn't care since I myself would benefit.

If the judge agreed.

Given the hoops I'd gone through with Councilman Peterson, his bail set at a million buckaroos for the murder of his wife, I was guessing I'd get the same treatment. Which meant a hundred Gs in bond, forked over to Mill Creek Junction Municipal Court of Justice. None of which would be recoupable.

Had no clue what I would be charged with. Apparently murder. But what degree, what sort? Didn't have a clue. Supposed I'd find out soon enough, but one thing I did know— without a doubt.

I'd been framed.

That much was obvious. To me, anyway. And I was champing at the bit to get my hands on discovery and see what sort of friggin' bull Dean Lawlor and his Junction PD cronies had trumped up to exact their revenge on me beating his office and the boys in blue case after case, year after year.

I'd beat 'em again, too.

And Mill Creek Junction would know who the best attorney was in all of Michigan.

Gideon Friggin' O'Donnell.

A quick shuffle through the same stale hallway of dim fluorescent lighting I'd been familiar with even before becoming a guest of the Junction PD jail led to an almost as quick of a ride in an MCJPD van to the courthouse across the street. When I got out, I almost wanted back in my cell.

Normally, the accused was brought through the back, to a loading dock of sorts that actually was a loading dock for the courthouse. Where foodstuff and printer paper and Judge Heller's cases of Kentucky bourbon were shuffled inside.

Not this time.

It was the walk of shame for me, the van motoring around a semi-circle drive and up to the main entrance into the Junction's own Lady Justice temple.

Where the same circus that had met me upon my arrest was waiting at a set of ornate brown marble stairs rising a story to a set of walnut double doors.

Those blasted vans, with their ears to space raised for proper reception, were lined up like soldiers along the drive. Along with bozo reporters from ABC, NBC, CBS (those were still a thing?), joined by a few of the bigger dogs, CNN and FNC and MSNBC. Imagined a few of the rags left standing had sent their own gumshoes to write a blog post, maybe an article. Had always wanted to grace the pages of the Gray Lady, the paper of record for metro New York and the rest of the country. Even something closer to home, like the *Detroit Free Press* or a national newspaper like *USA Today*.

Not like this. Not *for* this.

"Are you kidding me..." I muttered as the side door slid open.

"No siree, princess," Marv cooed, sending that tongue of his licking the underside of his front teeth with a giddy grin.

Bert appeared behind, muscling past and yanking me out from the van.

It was a bright, hot day, the sunlight and summer heat slapping me in the face. The sunlight was blinding, and I went to shield my eyes—forgetting my hands were bound to my feet.

They snapped my hands back down. Bert and Marv wrenched their hands around my arms and shuffled me forward in my orange jumpsuit, hands cuffed in front and shackled to chains strung down to another set of shackles at my ankles. Overkill, as far as I was concerned, and definitely designed to send a message.

Eat it, O'Donnell.

Waiting for me was a gauntlet of reporters, larger and more aggressive than when I had been booked the day before.

And there she was, leading the pack.

Tracy friggin' Nolland.

I suddenly felt self-conscious of what I was wearing, of all things. I was handcuffed and chained between two police officers, ushered forward by their authoritative grip on my upper arms, accused of murdering my mother. And what was the first thought that popped into my head?

I should've worn my black Canali to the dance.

Shuffling forward in my jumpsuit, black **PRISONER** lettering emblazoned on my back, I felt my face flush warmer than I already was from the heat of the high-noon sun and stuffy ride over. But something in me snapped into autopilot, and off I went.

I held my head high, fixed my eyes on the double doors up ahead, and took the first step up the stairs.

When—

"Did you do it, Gideon?" Tracy shouted at me.

I ignored her, taking another step.

She followed close behind, unrelenting.

"Why did you do it?"

That yanked my attention, breaking through my foggy haze.

And broke something in me.

I spun free from Marv, nearly sending the guard tumbling backward, just as I came face to face with the ginger who had normally been an ally, speaking truth to power and keeping the Junction oligarchy in check.

"Are you friggin' kidding me, Tracy?" I growled. "Did I—"

My reply unleashed the Junction PD goons escorting me toward destiny. Bert tightened his grip and cinched his other hand around my wrist while Marv recovered, slapping a livid mitt on my neck and squeezing tight, the pair yelling at me to fall in line and step forward, double-time.

I did, the two guards forcing my hand.

Just as the rest of the jackal pack scampered after me, the mangy mutts they were lashing out with their mics and well-makeuped mugs—with their own questions.

The same did-you-do-it and why'd-you-do-it questions, joined by the do-you-have-any-comments and what-do-you-have-to-say-for-yourselfs.

Wanted to puke. Almost did, then and there.

Instead, I took to heart the advice I had doled out to umpteen clients over the years.

I shut the hell up.

Then faced forward and shut up some more until I was through those heavy walnut doors and into the courthouse.

Inside was a blessed relief, the air cool and conditioned in the round, cavernous entrance. Large chandeliers from the Roaring '20s lit by yellow LED bulbs were joined by bright white sunlight streaming down through windows high above a soaring ceiling. The rotunda, paved in a patchwork of red-and-blue tiles with whorls of green and gold, was closely watched by a beautiful fresco of Lady Justice swimming high above in a white cloud accented by pinks and golds, swarmed by cherubic guardians.

I threw her a glance, her outstretched arms holding scales and a sword taking on new meaning.

Somehow it all looked different coming through the front wearing my prison uniform instead of my lawyerly one. Like visiting your childhood neighborhood a few decades past. Like I was an outsider, like I wasn't welcomed.

Like I didn't belong.

The feeling was probably heightened by the normally echoey clatter of fancy shoes and lawyer-client whispers and yakking attorneys winding down to nothing but nothing as I shuffled across the old courthouse tiles toward a guard checkpoint. The vast room stopped and stared.

The only sounds I caught were the quiet mutters of shock and my squeaking flip-flops, joined by the rattle of chains that sort of put an exclamation point on the alienation I felt.

Actually, now that I thought about it, I *did* belong. Not as a lawyer but as the accused. Now I was on the other side of justice.

I worried whether Lady Justice, with her scales and sword, would find in my favor.

Bert and Marv bypassed the metal detector, which actually ended up being a kind gesture, the jackal pack left in their dust having their bags searched and arms wanded before being admitted inside. Those shouted questions faded as the pair took me down a side hallway to a familiar room.

A small antechamber large enough for a table and a few chairs sat next to the main courthouse chamber. A holding room for lawyers and their clients to confer before appearing in front of the judge or jury. It was cramped and dark, smelling of my musty Junction basement. Waiting for me would normally have been my own client, and I would have gone over the lay of the legal land, told him to keep his yapper shut and check his emotions, look not guilty and not a threat, remorseful even. Had I been wearing my black Canali, that is.

Except—

In my alternate reality, orange was the new black. Waiting for me were Reggie and Lizzy.

They stood on my arrival, the pair wearing matching gray suits, even sharing matching blue accents, with Reggie sporting his favorite navy Ferragamo with playful baby blue elephants set against a crisp white shirt and Lizzy looking her best in a soft blue blouse.

I had always sprung for a red Robert Talbott, the wide shiny silk conveying a commanding presence, and had gotten into it a time or twelve with my associates about what colors were best for trial. With blue signaling trust and wisdom, empathy and compassion, they thought it the best go-to color. Red was always my answer. Which was about what I was about: power and authority, strength and passion.

A corner coat rack caught my eye, a black suit with a white shirt hanging from it, along with a plain navy tie. It would have to do.

My attorneys offered nothing but a nod while the guards uncuffed me. Any words exchanged within earshot of the guards were fair game, as the attorney-client privilege does not apply if a third party overhears a conversation in a public place where there is no expectation of privacy. Until those doors were closed, and I was alone with my attorneys, those guards could testify about what they heard. So my lips were sealed until the goons left.

They did, and I sat and allowed myself a sigh, the tension of the last half hour draining some.

"How are you holding up?" asked Lizzy, sitting next to Reggie.

"Could use an extra pillow—or any pillow, for that matter—and the minibar needs restocking. Other than that, peachy."

She smiled, giving my hand a squeeze.

Reggie asked, "Any issues on your arrival?"

I snorted a laugh. "Any issues? Did you see where they brought me? How did that happen, them taking me in through the front like that instead of the rear?"

"Yeah, about that..."

"We had expected you out back," Lizzy explained, "as with every client."

Reggie added, "Chief Roller had other ideas."

"Let me guess," I said. "Some bull about *protocol*?"

"Something like that. Other than your embarrassing entrance, I assume all went well?"

"Almost got into it with Tracy."

Lizzy sighed. "Gideon, you didn't..."

"Don't worry. I didn't say anything stupid."

Didn't add the fact I couldn't, thanks to my handlers. They didn't need the added worry that their client was half-cocked.

Reggie said, "No use crying over nearly spilled tea. All that matters is the next hour. Obviously you know the drill on that one."

Obviously.

The judge would make sure I had read over and signed an advice of rights sheet, laying out my right to remain silent, my right to counsel, my right to a jury trial and to confront the accused and any witnesses that testify against me. There would be a formal reading of the charges, with me entering a plea. I would be asked if I needed a court-appointed attorney, which I wouldn't. My plan wasn't to even have an attorney, aiming instead to represent myself. Knew I'd have to get past Reggie's and Lizzy's dead bodies for that one, but I could handle them.

Next up was bail, which was iffy but not out of the question, and an absolute necessity. I had to get out of Mill Creek prison. Not for myself but for my mother, even my awaiting clients, though that adventure in class action litigation was on permanent hiatus until I got the other thing under control.

Proving my innocence, yes, but it was bigger than that. It was like I'd told Reggie and Lizzy in their Junction prison powwow.

I had to find my mother's killer—*would* find my mother's killer.

Flat had to...

Reggie glanced at his watch before nodding toward the coat rack.

"We're expected in court in ten. We brought one of your trial suits to change into."

"Figured it was appropriate," Lizzy said.

Contrary to pop-culture portrayals, a defendant has the right to appear in civilian clothes for trial instead of a prison uniform prejudicing the jury and risking their judgment. A nice shirt and pants or skirt did wonders to preserve a prisoner's right to the presumption of innocence by at least not looking guilty. Courts did have some discretion over the matter in some states, insisting the right was waivable, but Michigan wasn't one of them. And the Mill Creek Junction court allowed for such changes of clothing even at arraignment.

I went to the rack while Reggie and Lizzy remained seated, backs turned to my undressing, whispering to one another while I got changed.

It wasn't my Canali, but I appreciated the change of clothes just the same. Amazing what a change of clothes can do to a man's mood. Anything but the orange one-piece designed to dehumanize and domesticate. Just hoped I walked out of there in those threads instead of the Junction's prison garb.

There was a pounding knock at the door, and it opened.

Marv was first in, closely trailed by Bert.

Here we go...

Chapter Thirteen

I sucked in an expectant breath.

Here we go Gideon Paul...

This was it. Do or—

Never mind.

Adrenaline spiked. A surge of epinephrine pinged my gut, sending it lurching—more with a roller-coaster drop followed by butterflies this time instead of the clenching dread that had sent me reeling in my jail cell. Nevertheless, the fight-flight hormone coursing through my body ratcheted my ticker and snatched my breath.

Marv sauntered toward me, Bert towering from behind the short, squat man.

I stood still, unmoving, hands in my pockets and chin raised at an angle. A power play that made them come to me and leveled the playing field.

No way would I be treated like one of the J-Max scum serving twenty to life. I was their equal. I was Gideon Paul O'Donnell.

The best friggin' attorney in the Mitten State.

"You're due in court, princess," Marv said, licking those teeth of his with a grin.

"Hands," was all Bert said.

Reggie stood. "Aww, come on, really?"

"Yeah, come on, fellas," Lizzy joined. "He ain't no harm."

Predictably, Bert grunted "Protocol" and that was that.

I didn't fight it. At least the chains weren't part of the *protocol*. Just a simple pair of cuffs, cinched tight around my wrists. I complained, and Reggie (God love him!) convinced Marv to loosen them a bit.

Then off to the races we went.

Reggie led the way from the antechamber through a door into the main courtroom, with Bert following and me close after. Marv stood close behind, one hand gripping my left arm, the other at my hip—and far too close, uncomfortably so—with Lizzy making up the rear. The lineup was a good thing in hindsight.

Because the first glimpse of the accused the courtroom got, and the waiting press (and thus the public) was of the black man looking all supportive of the man accused of shooting his black mother like a dog. Same for the rear, with the perky blond woman standing with the same support beside the accused.

Accused...

The thought snagged inside my head as I emerged into the courtroom.

Gideon Paul O'Donnell, shackled and appearing before Mill Creek Junction Municipal Court—not for the defense, as a defense attorney.

But as the *accused*.

Every fiber of my being wanted to give the courtroom a once-over. Glare at the prosecution table across the aisle next to the jury box before flashing my pearlies at the awaiting audience behind like I always did. Did neither, instead holding my head high as I walked to the same table I had been at just yesterday.

Only then, I'd been the one defending the accused of murder.

Now look at things...

Sitting, the wood chair felt harder than I recalled. Maybe because I was often on my feet most of the time, springing to object to this or that, pacing the front of the court to interrogate a witness or coax a friendly into supporting the cause, fighting for justice and all that jazz.

Lemon polish was the same, the whiff that had been background noise now front and center as I waited for the judge to enter. I fixed my eyes on the grainy wood table, made of the same wood as the courthouse doors. Walnut, stained a muddy brown. In the light streaming into the courtroom from windows behind the judge's perch, tiger stripes popped with a brilliance I hadn't noticed before. Almost looked like the tiger eyes I'd collected as a young boy, golden to red-brown hued gemstones with the same silky luster, the centerpieces of my rock collection.

Something Ma and I had shared together...

The jury box sat empty across the way, next to the prosecution table. Which I glanced at now waiting for the judge. And instantly regretted it.

Passing a glance met the pools of azure I'd come to know the past several years going toe-to-toe in that very chamber. Eyes I'd come to love the past few months.

Annabelle Kirkland was second-chairing, and she'd glanced over with the same idea, our eyes connecting with instant surprise.

Sending her head snapping back to a blank yellow legal pad in the fuchsia leather folio that had been her trademark, her strawberry blond hair falling down past her face and shielding her embarrassment.

Just as Dean Lawlor's mug snapped my way. With narrowed gray, hateful eyes and the smirk to match sending me snapping my own gaze back to the blankness of my table. No legal pad for me. That would change.

"All rise!" Silvia bellowed, the court clerk.

Right now, in fact.

She continued, "The Honorable Judge Staggs presiding."

The call to attention revived that ping of adrenaline that had assaulted me earlier when Marv fetched me for my date with Lady Justice. It also got my head in the game, the adrenaline fueling me for the biggest legal fight of my career.

My legal fight.

It was go time. To save Gideon Paul's bacon.

The courtroom rose to their feet, shoes clattering and benches groaning.

Entering was a thin man with a round jaw and a full shock of dark hair that reminded me of Paul McCartney from back in the day. Also looked like a Russian ushanka hat was planted on his head, like the one I had hanging in my office, a souvenir from a college trip through Eastern Europe I'd picked up in Ukraine.

Stuttering Stanley Staggs, as he was known around the courthouse, on account of an odd tick that was sort of a stutter, the man often repeating the last syllables of a sentence, sometimes mid-sentence. I'd had to counsel each of my clients to hold their tongue if and when His Honor slipped that extra syllable or even word at the end of his thought. Sometimes they would snicker, which would send Stuttering Stan into a scowling mood, and then a lecture.

With a story.

The monkey-beating story that would then often land my clients in contempt.

Recounted it as the man strode into the courtroom from his chambers, the heavy door thudding behind and his stiff shoes clattering across the old, scuffed wood, before he sank into his chair. He muttered a "Be seated," and the room echoed with his orders, the man's voice triggering the memory.

"There was a boy from Hudsonville," the judge would begin his story. *"Poor, hungry. A Spaniard, as they were called in those days. He would pick onions from the fertile soil of the former river bed of the mighty Grand River that used to run through those parts. Blind. But he had a gift. The gift of gab. Oh, he would regale that small farming town with stories and jokes until people were either laughing from tears or crying from emotion. People loved listening to him."*

Then he got serious: *"But he also had a dark side. A monkey. On his back. He was addicted to pot. And I'm not talking about your grandma's Mary Jane. No, the stuff of legends from back home, across the border. Lord Almighty, he loved to toke on weed till he was green in the face."*

It was at this point his voice rose into a crescendo: *"And yet—"*

Judge Staggs would scoot close to his bench, leaning both arms on top as he craned his neck forward and fixed his over-sized eyes on my clients.

"Blind, Spaniard, addicted to drugs, he beat it. He beat that monkey till it was blue in the face. Beat it, I tell you! Beat it—strangled it between both fists clenched tight! And he went on to become a hero of his small town, eventually owning the very farm he'd pulled those onions from before he beat his monkey silly—often with the help of his friends!"

Yes. That happened. The monkey. The beating it language.

The friends bit. Even clenched his fists together and squeezed as he pounded them up and down on his bench.

Then the clincher: *"So let this be an example to you. Beat your monkey, young man—till you're blue in the face from exhaustion! Live a drug-free life. Go forth and make this world a better place!"*

One time, my client lost it. Who wouldn't? Could barely hold it together myself. But this was a laugh that totally exploded from him, spittle flying and the echo filling the courtroom.

Which he instantly regretted. And later rued.

Got eighteen months at J-Max for it. And now, recalling that episode, I snickered to myself just thinking about—

"Is there something funny-nee, mister?"

I sucked in a startled breath, snapping my eyes to Judge Staggs.

He fixed me with oversized eyes that made his head look too small for his already thin frame. Lips were pursed and head was jutted out like he meant business.

I quickly cleared my throat, straightened, and apologized.

"No..." I glanced at Reggie, who had the same look about him and subtly shook his head.

Another swallow, further stiffening. "No, Your Honor."

"Goodie! Let's get on with it then."

Silvia returned to bellowing, a short, pudgy woman I had never liked. Mostly because I could never ply her with cookies and cakes like I could the other clerks. Nate Reese was especially pliable, the man giving me some court-docket love with better times and more amenable judges when I brought by his favorite red velvet cupcakes from Millies on Main.

"Calling the case of The People of the State of Michigan versus Gideon Paul O'Donnell, Case Number 43623-59."

And with that, the wheels of justice started cranking.

"Mr. O'Donnell," Judge Staggs said, "please step forward with your counsel."

Reggie was to his feet first before I could intercept him with my own plans.

"Reginald Wilson, counsel for the accused, joined by Elizabeth Seward as co—"

"Actually, your honor," I interrupted, rising and buttoning my suit coat.

Attracting Reggie's and Lizzy's pinched-face (hers) and raised-brow (his) stares. "I will be representing myself."

"Say *waaa*?" Reggie replied, cocking his head.

"I have to agree-ree," Judge Staggs said. "Did I hear you right-right?"

I cleared my throat. "That's right. I wish to enter a waiver of my right to counsel and proceed pro se."

"Like hell you will!" Reggie blurted, eliciting a wave of echoey chuckles from the onlookers.

He cleared his throat and turned to the judge, who slouched back in his chair and crossed his arms in a scowl.

"Apologies, Your Honor."

"I have a court to run-run," Staggs bit with irritation, "so perhaps we could clear up this confusion. Who is representing Mr. O'Donnell?"

"*I am*," Reggie and I both said at the same time.

"Gideon," Lizzy hissed from my side, giving my suit jacket a tug.

Reggie turned to me. "We'll talk about this later. For now—"

"Your Honor," I interrupted, "I would like to represent—"

"*Later!*" Reggie snapped with his own interruption, actually snapping his big, bald head and even bigger brown eyes to me.

"I agree-ree with counsel—that is, Mr. Wilson," Judge

Staggs corrected. "For now, until we have a formal hearing on the matter, you will be represented by counsel, Mr. O'Donnell."

I went to retort with a clever constitutionally relevant argument, but instead shut my mouth and nodded.

First loss of my trial. And last. I would fix it once I was sprung with bail.

"Now that we've got that sorted..." Dean Lawlor grunted with a smirk, rising and buttoning what was surely an off-the-rack Men's Warehouse special, "Dean Lawlor, lead prosecuting attorney, representing the interests of the State of Michigan and the people of Mill Creek Junction, joined by Annabelle Kirkland, assistant prosecuting attorney."

I clenched my jaw. *People of Mill Creek Junction my... whatever.* Then my stomach sank knowing I was being prosecuted by the love of my life.

Judge Staggs returned: "Mr. O'Donnell, you are here today for your arraignment, a formal reading of the charges against you. I assume you've received a copy of those charges?"

Reggie answered, "No, actually, we have not."

"What?"

"Apologies, Your Honor—" Lawlor started.

"There's been too much of that this morning-ning."

Couldn't help but smile at that. Go Stuttering Staggs!

"Yes...well, we had to amend the charge in light of new evidence."

My stomach sank. New evidence?

Good for Reggie, he pounced: "First of all, bad form for not submitting a copy of whatever trumped-up charges you did have before your *amendment*."

"Watch it, counsel..." Staggs *tsked*.

"Second, we were not made aware of this new evidence—"

"It's the arraignment," Annabelle joined in now. "The judge doesn't consider evidence."

"My point, if I could finish..." Reggie swung his head toward the prosecution's table with emphasis before continuing. "Your Honor, I am distressed the city would refuse my client a due diligent awareness of the charges he is facing."

"Distressed?" Annabelle mumbled with a snicker.

"As I said," Lawlor continued, "we had to amend the charges in light of new developments. Which we will fully disclose to the defense in discovery."

"Very well," Judge Staggs said. "What do you have for me? Please read the charges."

What came next was expected.

And not.

Chapter Fourteen

I shifted, preparing myself for what came next.

My charges.

I wasn't ready...

"Yes, Your Honor," Lawlor began. "The defendant, Gideon Paul O'Donnell, is charged as follows. Count One: Murder in the First Degree, in violation of Michigan State statute 750.316, a Class A felony."

A murmur rippled through the room.

I felt it. Deep down, inside.

My own body rippled with the revelation, a coldness flooding my veins. It was joined by a tremor when I fished the rest of the statute from memory: *'Perpetrated by means of poison, lying in wait, or any other willful, deliberate, and premeditated killing.'*

There it was. Murder One.

Those words, from that statute, clamored for attention a second time.

Premeditated. Willful. Deliberate.

Are you kidding me...

That's what the Junction PA office thought of me?

That's what they had *evidence* for?

The prosecutor continued, "The charges allege that on or about August 10, in the County of Kent, from the State of Michigan, the defendant, Gideon Paul O'Donnell, did unlawfully, intentionally, and with premeditation cause the death of Florence O'Donnell by shooting, thereby committing the offense of murder in the first degree."

My legs almost gave out. Didn't. But—

Hold it together, O'Donnell...

"Thank you, counsel," Judge Staggs said. "Mr. O'Donnell, how do you plead to the charge of murder in the first degree?"

Time stopped. Reality itself ground to an unmoving halt.

And the room started to spin, with starlight sparkling across my vision.

I heaved a breath and placed my hands on the table to stabilize me.

This is not happening...

"Your Honor," Reggie replied, "my client pleads not guilty."

"Very well-well. The plea of not guilty is so entered into the record."

The faint clattering of the stenographer refocused my attention.

Another deep breath, then a shaky drink from a cold glass of water stabilized me.

I needed a drink...

The judge said, "We will now consider the matter of bail. Does the prosecution have a recommendation regarding bail?"

Lawlor nodded. "We do, Your Honor. Due to the severity and nature of the charges, along with the extenuating circumstances, combined with the potential flight risk—"

I scoffed and shook my head. *Flight risk my ass!*

Apparently loud enough to throw Dean off his game and draw a scowl from Staggs.

I shifted. Lawlor got back to it.

"Combined with the potential flight risk, the City recommends this court deny bail."

Reggie was all over the preposterous request: "Your Honor, the prosecuting attorney knows well enough that the right to bail is constitutionally protected in Michigan—"

"And defense counsel knows well enough," Lawlor butted in, "that circumstances can warrant a judge denying bail entirely."

"But only when the proof of which is self-evident or the presumption of which is great, due to the preponderance of evidence."

Lawlor snorted. "Oh, it is self-evident, the evidence is exceedingly great!"

Judge Staggs interrupted with a loud, deliberate clearing of his throat.

"Gentlemen-men. Let's not turn my courtroom into *Judge Judy*!"

He glared at Dean Lawlor with a frown, which made me grin.

And the PA reddened. "Yes, Your Honor..." he muttered. "May I continue my argument?"

Judge Staggs motioned with his hand for him to continue.

"Due to the severity of the charges, the PA's office recommends that bail be denied. In the alternative to such denial, we ask that it would be set at two million dollars, with conditions including GPS monitoring and surrender of all travel documents."

A gasping murmur rippled through the courtroom. I agreed.

"And what are your reasons for such a request?"

"First, Your Honor, the defendant is charged with murder in the first degree, with indications of premeditation and intent. This particular charge and the nature of this particular crime is obviously an extraordinarily serious offense, one that carries the possibility of life imprisonment without the possibility of parole."

It took everything within me not to rush the man. I'd seen it done before, to Dean Lawlor, in fact. A few clients, charged with the same violent crimes flying off the handle at being accused of such a thing.

Flat knew how they felt now.

"Furthermore, Mr. O'Donnell poses a significant flight risk. He has the financial means that would allow him to easily flee the jurisdiction and evade prosecution. In fact, the lengthy prison sentence incentivises him to flee. The more important point, however, is the belief that Mr. O'Donnell poses a grave danger to the community. The crime—"

"Alleged!" I blurted. Couldn't help it.

Earning me the gavel.

"Control your client, Mr. Wilson," Judge Staggs instructed, actually pointing his polished wooden mallet our way.

Now Reggie's head swung my way, with those eyes that told me what was what.

He said, "Oh, he'll be controlled alright, Your Honor."

"Very well-well. Continue, Mr. Lawlor."

"As I was saying," he said, "given the *alleged* crime is a violent one, and particularly violent in this case, there is the concern that Mr. O'Donnell could further perpetuate similar acts of violence against the community if released."

"Really-lee? You're suggesting the allegations are serial in nature?"

"Uh, well, sort of..." That seemed to trip up the bozo.

"You're alleging a pattern of criminal behavior that isn't isolated in nature to this one act?"

More hemming, more hawing, clearly tripped up.

Go Stuttering Staggs a second time!

Lawlor let a huff slip before adding, "All we are suggesting, Your Honor, given the charge of murder one, for this and other reasons we strongly urge the court to deny bail."

The judge nodded, turning his gaze to Reggie. "I assume the defense has a response?"

Reggie said, "Yes, Your Honor. We respectfully request you set a bail amount that is reasonable, given the accused. Obviously, Mr. O'Donnell has strong ties to the community. His record and relationship with Mill Creek Junction speaks to this. He has lived here his entire life, owns a home, and operates a local business. He doesn't pose a flight risk. In fact, Your Honor knows he is due in court to litigate a massive class action lawsuit he would be remiss to neglect. He has people who depend on him. These factors significantly reduce any risk of flight."

"I don't know...I'm inclined to agree-ree with the prosecuting attorney."

Reggie continued, "Mr. O'Donnell has no prior criminal record, not even a speeding ticket. He has been a law-abiding citizen and has demonstrated good character and responsibility throughout his life. The notion that he would suddenly become a danger to the community is not supported by any evidence beyond the current charges, to which he has pleaded not guilty, and of which he is presumed innocent."

"Except those charges are significant. Rarely do I let murder suspects free on their own recognizance."

"Yet, the prosecution's claim that Mr. O'Donnell has the financial means to flee is speculative, not to mention factually inaccurate."

"Explain-plain."

Reggie frowned, having been roped into disclosing the firm's disastrous financial situation.

"He is far from wealthy enough to evade law enforcement effectively, especially given he is not financially stable. His business has fallen behind on payments to its landlord, and its electricity was recently shut off."

That got a reaction, a flurry of murmurs and snickers racing from behind. And a snorting laugh from my right. Didn't look to see who. Probably Lawlor.

An embarrassed heat raced up my neck and bloomed hot and heavy in my face. If the charge of murder didn't trash my reputation and street creds, the revelation I was a financial loser would.

Reggie continued, "We propose that bail be set at a reasonable amount. If the court would need further assurance of his cooperation, conditions such as GPS monitoring or house arrest would be reasonable, ensuring my client shows up to trial and allowing him to prepare for his defense."

Didn't like that last condition. Not in the slightest. Especially the house arrest part. How would I be able to solve my mother's murder—much less come to my defense!—if I was housebound?

Judge Staggs pursed his lips together and leaned back in his oversized chair, the brown leather almost enveloping him as he considered his ruling.

"I do believe," he finally said, "a little bird told me recently that your client successfully arranged for a similar bail for his own client. So, bail shall be set forth at one million dollars-lars, along with an ankle GPS monitoring device restricting Mr. Donnell's movement to Mill Creek Junction. He shall also surrender his passport forthwith."

I sighed. Both with relief at not getting house-arrested, but also with frustration at the ankle bracelet.

And the dough.

That was a significant chunk of cabbage. I would need to arrange for a cool hundred Gs, which I could do. It'd be tight, given the nature of things with the practice, and the bond would be non-returnable, which sucked. But I could do it.

I would do it. *Had* to do it.

If not for my sake, for Ma's.

"The next court date for the pretrial conference," Staggs continued, "is set for next Monday. Mr. O'Donnell, you are to appear in this courtroom at nine o'clock on that date. Do you understand?"

I nodded. "I do."

The gavel fell with a smack.

"Very well-well. Court is adjourned."

Judge Staggs stood. Silvia instructed us to rise. His Honor shuffled off stage.

And I was brought back into the cramped antechamber by my two goons, joined by two irritated defense attorneys.

Same table, same chairs awaited to confer with my lawyers before I was brought back to my jail cell to await the posted bond. Same for the cramped, dark, nature of it. With the same musty Junction basement smell.

Bert and Marv guided me to the table and began securing me to a metal anchor at the center. I didn't fight it, neither did Reggie nor Lizzy. My guess was they didn't care one bit given what I had pulled in court.

Which I had to explain: "Look, I did what I did—"

"Save it, Gideon," Reggie barked, jaw clenched and nostrils flared. He nodded to the two goons continuing their goonery.

Probably best to wait for them to leave.

They did. Then it came.

First by Lizzy: "What the hey-ho day was that, Gideon?"

She paused, putting up a finger and joining Reggie with a clenched jaw and flaring nostrils.

"No, Gideon, what the hey-ho day were you *thinking*?"

"It's my future on the line!" I barked back.

"Don't even go there, Gideon!"

Reggie added, "You know how stupid it would be to represent yourself? No, you know what? I *know* you do. Number one rule, drilled into us from, like, Day One of law school. Never represent yourself!"

"I'm with Reggie, Gideon," Lizzy added. "You know what they say about a lawyer who represents himself."

I frowned. I did.

Reggie said, "He has a damn fool for a client."

Lizzy nodded. "Darn right. That's, like, basic!"

I sighed. "Come on, what did you expect me to do?"

Reggie huffed. "I expected you to let us do our damn jobs, Gideon!"

"Look, it's my life on the line here—"

He laughed with interruption. One of those big, from-the-belly guffaws I usually smiled at.

Not this time. Not when it was directed at me with mockery.

"That's right. You're Gideon friggin' O'Donnell. Lawyer extraordinaire! The mister-mister who's the Junction's shiznit!"

"Reggie..." Lizzy started.

"And we're just chopped liver, right? Your less-than lackeys who didn't go to no fancy capital B and C big-city law school!"

"Come on, Reggie, cut it out. That's not what he meant."

He spun to her. "Then what *did* he mean? Because you know as well as I do that lawyers are their worst attorneys!"

The door opened and in popped Marv.

"Everything alright in here?"

"*Yes!*" we three replied as one.

"Oh-kee-dokey..."

Easing the door closed, he announced he would remand me back to jail in five minutes. I'd sit there until I posted bond. I needed Reggie's and Lizzy's help on that front. Which meant I needed to tread lightly while also winning the argument.

I sank into the chair and huffed a sigh. A bone-deep weariness overtook me, the adrenaline high wearing thin even as the stakes continued to ratchet into the stratosphere.

"I didn't mean to imply," I started, "that neither one of you were capable of defending me. And no way you think I think you're my lackeys. You know that's not true. You're my partners now, remember?"

Reggie said nothing. Lizzy offered an "I know" before jamming an elbow into her silent partner's ribcage and forcing a "Right?" from the man. He grunted an affirmative reply.

I got on with it: "But this is my life on the line here. Not yours."

"And?" asked Lizzy. Fair question.

"And..."

I couldn't finish the sentence. Couldn't think of a reasonable response. Because Reggie was bang-on the money: Lawyers really were their worst attorneys. The adage was a tongue-in-cheek way of reminding juris doctors that, in representing themselves, their judgment would be clouded, no way could they be objective, and more often than not it led to overconfidence and under preparation, even neglecting candid advice that would normally come from professional distance.

That wasn't even touching on the pressure and stress from the time and resources it took to mount an effective defense while still taking care of business—in my case, my in-progress class action suit.

Reggie and Lizzy were just as good, just as fierce litigators as I was. Knew of no one else in all of Michigan who could win the fight I was up against. Except myself, of course. But...well, I'd be flat stupid to sideline them and reject their help.

So, yeah, they were right. Big mistake. I knew that.

Taking a deep breath, I stood and offered a hand, those blasted chains rattling again.

Reached out to my friends, my partners.

My lawyers.

Reggie regarded my hand with a raised brow. "What's this?"

"This means you're hired," I said with a wry grin.

He smirked and shook it. Lizzy just threw an arm around my shoulder and pecked my cheek.

"Knew you'd come to your senses," she said, "and see it our way."

I laughed. "No offense to you, Lizzy, but if this goes to trial, I want Reggie as the first chair. He's stronger with criminal proceedings and...well—he'd be sympathetic to a jury."

Didn't need to say the quiet part out loud: as a black man.

She nodded. "Alright, Gideon. We'll play this your way."

"Where do you propose we start?" asked Reggie.

I knew exactly where to start.

And who to call.

The exit opened with a shudder. In walked Bert and Marv.

Back to prison for me.

For now.

Chapter Fifteen

I eased my coupe into the single-stall garage attached to my two-level craftsman and promptly closed my garage door.

Then huffed a relieved sigh.

I'd made it. Home.

Didn't move. Didn't want to. Because part of me didn't think I'd ever see the inside of my life again.

If Mill Creek Junction PD had had a say in the matter, I wouldn't have. Ever. Took their sweet-ass time getting me out of jail after Reggie and Lizzy secured the bond for bail. They leveraged a line of credit from our business account, figuring it was in the best interest of the practice that its principal business owner was sprung from the clink. I would pay back the firm with a personal line of credit from a second mortgage, but for now it worked.

Until it didn't, the boys in blue claiming there had been some paperwork error at the court side of things when the bond had been posted. Took several hours, and several back-and-forths from Reggie and Lizzy to sort out the "mess." Which really wasn't a mess, because everything was exactly in order, in the way it should have been.

It was only after the two brought a certified letter from the court attesting to the bond's posting that Junction PD got its act together. Even then, they'd dragged their feet until it was dusk, claiming work-load this and trouble-locating-the-GPS-tracker that. Had to take Reggie—God bless him!—threatening to sue the Junction, along with every one of the officers involved personally, for violating my due process for the gears of justice to finally activate.

Waiting for final processing was an even more remarkable experience.

Getting my clothes and dressing back into what I had been arrested in, Bert and Marv made these odd comments about being careful on my way home. Said they'd heard "chatter" about "some folks" who were "riled up" over my release.

When I pressed them about it, they pivoted back to the vague "chatter" nonsense. When I said such claims could constitute police intimidation, a serious rights violation, they shut their traps and got to strapping that GPS tracker around my right ankle. Hurt like a mother, the one short, squat goon with a handlebar mustache cinching it tight against my skin, down to the bone. I complained, but Burt predictably claimed "Protocol" and that was that.

The only saving grace was that Lizzy was waiting with the keys to my car. She and Reggie figured I'd want to drive home alone. She was right, and I was finally stumbling toward my vehicle in the sticky August night.

When Chief Roller and Mayor Goodall met me on the walkway.

The chief asked if I wanted a police escort. Said he was worried for my safety, given all the news coverage. The mayor echoed the man, adding his own worry over the impending class action suit that lots of unnamed people were angry about. Said that the investment from London money was the start of a new Junction era, that it was fixing to do a lot of good for a lot of people. Said people were liable to get violent if they thought I was messing with a good thing that might secure their futures.

I demurred, waving off their offer, and went on my way, shaking my head over the odd conversation. And not a bit unnerved by the veiled threats, echoing the ones Burt and Marv had offered up.

That was over an hour ago now. After leaving, I hadn't driven straight home. Ashamed to say I'd been a bit shaken by the encounters, the veiled threats, not to mention the last few days in jail.

Now I couldn't move. Couldn't leave the cozy comforts of my German import. An Audi RS5. Nothing overly fancy, like a BMW or Mercedes, but the silver coupe certainly stuck out like a sore thumb in the Mitten State famous for GM and Ford. Instead of turning off the engine and slipping inside, I lingered in the moment.

The heavy, throbbing purr of the powerful twin-turbo V6 engine was a mental, calming balm for the chaotic past few days, relieved to be free from the six-by-eight that I had worried would be my forever abode.

Just sat like that, for the longest time. Enjoyed the simple pleasures of the steady hum in the quiet comfort of the moment, wrapped in the soft, sturdy charcoal leather that reminded me of my upper-middle-class professional existence that was on the ropes.

What the heck...

This is ridiculous! Get. Out.

I did, heaving a stabilizing breath and making for the side entrance into my house.

Fumbling with my keys, I finally managed to unlock it and

slide inside. Promptly shutting the door and locking it again. Both knob lock and deadbolt.

I stood still, silent in my living room, the cavernous house beyond dark and shadowy. Listening, intuiting, discerning any movement, anyone.

Nothing but the sound of silence.

I sauntered across the walnut hardwood floor, the bone-weariness from the past few days heightened by the anticipation. The flaring bark of a dog from somewhere in the neighborhood sent me to the front window. A quick peek outside through a part in heavy silk curtains confirmed an empty street. After another beat, then another confirmation, I drew them tight and withdrew, running a relieved hand through my greasy, unwashed hair.

I wanted to sink into my leather couch but didn't. A ticking clock kept time on the mantle above a marble fireplace and filled the silence of my nice-size, two-story house as I beelined it for my kitchen. I was hungry. I needed food.

I'd often thought of my kitchen as the pride of my home. Today it just looked sad. Just a sad gray greeted me, compounded by stainless steel appliances. I'd had good intentions to add some color to the joint after the lockdown those years ago. Best laid plans and all. A bright moon shone silver through a bay of windows in the rear breakfast nook as I rummaged through the massive Kitchenaid fridge built for a family of eight. Overkill, considering it was me and only me.

A carton of eggs left me one left, which wouldn't do. Same for a carton of orange juice that had gone bad. Sour and fermenting in all the wrong ways. Which fit the day to a T, considering the past few days. Then some cheese slices going green and a gallon of milk past its prime. Frozen meats in the freezer would take too long, and now I wasn't feeling so hungry anymore, standing with the molding remains of my refrigerator, my life.

So I sauntered back into the living room and sank into that leather sofa, a headache beginning to needle the center of my head.

The last time I remember feeling this way was those years ago when the governor put the state in a temporary timeout during that crazy coronapocalypse that just happened to coincide with a personal apocalyptic moment.

My Big Four-Oh.

I'd had a big bash planned that was sidelined by the stay-at-home order, with Ma and Dad, a few former clients from the firm, along with Reggie and Lizzy, then some of the fellas from Max's Place, Max Blade himself providing the alcohol and catering in a feast fit for a forty-year-old king. Even the Rev and a few of his parishioners from my childhood church were set to join in the festivities.

Until my cell phone vibrated with the emergency order from the governor locking us down, and my massive fifty-incher anchored above my vacant fireplace outlined the terms from the plush comforts of a hermetically sealed news studio. With that Merriam-Webster's Word of the Year shoo-in we all came to know as "social distancing" along with no unnecessary travel.

Not that the restrictions didn't make sense, given all the reports of the zombie apocalypse descending on the world. My own state had run third behind New York and New Jersey for most cases and most deaths. So, yeah, I was fine to sign up for social distancing! Didn't make it any easier knowing I was doing my part to flatten the curve.

On, of all days, the day I'd slammed into middle age.

Someone somewhere said life begins at forty. Not for Gideon Paul O'Donnell that day.

My leg vibrated with an incoming text.

I retrieved my phone and frowned.

Annabelle Kirkland.

Flat didn't know what to think, how to feel seeing her name.

Of course, she had all the Southern charm of a pixie, with that smile and wink and twangy *'Bless your heart'* wielded like dust to lull you into acceptance.

Right before she stuck a shiv in your belly at trial.

Luckily, two could play at her game. And I had, holding my own against the feisty woman and winning enough verdicts to keep a batting average that brought in more clients than I'd known what to do with.

Except she had won me over. And we had started dating. Making my life uber complicated. Who knew where we stood now that I'd been accused of murdering my mother, and she was helping prosecute my guilt.

I shook away the thought and read the text:

> Hey, Paulie. How's life back on the street?

Paulie. I smiled. Her little pet name for me, an endearing use of my middle name like that, as Annie was for her.

That was promising.

Three dots appeared, indicating she was typing.

I waited. They fell back into the internet ether.

My thumbs hovered over the keyboard. Respond or not? If I did, what would I say?

I went with one word, which spun into a few back-and-forths:

> Fine

> Good to hear

Yeah

Hope you didn't drop the soap ;)

My smile widened at that last line, followed by an echoey chuckle. Classic Annie. But I wasn't in the mood. Not only because I was just flat tired. From it all. But also because she was technically my adversary.

Prosecuting me for murdering my mother.

And wasn't this some ethical violation? Yeah, we were dating and all that jazz. Still...she wasn't supposed to contact me, the adverse party, without the presence of my lawyer. Supposed that technically was Reggie and Lizzy, although I still intended to represent myself. So I let the ethical violation go.

Except—

Except she was on the other side of this—whatever *this* was. And I was in no mood to engage.

I replied with two words:

Good luck

I sighed, tossing my phone to the side.

What a day.

Taking in my empty living room, bare walls complementary shades of sanitary gray—with pretentious names like Pewter and Pearl River and Anchor—a sudden coldness flooded my veins, and my head began to swim with a familiar friend I'd kept at bay during my teenage years, and even through college and law school when I kept my focus on working hard and making something of myself.

Loneliness.

Took me back to the pandemic, when I was on lockdown

and had the exact same feeling wash over me on my fortieth birthday. I hated it then. Hated it now. Almost as bad as being in that six-by-eight.

Suddenly, I felt very small and unseen. Alone and aware of the emptiness of my surroundings—of my life, even—in a way you're not supposed to.

Most of life is background noise. The house or apartment, the car and commute, the blanket tossed casually across the back of the couch when you need it on a cold night, the dishes ready to use and a refrigerator stocked for three-square meals, the magazines piled next to the couch you always mean to cancel but never get around to doing.

It all just exists. It's just there. A steady eclectic presence of stuff waiting to be tapped into, to be enjoyed, to be leveraged to live and survive, to function with perfunctory servitude.

Except—

Taking in my living room—the flat screen above my fireplace, the shelves of books in one corner, the nice leather furniture arrayed around the large space. Glimpsing the mahogany dining room set in the next room, with the fine china chilling forgotten behind glass. Catching my study farther on, iMac and MacBook resting on a walnut desk piled with work and legal tomes, JD diploma hanging proud on the far wall with the imprimatur of Georgetown Law. Then feeling the weight of my four-post king bed and suits and ties and sweatpants directly above, with still two more unused rooms waiting to house nonexistent guests and nonexistent children full of exercise equipment and childhood sports trophies—

All of it pressed in against me with lonely suffocation.

All that stuff. The abundance and gluttony and utter vapidity of the life I'd crafted the past decade. Just sitting there, trinkets and trophies of success, not service.

Yup. I'd arrived. With all the trappings of bourgeois respectability and comfort.

Except—

Who was I kidding?

Loneliness had been my best friend and worst enemy. My frenemy, since childhood. And now, back in the land of the free, what I had often kept at bay for a few decades—it all smacked me in the face like a jilted lover. I couldn't deny it, couldn't escape it.

All I really had was me, myself, and I. Always had been that way, really.

Started with my adoption, after my birth mother left me at the fire station over forty years ago. As an introvert, I normally relished the alone time at the end of a long week going to the mat for my clients and the extra class I taught at the college in town. Even those brief days in jail were a bit of an all-inclusive-resort respite—sans mojitos and white-sand beaches.

Now it was all suffocating, ringing hollow without anyone to share it with. Without anyone to feed and nurture and shelter other than my own ego.

Without Ma...

The thought wreaked me. Undid me. And for the first time since being arrested—being *fingered*—for her murder, I allowed myself to be undone.

Emotion seized my throat and flooded my eyes. Soon I was blubbering like a baby, my body wracked by convulsive sobs sending me to the floor curling in on myself, cries of agony echoing with the sounds of grief.

Joined by one haunting question.

Ma...what happened?

Chapter Sixteen

I was not a crier. Rarely shed a tear. When I did, it took a lot to turn the faucets on. Really never saw the point in it.

What does crying *do*? I mean, for the situation, for the thing? Nothing but a waste of hydration and energy, as far as I was concerned. Was more the type to hold in my emotions, especially the sorrowful and sorrow-filled, gut-wrenching ones. Took after Dad in that way. When they did show up, they often came in an angry outburst of frustration. Never in tears.

But this felt good. The tear-shedding, the mixture of sorrow and rage exploding from the very center of my diaphragm and throat, the heaving sobs wracking my body until I ached from head to toe.

All of it felt right—*was* right. Felt just and good and true.

Supposed crying over the loss of one's mother was about as right and good and true as a cry could be, beautiful even. Doubly so when she was murdered in cold blood.

Except—

Except I couldn't handle it any more. I needed air.

Needed...something other than the shallow confines of my self-absorbed, lonely world. Needed to be around the hustle and bustle of people, eating and drinking and having a good time. I needed my go-to haunt.

So I jumped to my feet, a coldness spreading over me as I stood still in the belly of my professional-class existence. I had to get out of my house. Out of this prison and back out into the real world. I knew exactly where to go.

Instead of taking my car, I opted for a walk. The fresh air and movement of limbs and muscles that had sat unused the past few days would do me good.

But first things first: a shower.

After washing away two days of incarceration, I threw on a white linen T-shirt and gray linen shorts then slipped into my favorite casual walking shoes and hiked it the seven blocks down to Main Street. Thankfully, the humidity had lifted, and now the sun had set, dipping below Mill Creek Junction's skyline at half-past eight in a blazing display of orangey purple brilliance. Just beautiful, the giant dwarf star setting the horizon on fire. Supposed those old Jewish poems were true: *'You have set your glory in the heavens...The heavens declare the glory of God; the skies proclaim the work of his hands.'*

Hustling across Straight Street, I smirked to myself, wondering why Psalms 8 and 19 popped into my head. Supposed you could take the kid out of church but you couldn't take church out of the kid. I also supposed prison will do that to a guy, bringing a person back to the Almighty after not darkening his sanctuary in years.

The Junction's main strip of shops and eateries neared, illuminated by the flickering flames of gas-lit street lamps that reminded me of simpler times. The sounds of traffic and the joys of nightlife festivities began to drown out the other night life. That barking dog from earlier and insects and tree frogs faded into the background of grumpy mufflers and loud talkers and some instrumentalists jazzing it up in a brick building just up ahead.

I jogged across Main Street toward Max's Place, my stomach rumbling with hunger now and barking for relief. The evening air was laced with the smell of hops and grease and peanuts. Exactly what I needed—all of the above!

Entering through a screen door, it sure was nice to see the Junction's watering hole filled to the brim with familiar faces, joined by the competing senses of Max's Place. The grill flared seared beef and garlic, joined by saffron and mustard, Burt whipping up some special culinary creation from the back for the night. Those jazzmen I'd heard on approach were going at a modern rendition of Jimmy Smith's "The Sermon." Marvin and the Gang were doing their thing on a stage at the back, the headliner himself working his Hammond organ like it was nobody's business, joined by a strumming a bass and a *rat-a-tat-tatting* drum set and a trumpet.

All of it turned my frown upside down at the lively mood. Exactly what I needed, regaining my sense of place, my sense of purpose.

"Burt!" Max yelled. "Give me some hamburger love, would ya?" He poked his head up from behind the bar—his bar, in his bar. Or more accurately, Max's Place.

The mainstay eatery of Mill Creek Junction had been in the Blade family since the town's founding. Smelled like it too. That old, woody smell of earth and spice and tar. With peanut shells ground into the hardwood floor, and all that spilled pilsner beer, even moonshine they'd brewed and smuggled during Prohibition still flaring. Add to that the lingering stench of a century worth of cigarettes and cigars, it's no wonder people still frequented the joint.

No, that wasn't true. I knew exactly why. It's why I had left the safety of my house for the joint.

Community. Family. Home.

Sure is true what they say: *Absence makes the heart grow fonder*. Especially when you've been in jail.

"Gideon!" Max shouted now, throwing up a *yee-haw* before beelining it for me. The whole dining room seemed to stop, on a dime. One of those corny record-scratch moments from those '90s sitcoms I loved as a child. Those were the days, but I much more preferred those sorts of moments from television shows of yore. Not from the good folks I had to live with.

Who now, no doubt, suspected that I'd killed my own mother.

Probably only my imagination, most of the place resuming its revelry while catching a few cross-eyed glances between mouthfuls of beer and bites of food.

Max bounded over in a Pink Floyd t-shirt and ripped jeans running a bit snug for the man my age. He threw his arms around me in a bear hug then pulled back, eyes misting over.

"Sorry for your loss, dude. She was a good mama."

Emotion returned to my own eyes. I had trouble voicing a response, my throat clenching again with the same. I managed a smile and nodded.

"And what the bleepity-bleep is that gigolo Dean Lawlor thinking!" Max hooked a thumb in his direction, a scowl deepening with solidarity. "Arresting you—accusing you?"

He huffed a sigh and crossed his arms, shaking his head. "Almost didn't serve the dude but feared he'd throw my own skinny heinie in the clink. Hey, you didn't drop the soap did you?"

A wink, a smile, a back-slapping laugh that lightened the mood.

I laughed, shaking my head. "That's what Annabelle asked. And no. Didn't even have a chance to shower."

"Annabelle..." Max whistled and gave his head a shake. "*Oo-wee!* Now that there's some complicated shiznit."

"Pretty much."

"Girls...Can't live without 'em. Can't live with 'em. Especially when they're fingering you for a crime you didn't commit."

Could only nod at that. And smile, knowing at least one person thought I hadn't killed my mother. The thought sent my eyes darting a quick glance through the dining room.

Wondered how many were waging bets I was guilty as sin?

Max slapped my back and guided me to the bar, and that was that. The room resumed its pace and I was ushered to a stool while Max hustled around to pour me a drink. Asked me what I wanted, and I mumbled some local grapefruit IPA, and he went to work.

I sat and slumped against the polished dark wood smelling of lemon polish.

Pouring my drink, Max peppered me with questions about life inside the big house before launching into a story about his grandpappy from somewhere up the Blade family tree getting busted for illegal moonshine during Prohibition.

Didn't pay him much mind. I was more interested in the foaming India Pale Ale, which he handed off as he went into how he'd busted out and made a run for it up north.

Took a whiff, citrus and tropical fruit heavy on the nose. Good start to what promised to be a good drink. Throwing one back, my mouth filled with a delicate tartness and—well, the taste of grapefruit. Had a nice sweet, malty backbone to it with a clean finish at the end.

I *ahh*ed. The simple pleasures of a cold drink on a hot

summer evening. Something I would never take for granted again.

Max kept at his story. I glanced around the place.

And smiled. A cross section of town all gathered together under one roof, with Max Blade the ringleader of the circus. It was nice. A nice town of nice people, dealing with their fair share of issues, but getting by and getting along.

Chief Roller had just shown up, head shiny beneath the lights overhead. He came in with a few of the boys in blue. Big-boned bruisers sauntering in like they owned the place. Roller led the pack and poured himself a drink from a half-drained pitcher a table from the stage, all big-toothed and full-on belly laughing. Old Man Nugent was doubled over now, adding to his own drink. Nice guy who gave a decent haircut for a good price. But seeing him with the chief like that made me queasy.

Ken and Barbara sat together across the room, enjoying a moment alone after adding a newborn to their family last year. Looked the part, too. Tall, blond, fit. Their baby girl was a perfect blend of their perfect all-American features. I was happy for them.

Then there was Dean Lawlor, commanding another table of his cronies. Annabelle Kirkland was nowhere to be found, thank the good Lord above! Couldn't imagine showing up for a quiet night and having to face her after the past few days. Could barely stomach seeing the blowhard who'd gone after me like that. How could he accuse me of killing my own mother, after all she'd done for me—after all Lawlor *knew* she'd done for me, the two of us childhood friends?

That comment Max said earlier snagged in my ear. About how you couldn't live with a girl who fingered you for a crime you didn't commit. Was that what Annabelle thought too—that I'd been accused of something I hadn't committed? We'd never gotten that far in our text exchange. Mostly because I'd cut it off with that lame curt reply wishing her *Good luck*. Didn't define what I meant, but the message probably came through.

Good luck prosecuting her case against me.

What a boneheaded thing to say.

I threw back another swig, then another, sweeping the rest of my gaze past a table of farmers and farmhands nursing their own pitchers and jawing it up over baskets of fries and burgers, with Fred Myers adding his two cents, the local grocer. I ended on an unexpected sight that set me flat.

Mayor Goodall was hamming it up with a table across the room, working it like the politician he was, joined by six or seven others. Made sense he'd be working the room like that, given it was an election year. His wife Millie rolled her eyes before grinning, shaking a finger before rolling her eyes again, eliciting a round of laughs at something.

I was more interested in the others who had joined him.

Chief among them, Gage Strauss, the CEO of Happy-Living Estates. The buzz-cut joker straight from an Army recruitment poster I was supposed to have deposed a few days ago before getting arrested. Wondered what he was doing with the mayor. Didn't know they were close enough to be drinking buddies.

And who were those other three with him?

Two Asian men in fine tan suits, one a darker complexion and built for a factory floor, the other a fair-skinned man looking more adept for the 52nd floor of some Hong Kong high-rise. Both flanked a tall blonde with a beauty mark on her upper lip. Reminded me of the Cindy Crawford poster I'd taped up on my bedroom wall as a teenager. This version was more the Wall Street type than Madison Avenue or Hollywood Boulevard sort of lady. The way she carried herself looked like she was the one running the show, the way the two suits deferred to her, the way that CEO leaned in and fixed his attention on her. Even the mayor was directing his conversation, his jokes her way.

"Burt, get this man a burger!" Max shouted with interruption into the kitchen. He yanked my attention back to himself and turned to me with a smile. "On the house."

I set my drink down and reached for my wallet. "You don't have to do that, Max."

"Naw, brotha-from-anotha-motha! A guy breaks free from the clink and he deserves a fine meal. And a second beer."

I looked down to find mine almost empty. He twisted off the top of a brown Budweiser bottle and plunked it down in front.

Draining my IPA, I nodded my thanks and slurped back a mouthful of the brew. Not really a low-brow wheat beer guy, going more for hoppy craft-brewed liquid pleasure. Didn't matter a lick. Beer was beer when you broke free from the clink. Even a Bud.

I scooped a handful of peanuts from a red basket Max kept up at the bar, and started crushing them, popping each one into my mouth. I turned around toward the band striking up another tune from the stage in the back. The organist switched from one of Smith's earlier bluesy numbers to a later groovier one from his fusion days. Something from the late 1960s evolution in jazz when musicians combined jazz harmony and improvisation with funky rock and bluesy rhythm. "Root Down," if I recalled.

Good number, with the man on the whites-and-blacks working the ivory of the old, boxy, honey-stained contraption like it was nobody's business, the drums keeping up a nice rhythm, a youngster strumming his electric guitar, working the strings with a twisted face that said he was feeling what the organ was putting down.

Before long, Max handed off a thick burger piled high with

the fixings and a side of his crack fries, as he called them. I thanked him, and he told me to holler if I needed anything else, then I dove in.

Nothing in all the world like a burger made special by Burt. With that thick, juicy patty served rare with an extra amount of moo, still bloody yet warm enough to ward off the salmonella, dripping with sharp Wisconsin white cheddar and smothered in ketchup and brown mustard and that special spicy sauce he whips up that made my eyes spill over.

Especially just out of prison.

The bite was heaven. More than heaven. Nirvana.

Same for the side of hot fries soaked in grease and sprinkled with a dash of pepper and a generous amount of salt to burn the lips. Crack fries was right! Swallowing the first bite of cow, I stuffed a handful of greasy fries into my mouth, savoring the mashup of flavors.

All of it complemented by the cold bottle of Bud. Which I promptly threw back to wash it all down.

The first meal I'd really had since entering into the Junction PD jail. And boy, did it taste good.

Except—

Something sat sour in my stomach and snagged for my attention.

Mayor Goodall, and that table of mystery guests.

Swallowing, I reached for my bottle and twisted back for a look.

There they were. Goodall and *Fraulein Geheimnis*, the young mystery woman who smacked of foreign money. The handbag certainly screamed it, a shiny black patent leather purse with two gold intersecting Cs and a matching chain indicating she definitely wasn't from those parts. Same for the large pearls clinging to her ears. Maybe East Coast money, maybe European.

Bigger question was what she was doing palling around with Gage Strauss, that CEO bozo who'd stood him up. And flanked by two Asian men, with the powerbroker of Mill Creek Junction leaned in all conspiratorial like while a woman straight out of the *Sound of Music* spoke.

Had half a mind to march over there and have it out with the man, both of them—the CEO and Mayor.

Instead, I snapped a few pictures on my phone, took another swig of Bud, then turned back to my burger.

Except—

That table, with Goodall and Strauss, those men and that woman.

Something flared at the back of my brain and worked its way through my chest, skating cold through my veins. A spidey sense I'd hammered and honed through a decade of litigation and investigation.

You develop a sixth sense about these sorts of things in this line of work. And with the way my trial was set to start soon, and that CEO pulling out and those threats from the mayor about discontent from my class action—then these new actors, who were probably bad actors, knowing the bull Strauss was trying to pull...

Something didn't sit right. Didn't know what or why, but—

Another burger bite before another glance across the shoulder.

To catch Fraulein and Strauss and Goodall leaving, joined by those other two goons. And was that Chief Roller and his boys in blue trailing them?

Nope. This didn't sit right at all.

And I aimed to find out why.

Consequences be damned.

Chapter Seventeen

What the heck was that text about?

Annabelle Kirkland didn't have a cotton picking' clue what the bloomin' blazes that Yankee Doodle Dandy Gideon O'Donnell had meant by that bloomin' cryptic final text last night.

Good luck.

Huh? Couldn't figure that boy out as far she could throw him!

Hustling in a pair of boots that were not made for hustling, she rolled that text around in her noggin'—for the umpteenth time.

Good luck.

At what?

Her next pickleball tourney? At trying to revive her vegetable garden that had befallen both her backyard critters and black thumb?

Good luck.

She scoffed, her pace only outmatched by her irritation.

Luck at what? Life—*her* life?

She had a sudden, sinking realization that slowed her roll right quick.

Were things over between them? Was that a final send-off text ending their relationship?

No, that couldn't be it. Was sure it wasn't.

Wasn't she?

The context surrounding the text had been about Gideon's incarceration. So maybe he meant the trial, her prosecution of him. Or *persecution*, because surely that's how he felt. Maybe what she wondered was right.

He's eighty-sixed our relationship!

She had no cotton pickin' clue! And it had kept her up until all waking hours figuring out his meaning. Just her, a package of Toll House cookie dough, and Rory and Lorelai Gilmore from her go-to television show.

Now she was cranky and running late for work.

Hence the midmorning stop at Starbucks.

"I'll take a grande extra hot flat white latte with sugar-free vanilla, please."

Annabelle slung her purse up on the counter and started rifling through it for her drink card. She knew it was in there somewhere. But between the mascara, lipstick, eyeliner, deodorant, and extra pantyhose—because Lord knows a girl has got to keep an extra pair just in case!—she was having about as much luck as a cat in a swimming pool.

Still rummaging, she added, "Oh, and would you be a good dear and add an extra shot?"

"One of those days, Annabelle?" asked Trisha, leaning over the counter and eyeing her oversized purse that serviced as an office away from office.

Annabelle sighed, pushing a stubborn lock of strawberry blonde hair her mama had blessed her with back into place. "That it is. If only I could find my card..."

"Don't worry about it, sister. It's on the house this morning."

She looked up with no small amount of embarrassment. "Really? Are you sure? You're not gonna get fired or anything?"

"Naw. We do it all the time for our fave customers."

Annabelle went back to the purse, rummaging through it with about the same amount of luck.

"Because I can certainly come back later once I find the darn thing..."

"Seriously, sister. Not a problem. Doubt Howard Shultz is going to miss the fiver."

She smiled and clutched her chest. "Bless your heart, Trish. I owe you one!"

"Next time Chief Roller gives me a speeding ticket, I'll come knocking."

"Deal!" Annabelle tossed her the only buck she had for a cheapskate tip then slid to the end of the bar to wait for her drink.

The morning was looking better already. Especially with who was waiting for her at the end.

"Howdy, Cameron," Annabelle said to the college kid manning the espresso machine, ears pierced with quarters that looked like they hurt something fierce! A shock of blond hair swooped down from underneath a charcoal stocking cap that looked out of place in the dead of an Indian summer that was ruining her hair. He had that boy-next-door look about him but was trying to pull off a bad-boy look that looked like fake news. Didn't mind one bit, though.

The kiddo looked up and brightened. "Hey, Annabelle! Or, should I say, good morning, Miz Kirkland, assistant prosecuting attorney extraordinaire," he added with a bow.

She giggled. "Oh, stop that miss nonsense! How many times have I told you that you make me sound like an old windbag? My mama and my meemaw are Ms. Kirkland. Annabelle is fine for you."

Cameron chuckled and held up his hands in surrender. "Sorry! Annabelle it is. Figured it was you when I saw the flat white latte come through."

He held up her cup and winked, flashing her those perfect white teeth with that perfect dimple that threw off the whole bad-boy gig.

Annabelle flashed him a smile and winked back, throwing up her hands with another giggle. "Guilty as charged!"

Then felt foolish, glancing around the cafe at the banter.

No one seemed to be paying them any mind. Anyhow, what bloomin' business was it of theirs anyhow? Can't a forty-ish woman flirt with a small-town college kid?

A depressing thought muscled its way in: Had she married her high school sweetheart like she'd planned before he left her at the altar, literally, she very well could have been old enough to be Cameron's own mama.

The smile quickly faded, and she lost her appetite for the flat white.

They shared a laugh and the shrill of her phone gave her an excuse to exit stage left, pronto.

Annabelle fished it out of her purse, finding her Starbucks card nestled inside a We Will We Will Wok You Chinese takeout menu on her way for her phone. Ahh well. Sort of happy to have stuck it to the Shultz Man getting her flat white comped, as cheap of a middle finger as it was.

Retrieving her phone, she yanked it out and frowned.

Dean Lawlor. The Bossman.

Now there was a man she wouldn't mind giving the single-finger salute to.

She sighed. Never a good sign when Lawlor was ringing.

And the fact she'd just been flirting with his son made it doubly bad.

Grabbing her finished drink from the counter, Annabelle tossed Cameron a buckaroo she'd found on her way for the phone and nodded goodbye as she jostled the phone against her head.

"Mornin', boss. Sorry I'm running late. Didn't mean for you to have to ring-a-ding-ding. Hope all is well at—"

"Have you gotten a call yet from O'Donnell?" asked Dean with an interruptive rush.

"Gideon?" she said, cursing herself for getting too casual with the other side of the aisle.

Dean totally disapproved of them dating, given the nature of their adversarial relationship at the courthouse. Mostly it was because Dean hated Gideon's guts. Probably because Gideon was good at what he did, and word on the street was they'd had something of a rivalry stretching back to childhood. Didn't get it one lick of a popsicle.

She heard him clear his throat on the other end, as if swallowing back a shot of vinegar at her mentioning his name. Dean said, "That would be the one. Anyway, he was released on bail."

"I heard..."

"So we've got to get our crap together. Go over the evidence again. Replay that recording, get it verified—"

She snorted. "The recording..."

"Yes, Annabelle. The recording!"

She set her drink on an annoyingly tiny table in front of a picture window, and squeezed into a seat with her back to the door. That recording had unsettled her from the start. Sure sounded like her boyfriend. Tone and timbre and all. Except for the substance, the content of the recording. She knew it didn't look good, the accusations. From both sides of the convo.

It was also no smoking gun. Not like Dean was trying to make it out to be. And besides, she knew Gideon better than what the recording indicated.

"Helloooo?"

Annabelle threw back a sip, wishing for something stronger than the earthy, caramelly espresso-and-milk.

"I'm here. I'll get it over to my contact in cybersecurity at the FBI field office in Grand Rapids."

"Good. Where are we at with the rest of the evidence, especially the physical side of the collection?"

"Still working on tracking down Florence's dental and bloodwork. There's been a...snafu."

"Don't worry. That's being handled."

She sat straighter. Handled?

Sounded about as vague as the *Good luck* text she'd gotten from Gideon.

Men!

And yet Annabelle could gather his meaning without plumbing its depths. She'd seen how the man had operated since arriving in this humble town a few years ago. The Pentwell case was—well, a case in point.

She had assumed it was a simple drug possession case. Well, that's how it started, anyway. Right before Dean laughed her off and clued her in that nothing was ever simple in Mill Creek Junction. Especially when a city council member's son was involved, and up against the mayor in a dog-eat-dog election.

Annabelle popped the top to her cup, recalling that wake-up moment, slurping some foam off. It was laced with dark espresso, the earthy, smoky notes tingling her taste buds and taking her away for the slightest moment.

"Annabelle, you there?" Dean asked.

She swallowed. "I'm here."

"Verify that recording, you hear? It all hinges on its authenticity."

That's for sure. Because the dang thing offered up the big Mo on a silver platter.

Motivation.

He went on, "Were you able to interview the CEO?"

"I was. He had quite the story to tell."

Dean snorted a laugh. "I'm sure he did! From what I gathered, Gideon was eager to nail the guy until his mother's death. Which could be perceived as a clear motive for his crimes."

She shifted. Again, the whole thing reminded her of the Pentwell case, when she was planning to kick the thing to the curb because a few marijuana joints weren't worth her time. Turned out the amount weighed enough to peg him with intent to distribute, which Dean had pressed her to try the kid on. Even though the Mitten State legalized recreational marijuana use, and even though his mother was the chief rival to the Junction's mayor, posing all sorts of entanglements that'd give Southern politics a run for their Deep South money.

Supposed you skinned small-town politics the same way, no matter which side of the Mason-Dixon the cat hissed.

"Don't forget how important this is for the Mayor, Annabelle. His plans, for Mill Creek Junction—for us Juntioneers."

Annabelle frowned. There it was. Same MO from the last several go-arounds on the small-town merry-go-round.

She shifted in her chair and took a mouthful of espresso-laced milk this time. "The mayor has plans? What the heck does that mean?"

"Look. There's been some trouble, apparently. And with the upcoming election, he needs this win. We all do! With the way small towns are going nowadays, the way of the dodo bird is the way of our future if this HappyLiving deal don't go through."

"But that's politics, Dean. We're about the law. Justice."

"It's politics all the way down in the Junction, Annabelle. Same for justice. Anyway, as you know, our office is staffed by appointment. Not me, of course, as an elected judicial representative. And the way the Mill Creek Junction charter was written way back in the olden days of yore, that appointment comes by the chief executive."

Now Annabelle needed a shot of Baileys, because she got where he was going with this one.

Mayor Goodall was that chief executive of Mill Creek Junction.

"Spell it out for me, Dean. Just so I'm clear on my marching orders. From the chief executive."

"Now, Annabelle, I'm not giving you marching orders, per se."

"You just indicated how Gideon's case was politically convenient. And biffing it would be politically *in*-convenient."

"All I'm saying is, do your job. Keep a Mill Creek murderer off our streets. *That's* a matter of law and justice. Gotta go. Catch you later, and give me an update if you hear from O'Donnell."

The call ended, and Annabelle tossed the phone back in her purse.

"Oh, I'll give you something, you sorry sonofa—"

She was interrupted by the jangle of the bell above the door behind her.

Spinning toward it she half expected Gideon to come walking in. It wasn't him. Just some teenyboppers coming in for some froufrou drink in between classes.

It did bring back a memory, though. When Mr. McDreamy himself had come waltzing through those doors to order his morning drink of choice. Hair all slicked from just the right amount of product keeping those wavy dark locks in place, a golf umbrella keeping it perfectly dry and coiffed. That dark blue suit pressed to perfection with the starch-white shirt and bright-red power tie that told the world I'm Mr. Somebody, I'm Mr. McDreamy, in all of his—

Annabelle's flushing, warming face brought her back from McDreamy dreamland to her senses. She sank in her chair and promptly took a calming gulp of espresso drink goodness.

What they hey-ho day brought that on? All she had wanted was a smidge of peace and quiet before getting back to the farm. Yet there was McDreamy, surfacing in her mind's eye.

And the Pentwell case.

Annabelle smiled at recalling how she'd bit his head off after he had complemented her hair. Went all Gloria Steinem on him, thinking she needed to defend her feminist honor by questioning why it was whenever he needed something from her he complimented her hair. Never would a man compliment another dude's haircut, and she'd never seen him complement Dean Lawlor's hair! It's only women who get that sort of treatment when men come calling, hat in hand.

She was right, of course. And also not. Because he was just making small talk before he tried defending his client. Flipped when she suggested there was intent to distribute, as Dean suggested. Waved his negative DUI in her face, along with the probable cause issues and his youthful first offense—all before asking if she'd do him a "solid" for the "upstanding Eagle Scout."

The man had certainly tried to swoon her, but she was made of tougher material than most Dixie chicks. Instead of caving, she'd put on her big girl pants and told him she couldn't do the solid and would take it to trial.

Gideon hadn't liked that one bit, and off he stormed, ready

to go to the mat for his client who'd gotten screwed over by Dean Lawlor. Or his client, rather. All for the machinations of small-town politics. She eventually turned the tables on her boss and cut a deal with Gideon, but still.

After that convo with Dean, Annabelle could not help but think it was happening again, this time to Gideon O'Donnell.

Crapola...

She slumped back and took a drink of her flat white, grimacing at the cold milk and hating her morning.

What was she going to do?

Chapter Eighteen

Johnny Pope had been summoned by Gideon O'Donnell, and it sounded urgent.

About time, given what he had been trying to confirm for him, what he'd been trying to get to him after that ill-fated breakfast a few days ago. Actually, more like providential breakfast, given what he had heard, what he had translated, from those men, that woman, from Millie's on Main —who had spoken Russian.

And what he had confirmed.

For the better part of two days, Johnny had been sleuthing. Gideon paid him a nice, fat retainer each year as his go-to guy to get things done when he came calling. This rabbit trail wasn't exactly on-the-books, but he considered himself a private eye of integrity. When anything arose that seemed relevant to a case, he got to sleuthing work, regardless how tangential it seemed.

And this rabbit trail had proven to be far more relevant to what Gideon was up against.

It all started at Millie's on Main. After the commie pinko

trio had shared a quiche Lorraine and pot of coffee, they'd headed out walking about Mill Creek Junction. Strolled up one side of Main Street and down the other, pointing and jibber-jabbering in Russian about "earnings potential" this and "due diligence" that. Clothing and shoe stores and the local jewelry shop. Max's Place and even back to Millie's on Main. They talked about gross efficiencies versus net efficiencies before mumbling through multi-figure numbers that sounded like nothing but a bunch of hooey.

And super suspicious.

His suspicions kept ratcheting when the trio climbed into a Mercedes SUV and started tooling across the Junction, from one end to the other. Started at the regional supermax prison and spent a spell inside, which was real odd. Didn't follow them in, of course. Just waited for their return, which was late in the afternoon before they motored on to their next stop: Fred Myers General Store.

The modest grocer had been a hallmark of Mill Creek Junction for generations, stretching back through Johnny's childhood and to the Depression. He followed them inside, thinking they were in for some foodstuff and toilet paper. Nope. It was a conversation with Freddy himself, the mystery guests and grocery store owner retiring to his back office for a chit-chat.

Johnny would've given anything to be a fly on that wall. Instead, he settled for a nap in his Ford a few parking spots over —before being rudely awakened by the roar of a turbocharged engine readying for the next destination.

The local Holiday Inn for the night.

He had checked into an open room down the hallway from the commies to keep an eye on them and do a little digging with his laptop. Through some backchannels that weren't entirely on the up-and-up, he found the rental with a receipt connected to some firm he'd never heard of before. A quick internet search showed it was a major investment management company from London. Explained the expensive clothes and car and international accent, but nothing else.

The next day was much of the same, starting with an early morning tour of Mill Creek Community College that lasted an hour before an extended stopover at Warner Farms. At each stop the past few days, the two Asians and blond *koshka,* prowling like the pussycat she was around his town, visited for a few hours. After a stopover at Smiles Dentistry, even to City Hall, Johnny called off the tail when they rolled up to the local funeral parlor. Besides, he'd needed to connect with his boss.

Except with this mess around Gideon, getting picked up by Mill Creek PD, and this accusation by the Junction's prosecuting attorney about his mother, not to mention her tragic death—with all of that, he hadn't been able to connect with him on that front of his investigation. Which actually worked out, because that confirmation might work in Gideon's favor, as tragic as it was.

Johnny pulled up to the old brown-brick building housing the local Starbucks and Gideon's law office, then threw his pickup into park. A retro-style F-150 throwback model from the '70s. The kind from an era when Ford still knew how to make a pickup truck. Painted crimson with a cream panel ringin' the perimeter, fat tires with treads that meant business lifting his baby off the cracked pavement an extra few inches. Was a spittin' image of his first car, the one he'd picked out after gettin' home from Nam. Then Lynn happened, then seminary and taking a post with his childhood parish, Saint Thomas Catholic Church after Lynn passed, and he traded his original heart's desire for an Oldsmobile.

It wasn't as hot today, but still muggy. So he left his trench coat and opted for a light-weight linen sport jacket instead.

Had to look the part, especially for the boss. Snatching his fedora, he fixed it on his bald head and secured his Colt handgun to his waist underneath his jacket—then grabbed one more thing.

A gold crucifix.

With a name like Johnny Pope and a background as a former priest, supposed a guy in his shoes would be expected to carry around such a thing. Some added protection on top of his trusty Colt.

Except his last-minute grab was much less about some PI uniform and more a feeling about something that was rearing its ugly mug.

As in, demonic ugly.

Saint Paul was right, care of his letter to the Ephesians: 'our struggle is not against blood and flesh but against the rulers, against the authorities, against the cosmic powers of this present darkness, against the spiritual forces of evil in the heavenly places.'

Got turned on to an awareness of those principalities and powers of this supernatural darkness during the priesthood. Summer of '05 probably had something to do with that when he took part in the Exorcism and Prayer of Liberation course the Vatican opened to his fellow priests crazy enough to take them up on their offer. In the years after that, Johnny had seen a whole lot of spiritual warfare that would give his Nam experience a run for his eighteen-year-old money.

Which was why he also took seriously the other piece to that exhortation: 'be strong in the Lord and in the strength of his power; put on the whole armor of God, so that you may be able to stand against the wiles of the devil...'

The crucifix was part of that armor.

As was the Colt.

Johnny slipped the heavy gold cross of Christ around his

neck and stuffed it down his yellow polo, then went back for one more item. Almost forgot the thing that he'd been summoned for.

A manila envelope from MCJPD, care of the MCJPA.

Dean Lawlor hadn't been too keen on handing it over, but he threatened to raise a stink about him impeding his client's due process, a major Brady violation. Tried claiming he was only obliged to hand it over to the defense *lawyers*, until Johnny told him Judge Heller was an old lay ecclesial minister from his former parish and an ongoing golf buddy. The dude relented, grudgingly.

Johnny stuffed the envelope under his arms and stopped off at Starbucks for a large dark coffee. No, not a ventie-thingy or whatever made-up Italian crap word those yahoos in Seattle had concocted. Just like God created male and female, he created small, medium, and large. And black coffee.

He exited into a narrow, dark hallway adjoining a set of stairs stinking of wet wood and those hippie-roasted coffee beans. Trudging up the stairs, he gulped down a mouthful of his *large* brew, and grimaced.

Blech!

Tasted of cardboard and burned socks, it was so bad! He'd have to convince Millie on Main to start selling her joe to go, because this mud was for the birds.

Trudging to the second floor, Johnny recalled the first time Gideon had hired him, and he'd asked why, when he hadn't had a track record. Gideon said he liked his name. Sounded like a superhero name. Had to laugh at that!

Which wasn't his real name. Well, the Johnny part was. Papadopoulos was his given name. But Jonathan Aquinas Papadopoulos doesn't roll very well off the tongue. It also sounded like some East Coast yuppy who stepped off a sailing yacht—donning Sperry loafers, sporting a pair of loose-fitting khaki shorts and a plaid Polo shirt of bright oranges and reds and yellows and blues, donning a faded yellow sweater draped ever-so right across his shoulders.

Name didn't fit too good on a business card either, and most people couldn't pronounce it to save their life, let alone spell it or remember it. Which wasn't too good for the line of work he did, when fellas and felines alike needed a name at the drop of a hat to get an ounce of justice.

The musty smell of mildew was getting to him, each step up the rickety stairwell of hardwood flaring up a new bout—probably of mold spores, it was so bad. Could use an industrial-grade dehumidifier. Or maybe there was a leak somewhere. It'd been raining cats and kittens the last week nonstop, so that was a definite possibility.

Farmers on the west side of Mill Creek Junction weren't complaining, that's for sure! Neither were the celery and onions and cabbages, the beans and tomatoes and every other veggie under the sun that had put the Junction on the map back in the day after the place was cleared of trees, then milled and sent packing on trains that ran through town.

Reaching the top, Johnny had to chuckle to himself and shake his head. Back in the day, when he was a teenage ankle-biter, he'd hitched a ride on an eastbound train to Detroit. The line ran from Chicago clear through Mill Creek Junction and on toward Motor City, picking up produce and other factory odds and ends.

He'd hitched his way all the way to Detroit after hearing on the radio that Smokey Robinson & The Miracles was playing a sold-out concert. Didn't know who the heck that was at the time. Just thought the name sounded cool. So he snuck his way east, then snuck into Fox Theater—and was promptly kicked out at intermission. Coppers nearly read him the RIOT Act before calling up Pa—then he did read Johnny the

RIOT Act and kicked his rear from Mill Creek to kingdom come!

And good for him, too, because he was a terror. Would have kept at his terrorizing had it not been for the draft, and Nam, and all that had happened when he got back. But that's a whole other ball of ugly for another day.

His smile faded, the memory making him wish he'd stayed in Detroit. War is hell, General William Tecumseh Sherman was quoted as saying. During a speech at the Michigan Military Academy, actually. Johnny preferred the one by Alan Alda: *"War is war and Hell is hell, and if you ask me, war is worse."*

Got that right.

Hoofing it to the top, he threw back another mouthful of coffee, the cardboard socks less burnt and more sour now, making it bearable. He yanked out his handkerchief and wiped his sweaty brow. Should have gone for an iced tea. Was sweltering on top of the stickiness, the dead-of-August heat pressing in like crazy and thickened by midnight storms that had been flaring up all week. Didn't Gideon's joint spring for air conditioning? Jeez Louise!

Stuffing the hanky in his back pocket, Johnny turned his nose up and walked down to *O'Donnell and Associates.* Reaching the door, he grasped the burnished bronze knob and gave her a yank. Inside was about as bad as outside. And dark! Or dim, rather. And quiet.

No whirling of fans and definitely not the grumbly grunt of an HVAC working overtime. No copiers copying or printers printing, no faxes faxing, if that was still a thing. Was like Jesus Christ himself had returned at the end of the age to evacuate his chosen, if you bought that sort of end-times interpretive nonsense. With him left behind.

Except—

Something caught his attention, farther in. A cough, the rustling of paper, voices echoing back to him.

Gideon's office.

Johnny threaded his way through the main work area of old wood desks with a '60s vibe to them. Reminded him of those Sisters from Catholic school again, the sort of desks that teachers used from when he was a teenager.

Stacks of stained manila folders were piled on top, papers and sticky notes and paper clips sticking out from them. No phones on top ringing with waiting clients, not like the movies and shows from last decade. Plenty of pens, though, reds and blues and blacks. Each had nameplates of blocky, black letters set against fake gold. One with REGINALD WILSON, the other with ELIZABETH SEWARD. They each had a chipped mug from their law school, along with sagging black office chairs from Staples.

Johnny bypassed them for the cramped space at the back.

Where he saw the members of *Gideon and Associates* slumped and silent now.

"Who died?" Johnny snorted with a laugh.

The three jumped at the sound of his voice, Reggie springing to his feet and spinning around with his fists raised.

"Jeez! Calm down!" Johnny backed up with his own hands raised in surrender.

"Way to make an entrance..." Lizzy grumbled, a calming hand at her chest.

"About time you got here," Gideon complained.

"Yeah, sorry about that. I got a little sidetracked." He gestured to an open chair. Johnny waved him off wanting to stand. "I'm really sorry about your mother, Gideon. Haven't gotten a chance to extend my sympathies with your...well, other entanglements the past few days."

He nodded his thanks then scooted to his desk. "Thanks for answering my call. Did you get what I asked?"

Johnny smiled to himself. Always down to business, Gideon was. Couldn't deny the man trying his hand at solving his own litigation—or his mother's murder.

He brought out the envelope and held it up with a smile.

"What's that?" asked Lizzy.

"The autopsy report."

Chapter Nineteen

There it was. The envelope.

The thing I was most interested in getting my hands on to aid in preparing for my defense. It was also what I was most dreading to get my eyes on.

Because that envelope held what was also meant to prepare for the complicated case: investigating my mother's murder. Reading the medical examiner's notes and conclusions would force me to confront the reality of my situation. Which was really about confronting the reality of *reality*.

That Ma was dead.

Really, truly no longer alive.

All because some sick bastard took her life.

Couldn't think about that now. All that mattered was what was inside that envelope, then doing a deep dive into the evidence I hoped would clarify that reality.

I clapped my hands together and jumped to my feet. Lawlor had been a real pain in the ass about this piece of discovery, his office stonewalling on this crucial piece for the past few days. Claimed they still needed time to go over the preliminary findings, that it wasn't fully vetted, that they had to yada-yada-yada.

Preliminary-not-fully-vetted my yada-yada-yada backside!

I reached out a hand. "Good work. Hand it over."

Johnny walked over the envelope and passed it off. I snatched it and ripped it open.

A ping of adrenaline skated cold through my veins at the anticipation of what was inside—what I would read, about Ma. The fight-flight rush clenched my stomach and quickened my breath, ending with my mouth dry and coppery and wanting to down a shot of scotch.

Reggie asked, "Did the PA's office give you any trouble?"

Johnny P snorted a laugh. "You kidding me? Is the Pope Catholic? Of course! But I said I'd personally march down to the Michigan Department of Civil Rights and file a due process violation complaint if he didn't hand over the report."

"Say *waaa?* Look at you, JP. All Johnny-on-the-legal-spot!"

"That's my PI," I said, sliding out the thick mess of papers stuffed inside the envelope—

And nearly dropping the whole dang thing at what greeted me.

Photos.

Of the crime scene.

Where I was face to face with a bullet hole in the back of what I could only assume was a head, a mess of black curls matted by blood, face planted into a white pillow stained a wicked crimson. Pink matter and bone shards were scattered about in that mess of curls. The top of a baby blue nightgown had grown purple at the stain seeping down the neck and into the cuff.

Thank the good Lord above there wasn't a face to go along with that head.

Yet.

"That sicko…" Lizzy said lowly. "No way that wasn't on purpose."

"Ya think?" Reggie sneered. "How about I take these for now…"

He slowly released me of that burden, and a tremor suddenly seized my hand where the stack of papers had been.

I clenched it tight and took a breath. Swallowing, I settled into my chair and scooted to the desk. Reggie had taken the photos from the top of the pile and placed them face down.

"No need to worry about those just yet," he mumbled.

We were left with several paper-clipped bundles of papers, all related to the official medical examination of the woman's body.

The woman…

I couldn't face the fact the *body* was my mother.

I shook away the thought and reached for the top bundle of papers, removing the paperclip and scanning the first page, my grip tight, chest even tighter.

There it was: Case Number 2024-0529.

Name of the deceased would normally be withheld in these circumstances, pending notification of kin. That wasn't necessary since I had been notified the moment I was arrested.

Florence Gail O'Donnell was typed in bold.

Which made it all the more real, much more than it had been up to that point. With that case number, her name…

It was go time.

I kept reading:

Date of Autopsy: August 15. Autopsy Conducted By: Wayne Talbert.

I knew Wayne. Good guy, straight shooter, precise and professional. His medical examiner's report contained everything I would have expected, beginning with an external examination of the body habitus:

The decedent is a black female, appearing between the ages of 65 and 70 years.

Height: 163 cm (5 feet 4 inches)
Weight: 132 pounds (59.87 kg)
Body, average build; post-mortem rigidity, moderate; no signs of decomposition.

No surprises there. Pretty much lined up with the mother I knew. The mother I had last seen and spoken to before I'd been arrested.

The day before she had been killed...

The report listed more physical characteristics:

Hair: Black, with some age-consistent graying.
Eyes: Dark brown.

Again, as expected.

I slipped the page facedown to the desk and skimmed the rest of it, about markings and tattoos (Ma, with a tattoo? Ha!); her brown skin showing "mild skin changes related to advanced age, such as wrinkles and age spots;" her clothing ("light blue nightgown" and "barefoot at the time of the examination"); any personal effects present on the body, which were none, including no jewelry.

That was page one.

The next page would be titled *Evidence of Injury*.

I definitely wasn't sure I was ready for—

A hand jolted me, literally sending me bolting back. A squeaky wheel flared from my chair and the autopsy report fell from my grip to the desk.

Lizzy, who startled and apologized and jerked back her kind gesture.

I caught my breath and returned to the desk, gathering the report back together.

She asked, "Are you sure you're ready for the rest?"

Reggie leaned in. "Yeah, Gideon, we can take it from here."

"Can't imagine it's pretty, kid," Johnny added. "No one should have to read something like this about their mother."

I appreciated their consideration and solidarity, but I had to keep going. Had to face reality. Had to witness what that bastard had done to Ma.

Swallowing, I shook my head and retrieved the top few pages to the report.

"No. I'm fine. I need—"

Snapping paper drew me from the moment to my hand. Which was shaking with a tremor, the report flaring up the snapping shake.

Setting the sheaf of papers back on my desk I muttered an "I'm fine" and kept at it, Reggie and Lizzy leaned in to read along with me from above:

Entry Wound: Located at the head's posterior surface, 1.5 cm to the right of the midline and 3 cm above the occipital protuberance. The wound is a jagged circular entrance, with an approximate diameter of 1.3 cm. While expecting to find soot deposition and stippling around the entry wound, indicative of a close-range discharge, both are lacking in hair and matter, indicating secondary discharge augmentation.

I recalled an initial assessment of a pillow being found with the expected physical evidence, discarded after the fact. The assumption being, the perpetrator—which I supposed was assumed to have been me—had shot the victim at close range through the pillow to avoid blood splatter and muffle the sound of the weapon discharge.

I kept reading:

Exit Wound: Located on the anterior aspect of the face, exiting through the left cheek, 1.5 cm below the zygomatic arch and 2.8 cm lateral to the nasal bridge. The shape of the exit wound is irregular, measuring approximately 4.3 cm in diameter. Surrounding tissue is severely damaged and the exterior facial features lacerated, with the facial cavity having collapsed.

My stomach lurched at the revelation.

The bastard who shot my mother blew her face to kingdom come.

My head felt faint. The room wobbled, and now starlight flashed across my vision.

"You OK, Gideon?" asked Reggie above a whisper, voice deep and concerned.

It managed to pull me back from the edge. I nodded and read onward:

> **Trajectory:** The exiting bullet traveled in a slightly downward and anterior direction, passing through the occipital bone, brainstem, and frontal lobes, before exiting the face, indicating the perpetrator was standing above the victim at the moment of weapon discharge.

After the physics of it all, the report launched into associated injuries. Everything from "significant damage to the brainstem and cerebrum" to "extensive hemorrhaging and cavitation," all of which was to be expected from the "posterior exit and facial shattering" resulting from the back-of-the-head gunshot wound.

I blocked out any images that language might have conjured, reading about fractures to a bunch of bones, ranging from the skull to eye sockets to nasal to jaw. Didn't much get it, and nothing stood out. Again, all of it to be expected given the nature of the attack.

I quickly flipped the page over with a shaking hand, thankful to have gotten that out of the way.

That was it for the worst of the examination.

The next section was labeled *III. Internal Examination* and started with *Cranial Cavity*. It covered the laceration of the dura mater, thanks to that bullet at the back of her head and its trajectory through the brain and face. Again, massive hemorrhaging was noted inside the cavity "with extensive damage to the brainstem and left cerebral hemisphere." The brain's weight was given, which didn't matter to me.

I skimmed the rest, which dealt with the chest cavity, listing a bunch of details about the heart and lungs. Same for the abdominal cavity, listing the weight of several organs (liver, spleen, kidneys, gastrointestinal tract) and notations on their characteristics, with a side note on the musculoskeletal system.

None of it seemed relevant, so I flipped over that page to one I was much more interested in. The toxicology section.

So far, so good. Blood and urine samples had been collected for toxicological analysis, as was routine in criminal death exams. The preliminary results of the toxicology report showed no alcohol or common illicit drugs detected. No surprise there as both my mother and father had been strict teetotalers.

I smiled at that notation. Not a few times had my parents gotten into it with me about my alcohol consumption. Ma had been the first to remind me what the Good Book says about it, how it condemned it. When I asked my grad school roommate about it after one trip home, the son of a Baptist preacher actually, he had reassured me it wasn't drinking that the Almighty had a problem with, but getting drunk. So I listened respectfully, even endured a few more tongue lashings, but still enjoyed my nightcap.

Reading that part of the report, with that memory, made me wish for those tongue lashings again. Supposed the saying was true: You never know what you got till it's gone.

I shook away the memory and the thought and continued, reading that further testing was pending for prescription medications and other substances. Not exactly what I expected. I'd hoped to find some indication of—well, something. Something to explain how she could have been attacked like that without putting up a struggle, without alerting the staff to danger. Supposed her dementia wouldn't have helped matters, not to mention being almost seventy.

None of it made sense. Who would have wanted to hurt Ma? And like that?

I turned the page, coming to the end of the report. I was prepared for the conclusion—but also not:

V. Conclusion

Cause of Death: Gunshot wound to the head.

Manner of Death: Homicide.

The deceased black female, aged between 65 and 70, appears to have died from a fatal gunshot wound to the back of the head. The bullet exited through the face, the trajectory of which causing extensive damage to the brainstem and cerebrum, resulting in fatal brain injury and immediate death. While lacking chemical evidence of close-range discharge, the manner and physical characteristics of the wound indicate the shot was fired at a very short distance from the victim.

Looked about right. Except—

I wanted to check something first. Something I'd skimmed over from identifying marks related to dental records.

"Whatchya got, Gideon?" asked Reggie.

"Yeah, kid," Johnny added. "Something strike you?"

I mumbled a "Just a sec..." and started rifling through some of the supporting pages after not finding what I'd wanted.

There was something about this that was difficult—both in the gut-wrenching, emotional sense of it, but also the forensics side of it. Knew it depended on the caliber of the weapon, but in general a gunshot to the back of the head would have a small entry wound at the back of the skull with a large exit wound on the opposite—often resulting in what could only be characterized as an explosion.

Like someone's face being blown off.

The medical examiner's report noted the sort of damage you'd expect from that sort of wound. But there was one thing I was wondering—

There it was. I read what I'd been looking for, frowning.

"Only thing is..." I started, trailing off, confused.

"Only what thing is?" asked Lizzy.

This didn't make sense.

I went over the section again, then I went over the memory again.

One plus one didn't equal two.

"You're killin' us, kid," Johnny said.

I set down the page and leaned back, thinking. The seconds ticked by, more than I had realized. Loud throat-clearing and Reggie giving me his get-to-it look brought me back.

I jabbed at the confusing page. "The report lists the victim having a full set of teeth."

"What's the problem?" he asked.

"She got her wisdom teeth yanked when I was a senior in high school."

"Really?" Lizzy said.

"Really. I remember because she was so laid up from the pain that she almost missed my graduation. Didn't, because no pain could ever keep her down. But..."

"Maybe implants?" added Johnny.

"Maybe..."

"That sounds bonkers to me," Lizzy said. "Who gets wisdom teeth implants?"

"She did have bad teeth," I said, considering her point. "Ma had a few more pulled later in life."

"Did she ever get dental implants?"

I sat forward. "Actually, she did. She lost a few teeth in the years before her dementia really started showing signs."

Reggie said, "I did read once that tooth loss and dementia are linked."

"Right. After she started showing signs, she fell and busted her two front teeth. I know she got them replaced."

He winced. "Ouch."

Johnny said, "Your mother could have gotten a new mouth of implants taken care of in one fell swoop. Something to look into but this seems like a rabbit trail."

"I agree," said Lizzy. "What about making a positive identification of the body?"

"They wouldn't let me make the arrangements."

"Wouldn't let you?" I said. "You mean wouldn't let *me*?"

Johnny nodded. "Lawlor refused, citing conflict of interest."

Reggie added, "Suppose you can't let the accused give the thumbs up or down on a murder victim."

Lizzy asked, "But how will they make a positive ID without her only living heir giving that thumbs up or down?"

"I'm working on that," Johnny grunted.

I slumped back in a huff. Unbelievable.

Didn't stay that way for long. Because I knew what we needed to do.

I leaped to my feet and started for the door.

"Gideon," Reggie said, "where are you going?"

"Dreamscape Manor. We've got to get answers."

Lizzy stood, eyeing Reggie. "What, now?"

Heat flashed with irritation up my neck and bloomed hot in my face.

"Yes. *Now*. You have a better time in mind?"

She frowned and crossed her arms. She was not amused at the snapback.

I sighed. "Look, sorry I bit your head off. But we don't have time to waste. We have the right to talk to the staff. To her caretakers and other residents. To view the crime scene, see my mother's—"

My voice faltered.

Crime scene. My mother.

None of those words should have ever found their way into the same sentence...

I silently cursed myself for the weakness, then continued in a whisper: "—see her room."

Swallowing, I added, "I have to know what happened."

Johnny asked, "What about that other thing I got?"

"Tell me in the car, all of us. Reggie, you're driving."

Chapter Twenty

I rode shotgun while Reggie motored through downtown Mill Creek Junction on toward Dreamscape Manor Assisted Living. It sat on a rather nice piece of land south of town along that actual Mill Creek.

The property had once belonged to a logging baron who had cleared the landscape without thought of reforestation. Such was the way of things back during the early days of the Republic, when the wilderness was still untamed and untouched, at least by Western hands. Of course, it had been settled by several indigenous tribes long before Europeans arrived, especially Michigan. The Council of Three Fires, as those earliest of nations were known—the Ojibwa, the Chippawa, and the Potawatomi—bartered with French and English traders for flintlock guns and clothing and flatware in exchange for their highly sought after furs that made for a lucrative industry back in the Old World. That is, until they helped obliterate the major pelt population through trapping and the demands of the mercantile class.

Now Dreamscape was the only thing left of that ill-forgotten era, which was a bit appropriate since most of those elderly folks that were cared for in the assisted living center were themselves ill-forgotten by their children.

Not me. I visited Ma every Sunday. Without fail. And more with the trial. Especially with the trial.

I was just sorry about how I'd left things the last time I visited, just before Ma's death. And then our conversation...

I glanced at Reggie, whose eyes were focused on the road. I'd yet to broach the subject with him, and Lizzy for that matter. Johnny had been tasked with figuring out whether there was any truth to what I had called about.

Her reconsidering the suit, which didn't make any sense at all.

And threatened everything. The suit, her own livelihood, the others.

Me...

Which had freaked me the hell out ever since getting arrested. A detail I hoped to the good Lord above wasn't in the hands of the prosecution.

Because there had been a poison-pill condition with the class action suit, conditioned by an arbitration agreement attached to the property agreements themselves. It was archaic, and lousy—basically screwing the lot renters sideways without them knowing what was jacking them up the backside. Because what it allowed was for a majority of property owners to kill any suit outside arbitration.

Ma was the final hold-out who had the power to eighty-six months of work and a potential financial windfall that would set me right—us right, all of the participants, Reggie and Lizzy, the class representative.

Who happened to be Florence Gail O'Donnell.

Had a hunch someone had gotten to her. HappyLiving, a disgruntled neighbor who'd been gotten to—hell, even Mayor

Goodall or that weaselly sidekick of his, Milton someone (because, come on: with a name like Milton, you're a weasel!).

Although...I knew some*thing* also probably got to her.

Dementia.

It had stolen into her life like that famous Ernest Hemingway jingle about bankruptcy: at first gradually, then suddenly. And now it threatened everything.

Or, again, it could have been some*one*. Didn't have a freakin' clue.

It was stop-and-go for several blocks. Summer tourists clogged the streets, in town for the annual riverside music festival. The lunch crowd was out in force, with Millie's on Main packed. Same for Max's Place, a long line snaking a block. Looked like Max was enjoying himself, my pal hamming it up with the crowd in a Lollapalooza T-shirt from that time he'd gone with his folks in 1994. Hated my best friend for getting a glimpse of Smashing Pumpkins and Beastie Boys without me, my two favorite bands from that era.

Soon we were past the traffic crazy and cruising down a single-lane state route flanked by fields of onions and corn. The sour stench of manure and vinegary tang of onions made me want back in town for the grilled beef and fried chicken I'd smelled on the crawl out.

Then I remembered one of the reasons Johnny came calling.

I turned toward the back, where Lizzy and Johnny Pope were seated, squished really in the backseat of Reggie's Honda Civic.

"Alright, JP, you said you had something for me."

Johnny frowned, then corrected: "Might."

I nodded for him to continue. Knew his normal MO was to stand and pace. I smiled at that, knowing he worked better that way, the blood flowing from top to toes, working through a thought on the move. Then I had to chuckle to myself as he mumbled something under his breath and looked out the window. Sorry, Johnny.

"So I'm at Millie's on Main," he started, shifting like he was about to start pacing but settling for leaning toward me instead, "when these two cats come waltzing in. Real dandies, too. Dressed to the nines. With expensive Old World suits, silk ties, polished leather shoes. You know, your type, Gideon."

Reggie and Lizzy laughed. I frowned.

"Gee, thanks. So what's interesting about them?"

Johnny put up a finger. "Not them. The broad who came in after them."

Lizzy scoffed. "Broad? Really? Are we living in *The Godfather* or what?"

Had to smile at that. Always one with a Hollywood reference, Lizzy was.

"Dame, lady, beautiful woman, whatever is the correct post-MeToo lingo you kids are springing for these days."

"How about none of the above…"

Reggie said, "Alright, we've determined JP is politically incorrect. Let's hear what the man has to say."

"Yeah, Johnny, why do they matter?" I asked.

"It's not them that matters. Well, the fellas. Like I said, it's the—" he turned to Lizzy "young lady who came in after. It's the conversation she had with them. What they said and how they said it."

"And what was that?"

"First, they spoke Russian."

"Russian?" Lizzy said with a start.

"Russian?" I questioned as well, intrigue growing.

"Russian," Johnny confirmed.

"Echo…echo…echo…" Reggie said with a smirk.

I waved him off. "Guessing there's a punchline coming."

Johnny said, "I'll get to it. At any rate, they start talking investments. Like beaucoup bucks investments."

"How do Russians have money for investing?" asked Lizzy. "I thought the Feds seized all of their assets because of the war."

"Not these, apparently. The two guys she was with—"

Two guys. With a woman. In Mill Creek Junction?

The connection suddenly coalesced in my mind's eye.

So I interrupted: "Hold on a second. The broad, the dame —" Lizzy cleared her throat, loudly. I corrected: "the beautiful woman...are we talking Cindy Crawford beautiful?"

Johnny tilted his head. "That's a good way of putting it."

"With a beauty mark, a mole on her upper lip?"

"Where's the fire, Gideon?" asked Reggie.

Lizzy nodded. "Yeah, boss, you sound like you know who he's talking about."

Ignoring their questions, I got to my own punchline: "Tell me more about these guys who were with this woman."

Johnny shrugged. "What do you want to know?"

"Like who were they? What did they look like?"

"One on the taller side, one on the shorter. Both had black shoulder length hair, slicked and styled—"

I waved him off. "No, I was thinking more along the lines of their nationality."

He narrowed his eyes. "Nationality?"

"Right. Where did they look like they were from?"

Another shrug. "Looked Asian to me. Maybe from Japan, maybe Chinese."

Asians...

I straightened at that. Holy cow. Are you kidding me?

I recalled the two men I saw the other night after I'd left MCJ lockup, just jawing it up with Mayor Goodall, along with that Cindy Crawford lookalike.

"Wait a second—" I yanked out my phone, also recalling being aware enough after my two beers to snap a picture of the meet-and-greet.

I fetched my photos app, zeroing in on the one I had snapped of the same trio I saw at Max's Place. Yup, I'd recalled right. Definitely two Asian men. The one darker one, the other more light in complexion.

I showed Johnny the phone and asked, "Like these Asians and that Russian woman?"

Johnny leaned in and squinted, then snapped his widening eyes at me with confirmation.

"Yep. That's them. Where'd you get this?"

"Max's Place the other night. Saw them in deep conversation with Goodall and Gage Strauss."

"Mill Creek's Mayor and HappyLiving's CEO..." Johnny whistled. "Well, that makes sense, considering what they were jibber-jabbering about."

"Investments, right?" asked Reggie.

"Right. In multiple industries, across the Junction."

"Which takes a mighty high stack of Benjamins."

"Beaucoup bucks," added Lizzy. "That's what you said, Johnny."

Reggie nodded. "Right."

"Which takes an investment firm. Even then there are several types of companies and firms that specialize in buying and investing in other companies to achieve a rate of return."

"Such as, Dave Ramsey?"

"Well, there are a variety of these sorts of financial entities. You've got venture capital firms and hedge funds—which might be the case here. Multi-national conglomerates on the prowl for quick M&As, not to be confused with corporate venture capital. Then those pillaging private equity vultures and real estate investment trusts, sovereign wealth funds from banana republics and Middle East kingdoms, distressed asset investors —even your run-of-the-mill investment bank."

"How the heck do you know all this?"

"The interwebs, Reggie."

"Right..."

I asked, "Did you catch the firm's name?"

Johnny replied. "Sure thing. Perses Global Financial Group. Ring a bell?

I shook my head. "Nope. Should it?"

"Did some digging. Not often you get a trio of East Slavic speakers waltzing through Mill Creek Junction. Followed them taking a tour of our town, too. Real strange."

"And let's talk about that one," Lizzy said. "How did you understand what they were talking about anyway?"

"I was a translator for Uncle Sam during my time in Nam. Got real good translating communications between the Soviets and North Vietnamese. Saved a few lives too..."

He trailed off, eyes narrowing and casting down, as if reliving a painful memory.

She said, "Suppose one good thing came from that misadventure nonsense."

Johnny laughed. "Suppose so. Anyway, I did some digging —and I mean major digging. Which your absence, Gideon, allowed for."

Now Lizzy laughed. "Suppose one good thing came from *that* misadventure nonsense."

Had to smile at that.

I asked, "And what did you find, Johnny?"

"PGFG is a private equity firm out of London that recently bought a mobile home park not far from where we're driving."

At first, it didn't register.

Then it did.

"No..."

Reggie echoed my surprise: "Say *waaa?*"

"HappyLiving Estates?" Lizzy added.

Johnny said, "That'd be the one."

"And what did you hear?" I asked.

He replied, "One of the fellas asked the woman, 'Did you hear the good news?' She was eager for confirmation."

"Confirmation?"

"Right. 'Is it confirmed?' That's what she says."

"Is what confirmed?"

"Well, her partner nods. Says 'It's done. We got her.'"

"We got her?"

"Got her."

My head swam with all sorts of questions spinning out of that one. Which I voiced in rapid succession: "Did they identify this *her?* Did they explain what *got* meant? Did this have anything to do with my class action suit? My mother's waffling about moving forward? Anything to do with her involvement in—"

"Hold the phone," Lizzy said. "What's that mean, *waffling?*"

"Yeah, Gideon," Reggie added. "Sounds like your mama was thinking of bailing on the class action."

He slowed to a stop at a four-way and glanced my way.

"She wasn't thinking of bailing, was she?"

I went silent, saying nothing.

Hadn't even realized the slip. The reveal.

The one about Ma having had second thoughts about going through with the class action. Along with the other more complicated one that I'd had to talk her off a ledge, not a few times, from selling out to HappyLiving—to this Perseus Global or Perses, or whatever it was. She'd had it in her mind that a big payout was in store, which was a joke on many levels.

"Gideon!" Reggie shouted.

"What?" I shouted back, realizing he was still stopped at the four-way.

"What did you mean by waffling?" asked Lizzy again.

Reggie pressed, "Please don't tell us your mother was bailing—"

"She wasn't!" I snapped.

"Are you sure?"

"She wouldn't..."

I went silent again.

"Did you know about this, JP?" asked Reggie.

Could hear a sigh behind me, Johnny not thrilled to have been dragged into this mess.

He replied, "Gideon had asked me to do some digging. And, yeah, she had been waffling, as he indicated. Didn't find out anything that might have changed her mind. But, well, apparently she did. Some of the neighbors confirmed it."

Reggie said, "You do realize that doesn't look good, right?"

I turned to him and frowned. "You think?"

"As in, motive not good?" Lizzy added.

"And means not good," Reggie echoed, "given your access to her."

"You don't think I know that?" I snapped.

"Whoa whoa whoa! We're on your side here."

Should have apologized, but I didn't. Didn't really want to. I was tired. Of all the drama, of the implications.

"And we're your lawyers, Gideon," Lizzy added.

"And that!" Reggie exclaimed. "Which means no secrets, right?"

"You tell us everything that might matter to your case."

"I know, alright?" I said, irritation mounting.

Reggie kept at it: "We know what you know."

"That's, like, basic," Lizzy joined in again.

"You'd say the same thing to your client if you were us."

"Gotcha there, kid," Johnny said.

I frowned, saying nothing. Yep. Got me there.

They were right. It's exactly what I would have said to my client if I were in their shoes. Shoot, I *had* said exactly that to clients in my same shoes!

"I messed up, alright?" I finally said. "Not telling you everything from the get-go. When the others started dropping. When Ma had started raising objections to selling, and the back-and-forth arguments. When I visited her before she..."

That revelation died in the ellipsis.

"You visited her just before she was found murdered..." Lizzy said. Not really a question. More an acknowledgment of the revelation that confirmed Reggie's and her observations about my boneheaded move.

"Well, partner," Reggie said, gesturing at the country road outside, "we've got plenty of time for you to spill the tea now."

"I'll tell you everything. Just—" My voice faltered, frustration at myself and worry about this case—mine and the one I was supposed to be litigating—all of it crashing into me with sickening dread, literally clenching my stomach with worry.

"Just drive faster, Reggie."

He pulled forward then shifted into higher gear.

"Already on it, my man."

I felt my body jerk toward destiny.

Then I spilled the tea.

Chapter Twenty-One

I rolled down my window. Needed some air. Reggie still blasted the air conditioning, but he didn't complain at letting in the hot August air into the car as I gathered my thoughts. No one did, which I appreciated, the outside whoosh filling the silence.

We had left behind the onion and celery fields in favor of strawberry patches now, flanked by those low-growing fruit plants on one side and a stretch of trees on the other. A mixture of pine and some leafy variety—oaks or maples or cottonwoods or something—that sent the fecund forest flaring all around. I eased an arm out, the airspeed pressure against my skin cool and jolting.

I cupped my hand like a spaceship and rode the slipstream, as I had as a kid riding shotgun in Dad's Plymouth Horizon, shirtless and wearing dirty yellow shorts, just listening to the local jazz station and driving till dinner, maybe stopping along the side of the road to swipe some of those strawberries or get an ice cream cone at Coney Creek Junction. What a memory, me and Dad.

Bobbed my arm, up and down, the sensation grounding, same for the memory. Those were the days, when all you had was endless time, an open road, and a drive leading to nowhere in particular.

Now look at things...

For nearly a year now, endless time and those open roads had been out of the question. I'd poured my heart and soul into fighting HappyLiving tooth and nail to stop the lot rate increase. It all started after Dad had passed, and Ma's future was threatened. Something I hadn't fully explained to Reggie and Lizzy. They were mostly out of the details, knowing enough to support me in the suit but working other cases to keep the ship afloat while I chased after my white whale.

Which was where I started in my tea spilling.

Bringing my arm back inside the car, I rolled the window back up, then got to it.

"I haven't shared the full story on this..."

Reggie and Lizzy said nothing.

So I filled in the gaps.

Beginning with my pursuit of the case not really being about the equity she had in her mobile home. They knew I took on the case because of Ma, her ownership of the home and rental of the lot, but the bigger reason was about the physical location from an era before her mind started going that kept her grounded and helped with symptoms. It's why I had held off taking Ma to Dreamscape to begin with after Dad passed, keeping her in a familiar place with familiar objects and memories beyond what even her doctor had recommended.

Reminiscence therapy, it was called, based on research and medical findings that objects and locations from a person's past can have a significant positive impact on their mental health. There was some evidence that the approach helped manage not only symptoms but also dementia's progression. The idea was to use familiar items—a favorite book or chair, photos and music, visits to meaningful, familiar places—to stimulate memories and cognitive function.

The jury was out on how it slowed the progression of dementia, and whether it even did. But I was willing to try anything once Ma started showing signs. And it was actually her who had insisted on managed care when she realized she'd gotten the mental bug. Even pointed me in the right direction with Dreamscape Manor. Said she'd seen it in a TV ad or something. Thought it looked homey.

So after Dad passed and Ma started slipping, it was then I decided to place her in Dreamscape Manor's care. I also kept the property to help with improving her mood and reducing the agitation that had overtaken her at times. It seemed to work, too, periodic visits home improving her mood and memory that were definitely worth it, on top of the equity she still had in the home itself.

The sale of HappyLiving, apparently to this Perses Global Financial Group outfit, threatened everything. Threatened Ma—or had threatened her until her death.

The funny thing, or sad thing, really, was that Ma's insistence to bail from the class-action suit, as Reggie and Lizzy framed it, was because she expected a massive payday if she sold out. Which wasn't at all the case—mostly because there wasn't anything to buy!

None of the residents in HappyLiving Estates owned their property. The tenants, thanks to the arrangement between them and the mobile home park, basically lived just a step above indentured servitude. Most of the residents had a sort of revenue share with the existing landlords, literally. Happy-Living rented them their lot and then financed many of their mobile homes. Now that the park had traded hands—into private equity hands, of all places—they were set to raise the rent, which would crash whatever equity they were hoping to squeeze out of their property, the mobile home itself.

Even the more conservative market analysts I had hired predicted a crash, and then burn, of epic proportions, when the residents were squeezed with rate increases. They would be hard pressed to find potential buyers interested in renting from the freshly raised lot rates. In turn, the value on their real property would be severely depressed, limiting their ability to sell and find greener (read: *cheaper*) pastures. They would be shackled to rising rates with no chance or incentive to stabilize in a market with little new homes being built and astronomically priced starter homes. That wasn't even touching the breach-of-contract issues connected to the rent-stabilized properties proffered under the original lease agreement, joined with the profit-sharing agreement the residents had entered into.

Including my mother.

So, yeah: These residents had experienced real harm. My mother had been screwed over. And I wasn't going to take it lying down.

Except—

Except the new HappyLiving owner, apparently this PGFG outfit, had tried sweetening the deal to mitigate any litigation. They promised either a one-year stability on rents or a generous buy-back option for the remaining balance on the financed portion of their mobile home, paying off what remained plus ten percent on current market value. For most of the residents, they thought they'd won the lottery. Only one problem.

It was all upside for PGFG and all downside for the residents.

Either they faced a rate hike now while losing out on their property ownership, or they kept their value-depressed property while suffering a rate increase. Rumor also had it that some backroom dealings had been going on to get the members of the class action to drop their claim. Part of what Johnny had been looking into. They'd already been able to peel enough people away with their crappy enticements.

With only one hold-out left.

"Your mother," Lizzy said, finishing what was unsaid.

I said nothing. Didn't need to.

"And with her being—" Johnny paused, taking a breath, then: "well, shall, we say, *eliminated*—her death changed things for that class action suit."

A coldness flooded my veins. In all the drama, in all the chaos of my own life, it hadn't dawned on me that things in the lawsuit had changed. Was too focused on dealing with my own nonsense case to think about my other one—not to mention dealing with the loss of my mother.

"Is that true?" asked Reggie.

"Must be," Lizzy said. "Gage Strauss pulled out of the deposition the day after she was killed."

"*Murdered*," I clarified.

"Right. Obviously by someone who had a motive to eliminate her. I'm guessing that with her being the last hold-out the others who wanted to settle with HappyLiving can go about their merry way. Am I right?"

I frowned, saying nothing, that coldness sending a dreadful tingle racing up my spine at the thought. Both that her vote had tipped the scale in favor of continuing the class action, and now the scales had been tipped in the other direction in favor of ending the suit. But also that what Johnny had said, that word he had used, was spot on the money mark.

She had been eliminated.

"You're thinking the class action had something to do with it?" I looked back at Johnny, adding, "Maybe something to do with those newcomers, the two Asian men and that Russian woman?"

Johnny frowned. "You might be onto something there, kid."

"Hey, what am I, chopped liver?" Lizzy complained.

He threw her a wink. "You too, Nancy Drew."

She laughed, then grew serious. "Why do I get the feeling we've suddenly walked onto *The Firm*. Russian speaking Asians, and an actual Russian, the three presumably repping this Perses Global outfit that just ponied up the moolah for HappyLiving Estates."

"You're thinking PGFG got rid of Gideon's mother?"

"All I know is there are bad, bad juju vibes here."

"But why?" asked Reggie. "That doesn't make sense."

"Why not?" replied Lizzy.

"If what you're saying is true, Gideon, that your mama had been having second thoughts, why would it matter if she was— eliminated, putting it in that way? She was pulling out. Perses would get their way and avoid costly litigation, not to mention a potential costlier judgment."

"Ahh, I see where you're going, Watson."

"Don't you mean Sherlock?"

"Nope. Watson was the real genius of the duo. After all, every book is about him."

"They are?"

Lizzy scoffed. "Of course! He's the main viewpoint character—oh, never mind. It doesn't matter. What does is that you've put your finger on the prob, Bob."

Reggie nodded. "Florence was no longer a problem if she withdrew from the class action. Especially as representative of the class."

"Bingo-ringo."

"Unless something had changed..." Johnny said.

Which got a duet of hums and muttering agreement from Reggie and Lizzy.

I didn't want to ask, but: "What changed?"

Johnny just grunted an affirmation of my question.

"What, indeed," Lizzy said.

"Suppose she was waffling," he said, "as you described it, Gideon. So maybe she had changed her mind, going back on pulling out, ticking off the right people who thought they had avoided a potential multimillion dollar judgment."

I said nothing, knowing that couldn't have been it. Not after the conversation we'd had just before she had died.

"Or maybe it's something entirely different," Johnny added.

"Either way," Reggie said, slowing the car, "we're about to find out..."

He turned into the main drive leading to Dreamscape Manor, a sprawling campus that looked more like a wellness spa or West Coast recovery center for LA washouts. Him and Lizzy and Johnny whistled their approval. I understood what they meant.

It was a magnificent compound of rolling hills, all green and manicured, dotted by gardens and shaded by trees. At the center was a large nineteenth-century mansion of white brick, wrapped by generous porches filled with wheelchairs holding residents and caregivers going this way and that and other residents wandering for a taste of fresh air.

When I visited, sometimes I wanted to stay. Just let people wait on me and let the cares of the day sieve away to nothing but nothing between games of euchre and gin rummy before afternoon painting lessons and evening ballroom dancing. When I was scouting out the place for Ma after she suggested it, I'd worried the food would be a replay of my '90s school cafeteria lunch—with rubbery cheese pizza and mystery-meat tacos, served on those yellow Styrofoam quintet-divided plates, joined by soggy, overcooked green beans and stiff sugar cookies. I'd only survived thanks to the small carton of chocolate milk.

Dreamscape Manor was a far cry from that, offering made-to-order omelets and fresh fruit in the morning, homemade soups and sandwiches for lunch, and carved meats and fresh vegetables in the evening. The food had given me some peace of mind letting Ma go, and I'd wished for the same catering service.

On approach, fruit trees loaded down with their wares lined the brick-paved drive funneling us to the original logging tycoon's mansion, a stately antebellum affair painted white that actually looked like it belonged in the Deep South. Made sense, since the original owner had been a former plantation owner who jetted north of the Mason-Dixon when the Confederates surrendered and the Union was preserved.

Soaring Corinthian columns upheld spacious porches that wrapped around the original sizable square manor, with two white staircases leading to the second floor. In the winter, winding woodsmoke would lace the chilled air rising from two red-brick chimneys planted on top a black roof that serviced the dining hall and recreational area.

Jutting off from that main building that was the hub for Dreamscape Manor activities was a more modern wing off the back, with kitchens and examination rooms filled with state-of-the-art doctorly technology that meant they rarely needed to hail an ambulance for emergencies or routine procedures. Flanking the center building were two more that held the residential rooms, all modeled after the main building that had withstood the test of time, harkening back to those glory days that would have meant the world to the residents. If they could remember them, that is.

The throwback architecture, mirroring the white brick and gabled roofs and even generous front porch on the lower level with matching black decorative shutters and chimneys up top—all of it was a collective environmental signal meant to ground the elders in the cozy comforts of their previous lives from decades ago. Ma sure commented about it. Reminded her of a childhood long forgotten, the trace elements of those memories enough to keep her lucid and comforted.

Billing itself a retirement retreat, it had been the best option to care for her with her dementia. Upon Ma's recommendation, I had researched it through and through and was satisfied with its record of care and commitment to "redefining retirement living with warmth, care, and vibrant experiences," as its website said. The admissions rep showing me and my mother around was even more convincing, priding themselves on "providing not just care, but a fulfilling lifestyle for our beloved seniors."

Everything about it had seemed great. Their dedicated teammates offered personalized attention in a safe, nurturing environment, where the well-being of their clients were their top priority, providing specialized dementia treatment and care. It was exactly the sort of care Ma had needed. Something she suggested, actually, nudging me to finally take the steps to sign her up and scoping out Dreamscape before I did my own due diligence.

Every room was built for two, which cut down on costs but also fostered connection, with a myriad of activities designed to stimulate both mind and body. They offered art classes, group outings to the Grand Rapids zoo and museums, wellness programs, and engaging social events, like in-person concerts, dancing, and comedy hour on top of happy hour. Everything anyone would want in a managed care facility for their loved one. Shoot, it was everything anyone would want for themselves!

When I had visited for a tour of the place, most of the residents were laughing and looking like they were enjoying themselves. Some were playing card games, others watching a show or movie on TV, then bunches gabbing over a meal. Their culinary team boasted delicious, nutritious meals catering to individual dietary needs with a rotating menu of options to suit individual preferences. Because, as their guide promised, "we believe that good food is essential to a good life." At the end of the tour, I had walked away confident I could entrust my mother to Dreamscape Manor, believing she would thrive in their care, be taken care of.

That she would be safe.

She was, for the longest time. Thriving, even.

Now she was dead.

I would find out what the hell happened.

Chapter Twenty-Two

As soon as Reggie parked in the visitor parking lot, I jumped out and headed for the front desk. For my crew's part, none of the three threw up an objection. Guess they understood I wanted answers.

Pronto.

Since taking over Ma's care, that's all I'd wanted. Answers. I had become an expert on the condition that had stolen my mother.

Dementia, the general term describing a person's cognitive decline, sucked a person down life's sewer day by day until they were a shadow of their former self. All thanks to damaged brain cells fueling the condition with misfirings and miscommunications between cells, turning upside down normal thinking and behaving and feeling, even eating and dressing and bathing. Alzheimer's disease was the most common and well known, but there were other versions.

Like everything in life when it comes to the decline of our bodies, mind and all, the way dementia progresses varies from person to person, where the three stages—early, middle, and late—depended on circumstances, genes, and those brain cells. However, it generally followed a pattern similar to that Hemingway quote: gradual decline, then sudden. That's the way it had been with Ma, with her middle stage really ramping up after Dad's death, leading me to find better care for her.

Early on, the most common experience of dementia is mild memory loss and confusion, which any normal elder experiences, often masking the underlying psychiatric condition. Symptoms grew and became more noticeable as dementia progressed, including: decline in a person's memory and disorientation (for sure Ma on both counts); difficulty communicating with those closest to them and other caregivers (not there yet, but Ma was on her way); changes in mood and behavior (thankfully none of those; Ma was still her pleasant self); a humiliating nosedive in their ability to take care of themselves, from eating to bathing to dressing (all three in recent months).

It was a sad decline in a woman who had meant the world to me, to so many, the different parts of her brain going haywire as the mental bug (as she had called it) advanced.

The more interesting part of it, which I hadn't known, was how they appeared to be normal and lucid, thinking and behaving as any elder would who wasn't suffering. She was often the woman I had known my whole life, for sure recognizing me (thankfully most of the time) and going on and on about childhood memories, especially trips we had taken as a family. These episodes were heartening for me at first, and actually made me reconsider my quest to get her permanent care, wondering (and often talking myself into believing) whether she was fine. Her doctor had popped that balloon, though, explaining that those lucid moments weren't really understood, rationalizing them as fluctuations in her brain chemistry or the temporary activation of less damaged parts of her brain. He had insisted that I not be fooled by those moments, and get her the kind of long-term, permanent care she needed.

He was right.

Because while Ma did have moments where she'd appear normal, more often than not she would slip right back into confusion or agitation with a suddenness that surprised me. Like a whole other person she was, with these crazy episodes triggered by stress and fatigue, changes in her routine and environment. For Ma, it was often in the calmness of her room or outside where she handled our conversations best. But get in a noisy, crowded place and she would become disoriented and distressed. I could never manage the triggers, and was grateful when I had secured a spot at Dreamscape Manor.

The managed care facility had provided way better care than I ever could have on my own. They had actually improved the quality of her life living with dementia. But something had happened.

And I was going to find out what.

A hot breath of midday August air gusted past, the flaring scent of roses and honeysuckle heavy. Gardens flanking both ends of the parking lot were managed by the residents, the outdoors doing them and their condition good. I bypassed the two winding staircases for the main front door, a pair of glass panes that whooshed open on arrival.

The inside was cool, with an almost bite to the air coming in from outside. It was laced by the scent of chocolate and a hint of vanilla. And was that peanut butter? Smelled like fresh-baked cookies, which made sense for the time of day. Midafternoon tea and coffee time was a daily ritual for the residents, especially Ma. Loved her sugar cookies and coffee, doctored with too much sugar and cream for my taste, but I smiled thinking about her preferences. And also those cookies, that strong smell of peanut butter and chocolate raising an even stronger memory of after-school treats, year after year. In my case, no bake cookies.

Could almost taste the soft and slightly warm gooey goodness in my mouth from the concoction of oatmeal and peanut butter and cocoa that was meant to harden on the counter. They were always the perfect coda to my school day from school hell. The smooth, creamy goodness was almost like eating peanut butter fudge, except loaded with oats. Dang, did I miss those cookies, those days.

More than that: I just flat missed Ma.

Though I visited her often, I hadn't made a single one of those midafternoon cookie and coffee rituals. Was too busy with the practice, with clients, with other people and other things.

Regret ran sour through me as I darted to the front desk in my favorite black suit and red tie. Both Canalis, crisp and expensive. Figured dressing the part of an upstanding citizen would put any worries to rest when I made my asks.

A young Hispanic woman with kind eyes behind narrow pink glasses smiled and welcomed me to Dreamscape Manor, asking how she could help me.

"I'm here about the matter regarding Florence O'Donnell," I replied. "I'm her son. And her attorney."

That smile quickly faded, and those kind eyes turned grim.

"Oh..." was all she said before picking up the receiver to a phone anchored to the desk.

"I've got questions. I want to see her room."

She held up a finger, nail painted a shade matching her glasses, before punching one of several buttons.

Reggie and Lizzy and Johnny caught up as she muttered to someone on the other end.

"What's the word?" asked Reggie.

I turned my back to the woman, answering, "I said I was

here for the matter about my mother. I think she's calling a superior."

"I bet she is," Lizzy said. "Can't imagine every day a woman is murdered in these parts."

Sure enough, a supervisor arrived a few minutes later.

"Mr. O'Donnell?" he said on approach, extending a hand. "Brock Sheldon, the chief administrator of Dreamscape Manor."

The man looked more like a linebacker than a managed care facility administrator, tan suit snug but trim, tieless and shirt open with a tan chest making a showing in the summer heat. I had never met the man, and I tried to get a read on him now. His pinched face, with furrowed brow and thin lips and clenched jaw, showed an indistinguishable mix of grief and remorse, worry and fear.

Given the dynamics, I bet all of the above were racing through his head.

Sheldon offered his hand. "Please accept my deepest condolences for your loss."

I smiled and took it, a loose grip meant to convey those condolences—until it tightened and switched to command and control. I returned the favor, the man's face loosening now, and his back straightening with eyes looking down with suspicion.

Had to imagine Sheldon knew of my arrest finger-pointing me as the accused, along with being the last remaining kin of the deceased on top of being a lawyer who was probably filled with all sorts of questions that spelled liability doom.

Letting go, the man said, "From everything I've heard from my employees, your mother was the sweetest, kindest, most pleasant resident we have had here at Dreamscape."

"Thank you, Mr. Sheldon. I appreciate the sentiment."

"Here..."

The man guided me with an open hand down a short

hallway to a modest sitting room. An ornate marble fireplace sat at the far end, flanked by walls lined of walnut bookshelves stuffed with neatly arranged books. Tall windows looked out on flowering gardens, and a collection of dark brown leather furniture anchored the center. He invited us to sit and asked if we would like anything to drink.

Sheldon sat across from me in an overstuffed chair, and I sat in my own. Reggie and Lizzy flanked my right on a couch, Johnny across from them at my left on another couch.

The man said, "A real shame what happened to her, and obviously we are cooperating with the authorities to assist in any way we can to help bring the perpetrator—"

He stopped cold, his eyes widening with recognition before narrowing and falling. His chest heaved with an uncertain breath.

"Well, we just want this matter resolved."

"So do I. Which is why we've come to see her room—" I swallowed, staring him dead in the eyes, then made my request: "—the crime scene."

"Oh..."

I knew this part was going to be tricky, because defendants did not have an automatic right to examine a crime scene. Such access was regulated by law enforcement agencies, and for good reason. It was in the best interest of their investigations to preserve evidence to maintain the integrity of that investigation.

However, there were ways for defendants to gain access to necessary evidence and information to prepare for their defense and ensure a fair trial, like discovery and even court orders requiring such access. The latter would take too long and the first option would be too late, gaining access to photos and samples and reports only weeks, even months after the fact, and filtered through the Mill Creek Junction police department.

I preferred to take the direct approach.

Reggie introduced himself as my lawyer and added, "Gideon wants to view the room where his mother lost her life. In your care."

Tried not to wince at both his appeal to authority and that last line. *In your care...* Seemed a bit too heavy-handed, with a slight emphasis on *you*, which I recognized was Reggie's way of currying compliance through a touch of guilt. I worried it would immediately turn Sheldon off to their ask.

The man's eyes flashed my way before returning to Reggie. "But I understand he is a suspect in the investigation."

Reggie replied, "He has the right to prepare for an adequate defense, which requires us to view the scene where his mother was murdered."

Sheldon shifted and crossed his arms. "I'm not sure about that. Crime scene tape is still fixed across the door, and Chief Roller himself said I was to keep the area cleared."

Lizzy jumped in now: "I understood the police had finished their work."

"They have."

"There you go!"

Her enthusiasm conveyed permission, which seemed to throw Sheldon, who cocked his head and just stared at her.

Reggie added, "It's been a few days since they've collected their evidence, correct?"

Sheldon nodded.

"And they haven't been back since?"

"No, they haven't."

"Sounds to me," Johnny joined in, "like Junction PD got what they came for."

Lizzy said, "Don't worry, we're pros at this sort of thing. We won't do anything that will compromise their work. We won't get you into trouble."

The man shifted again, rubbing his chin now, clearly torn.

"We can always obtain a court order," I said, keeping the momentum on our side, "and drag your facility through the normal legal process. But I don't want to bring any undue attention to a place that my mother loved so dearly. You understand."

Sheldon hesitated and looked off, the gears clearly turning. A few beats later, he sighed and stood, smiling and buttoning his jacket.

"That won't be necessary. As you suggested, it looks like the authorities have finished their work. And you'll be careful, you won't...do anything to compromise Dreamscape Manor?"

I got the man's meaning: You won't get me into trouble, right?

I stood and nodded. "Exactly."

While he led us back into the lobby, I added one more request.

"Oh, and we'll need to speak with my mother's nurses. Sammy and Kelsey, right?"

Sheldon spun on his heels, eyes wide and looking like he might put up a fight.

I quickly intercepted it: "Again, we could request a court order, depose them under oath and all."

Reggie added, "This way is easier. Fewer legal entanglements."

Same for Lizzy: "And way less public."

Sheldon frowned, then nodded. He conveyed his condolences again and left us alone to our investigation.

I prayed to the good Lord it bore fruit.

Chapter Twenty-Three

I knew right where to go. Room 527. She loved that room, situated at the back corner of the facility. The view opened up to a pond flanking the east side of the property, where she often watched the sun rise and the resident geese flock and flap and fly.

Aside from the sharp tang of disinfectants and cleaners, the wide hallway felt like walking through an upscale hotel. Little lanterns served as lamps outside each door, their soft yellow glow reflected off white cottage-style walls and black hardwood flooring. A crimson runner embroidered in blues and yellows and greens ran down the center, carrying on that Southern plantation feel.

Nurse stations divided the sections, with young and middle-age men and women in green and purple scrubs sitting at low counters filling out reports at workstation monitors or taking a breather from their important work. I passed the final one, leading the other three down the final hallway—spotting our destination.

Down at the far end, yellow **DO NOT CROSS** tape

made an X across the closed door—and an exclamation point on my mother's room.

Her *former* room...

Swallowing, I quickened my pace, noticing a pair of nurses standing guard, no doubt sent by Brock Sheldon, which I sort of appreciated.

A tall, lanky man with red hair met us. Joining him was a petite woman with curly auburn hair. They sort of looked like brother and sister. Really, they just looked like kids. And they were caring for my mother?

I frowned. Look at me, sounding like an ageist geezer. And look at them, clearly broken by the death of their patient, their eyes wide and brimming with emotion, pale and drawn. They extended their arms on my approach, as if they wanted to embrace the man who had been the son of the woman they had cared for. Loved, even.

I stretched out a hand, introducing myself. Kelsey took it, squeezing it with both hands while Sammy offered his hand, as if wanting to do the same. I obliged, Ma's two caretakers offering their sympathies while holding my hands, their eyes filling with the same empathy. I was touched by their support.

"Brock said you had wanted to see us," Sammy said.

Kelsey added, "That you wanted answers about your mother's death."

"We're not sure how we can help."

"It was a pretty busy day, and we had lots of residents to tend to."

"With not a lot of help."

"They were pretty much on their own most of the time."

"Been that way for—" Sammy turned to Kelsey for confirmation "gosh, I can't remember the last time we were fully staffed."

She smirked. "Tell me about it!"

The pair were nervous and talking at a rapid clip, sharing more than I had anticipated. Probably oversharing, but I welcomed it. It explained why my mother's killer could have slipped through, a lack of staffing supervision opening a window.

It also rang familiar.

Ma had shared the same complaints about the assisted living home my dad had been living in when he died. That one had also been caused by the sort of negligence Sammy and Kelsey were describing, staffing shortages thanks to funding cuts. Looked like this facility was like that one where Dad had been, both places putting profits over people.

I said, "Thank you for your time, and for caring for my mother this past year."

The pair offered weak smiles and nods.

"First off, do you know how she was—" I faltered. Swallowing, I added "*discovered.*"

"That was Kelsey," Sammy quickly said, looking at his co-worker to take over.

She swallowed, explaining, "With your mother, she always wanted an early morning wake-up call, before dawn. Loved to watch the sunrise, out her window or at the pond, tossing smuggled bread pieces to the ducks. She had said she hated sleeping in. Like she was waisting the day if she wasn't up by 9 o'clock."

Johnny snorted. "Ain't that the truth."

I smiled. Sure sounded like Ma.

Kelsey continued, "The medication she was on made her super sleepy, so she had insisted I wake her. That morning was like any other. I came in, eased the lights to a dull orange, like a sunrise to help her body wake naturally. But..."

She faded, not finishing the thought.

I did it for her: "But she didn't wake up."

She crossed her arms and clenched her eyes shut, a set of

tears pinching down her cheeks. "I thought she was sleeping. She hadn't stirred. Didn't make a sound. Here's the thing, though: There was a niggling—something in the back of my mind that things weren't right."

"How so?" asked Johnny, my investigator jumping into the fray now.

"The smell," Kelsey said.

"Smell?"

"And heat."

"Explain," was all Johnny said, crossing his arms and widening his stance.

"It was hella hot," Sammy explained, shaking his head. "The thermostat had been jacked up to almost 90!"

"So someone had cranked the room temperature."

"You're thinking intentionally?" asked Reggie.

"Intentionally," I confirmed. "No doubt about it."

"Why is that?"

"Ma hated the house hot. Hated it freezing too, but she'd always settled for just above 70."

"Makes sense," Johnny said. "And also why the room would be turned into an oven."

"Why is that?" asked Reggie again.

"Yeah, sharing is caring, JP," Lizzy said.

"Because high temperatures can wreak havoc with a crime scene by accelerating the breakdown of biological and physical evidence. DNA can break down more quickly, making it real hard, even impossible, to gather the sort of usable profile a detective would want for identification purposes."

"Like blood and what not?" I said.

"Especially blood. Raised temperatures kick-start the coagulation of bodily fluids, drying them out and even affecting the analysis of splatter patterns. Really wreaks the timeline when the state of fluids are messed with."

Sammy made a gagging sound, and Kelsey clenched her stomach. Both had gone pale and were leaning on the hallway wall. Clearly, this wasn't their cup of joe.

I said, "Same for physical evidence, I imagine. Fingerprints and whatnot?"

Johnny nodded. "Fingerprint degradation, evaporation of sweat and oils left behind—definitely."

Reggie added, "Making it hard to successfully lift prints from surfaces."

"Might explain," Lizzy said, "why the discovery file was thin on any prints."

"Right. MCJPD indicated little to no latent fingerprints present at the crime scene, including expected staff."

Johnny said, "Other chemical compounds, like drug residue and GSR, not to mention the decomposition of a body—"

"GSR?" Sammy asked, having recovered.

"Gunshot residue. The more volatile, organic components can evaporate in high heat, even alter their chemical composition."

"Egads!" Lizzy exclaimed. "All of that from jacking up the room temp?"

"You'd be surprised. Biological evidence starts to degrade once the temps start pushing into the mid-80s. Now, it takes a bit more to mess with DNA, but prolonged exposure to high temperatures ain't good news for criminal investigators, especially depending on how close the evidence is to a heat source."

I shifted, looking at the floor and scratching my chin, taking it all in.

Then I turned to Kelsey: "So what did you do when you found my mother like that?"

She straightened, pushing off from the wall to reengage.

"First thing I did was crank the air conditioning on, like full blast. Then I opened her window to air out the room. Like I said, the smell was super bad. Almost puked. Thought Florence had—well, I thought she'd had an accident."

"You didn't notice her lying facedown on her bed, in a pool of blood?"

Kelsey shook her head, her face draining of color some more at the memory. "Not at first. I remember turning from the window to her dresser to grab her pillbox and fill it for the week ahead with her medication, making light chitchat about the day. Then I started singing a song."

"What song?" Reggie asked.

"'Bye Bye Blackbird.'"

My heart stopped. So did my breathing. I braced a hand against the hallway wall. "The one by Ella Fitzgerald?"

"That's right! She loved that song. Said it was her favorite."

It was. Dad had sung it to her for years before he himself had slipped into dementia, a favorite of those early jazz singers. Was one of those touchstones that had kept him grounded when the mental bug had started setting in his own mind, something I had carried on when Ma started suffering. Fitzgerald had brought her back to reality, *grounded* her in reality, us two singing the song together, even just weeks ago. I had marveled at how she had still hung onto those words after all these years, after her mind had started to go in other ways.

"Then what?" I said.

"Then, well..." Kelsey trailed off, as did her gaze. She crossed her arms again and frowned, her lower lip trembling at the memory.

She recovered, plowing ahead: "Then I knew something wasn't right."

"How so?" asked Reggie

Normally, after I sang *'Sugar's sweet, so is she'*—"

I interrupted, "She would come back with *'Bye, bye, blackbird.'*"

She brightened. "Right! How did you know?"

I smiled weakly. "A family tradition. What happened next?"

Her face fell, and she swallowed. "Then I turned around, and I—"

She faltered, her tongue stumbling over itself on a throat I could tell was clenching with emotion. Her eyes filled with the same, and Sammy picked up the story.

"I heard her scream down the hall," he said. "I'd just finished with another resident, a few doors down, then came rushing to help. Like I said, it was hella hot, and she was right about the smell. I actually did retch a little."

He actually swallowed back the bitter bile and sour memory.

"Kelsey had fallen to her knees. I went to help her, thinking she had fallen, but she screamed again and pointed a trembling finger at Mrs. O'Donnell's bed. Well, at Mrs. O'Donnell."

I could hear my heart in my ears now, my chest heavy with its racing beat and breath hard to come by. I didn't want to ask, but I needed to know.

I simply said, "And?"

Another swallow, then a beat and a heavy breath.

Then: "And I saw her. Face down on her pillow, blood all around."

The soft clattering of keyboards and squeals of chairs, ringing phones from the nurses station and gentle footfalls echoed through the hallway.

"We already told all of this to the police," Sammy said.

"Yeah, why do you need all this?" questioned Kelsey.

Reggie answered, "It's helpful for us to hear the context of the events for ourselves. It will help our own investigation, so thanks for your time."

I asked, "Can I see her room, please?"

The pair exchanged a look between them. Short and quick, but definitely a look.

Then, from Sammy: "Are you sure?"

I nodded.

Kelsey sucked in a breath and puffed it out. "For *sure* for sure?"

There was that exchange again, their faces even losing some color.

For a second I wasn't sure, and I almost took back my request. What good would it do? We'd get the report in discovery, photos and analysis of samples and documentation of evidence. Did I need to see the last place my mother had been before she passed—the last *way* she had been before she'd died?

Did I want to? Heck no! Flat didn't want the last thing in my head about Ma to be how she had died.

But I plowed forward anyway. I knew I needed to. Needed to see the way she'd died.

Not only for the case—for *my* case—but for myself. Even for Ma. I owed it to her to get to the bottom of her murder by doing all I could.

Which meant seeing the crime scene for myself.

I swallowed and nodded. "I'm sure."

Sammy gestured to the door. "You know the drill. Put in your key code and you're good to go."

Johnny helped me carefully remove the crime scene tape from the door.

"What do you mean by key code?" Reggie asked as I pecked mine into the lock.

Sammy replied, "A unique personal ID number, assigned to each family member and the nursing staff."

"So no one can get in or out without this code?"

"That's right."

The door flashed a successful **GREEN** and unlocked. I

turned the knob and almost went inside when Reggie intercepted me.

He grabbed my arm. "You do know what this means, don't you?"

I looked at him, frowning, leaving the truth unsaid.

Lizzy said it for me: "So Gideon and the nurses...Those are the ones who had access to Mrs. O'Donnell?"

"That's right," Sammy answered.

"Anyone else have access to this room, the day she was murdered, maybe visit her?"

"That we know of?" He looked to Kelsey. Now she answered for him.

"Besides you, Mr. O'Donnell...not that I can recall."

Lizzy did one of her inaudible gasps. Mouth opened without a sound, eyes mirroring the same. Same for Reggie, the same dumbfounded disbelief etched on his face that would have normally come out as a *Say waaa?*

I imagined that would come later.

"You know..." Sammy said, scratching his chin, "there was that one dude who met with Florence, remember?"

Kelsey replied, "Oh, yeah! Forgot about him."

Johnny asked, "Did you get a good look at him?"

"Not really. It was one of those days, running in and out. I only know because of the log sheet."

"Log sheet?"

Sammy added, "Right. When residents are checked out by non-approved people, there's a log created with their credentials. Time in, time out."

"And name?" Reggie said.

"Yeah."

Johnny shifted, asking, "How can a non-approved person check out a resident?"

Sammy shrugged. "Not sure. I just work here."

He grunted an acknowledgement. "I'll follow up on that one."

Lizzy turned to me, lips drawn into a thin line that meant business. "And follow up on the *other* one."

Reggie crossed his arms and regarded me. "Yeah, me too."

Knew exactly what that meant.

I hadn't exactly told them about my meet-and-greet with Ma the day she had been murdered. They would not be amused. Clearly they were already not amused, no thanks to Sammy!

Not good, Gideon Paul...

I'd deal with them later. Right now, I needed to deal with the other thing.

My mother's room. Her crime scene.

Turning away, I shoved inside.

Not at all prepared for what I found.

Chapter Twenty-Four

I took a breath and completed my entrance, leaving the door open for the others filing in behind me.

And was overcome by exactly what Kelsey said she'd experienced when she had arrived to find my mother dead. Murdered.

The darkness, the heat, the smell of rot.

Hadn't they turned down the air?

A short hallway led from the door through a small foyer and into the main living area. The bathroom door at the left was open and dark, white marble tiles on the floor and counter, the white ceramic toilet and shower, covered in black fingerprint powder.

What little light seeped through the only window in the small apartment cast itself on a familiar, familial token. At my right. Clenching my throat tight.

A wooden coat rack sat against the wall. The one Dad had built for our family—what, thirty years ago? It was wide, about four feet across, and almost fit the height of the wall. The back was solid oak, stained a nice, warm brown, with three solid-brass pegs anchored to that backboard, along with a mirror still holding its reflection after all these years, now covered in more of that black fingerprint powder.

Still remembered helping Dad carefully sand and stain the wood. He let me do it all, too, after he had cut and carved each of the pieces himself. Then we fit every piece together, the two of us side by side, before I applied wood glue and he drove in the nails. Dad was always like that, bringing me along for the ride on his projects. Loved that about him. And Ma had made sure I did my part in using what we had made. Would pester me about my coats or shoes lying around, snapping her fingers and pointing at the door where the piece of furniture rested, the command unsaid but fully delivered.

Dreamscape Manor provided most of the furniture, but Ma had insisted they move it into her apartment. Said it made it more like home. I figured it grounded her in reality when her mind wandered into confusion, seeing something from the life she had shared with her soulmate, her family all those years.

I walked to the heirloom, smiling at the notches etched along the left side, each one marking my growth from over thirty years ago. I traced a finger through my timeline running down the side, the rough cuts taking me back down from teen to toddler.

Ma's faded red coat, bulky and well-worn, still hung on her peg, a lighter Mackinac Island zip-up hoodie on Dad's, our favorite family haunt up north at the tip of Michigan's mitten, where we would enjoy fudge and bicycle rides and swims in the hotel pool and pub fare for several days almost every summer. Another pleasant memory made bitter by the crime scene that awaited

A pair of navy rain boots sat dirty beneath a bench, along with pink running shoes. Missing were her pink slippers, which she went everywhere in, even more than her regular shoes. I would have to ask her nurses about those. Not sure why, maybe because I wanted them as a token of her memory, but I'd have to follow up on that one.

After the next thing.

Which was getting to it.

The crime scene beyond.

A hand rested on my shoulder, startling me into action. I appreciated the gesture of solidarity, not knowing who it was. Now I felt silly at the emotional show, and embarrassed. So I strode inside.

The window Kelsey had referenced was straight ahead, blinds down and curtains drawn. I went to it first, giving me some time before facing the inevitable, but also walking through the steps she herself had taken to sort of retrace the moments when my mother had first been discovered.

Walking past the dresser, this piece a Dreamscape furniture addition, covered in the same black fingerprint powder, I threw back the white laces—another home-brought token from Ma's former life, the ones that had decorated her and Dad's bedroom. Raising the blinds flooded the room with bright sunlight. A click from behind turned on a lamp.

A beat, a breath—deep, from the mouth, not caring for the lingering stink of blood and other fluids—I turned from the window.

And froze stiff. Unmoving and unbreathing.

The room opened into a modest square. A navy cloth reading chair was shoved into the far corner, with a lamp glowing a faint yellow sitting next to it. Then the bed, stripped of the floral duvet that normally would have been neatly draped across the well-made bed, sheets crisp and tucked and orderly, just as Ma liked things. Instead, the sheet and duvet had been pulled back, slumped over the bottom edge. A cream fitted sheet was all that was left.

And the pillow.

Stained a wicked crimson that had turned a rusty brown, the blood caked and coagulated, cracked and dry from heat and time. The size and shape of the mayhem was like a large water balloon of red paint had fallen from the ceiling and splattered on the head of the bed—the blood having spread in a meandering, stretching pattern across the pillow and down onto the fitted sheet at the neck.

I closed my eyes to catch my breath. It was no use, and actually worse than keeping them open.

All I could picture was Ma in that bed, in her light blue nightgown, face down in the pillow, head shattered by an explosive shot at the back, hair spread around her in an unholy nimbus of black curls streaked silver, blood pooled beneath her face, bits of brain matter and bone shards pockmarking those curls.

I snapped open my eyes and strode to the bed.

Shuffling feet behind across the carpet flared as I approached the right side of the bed, Lizzy and Johnny and Reggie joining me. JP sidled up to the left, a penlight in hand as he examined the stained mattress, then the wall behind. The light reflected off from bits of blood and other matter that had sprayed from the gunshot.

"No one heard a gunshot..." Johnny said to no one in particular.

"That's right," Lizzy confirmed.

"Not that anyone reported," Reggie added. "The discovery file indicated a secondary decorative pillow had been used to muffle the gunshot."

"MCJ took it for analysis, didn't they?"

"That's right."

Yes, the pillow. The one used to suppress the shot while my mother—

I couldn't finish the thought. Couldn't bear thinking about her sound asleep while someone crept from behind, clenched that secondary decorative pillow, as Reggie described it, against her head. Right before he (or she; I was certainly equal opportunity when it came to murderous criminals) jammed a pistol at the back of Ma's head and pulled the trigger.

I braced a hand against the wall at the thought and heaved a breath.

I wasn't sure about this any longer...

JP bent over the bed, drawing closer to the pillow before craning toward the back wall.

He said, "This doesn't look like anything a nine millimeter would do. Either a three-fifty-seven or forty-four magnum."

"Bingo on both counts," Lizzy said. "The ballistic report indicated either a .44 or .45. Both were consistent with the size of the entry wound and the level of damage out the other end."

He just grunted at that, withdrawing and scanning the surrounding area, which wasn't much.

I closed my eyes and bowed my head. It felt light, and I was boiling in the stifling, staid air, my head filling with the scents and sights of death.

"Say, Gideon, you own a gun, right?" Johnny asked, snapping me from my moment.

I shoved off the wall and shifted, suddenly feeling like the interrogation light had swung my way.

I swallowed and nodded. "That's right."

"What kind?"

"A Glock 37."

Another Johnny grunt, then the folding of his arms.

"A forty-five..."

Reggie said, "MCJPD hasn't executed a search warrant for your place yet, Gideon."

Lizzy added, "Though that could come at any time. So..."

I turned to her. "So...what?"

She glanced at Reggie, and I took a step toward her, repeating the question.

"So what, *Lizzy?*"

I said her name with more snap than I'd intended. Still, I was irritated by her meaning. Lizzy held up her hands in surrender.

"I'm on your side, Gideon." She gestured to Reggie. "We both are. I just want to make sure there aren't any surprises."

"What, like the murder weapon happening to be a Glock 37, showing up in my chimney?"

I huffed a sigh and spun away, taking a step, then a breath, then moving clear from the bed entirely back to the window. Geese were grazing on the bright green grass, and I imagined my mother taking in this very view. It made me angry. All of it.

"This is stupid..." I complained, raking a hand through my hair, sweating now from the stifling heat. "What the heck was I expecting to find?"

Johnny answered, "It's always good to take in the lay of the land, kid. Get a sense for the site of sin."

Supposed he was right.

"All I know is that it's hot as hell in here!" Reggie complained.

"Isn't there air conditioning?" asked Lizzy.

"There's supposed to be," I answered, taking off my tie and unbuttoning my top shirt button.

"Maybe Dreamscape cut back on that part of the amenities too."

I turned to her and frowned. "Maybe..."

"Didn't the Bobbsey Twins," Johnny said, jerking a thumb toward the hallway, "say they had cranked the air?"

Lizzy replied, "Kelsey said she did, then opened the window when she came to check on your mother."

I turned around, noting the window was sealed shut. No surprise. The staff would have locked it tight after finding the body, and Junction PD would have wanted to make sure it was secure to make sure the crime scene itself was secure. And maybe Dreamscape Manor figured they'd save a few dimes letting the room's air go. No need to keep the temperature low when no one was living in it.

The thought angered me even more than I had been, sending me to the thermostat to investigate.

Sure enough, it was just shy of 80 degrees. But the air was set to *COLD*. Looked like HVAC maintenance had gone to pots in this place from Hades. Or maybe it was just the mid-August heat playing havoc with the HVAC unit. Ninety-degree temps would do that to a—

Hold on...

I spun around, searching for signs of that HVAC unit.

A breeze, a sound—a *something*, anything that would tell me it was on and engaged, at least giving it a good college try to cool the room.

Nothing on all fronts.

Except there was a muffled rattle. Or was that a buzzing sound? Almost like my childhood kazoo Dad had bought for me at a local Junction carnival that had rolled into town. Loved that thing, my lungs blowing a hot breath through the plastic tube.

Ma didn't care for it one lick. Said it plucked her ever living nerves. And one day it went missing. Only later did I find out she'd hidden it away so she wouldn't go crazy with my kazooing. Didn't stop me from making my music in other ways.

"What's up, boss?" asked Reggie.

I put out a hand, searching the room, the ceiling, waving my hand around to find what I was—

There it was. Above Ma's bed.

I said, "When I was a kiddo, I had a favorite kazoo my mother hid from me when she got sick of hearing me blow the thing to death."

I gripped the headboard and shoved the bed, moving it a few inches.

"Hold up, kid," Johnny cautioned. "I'm not sure that's wise, Gideon..."

"Yeah, don't forget our promise," Reggie said. "Nothing that would get Dreamscape into trouble, especially that administrator dude."

I scoffed. "Who cares about Brock Sheldon?" Then shoved the bed another few inches. "All I care about is the kazoo..."

"Huh?" said Lizzy.

Another nudge, harder and more insistent. The bed slid farther than I'd intended, slamming into the lamp next to the chair near Ma's bed—toppling it to the floor.

It fell with a crash that sent the bulb winking off and worry flooding me that I'd wake the residents on either side. And send Sammy and Kelsey and their boss racing in to investigate.

No one moved. No one made a sound. Except for Johnny, who gently picked up the lamp and set it back on the stand. He turned the switch and on it came.

I eased out a breath I hadn't known I was holding.

Then promptly moved the nightstand at the bed's right underneath a vent I spied up top above her bed.

"Like I was saying," I went on, "Ma tossed my music maker, except it didn't stop me from making music. Found all sorts of things. Including my father's comb and a piece of wax paper."

Lizzy turned to Reggie. "He's lost his marbles."

He replied, "Have to agree. What's that sad story have to do with—"

"Listen!" I snapped, pointing at the vent.

All eyes followed.

It was throwing up a hissing wheeze.

"Like a kazoo..." Johnny said, snorting a chuckle.

I grinned. "Exactly."

"Say *waaa?*" Reggie said.

"Oh my heck..." Lizzy added. "A kazoo!"

I climbed on top of the table, steadying myself and straightening to take a look.

Johnny said, "There must be something stuck inside to create that buzzing sound."

I waved my hand in front of the vent. "Hardly anything coming out of this dang thing."

Reggie said, "No wonder it's hotter than a Texas roadhouse."

"The restaurant chain," Lizzy said, "or, like, an actual—"

The scraping of the vent cover as I removed it intercepted her.

"Jeez Louise! Can you make any more racket?"

The screws to the cover had been removed. It was one of those that fit inside, with the outer covering originally screwed on to keep residents from pulling it out—

Until someone had removed the screws.

I tossed it to the bed. Probably not the best idea, contaminating the crime scene and all. Didn't care. All that mattered was reaching in to see what was inside.

Reggie picked it up. "Where are the screws?"

"Good question," Johnny said. "Anything inside, Gideon?"

"Checking now..."

Couldn't see into it, so I stepped on my tiptoes and stuffed a hand down into the vent.

When my hand punched into a thick—*something!*

Large and flexible and wedged in the HVAC ductwork.

There was something blocking the airflow!

Chapter Twenty-Five

"Guys, there's something inside!" I stammered.

My heart leaped with a mixture of excitement and dread, snatching my breath and sending my stomach plummeting in one of those roller-coaster plunges you only read about in bargain-bin Kindle thrillers, but don't realize is actually the case when adrenaline floods your veins in a fight-flight release to activate the body and all of the responses baked into our lizard brain thanks to our ancestors' collective wisdom from being chased down by mastodons and saber-tooth tigers, running from mudslides and a stirred-up hornets' nest, avoiding plagues and warring tribes.

And, I supposed, finding hidden packages stuffed away inside an HVAC vent above the bed where one's mother had slept for months—and then was murdered just a few days ago.

Not good, Gideon Paul...

Or maybe it was.

Because that dueling mixture, the excitement and the dread, spelled one of two possibilities.

Excitement that we had actually found something that might be useful in our investigation into my mother's death—and then defense of my impending criminal trial. Excitement that this...*something* might actually mean something, that it might clarify something or prove something. Excitement that the police had overlooked it, and now it was in our possession, which might be crucial for said investigation and impending trial.

Then the dread part—which was curiously like pennies and chalk heavy in my mouth. Must be the adrenaline, drying it and flaring up that metallic tang, along with the tremor overtaking my hand. Dread at the flurry of questions the package sparked. The what and how questions, along with the why and who ones. Dread at their meaning—the implications.

For Ma.

Couldn't worry about that now. Answers would come later. At least I hoped they would.

So I clenched my hand to stay the tremor; it worked. Then I slipped my fingers around the top of the package and wrenched it loose from the ductwork, wriggling it from side to side until I managed to yank it out from its dang hiding place and out into freedom.

Fresh, cool air hit me in the face, actually chilling the sweat beading down my forehead and blowing my hair. Boy, did that feel good.

The cool air, the find, clutching the buried treasure—all of it!

"Say *waaa?*" Reggie said, mouth wide and eyes wider. "Who stuffed that up in there?"

Who indeed.

I hopped down and hustled to the dresser, then knelt to the floor.

"Mother Mary and Joseph…" Johnny said, coming around to join me.

"What is this?" asked Lizzy, hovering over my shoulder.

The question startled me. Jolted me. Because what immediately came to mind was a possibility too horrifying to comprehend. To voice, even.

But I did.

Before I tore into the package, I looked up at her, that possibility growing with conviction into a probability.

"Something that got my mother killed…" I said lowly.

The revelation settled hard in the stifling room that now felt a tad cooler, a river of fresh air pouring down into the space as my teammates shifted and hummed before going still and quiet.

For a few beats, I just stared at what I had just extracted from the HVAC vent above Ma's bed. We all did. Flat made no sense.

What we had, how it had gotten up there.

Whether Ma herself had put it there!

That made far less sense than the fact of the matter lying on the floor before us.

Which was a manila envelope. Yellow and classic and officey. With those two metal butterfly clasps and the flap that licked close. Ma had brought them home from her work all the time working for Mercy General as an accountant. Stuff she had taken home to work on for the evening over a glass of Chardonnay. Not the good Old World stuff. We're talking Yellow Tail, which even then had been a bit of a splurge for Ma.

This one was about as thick as the ones she had brought home. Half a ream of paper thick. It was sealed shut, by both the metal clasps and lickable flap.

A knock at the door snatched my breath and flooded my veins with frigid fright.

Two raps and a muffled "Are you alright?" voice beyond.

Which sent me scrambling from the floor with the package.

"Here!" Johnny said, extending his hands for a handoff.

I did, without thinking.

Just as the door eased open. And in popped Sammy, his head then shoulder then a kneecap.

Brow raised, he asked, "Everything alright in here?"

"Yeah, we heard a crash..." Kelsey said from behind, out of view.

"Tripped," I said, voice hoarse and dry and stumbly.

"Oh..." Sammy glanced behind, then took a step farther inside, Kelsey joining now on bobbing tiptoes seeking a viewing of the room.

I moved to intercept him, catching Johnny stuffing the package under the mattress.

I said, "We're almost through here. Will only be another few minutes."

Sammy stopped his advance, hesitated, then took a retreating step, bumping into Kelsey.

"And you'll leave the room the way you found it, right?"

I nodded. "The way we found it."

"Because if it's messed...Sheldon will have my hide."

"Not to mention Junction PD will," Kelsey added.

I neared closer, smiling and reaching for the door. Sammy and Kelsey both stepped back out into the hallway.

"We got what we needed," I said, easing the door closed. "Appreciate the help. We won't be long. And we won't mess the room. Promise."

"Alright, just let us know—" Sammy's offer was interrupted by me closing the door.

I heaved a breath and hustled back inside, wiping my brow.

More out of instinct at having dodged a senior living bullet than actually swatting at sweat. The room felt mercifully cooler now, and I was actually feeling a bit chilled from my sweat cooling and me crashing from the adrenaline.

"The envelope, Johnny." I reached out a hand, and he was already a step ahead, handing off the thick package.

Of what...

To be determined.

And fast.

I sank to my knees again and sent my fingers tearing across the envelope's mouth.

"You think your mama shoved this up in there?" asked Reggie, nodding toward the open vent.

I said nothing. Just shook my head. Couldn't process anything—couldn't *think* about anything except for what was inside. There was one lingering question from when my fingers had first touched the cold softness of that paper envelope, and then dragged the thick package out from its hiding place.

How?

How had that envelope, with that stash of papers—documents, really, of what I hadn't a clue...

How had it gotten up there?

Even more crucially: How had *Ma* put it there? Because that's the assumption I was working on. Hadn't voiced it. Hadn't *dared* voice it, barely even to myself. How else could it have gotten up there? Unless someone else had used her room as a safe house for whatever it was this was. Which was a whole other ball of ugly. Could hardly face the how, much less the what, which would come sure enough once we examined the contents. Then there was the *why* of it all—more ugly.

Wrenching my finger across the envelope's closed mouth, the questions kept avalanching until it reached the edge.

Success.

I was like a kid again on Christmas. Had not a care for the packaging. All that mattered was the present.

Which—

Pulling it out was indeed a sheaf of papers. White copy paper, covered with two-sided black toner. Text and charts and graphs. One of those massive black clips held them together, with smaller bundles of papers held tight by paper clips, some silver, some others of various blue-red-green colors.

My peanut gallery just *hummed* and *ooed* and *huhed* behind, saying nothing more, which I appreciated. The interrogation would come once I unclenched that black hand from the stack.

Which I did. Tossing the clip aside, I started flipping through the various bundles of papers.

Now I was sweating, despite the chilled air pouring down into the room. A bead of sweat tickled my brow as it wound down, and a whiff of body odor made me flinch as my arm moved, flinging those bundles of—whatever they were from hand to hand.

I didn't know what I was staring at. Spreadsheets with numbers. And not just numbers. Dollar signs joined by numbers. And—

"Names..." I said on a disbelieving breath.

"Say *waaa?*" Reggie leaned over my shoulder.

Lizzy came up around the other, with Johnny crouching next to me now as well.

He said, "No wonder it was still so freakin' hot in here."

Reggie added a grunt. "A stash of—well, whatever this is was blocking the vent."

I didn't know what I was looking at, but it looked important. Important enough that Ma had stuffed it inside this vent. At least that was my working theory. But how?

And why?

Then, again, that first question: How? With her condition, how had she managed to get these documents up in that vent? And what was she even doing with them in the first place? What did they mean, if anything at all?

No, they meant something. Meant something to Ma. Something enough that she swiped them or printed them after finding them, then stuffed them in an envelope and shoved it up in that vent for safekeeping.

But what was their meaning?

And, again, that question returned: How had she even figured out their meaning, that they meant something, with her dementia?

The questions kept coming, and none of them flat made any sense. Neither the questions themselves, nor the answers, which were pretty much nonexistent.

But they sure meant something. The questions, yes, and where they led. But more importantly, the stash of papers Ma had stuffed away.

Except—

Again, flat made no sense.

And I just flat had no clue what any of it meant.

A rapping at the door intercepted any further thought about it. Followed by a pounding that changed in tone. And changed the mood. Hard, loud, insistent. Followed by an announcement that Sammy was about to enter again.

"We better go," Johnny said. "The help has returned."

Lizzy added, "And is in no mood to wait."

I muttered a curse and assembled the papers into a stack.

"I'll get the vent cover," Reggie said, hustling toward the bed.

"Good idea," Johnny said. "We better put this room back together again."

I didn't worry about them or the room. All I cared about

were those papers. And getting them clear of this room and back to the safety of my office.

I stuffed the papers back inside the manila envelope, then stuffed the envelope at my waist.

"Give me my jacket," I said in a rush.

Lizzy handed it off as I stood. I slipped into it as Reggie finished with the vent cover, hopping down from the side table.

Just as Sammy knocked again—once, then a firm pound. I promptly buttoned my jacket.

When the lanky redhead barged into the room.

With Brock Sheldon in tow. He didn't look happy.

And I wasn't sure things were put back in order.

Couldn't worry about that now. All that mattered was what we had found.

"We were just leaving," I said, hand pressed against the package that was pressed against my soaked shirt just inside my jacket at my waist.

I prayed to the good Lord above that no amount of orangey yellow was visible peeking out from behind my Canali best hiding place. Then nodded off as I strode out into the hallway.

Didn't even look back to confirm my teammates were behind me. Just kept threading through the hallways and out into the main lobby. Then out into the waning day-turned-evening now.

Parking lot lights fluttered to life as I made for Reggie's car. A quick glance over my shoulder confirmed the others had made it out with me, the trio hustling too fast for my liking. Yeah, we needed to jet, but no need to draw attention to ourselves.

I slowed my pace, and took a breath, that package heavy and feeling like it was about to flop out.

Reaching Reggie's Honda, I could hear it unlock, my partner coming up to the driver's side now, key fob in hand.

"Let's get out of here," I said, sliding inside.

"No complaints from me on that front," Reggie agreed.

Lizzy and Johnny slipped into the back as Reggie brought his car to life.

Then we left, the sun setting behind a place I never wanted to return to again.

Chapter Twenty-Six

Annabelle Kirkland was not a happy camper. It had been a no good, very bad day that started with a sleepless night. Mostly because of the thing that had been coming for some time, and some day.

She had slept like crap last night, a migraine needlin' her noggin from half-past midnight that still smarted through the day until that hot minute. Her afternoon fix of Starbucks froufrou had worn off long ago. Which, let's be honest, was much more about the froufrou than the caffeine. And now she was turning the screws on her boyfriend, helping execute dual search warrants for Gideon O'Donnell's residence and law office.

Behind his back.

Which had a measure of high-heaven stank about it that boiled her blood.

Annabelle threw back four Advils and gulped down the brown pills with a bottle of Perrier in the quiet comforts of her Nissan Altima. Gideon might drive an Audi, thanks to a few well-earned civil judgments and landing even more well-paying settlements thanks to those civil-judgment street creds, but her driving life was one of middling Japanese automotive engineering. An assistant prosecuting attorney doesn't earn squat compared to a mixture of civil defense and civil litigation.

The water felt nice, especially the Perrier, the bubbles tickling her nose as she swallowed another mouthful, even though her sedan was nice and cool. She had thought Tennessee heat was bad. The Volunteer State had nothing on mid-Augusts in Michigan, that's for darn tootin'! She might drive middle-class, but she sure drank like the upper crust she had always pined for.

And thinking about what she was waiting to do, now she wanted a shot of some Gentleman Jack to get her through—especially after what Dean Lawlor had pulled. Or almost pulled, had she not made friends with sweet Eleanor at the courthouse, Judge Jackson Bock's clerk who alerted her to the warrant being rammed through for her boss's John Hancock.

'Parently, Lawlor had been coordinating with Chief Roller on searching Gideon's home and office for the past few days. That's where Dean was, tending to the search of *O'Donnell and Associates*. Or hadn't she heard it was now something like *O'Donnell, Seward, and Wilson?* She hadn't had a chance to catch up with Gideon the past few days on that major business change since—

She let the thought die. Didn't even want to think about what had happened. None of it. His arrest and arraignment. Her sitting on the other side of the aisle in a way she wouldn't wish on her worst enemy. His mama, dead and not-yet-buried—*murdered* for Pete's sake!

With the evidence so far pointing the finger Gideon's way.

She still disbelieved her eyes, and ears for that matter, even though her brain told her otherwise.

On the face of it, Gideon sure looked guilty. The Happy-

Living CEO had confirmed his mama was set to scuttle the case he had been working his Yankee patootie off to pull off for the past year. He was promised a major payday if—let's be real: *when*—he won, or at least got HappyLiving to settle. And boy, did he need the money. Landlord said there was back rent due stretching several months past. He was so broke he had been tapping a line of credit on his house, which he ran dry to spring that Yankee patootie of his out of jail after paying back his firm. Those firm lights had even been turned off to boot!

So Gideon needed money. Which meant the big Mo was a strong contender in the finger-pointing business.

That motivation was partly confirmed by the suit against HappyLiving itself, with some interesting poison-pill clause allowing a majority to sever the suit and drop the matter all together. Something about some of the initial residents having cold feet at the start of it all, and Gideon extending the olive branch to reassure them enough to keep at it.

So, if Florence O'Donnell had bailed the old-fashioned way, actually bailing from the suit, then she would have poisoned the well, salted the fields, performed whatever karate-chop metaphor there was to eighty-six the suit since some had already wanted to drop the matter after having had some sort of come-to-Jesus moment.

Which, let's be real, was really them having a come-to-HappyLiving moment after having been bought off.

Except if Florence bailed the other-fashioned way, dying of some cause, there was speculation that property would be transferred to Gideon through his mother's estate. Giving him a vote to carry on the suit.

And motivation.

The numbers game would have shifted, the remaining litigants would have all the people they needed to forge ahead, and Gideon would have had what he needed to carry on.

So, yeah, lots of Mo flying around. Which wasn't even touching on the audio recording of a conversation Gideon had had before his mother had been murdered. A heated conversation that spelled out exactly—word. for. ever-loving. word!— that exact scenario. The two really got into it, too.

Only strange part of it was that no one else had heard the conversation. Claims of being short-staffed sounded iffy, but the provenance of the recording checked out, the terms of service for Dreamscape Manor (that's right, a flippin' TOS for a senior care center!) spelled out their right to keep audio and visual recordings of all spaces inside the managed care facility, including the residents' apartments. For their safety, of course.

Yeah right. What good was that sort of techno-nonsense when a resident could be *murdered*?

But that wasn't Annabelle's jurisdiction. Something more for the civil side of litigation than criminal. What her side did have was Gideon O'Donnell with a convincing motive, definitely clear opportunity, the son of the deceased having exclusive access to her room via a passcode. Two of the three requirements for trying a criminal conviction looked pretty solid.

Sure, a jury might disbelieve such an upstanding citizen of Mill Creek Junction would go to such lengths to kill his own mother. But Dean Lawlor was banking on that audio recording to seal the deal and seal Gideon's fate.

Once and for all.

Now she sat idling outside his house as Mill Creek Junction's boys in blue started arriving, their lights off but the show of force, with the five squad cars plus ambulance, a sight to behold. The SWAT van and Mass Casualty Unit RV were both overkill. Vowed she'd have a word or twelve with Dean once she played her part in this sad song.

Especially since he had been all sneaky about it, sending

one of those same boys and girls in blue to keep tabs on Gideon. 'Parently, he had been at Dreamscape Manor the past several hours. The Junction PD lackey hadn't gone inside to confirm what was what, but it didn't take a genius to know what he was up to.

Scoping out his dead mama's crime scene.

Not that he needed to be at his home in the first place. Any first year law student learned that law enforcement officers have the authority to execute a search warrant without the presence of the defendant or property owner. All that's required is a judge's John Hancock and they've got all the power they need to search to their heart's content, without any obligation to wait for the defendant to show up.

All that was required of Mill Creek Junction police was to provide notice that they were authorized to execute a search warrant and the purpose of such a search. A simple "knock and announce," as it was known, was the minimum. Yeah, there were exceptions, with those crazy no-knock warrants allowed if there was reasonable suspicion that showing up and announcing themselves would be dangerous or result in the destruction of evidence.

Which is exactly how Dean had wanted to roll. I put the kibosh on that real quick. At least on my end. Not sure what he was up to down in Mill Creek executing on his half of the search, Gideon's law office—a super dicey proposition that raised my brows. And my hackles.

Law offices were sacrosanct domains. Filled with all sorts of privileged documents and information governed by a whole host of doctrines. Work product, attorney-client privilege, not to mention the Fourth Amendment of the United States Constitution itself that stiff-arms unreasonable searches and seizures—which extended to lawyers as well as to clients.

So, yeah, Dean was skating on thin ice. Didn't know how

he managed to wedge his way into the office to begin with. Sure, the warrant only allowed for specific evidence and items used to commit the murder of Florence O'Donnell. Which was basically the murder weapon. Even then, any reasonable person would sniff the brown-shirt overtones of letting the government go barging into the domain shared by lawyer and accused.

Dean must have friends in high places to work that sort of hocus-pocus magic.

Sure, Gideon would have legal options to challenge the maneuver. She and Dean were sure Gideon would march his way into court and challenge the search and seizure, if anything came of their sunset hunt. The obvious goal would be to suppress any evidence we discovered on the basis of an improper execution of that warrant or an improper issuance of it in the first place without probable cause—then trying to trigger the fruit of the poisonous tree principle to invalidate whatever was found, arguing it had been legally tainted by the illegal search.

Except she knew he would fall flat on his face on both counts. Because, again, she was there to make sure the warrant's execution was squeaky clean. And they for sure had the reasonable articulable suspicion necessary to establish probable cause for the search in the first place.

The tape...

Annabelle had wondered why they hadn't moved on the search sooner. All Dean had said was they needed to button up a few things to make sure the search was airtight. And then all of a sudden it was green-light go. What changed, and when... she wasn't sure.

Now, there were certain legal safeguards and procedures in place to make sure the search would be lawfully conducted and that a defendant's rights are kept from being violated. One of which was the presence of a member of the prosecuting attorney's office.

In this case, that someone was lil ol' Annabelle Kirkland.

So there she was, idling outside Gideon's bungalow in the late evening hours, the horizon a nice golden orange stretching to a bruised purple far up top, the sun having set a bit ago. Popping sunflower seeds and sipping Perrier until—

A black Suburban SUV raced by and turned into Gideon's driveway.

Annabelle stiffened, swallowed, and stuffed her snack into a cupholder.

Out stepped the one person she had not wanted to see that evening.

Jamie Ramos. Mill Creek Junction PD detective extraordinaire, who had made her life a living you-know-what on more occasions than she cared to count.

The last of which had been going up against Gideon O'Donnell, in fact. That renegade weasel had last costed Annabelle the case that should have been a shoo-in. She had lost the Gerald Peterson case no thanks to that woman's law-skirting—well, skirting!

Annabelle swore hell would freeze twice over before she let her work her funny business on this one as well.

Tossing back a final mouthful of bubbly mineral water, she swallowed her final sunflower seed indulgence, shut off her Altima, and stepped out into the waning August Junction evening.

Gunning for Jamie Ramos, Perrier in hand.

Since her boots were made for hustling, hustle she did. Down Springdale Road right quick to intercept the detective and her entourage of officers exiting their Suburban.

"Fancy meeting you here, detective," Annabelle said, smiling and throwing in a chuckle for good measure.

Ramos snapped her head her way and frowned.

"Surprised to see you here, counsel."

"Why is that?"

The woman swept a hand toward Gideon's bungalow.

"Why, given you're—*Que es la palabra?*" she said in Spanish. Then she had that word she'd been searching for: "entangled."

Annabelle took a hesitant sip of water, face on fire from the finger-pointing. And, let's be real, finger-wagging.

"Dean wanted to divide and conquer," she simply said, laying the blame at her boss's feet. "So let's get to it, shall we?"

She gestured with her free hand toward the front door. Ramos nodded and took off, instructing a few of the officers in her entourage to stand guard at the bottom of the drive and front door. What did she expect? That Gideon would come racing home and barge into his house, put up a fight and impede the investigation? Maybe play fast and loose with whatever evidence Ramos and her cronies were expecting to find?

What a load of hooey!

Regardless, Annabelle followed her to the door—shocked by what happened next.

Jamie Ramos herself approach Gideon's house and offered a curt rapping knock on the front door Annabelle had come to and gone through countless times. The detective announced, "Mill Creek Junction Police Department. Open the door! Gideon O'Donnell, we have a search warrant. Open the door, please."

A breath, a beat.

Then: "This is the police. We have a search warrant and we're entering your premises, Mr. O'Donnell."

And that was that.

With a wave of her hand, a big-boned bruiser of an officer Annabelle couldn't identify approached with a battering ram.

A real mean looking thing that splintered the door jamb and sent the door sailing inside on well-oiled hinges before smacking against the wall.

Ramos continued, "Gideon Paul O'Donnell, remain calm and please stay where you are. We are here to administer a judicially executed search warrant, so please follow our instructions."

Had to smirk at that. As if Ramos didn't know exactly where Gideon was. Which wasn't at all inside the house! But I knew what she was doing. Following this protocol ensured she and Junction PD executed the search warrant legally and constitutionally by doing due diligence to protect their safety and Gideon's rights. That discretion had been taken to ensure all was on the up-and-up legally.

Really, though, it was just a big, fat CYA move to make darn tootin' sure whatever—if anything—was found could be used at trial.

Ramos strode inside, waving the boys and girls in blue inside with her, and stopping in the middle of Gideon's living room.

"*Está bien,* ladies and gentleman. Get to work. Leave no drawer or box or corner unturned." She spun around, one end of her mouth curling upward. "And I do mean *nada.* We're here for the murder weapon and any other piece of evidence connecting Gideon to the murder of Florence O'Donnell. Turn it all upside down and inside out. *Vamos!*"

She clapped her hands together and off the officers went.

The next few hours turned Annabelle's stomach, the way they destroyed Gideon's place like that. The place where they had watched rom-coms, chatted about life, about their futures— together even. And, yes, made out. Nothing else, of course. She was too much of a good Southern-bred gal to run all the bases to home. Mostly she was just a committed Christian gal who took seriously Jesus' teachings about two becoming one flesh, in the holy bonds of marriage.

Annabelle was there to supervise, to make sure there wasn't any funny business legally. Mostly she was there as Dean Lawlor's own CYA maneuver, to make sure his and Chief Roller's backsides were covered, when Gideon challenged the search in court. She performed her duties admirably from the granite island at the center of his expensive kitchen, her own backside planted on a cold steel stool, elbows propped on the cold black stone, head resting against her hands—

Some raucous flared from behind. In Gideon's living room.

She spun around and raced inside as some young buck scrambled from all fours.

"What is it?" asked Annabelle.

The man turned to her, grinning. "We've found a weapon."

Her breath caught in her chest, her heart lurched forward, her veins ran cold, her bowels went all watery.

Never believed those bargain-bin Kindle thrillers that used that over-the-top lingo to paint the internal physiological reactions to dumbfounded disbelief, even fear. But, yeah, all of the above had swept through her. Gripped her!

Her fancy fizzy water had gone warm and flat an hour ago, but she took a sip anyway.

Then swallowed.

Then: "Where was it?"

He nodded toward the large marble fireplace.

She tilted her head, confused. "Buried in ash?"

"No, up in the chimney."

"In the chimney?"

She walked toward it, crossing her arms. "What, just stuffed down inside?"

"Basically. The damper had been closed, and when an

officer opened the two metal plates above the firebox—well, out it came."

He held up the weapon by its grip with a blue-gloved hand, like a dead animal by the tail, all rotting and stinky and stiff.

There it was. The weapon. Gideon's weapon. His Glock 37.

She corrected herself: *a* Glock 37.

Because no way on God's green earth did she believe Gideon Paul O'Donnell had shot his mama in cold blood. No matter where the evidence pointed—who the evidence pointed at.

Which, with that motive and opportunity, and now presumably these means...

"Dust for prints," Annabelle said. "Bag it and log the chain of custody. Then keep that chain intact. Don't leave anything to chance."

"Yes, ma'am."

She watched as the officer walked away, and as Ramos came around the corner. The two had a powwow about the find, him cradling the weapon in those blue-gloved hands, her backslapping him and promising a drink after he cataloged the evidence.

It was looking harder and harder for her to deny what was becoming increasingly obvious.

Gideon's guilt.

What was she going to do?

Chapter Twenty-Seven

I still didn't know what I was looking at. Didn't help matters I was flipping through the stack of papers by a mixture of Reggie's dome light, the setting sun, and the light of my phone. My passenger courtesy light wasn't working, so I sat with my passenger's door open and feet planted on the dirt road outside trying to make sense of what we had.

An hour ago, Reggie had raced down the drive leaving Dreamscape Manor a little too fast for my taste. Was worried watching eyes would be wondering who was speeding from the joint—and why. Soon we were bounding through the open gate and onto the country road headed back to Mill Creek Junction.

Everyone had breathed a proverbial collective sigh of relief, literally us four exhaling in a huffing sigh breaths we didn't know we were holding before heaving deep relief. None of us had made a sound, none of us had moved, letting Reggie drive far down the road and out of sight of the compound. Then he switched it up and took us down a dirt road to go over what we had taken.

That's where we had been sitting as the minutes ticked by,

each of us with paper-clipped stacks from the larger stash of papers. We wanted to get a handle on what we were dealing with before we got too far. Take in the lay of the paper-trail land and offer early assessments.

For my part, I used my phone to snap some images that might be useful later. Graphs and charts and numbers that didn't make sense but seemed useful, especially a bunch of money that had been funneled into political donations—locally, regionally, nationally. Had a buddy in DC that I'd gone to Georgetown Law with who worked on Capitol Hill. Jayce Robinson, working as some legislative aide to some congressman or senator or something. Wondered if he could make sense of it all.

Insects chirped and tree frogs croaked all around as we continued reading and humming, flipping and reading and humming some more. The air had cooled, a nice breeze blowing lazily through the countryside, tinged by leafy vegetation and woodsmoke and oddly cooking oil. The perfect Junction summer night, for a cookout and cold beers, telling stories and jokes with friends. Wished that was my night instead of sleuthing it in the backwoods of Mill Creek Junction with a pile of stolen documents that meant diddly.

My battery was dying and I worried the car battery would as well if we didn't get moving soon with this dome light feeling like it was fading. But it couldn't wait, our collective sleuthing. We had to figure out what the heck we'd found.

What the heck Ma had found...

"You're sure we weren't followed?" Lizzy asked from the backseat, what felt like the sixtieth time in as many minutes.

Reggie huffed a sigh. "For the fifth time, no. We weren't."

"Relax, kid," Johnny said next to her. "Gideon ain't Tom Cruise and you're no Jeanne Tripplehorn."

Now Lizzy huffed a sigh. "Well, this sure feels like *The*

Firm! Because that was sure a close one, Brock Sheldon walking in on us like that."

"I'm thinking more along the lines of *The Pelican Brief,* maybe even *The Street Lawyer.*"

"Really? Do tell," Reggie said.

Lizzy snorted a laugh. "Yeah, I'm getting an assassination vibe here. Albeit not a Supreme Court justice. But where's the David and Goliath battle?"

"Yeah, I'm not seeing the homelessness play here. Although..."

Reggie went silent, the void filled by page-flipping.

I waited for him to make his point. He didn't, flipping through more pages, even taking a few snapshots himself with his phone.

Finally, I turned back into the car and asked him, "Although, what?"

Reggie set down his papers and looked at me, frowning before looking out into the waning evening turning night now.

He said, "Your mama was an accountant, right?"

I nodded. "Right."

"So what we're seeing here—these graphs and charts, these numbers...they would have made sense to her."

"Right."

"Would have *meant* something to her."

"Right," I said again, wondering where he was going with this.

"Then why don't we go with Occam and call it a day?"

"By Occam," Lizzy said now, "I presume you mean William Occam?"

"As in Occam's razor?" asked Johnny.

Reggie grunted an affirmative. "The simplest explanation is the obvious one in my book."

"And often the right one in mine."

"That's what I'm saying!"

A headache needled for my attention, right between the eyes. Had been forming the past hour pouring through all of these documents in the dim light. Now all the double-talk was blooming it into what I feared was a migraine.

"And what is it you're saying?" asked Lizzy, saying what I was thinking.

He looked at me, dead in the eyes. "That your mama found something—"

"That got her killed," I finished.

He nodded. "Just like you said. Maybe some scandal. Something that pitted her against Big Managed Care."

The thought had certainly crossed my mind. It was basically the secret assumption I'd had when I found the package. That mama had found something, had stolen it, then hid it up in a vent in her room above her bed.

Then died.

"Hold the phone," Lizzy said. "That assumes Florence O'Donnell went looking for something."

Reggie responded, "Or at least found something."

"Still, that's a stretch."

"Is it? I mean, look at all of this stuff." Reggie swept an arm around the car.

"Kid has a point," Johnny said. "And with the amount of stuff hidden in that vent, I might be leaning on the looking-for-something angle than the found-something one."

"But–But–But," Lizzy stammered, then laughed, "the woman had dementia! No offense, Gideon."

I waved her off. "She had an illness. No offense in calling it what it was. And you've got a point."

"How lucid was she?" asked Johnny pointblank, getting to it.

I sighed, raking a hand through my hair. "She had good days and bad days."

"Mostly good or mostly bad?"

"I don't know...I mean, she knew who I was, knew where she was, even who *she* was. But she forgot things, and needed help with the basics."

Reggie said, "So she was neck-deep in the—what do you call it, a sort of illness?"

I nodded. "Dementia is a cognitive illness. Eating, dressing, bathing—she needed help with it all."

"Which means you're sure she had the cognitive illness?"

That took me aback, actually making me shift and straighten. "Pretty sure...She had all the classic signs of dementia."

"See, there you go, Reg," Lizzy said.

"I don't know..." Reggie trailed off, going silent.

"Don't know what, kid?" asked Johnny.

Reggie paused, looking at me. "Whether she was legit."

Now JP laughed. "Legit? As in legitimately had dementia?"

Lizzy said, "Supposed OJ said it best: If the glove don't fit—"

"You must acquit," Reggie finished. "That's what I'm saying!"

"What, that she was a mole?"

He just did one of his wide-eyed, head-cocked looks of his, not replying but saying all he needed to say.

"Come on, Reg. You can't be serious."

"Believe me, she was legit," I replied, not liking what he was implying, and actually sort of taking offense at it.

"Well, how else do you explain all of this, then?" Reggie held up his pack of papers. "These—whatever they are. Documents related to some important something, which I presume were stolen. And how did all of this get stuffed up inside some crawl space in your mama's room?"

"Aliens?" Lizzy said.

He sputtered his lips and went back to his stack of papers, grumbling something under his breath.

I did the same, shutting down the conversation by ignoring it and flipping some more. I switched my phone's light on again in search of something—anything to make sense of what this was, and whether what Reggie was implying made any sense.

To be honest, the idea that Ma had found something, then stashed it away was totally in line with the kind of person she was. She was all about justice, with a capital J. And not just any Justice, the Lord's kind of justice. Which for her meant God's righteousness, and his right ordering of things in the world. None of that Rawlsian idea about justice as fairness, the 19th century American political philosopher whose theories had so seismically influenced the liberal tradition.

No, Ma's understanding of justice was about rightly ordering the world according to the way God intended things to be when he created it. And she let me know, too. Which always made me wonder what she thought about what I did, defending the guilty and all, playing my part in the march of justice, as it was in this country, in the Junction.

So, yeah, it wouldn't surprise me at all if she had found something that ticked her off—and then did something about it.

But the other side of it, the first side Reggie had suggested... that she had set out to look for something—that flat made no sense! Made her sound more like a crusader for justice, a sort of secret agent, than a retired accountant with dementia. What would have motivated her to set out looking to begin with? What would she have been looking for? And what did that even mean, that she was looking for something, only to find it and then hide it away in—

Something jumped out at me. On the next page.

A name. And not just any name.

A business name.

"Are you kidding me..." I said on a disbelieving breath.

The page I had flipped to was a contract. A sort of bill of sale, actually. Between a global private equity firm and—

"CareBridge Senior Living Oasis..."

"What's that, kid?" asked Johnny.

I glanced up and repeated the company that brought instant recognition. And brought up all sorts of memories.

"What about it?"

"What was that outfit that bought out HappyLiving? What's it called again?"

Reggie said, "Perses Global Financial Group."

"That's right..." I returned to the contract, confirming the name, the details of the terms of sale. Flat couldn't believe what I was reading.

"Another few rounds of this stalling, kid," Johnny said, "and I'm gonna be six feet under."

Reggie chuckled. "Yeah, Gideon, what'd you find?"

I explained, "I'm looking at a contract here between Perses Global and a company called CareBridge Senior Living Oasis outlining the terms of a financial acquisition."

Lizzy said, "Sounds like the same sort of old folks home we just fled."

Johnny smirked. "Old folks home? Really?"

"No offense intended. You know what I mean! Sounds like Dreamscape Manor."

"That's because it is—" I swallowed back a rise in anger. "It was..."

"Was?" Reggie asked. "What are you getting at, Gideon?"

I turned to him, then looked back at Izzy and Johnny before sweeping my gaze back to that contract in my hand.

Another swallow, that anger spinning out into grief, wondering if this was what it had all meant.

Thankfully the car waited for me to get to it.

Another beat, a breath, then I did.

"CareBridge was where my father had died."

Lizzy said, "I remember when he passed. But I thought he had died in his sleep."

I shook my head. "There was an accident."

"Accident?"

"What sort of accident?" asked Johnny.

Reggie said, "And why didn't we know about it?"

Lizzy added, "I'm more interested in the deets than the blame. What happened?"

I explained, "He wandered out into a storm and basically froze to death."

A beat, then a trio of gasps, then competing reactions.

First Reggie, with his predictable, "Say *waaa?*"

Then Lizzy: "Egads!"

"Hold up, hold up, hold up," he said, waving a hand for attention. "You're telling me the same private equity firm that bought out your father's senior living center, who died because of an accident—"

"Negligence, actually," I corrected, "thanks to staffing issues from budget cuts."

"*Oof.* Even worse! And that same outfit bought out your mama's abode?"

Johnny put it plainly: "That's too coincidental for it not to be something that matters to what happened to your mother."

"Or what your mother did," Reggie corrected.

"Or that."

"You mean what she found," Lizzy said.

Reggie clarified, "I mean what she went after."

"What's that supposed to mean?" I asked, confused.

"Let me ask you this: After CareBridge's negligence led to your dad's death, did you sue their asses?"

"Ma had wanted to take them to civil court and nail them for negligent homicide. I counseled her against it and instead arranged for a cash settlement."

"With no admission of liability, amiright?"

I nodded. "With no admission of liability."

"How much did she get?" asked Lizzy.

"Nothing."

"Nothing?"

Johnny snorted a chuckle. "Some fancy lawyering that was, kid."

I said, "Oh, I did some fancy lawyering alright, JP. Got CareBridge to pay a two million dollar settlement, with a million going to a national dementia research foundation and the other going to a local Grand Rapids medical institution."

"There you go! That explains it," Reggie exclaimed, as if offering a self-obvious assessment.

"Explains what?"

"Think about it. Your mama ends up in Dreamscape, finds out the same Wall Street fat cats that were responsible for her husband's death up and bought his old folks' joint, then her own actual joint, then went gunning for them with this."

Reggie held up his stack of papers and gestured to the others around the car.

"That's ridiculous!" I scoffed, shaking my head.

"Is not!"

"Sort of is, Reg," Lizzy agreed.

He sputtered his lips. "Thanks for the vote of confidence, partner."

"How could she have known that Perses bought out her husband's senior living center?

"Not to mention her mobile home park?" I added, skeptical but now wondering about the line of thinking.

"Yeah, kid," Johnny engaged now, "you're forgetting she's in cognitive decline."

Lizzy nodded. "What Johnny said. Can't imagine someone with dementia is capable of getting revenge on a private equity firm!"

"Unless she was motivated to get that revenge. Unless..."

Reggie sounded like he had another thought that died. I was too caught up with his first meaning. The one about Ma exacting revenge against Perses for Dad's death.

I went to respond when a vehicle pulled out of nowhere. An SUV, down the road. Emerging from the darkness. Lights bright and headed our way.

Something in me flared a warning.

So I slid inside and shut the door.

"Turn off your lights," I whispered, which was sort of lame. No way that car could hear me, but it seemed right. The others complied.

The dome light took a merciful seven seconds before it also complied and we were plunged into darkness.

With that mystery car waiting at the other end.

Chapter Twenty-Eight

The back county road where we were planted was pretty out of the way, butting up against a grove of trees on one side of the road and a stretch of corn on the other side. You really had to work for it to get out this far, and on this road. Be intentional, even searching.

We were at least fifteen minutes outside downtown Mill Creek Junction, maybe twenty. It was so remote, the only sounds I heard were the continued droning chorus of insects and tree frogs, joined by my ratcheting breath. Couldn't even see the city lights glowing in the distance, neither the Junction's (which wasn't much because it was so small-town) nor Grand Rapids's (which was larger and brighter). Just the silverlight of the full moon shining down, floating in the night's bruised sky amidst a sea of stars.

Reggie said lowly, "A little out of the way for a moonlight stroll."

He slumped a bit, keeping his eyes trained ahead. I did the same.

"It's probably nothing," Johnny said. "Just some teenybop-pers out to find a spot to neck."

"What's it doing?" asked Lizzy, pointing outside.

"What do you mean, kid?"

"It's just sitting there."

I squinted, following her pointer out through the windshield.

She was right. It was just sitting there. Down at the other end of the road, lights casting a bright glow across the dark pavement, exhaust billowing out the back, the faint hum of an engine rising above the din of the nighttime chorus.

Until it drew closer. Slow and plodding, growing by the second.

"Quick, act normal," Lizzy said, shuffling her papers back together and fingering for her paperclip.

Johnny snorted a laugh. "Normal? Us four stuffed in this Japanese tin can ain't gonna look normal, no matter how we dress up this pig."

"Hey, speak for yourself!"

As the vehicle approached, I shielded my eyes, trying to catch sight of who was inside, what they might want with us.

Instead of seeing who, I saw the what of the arriving SUV.

And it wasn't good.

"Shiznit..." Reggie cursed.

Had to agree with him.

Because this was police-cruiser not good!

White and almost glowing with unholy arrival under the moon's gaze in the cloudless sky. Emblazoned with **Mill Creek Junction Police** on the hood and side in black that spelled nothing good.

Not racing, not rushing off to nab some criminal.

Slowing. Coasting, really, the driver making time for a look-see as it passed us on the shoulder.

Which surely looked suspicious, the car angled off the dirt road on the outskirts of Mill Creek in the middle of the night. With one door open and the dome light on, three people all huddled inside.

The moment happened faster than I could plan for, the vehicle passing with mozying interest.

And two officers inside, locking eyes as they passed.

With me.

Not good, Gideon Paul...

"That can't be good," Johnny grunted.

"Nopety nope..." Lizzy said lowly.

Reggie said what I was thinking: "Let's get out of here."

"You read my mind," I said, gathering up the documents as Reggie cranked the car.

With nothing but a wheezing cough in reply.

Reggie cussed like a grown man now and hit his steering wheel.

"What's wrong?" I asked.

"Did we drain the battery?" Lizzy added.

"Like I said," Johnny grunted, "Japanese tin can."

I spun around watching the Junction PD cruiser continue down the road, red tail lights casting a haunting menace across the packed dirt.

Lizzy turned as well, and we both held our breath as Reggie turned over the engine again—with the same wheezy result.

"Maybe it'll keep going," she whispered.

"Maybe..." I muttered, doubtful.

Another crank at the ignition and the Honda roared to life.

"Thank the Lord Almighty," Johnny said with praise. "Let's get out of here."

"Don't have to tell me twice..." Reggie replied.

He cranked the wheel and sent the car sailing toward destiny. Which at that point was anywhere but there.

Except—

"Aww crap..." Lizzy cursed.

"What?" I said, turning toward her.

Seeing exactly what the crap she was talking about.

The county mounty's brakes had flared something fierce, jolting to a stop and spinning around, spitting up a cloud of dust and dirt. Its headlights scythed through the night against the forest before angling back on the road. Our way.

Right before the vehicle started heading our way.

"Not good, Gideon Paul..." I muttered.

"Not good is right," Reggie said, glancing in the rearview mirror.

Johnny said, "Looks like one of the Junction's finest is set to spoil our night."

"Well, I won't let it." Reggie gripped the wheel and glanced back again in the mirror before jerking the car faster.

I also spun for another look—not at all liking what I saw.

Wheels were spinning and gaining on us something fierce. Which only meant one thing.

Sure enough, the reds and blues started up, in hot pursuit.

Except Reggie just went faster.

I shifted, looking behind again and not liking at all what I was seeing.

"Uhh, Reg, shouldn't you be slowing down?"

Instead of responding, Reggie actually sped up, sailing down the country road at a speed that matched the back-country speed limit but risked bringing down the swift hammer of law enforcement.

"You sure about this, kid?" Johnny said.

Lizzy added, "Yeah, I'm not sure poking the Junction PD bear is the way to go, given our circumstances."

I frowned. What she really meant was *my* circumstances, but I agreed.

"We ain't done nothing wrong," Reggie insisted.

"Tell that to the copper gaining on our butts!"

My ankle bracelet barked for my attention now. Was sure I was within the electronic boundary markers imposed by the court. But with that county mounty racing after us, its lights flaring and no doubt gunning for us after making us—which begged a whole host of questions, primarily whether they had been looking for us to begin with. Given all that and my bail status, I wasn't at all interested in getting into a high-speed chase with Junction PD!

I glanced over at the speedometer. Reggie was pushing it past what he should. Under sixty by over fifty-five, the limit out in these parts.

I said, "I'm not sure this is a good idea…"

"Yeah, kid," Johnny said. "Maybe it's about time to give up and pull her over with the way Junction PD is gaining on your tail."

I looked back again—the Junction's finest indeed closing in.

"Come on, party's over, Reggie," Lizzy said.

"Yeah, partner, pull her over and get this over with."

I braced myself, agreeing. "Isn't there something in the Good Book about rendering unto Caesar what is Caesar's, and all that jazz?"

Johnny grunted an affirmative. "Yeah, Jesus Christ himself said something to that effect."

"I say we outrun 'em," Reggie said, glancing in his rearview mirror again, plotting and scheming as those blues and reds closed the gap.

"Are you high?" Johnny said from the back.

"I can't be part of this," I complained. My ankle GPS monitor felt heavier, much more significant, almost throbbing for attention now.

White light suddenly flared from behind. I worried the police cruiser had thrown on its search light.

I glanced in the back seat to find Johnny snapping shots of his pile of papers.

Good thinking.

Attorney-client privilege and the work-product doctrine extended to private investigators who were hired to assist in providing legal services to a client. In Johnny's case, he was on retainer by the firm to assist us in our cases. Including mine. While Johnny's extension of work-product protection wasn't as firm as it was between me and Reggie and Lizzy, his fact work product, as it was called, the information he collected, was still protected.

Like the information he was snapping up using his camera phone as fast as his fat fingers would allow him.

Reggie slammed on the brakes, cranking the wheel just before another dirt road jutted west, back toward Mill Creek Junction, slicing between the property lines of several farms anchoring the town's east side.

Remarkably, the Honda made the turn, spitting dirt and a dust cloud behind. Sending Lizzy raining down curses on Reggie's head for the move. He just laughed it off and sped off.

I spun around to check the status of our Junction county mounty.

Catching him slipping and sliding to make the turn.

Had to laugh at that! But not for long.

Because joining its brake lights flaring livid behind while its white headlights sliced through the wake of our dust, those blues and reds that had been silent and searching were now joined by a livid siren that meant business.

As in pull-the-heck-over business.

Which confirmed what I'd known from the get go.

"They're after us, Reg," I said, turning back around.

But instead of slowing to a stop on what little shoulder there was, he braked for another dirt road and yanked the wheel, making another hard left turn that just pissed me off now. Last thing I needed was Junction PD on my backside—

Pulling my backside over!

And sending it back into the clink.

"Are you insane?!?" I bellowed, punching Reggie in the shoulder.

"*Ouch!*" he complained, jerking the wheel to the left on instinct.

Which sent the Honda veering until he corrected his mistake and almost sent it careening into the cornfield on our right.

I turned to the rear. That county mounty made the turn.

Speeding toward us—and gaining on us!

Could almost hear all eight cylinders of that Ford Police Interceptor SUV using all of its ponies to claw toward us across the dirt road.

Lizzy said, "I'm not so sure this is a good idea, Reg."

Reggie huffed. "What's not a good idea? Driving down a country road?"

Johnny said, "You forgot the part about the po-po hot on our tails, lights twirlin' and siren blarin'!"

"We don't even know they're after us."

"Ha! Who are they after? Smokey the Bear?"

Lizzy said, "Maybe you should just pull over, just to be sure."

"Finally, a voice of reason!" I huffed.

"Yeah, kid," Johnny agreed. "I ain't interested in getting slapped with some accessory to evading the po-po charge."

"I think I'm going to be sick," I moaned, propping an elbow up on the window and leaning my head against my palm.

Reggie laughed. "Oh, come on, Gideon. Don't be so

dramatic. It's not like we robbed a bank or anything. Just failed to stop for some lame-ass traffic stop without any probable cause."

"Right after we robbed Dreamscape Manor!" I yelled now.

"Naw. We just retrieved your mama's property."

"Can't imagine Brock Sheldon sees it that way."

"Man, you don't even know why they're coming up on us like this."

"I know! That's why we need to pull over for that county mounty."

The siren squawked for attention—three short bursts, followed by a long blare before one of the officers bellowed over the loudspeaker for us to pull over.

"Reg, pull over!" Lizzy commanded.

"Finally, a voice of reason," I said.

"But we didn't do anything wrong!" Reggie complained.

"That was then," she said. "Now we are. You've been clearly signaled—commanded, to pull over!"

"But—"

"No buts about it."

Reggie hesitated, but huffed a mumbly complaint and offered a grumbly "Fine..." before the car's momentum eased up.

He braked, hard, the Honda skidding a bit as he angled for the side of the road. Worried we'd fishtail and get into a vehicular altercation, but we managed to finish our stop in one piece.

So did the Junction PD SUV cruiser. Now things would get interesting.

And they did. Quickly.

A door opened, then another.

Then: "Out of the vehicle with your hands raised!"

"Say *waaa?*" Reggie said, looking at me. "Did he say what I think he said?"

"Now you've gone and done it, kid," Johnny said.

"Are they doing what I think they're doing?"

Now the loudspeaker: "Driver, turn off your vehicle then slowly exit your vehicle, hands raised!"

"Same for yous other guys," the other officer bellowed.

I caught him in the taillight, the red ratcheting the menace, along with his outstretched Glock.

I said, "We better play ball before this gets any worse."

Reggie sputtered his lips but agreed, shutting off his engine, rolling down his window, and yelling he was coming out.

"Slowly!" the other officer on the loudspeaker yelled.

Reggie did, as did I, opening my door next and throwing my hands outside before stepping out into the night.

White light flashed from a light extended under the officer's Glock, blinding me. I dared not move my hands, so I squinted.

"Up against the hood!" he bellowed. "Same for you."

That instruction was given to Lizzy, who had joined me. We walked together to the front, Reggie and Johnny obeying a similar command by the other officer still on the horn.

"Fine kettle of fish we are," Johnny complained.

"This is bull," Reggie mumbled. Then he addressed the approaching officers, weapons still outstretched. "Why did you pull me over?"

"Resisting," the one officer from the loudspeaker said, a heavyset man with a few days salt-and-pepper scruff.

"Resisting?"

"You refused to pull over when I approached."

"Without your lights and siren!"

The officer yanked Reggie's hands behind him, slapping cuffs around his wrists.

"Then I put 'em on and you refused to pull over."

Reggie scoffed. "How was I to know you meant me?"

I closed my eyes and sighed. What a night.

Now the other officer approached me, younger and athletic, hair buzzed and face clean-shaven. He instructed me to place my hands behind my back, and he waved his flashlight inside Reggie's car as I did.

I held my breath, knowing what was inside, wincing as I got the same cuffing treatment

"What is this really about?" I said.

Young Officer reached inside an open door and held up a fistful of photocopies, grinning.

"Stolen property."

"Stolen property my ass!"

He tossed the contraband back inside then wrenched a hand on my arm. "Hold it, partner. Don't make me get physical."

"Don't make *me* get—"

"Gideon..." Lizzy said, "you better slow your roll."

Scruffy Officer got in my face, grinning with a mouth full of teeth stained brown from chewing tobacco. Could see a pinch pressed between his bottom lip and gums. I wanted to puke.

"There's also an APB out for you."

"Say *waaa*?" Reggie said.

Lizzy asked, "An all points bulletin...for what reason?"

That grin widened: "His arrest. We found the murder weapon."

Didn't catch him at first, it was said so matter-of-factly. It was only after Lizzy confirmed what he said that it actually sank in.

Young Officer jerked me from the front of Reggie's car and started leading me to the rear. "And your bail has been revoked, partner."

"Say *waaa*?" Reggie said.

Scruffy Officer laughed. "That's right. At least until one of your attorneys pulls a fast one again and gets you back off the hook."

This was not happening. But I knew it could.

Revoking bail was a perfectly valid legal mechanism in the interests of justice and public safety. Bail was often revoked if the terms of the release agreement were violated. Sometimes if new evidence came to light, where additional facts implicated the defendant of a crime more conclusively. Either way, the prosecution could request a judge to revoke bail, arguing that flight risk or community danger had increased.

Young Officer halted, looking back toward Reggie's car. "Looks like we've got two for the price of one tonight, right boss?"

Now Scruffy Officer started man-handling Reggie, leading him in my direction.

"That's right, Cole. Must be our lucky night."

"Give me a minute with my clients," Lizzy said, coming up behind.

The two officers hesitated but relented, the pair bringing us to Reggie's trunk.

"Sixty seconds," Scruffy Officer said. "Starting five seconds ago."

They left, and Lizzy got to it: "We'll deal with this in the morning. Both of you."

I nodded, saying nothing.

Reggie grumbled a cussing complaint.

"And Gideon—" Lizzy looked at me "remember the cardinal rule of incarceration."

I frowned and nodded.

"Keep your mouth shut."

"Damn straight."

"I will."

For the second time in as many days.

Chapter Twenty-Nine

Today was a special kind of stupid.

Annabelle Kirkland had awakened to a text message from Dean Lawlor instructing her she had to take his place in court that morning. 'Parently he had contracted a wicked respiratory virus that had laid him out flat on his back the night before. Wondered straight away if the coronacrazy had come back to haunt Mill Creek Junction, but she had bigger things to worry about.

Like the fact she had to appear in court that morning to deal with two arraignments that ticked her off to high heaven. Because both were for fellow lawyers, one of which happened to be her boyfriend.

For the second time in as many days!

That one, for Gideon, made sense. Sort of. Because revoking bail was a pretty serious thing to bring before a judge, one she was normally not inclined to do except in the most extreme circumstances.

Like some evidence being uncovered for an accused murder running around Mill Creek Junction.

Annabelle had been fighting the rationale for it since the night before. Mainly because she had been fighting against the possibility that had spun out into a probability implicating her boyfriend in the cold-blooded murder of his mama.

Except she couldn't escape the obvious. Escape what the evidence pointed to, with motive and opportunity now joined by means adding up to a major cluster embroiling Gideon.

Even her...

When a weapon turned up—presumably *the* weapon, the murderous sort Jamie Ramos and Dean Lawlor had been champing at the bit to lay their grubby little hands on ever since his mother's body had been found shot to death in an apartment at Dreamscape Manor—she couldn't deny it any longer. Yet something still didn't sit right. Didn't feel right. Still...she had laid awake all night with the sneaking suspicion that she had been wrong—about so many things.

Suppose it must be true: You never really know a person until you travel with them, you live with them, and you discover a handgun stuffed down the gullet of their chimney connected to a heinous murder.

Except Dean Lawlor had said he would take care of all that. Revoking bail and the hearing justifying it before a Junction judge. Now it was left up to her to plead the city's interests. Along with the other thing that was just as stupid, maybe even more so. The matter about Reggie Wilson.

Made not a lick of sense why the Mill Creek Junction police department had dragged him into all of this, arresting him on some fleeing and resisting charge. Didn't pass the smell test one bit knowing how Junction PD, not to mention the prosecuting attorney's office, had been seeing red the past few months after *O'Donnell and Associates* had whipped their butts in court.

And yet...

Aspects of the case did point a finger. Gideon certainly appeared to have motivation, and he certainly had opportunity. Now it looked like he had means with this new discovery. She hated to admit it, but she knew what was what, what she had signed up for regardless of how personally uncomfortable and inconvenient it was.

She had an obligation to fulfill her oath as an assistant prosecuting attorney, which was a responsibility to Mill Creek Junction itself. Whether she liked it or not, or could wrap her noggin around the turn of things that had upended Gideon's life—and her relationship.

So, two hours later, she was running up the stone courthouse stairs, nearly slipping on the final one before lunging into the back end of an officer whose name slipped her mind.

They exchanged pleasantries, and she managed to make it through the metal detector without incident. Those things always seemed to have her number, fingering her for the most mundane of offenses. Stray rings, keys, coins. Not today, thank sweet Jesus! Because in one minute she would kick off a hearing with tardiness, and that's the last thing she needed standing before—

She stopped in the middle of the hallway, her face scrunching up with dread.

"Judge Staggs?" she read off the nameplate attached to the courthouse chambers she had reached.

Things kept getting worse. She should have stayed in bed. Called in sick.

Just her luck...

Stuttering Staggs, as he was known around the courthouse. Annabelle frowned on that characterization, having had a speech impediment most of her childhood. Praise the Lord with the sound of trumpets she had gotten the speech therapy in high school she needed to overcome her flaw. So when others mocked the good judge for his own foible, she secretly burned inside, and wept. Both that the man was the butt of such nasty jokes, but also that she didn't say anything, didn't stand up for the good man who was generally a fair and kind judge.

Apart from the fact he didn't care for a one Annabelle Kirkland after she had spurned his not-so-subtle advances over the course of the year. Jilted lovers-in-waiting make the worst judges.

No matter.

She would rock this joint, or die trying. Probably get fired for it, given her sour attitude toward the whole darn set of cases —the pair of them trumped up by Dean Lawlor and Chief Roller, probably even by Mayor Goodall himself!

Finding a new confidence, Annabelle pushed through the double wood doors.

Just as the clerk bellowed an "All rise!" and in walked the presiding judge.

Hardly had a moment to go over the particulars of the cases hustling to the oak table when the judge instructed them with a sharp "Be seated."

Judge Staggs said, "Sorry for the late arrival-val. I was pulled into the case at the request of Judge Heller. He was taken away by a family emergency, so you have the distinct privilege of having me-me."

Annabelle threw a quick glance across the aisle to the opposition. Who were really her friends, both Elizabeth Seward and Reginald Wilson, and Gideon. Dean had finger-wagged a time or twelve catching her commanding a table at Max's Place, with Lizzy and Reggie and Gideon laughing at a well-timed punchline and a graveyard of polished pints. He positively flipped his wig when he found out she and Gideon were dating —from a courthouse clerk, of all people.

She didn't care. After transplanting to Mill Creek Junction

just before the pandemic got its coronacrazy groove on (her timing always was peachy), she had needed friends, needed community. The only people she found who cared one lick about her were the ones she was up against.

Glancing across the aisle, she caught Gideon, looking all spiffy in his best navy pinstripe suit. The one he had trounced her in just days ago, in fact. There they were again, on opposite sides of an aisle that now cut a divide through them she wouldn't wish on her worst enemy.

Prosecutor and accused.

"Is that alright with you, Ms. Kirkland?" Judge Staggs said, snagging her attention.

Annabelle snapped her head toward the bench. "Huh?"

"I said, shall we get to it?"

A wicked case of embarrassed heat flared up her neck and bloomed hot in her cheeks.

He smiled, regarding Annabelle, raising his brow and bobbing his head, as if to signal let's get on with it.

Taking a breath, she stood to address the court: "Your Honor, this first matter is a simple one. Last night, Reginald Wilson was observed driving at a high rate of speed down a dirt road on the outskirts of Mill Creek Junction. He was instructed by two Mill Creek Junction police officers to pull over. He refused, speeding up to evade—"

"That's a bunch of hooey!" Lizzy interrupted, sending her chair scraping across the hardwood floor as she leaped to her feet.

"Pardon me-me?" Staggs stammered, eyes wide with surprise.

"I'm sorry, Your Honor, but that's a flat lie."

"Your Honor!" Annabelle intervened, gasping. "I am offended at the accusation that I would bring a lie before this court."

"I have to agree-ree, counsel," Judge Staggs replied. "That is quite the accusation—on top of quite the interruption!"

Lizzy said, "I'm sorry, Your Honor. I wasn't suggesting the assistant prosecuting attorney was lying. I was merely suggesting that her account of things was a lie."

Judge Staggs leaned forward. "Are you suggesting the prosecuting attorney is bringing forth false evidence?"

"Yes, Your Honor," Lizzy offered without missing a beat.

Annabelle offered a huffing scoff. "That is preposterous! And quite the accusation."

"I have to agree-ree, counsel—a second time," Staggs said. "Suggesting the police are lying isn't something I take lightly. Can you substantiate this claim of yours?"

"I can."

He leaned back. "How?"

Annabelle glanced at Gideon, who was wearing a smug smile that sent up all sorts of spidey-sense flares that she had walked into a trap.

Lizzy replied, "Why, because I was in the car when it was pulled over."

There was an audible echoey gasp from somewhere in the courtroom. It was only after Judge Staggs glanced her way, brow raised, that Annabelle realized it had been her.

She cleared her throat and announced, "May we approach the bench, Your Honor?"

Judge Staggs offered a come-hither gesture with both hands, and she and Lizzy approached.

Annabelle had to think quick to salvage this one. After which she would string Dean Lawlor up by his ten toes!

"Your Honor, I was not made aware the defense counsel was present at the stop."

Lizzy said, "And I was not made aware of the two officers'

testimony until now. Which, I'm sorry to say so, smells super suspicious!"

"Careful, counsel," Judge Staggs said.

"I'm just saying that on the face of it, there are major discrepancies in the account."

Before Annabelle could insert her own thoughts on the matter, Lizzy explained what she herself had experienced.

How they had been parked on the side of the road, just chit-chatting about the case (yeah, right, based on the other thing she was there to litigate). When all of a sudden, the Junction PD cruiser came out of nowhere, passing them, glaring at them (an overly dramatic insertion she let go) before Reggie and the rest started motoring back toward town. When all of a sudden (gasp!), the cruiser pulled around and headed their way, and Reggie kept going until he finally realized the officer was instructing him to pull over.

"So, Your Honor," Lizzy concluded, "the testimony proffered by the Mill Creek Junction police officers in this affidavit is super suspicious, given that it contains falsehoods that I, as an officer of the court, vigorously contest with my own eyewitness testimony."

Annabelle snorted a chuckle. "Vigorously?"

Lizzy frowned, shooting her a look that could kill. "Yes. *Vigorously.*"

Now she frowned, because her opponent, her friend, was right. It did smell super sus. So Annabelle didn't put up much of a fight. Dean would flip his toupee—one of the worst-kept secrets in the prosecuting attorney's office—but she didn't care. Because she was there and he wasn't, cleaning up Junction PD's pile of bulldookie.

Judge Staggs sighed and swung his gaze at Annabelle. "What say you?"

Here we go...

She took a breath, then a beat.

Then got to what she needed to do, but her boss wouldn't like worth a lick.

"I agree, Your Honor, there are...suspicious discrepancies I would like to investigate before moving forward with this charge against Reginald Wilson."

He sat straight, cocking his head. "So you are dropping the charges-ges?"

"For now."

He rapped his gavel and "So ordered!" her request, then sent them back to their seats.

Now for the second thing that turned Annabelle's stomach.

"In the second matter," Judge Staggs said, "of Gideon O'Donnell. You are requesting the revocation of his bail due to the discovery of new evidence?"

Well, not me...

Annabelle didn't say that, of course. Instead, she swallowed and nodded, playing the part of the good assistant prosecuting soldier she was. Especially after goinking Dean's first hearing against Reggie.

She replied, "A weapon, matching the description of a handgun—specifically a Glock 37—registered to the defendant was found in the chimney of the defendant's home."

Staggs leaned forward, his head jutting out with intrigue and an eyebrow raised reflecting the same.

"Do tell-tell."

She did, recounting the previous evening's events. From the execution of the dual warrants issued by Judge Bock, to the discovery of the handgun stuffed down the chimney and resting on the metal damper plates.

"Yes," Lizzy interjected, "but does the handgun in question belong to my client, Gideon O'Donnell? And where is the evidence report on the handgun in question?"

Annabelle took a breath, passing off a preliminary report that was a dicey proposition, since there were several aspects of the report itself that were dicey. Lizzy snatched it and started scanning.

While she flipped pages, Annabelle explained, "A further search of the house did not turn up other weapons. However, a Glock 37 is registered in the State of Michigan to Gideon O'Donnell—"

"No prints and no serial number?" Lizzy giggled, then actually laughed out loud.

Judge Staggs cleared his throat, glaring at her. Annabelle folded her arms and frowned and regarded the judge to discern a reaction, whether favorable or unfavorable. Couldn't tell.

Lizzy's face fell, and she set down the report. "The prosecution can't be serious, Your Honor. The report stipulates no identifying marks were found on the weapon to tie it to my client!"

He wiggled his fingers and asked for a copy.

Handing one off to the bailiff, Annabelle explained, "The weapon is a match for the type of weapon the medical examiner believes was the cause of death."

"I see..." Judge Staggs hummed, biting the end of his pointer finger while lazily flipping through the report. "And the ballistics, is it a match-match?"

"We're still waiting on that."

He glanced up, yanking that finger from his mouth. "And you want me to revoke bail on a loosely tied string of circumstantial evidence?"

No, Dean Lawlor wants you to revoke bail on a loosely tied string of circumstantial evidence!

Annabelle didn't say that, of course. Instead: "At the arraignment, the prosecution stipulated that the defendant had motive to—" she could hardly bring herself to voice the argument; she did anyway: "—kill his mother. He was about to lose a multimillion dollar class action case because she was reportedly rumored to have been considering pulling from the lawsuit."

Lizzy scoffed. "Reportedly rumored...considering pulling. The circumstantial evidence just keeps rolling down hill, doesn't it?"

"Objection, Your Honor!" Annabelle said, stomping her foot with an echoey clack and throwing Lizzy a scowl.

Staggs rapped his gavel. "Sustained. You'll have a chance to rebut, counsel. And leave the Perry Mason references for bargain-bin Kindle thrillers, alright?"

She apologized and folded her hands, sufficiently chided.

Couldn't help but smile at that. She continued, "Opportunity is clearly established, given his exclusive access to the victim. In fact, logs show the defendant visited just before the crime in question, and there is a record of the two engaged in a heated argument."

Staggs nodded. "Yes, that is stipulated in your evidentiary report-port. Which was issued at the time of the arraignment, and went into the original bail considerations."

"Yes, but now we have the means and method of the crime."

"*Alleged*," Lizzy interjected. Staggs didn't stop her.

Annabelle almost objected, but didn't. She wished she would've.

Because Lizzy pressed further: "Your Honor, this is an outrageous request of the court, and is actually a gross attempt to undermine this court."

At that Annabelle scoffed. "It is nothing of the sort! Defense counsel clearly knows—" She turned to Lizzy "—or *should* clearly know..." Back to Judge Staggs: "that bail can be revoked if new, particularly inculpatory, evidence emerges to affect the defendant's danger to the community or risk of flight—"

"Of which this so-called evidence does neither!"

"I would say the discovery of a murder weapon stuffed down a criminal's chimney—"

"Alleged!"

"Fine, *alleged* criminal's chimney—I would say such evidence shows a defendant's danger to the community!"

"Except you haven't shown the weapon is my clients!"

"Ladies..." Judge Staggs finger-wagged, actually wagging that pointer he'd been biting on earlier.

Annabelle huffed a sigh. "Irregardless, Your Honor—"

"Not a word..." Lizzy mumbled, throwing her off her game.

Because now she wasn't sure it was a word, one she had used all her life.

Annabelle shook her head, plowing forward: "Regardless, then, we have the right to present an argument for the revocation of the defendant's bail."

"Yes yes yes," Judge Staggs said, raising a hand. "I've heard enough. And I am unpersuaded. Get me better proof that said new evidence is linked to the defendant and I will reconsider."

Rapping his gavel, he added with finality: "Prosecution's request regarding the defendant's bail revocation is denied."

Crapola. Dean would not be pleased...

Chapter Thirty

It was past time that Annabelle Kirkland put on her big girl pants.

And by putting on her big girl pants, that meant going back to the office.

She had been sulking at Max's Place nursing a gin and tonic the past hour. Sheila made a mean G&T with Tanqueray London Dry, of all things. Loved the juniper-forward gin with its distinctive pine flavor and faint lemon zest. Sort of middle-brow, but she liked the perfect balance of juniper, coriander, licorice. A sort of classic base for every G&T without overpowering it. Mostly, it reminded her of home. Of companionship.

Of Gideon, even...

He made her favorite sort, with some elderberry syrup and a hint of lime that curled her toes before Gideon himself did. Not in *that* sort of toe-curling way. The first-base sort.

Anyhoo.

She was nursing her third drink when she realized it was getting late, and Dean Lawlor would have been apoplectic wondering what had happened with the dual verdicts. He had called several times, which she ignored several more times. No more.

So she hiked up those pants and set out onto Main Street, the sun cresting toward the horizon on a brilliant show of oranges and reds that only the Midwest could showcase this time of year.

On the walk back to the courthouse a few blocks over, she couldn't help but go over it all again in her mind. Everything that she knew to be true about this Florence O'Donnell case.

About Gideon O'Donnell's case.

There was the motive, which was convincing enough for any jury beyond a reasonable doubt. Not for her, knowing money wasn't what made Gideon's world go round. For most people it did, so it wouldn't take much to convince twelve angry men and women that he had offed his mama when his golden goose was threatened.

Then there was the matter of opportunity. Gideon's keycard access to the building as his mother's only guardian and his access to her room certainly proved that part of the case. Since the logs showed he'd accessed the room that day before she'd been discovered with a hole in the back of her head and face blown to smithereens, opportunity was mostly in the bag. Final identification of the body had been a real pain in the patootie, which she needed to get on stat to tie up that last end of the procedural part of building a prosecutorial case against Gideon—the thought of which just turned her stomach fierce!

And now the murder weapon had been located, or *presumed* weapon, with a presumption that it was Gideon's. Although, as Lizzy brought up, the preliminary report showed neither prints nor a serial number to tie it to him. But she'd tried cases for less—and won bigly. The rule of thumb in her line of work was M and O trumped that last illusive M in more cases than not. Motivation and opportunity were a powerful combo in the minds of a jury, regardless of the means.

And yet...

Yet the man she knew—with intimacy, at a *heart* level!—wasn't capable of murder, no matter how the evidence stacked up against him.

Yet...she had to admit she wasn't as clear-eyed as she should be, given he was also a man she loved. What they say is true: love blinds.

But so does the truth. So maybe Dean Lawlor was the one in need of a good ophthalmologist.

Crapola...

What was she going to do?

About Gideon, about Dean—about this case?

Annabelle slumped her shoulders as she clickety-clacked back to the farm.

'*Let justice roll down like water,*' the good prophet Amos says in the Good Books, '*and righteousness like an ever-flowing stream.*'

Fat chance of either rollin' or flowin' in Mill Creek Junction.

Especially when small-town politics were involved.

With Gideon O'Donnell in the crosshairs, Dean's finger on the trigger.

And her playing the role of spotter.

Again: What was she going to do?

All she could do, she supposed. Which was her job.

After licking her wounds, Annabelle finally reached the courthouse and shuffled up to her office. Where she knew the seven-headed dragon from the Book of Revelation would not be happy when she called from her office to finally check in.

Pushing through the wood door that was the prosecuting attorney's office—guess who was waiting?

Mr. Prosecuting Attorney himself. Apparently, whatever it was he had been suffering from had passed, and he had come to collect. Made her think Dean had just wanted to throw her to the judicial wolves than deal with the hearing himself, in case anything went down that wasn't according to plan.

There was his smirk that irritated the snot out of her, and his arms were crossed, like a bouncer blocking her way.

"Well?" he asked, scowling now. Did he not know?

I took a breath and straightened, holding my head high.

"We lost."

He dropped his arms and huffed a sigh.

"I know. What the heck happened, Kirkland?"

Annabelle pushed past into her darkened office. He followed. She slung her bag on her desk and came clean, explaining what went down in court. Could have—*should* have!—blamed it on Junction PD for their falsified reports, but didn't. Instead, she finished and went silent.

His face darkened.

"My office," he commanded, then stormed out into the corner he'd snagged, shutting the door with restraint behind her. He grumbled something under his breath before moving behind his desk in some sort of macho power play.

"Lost," he repeated. Less a question and more an exclamation point.

Annabelle took a breath and raised her head. "That's right."

"Again, what the heck, Kirkland! We had them both dead to rights! Didn't you fight?"

"Give me a break, Dean! You're bonkers if you think all of this was nothing more than political posturing during an election season, snagging them two threatening Mayor Goodall's plans for Mill Creek!"

A furtive glance to the right, then the left said it all.

Dean clenched his jaw, then said, "It was a matter of law, not politics, clear and simple."

"Bulldookie! It was a matter of politics, clear and simple, mister."

He folded his arms. "Then what happened, huh?"

Annabelle waited a beat, considering his question. Then settled on: "What happened was a matter of justice. No way around it. Reggie was pulled over improperly. Which isn't even touching on the falsity of Junction PD's account!"

Dean huffed. "Well, what about O'Donnell?"

"We don't have enough to link Gideon to the weapon."

"Stuffed down his chimney!" he exclaimed, waving his arms.

"And did you ever consider how it got down there?"

Dean scoffed. "Obviously, O'Donnell got up on his roof and tossed it down there."

Annabelle crossed her arms. "With no eye witnesses?"

"Well, then he managed to stuff it up from the bottom."

Now she frowned. "With those damper plates?"

"I don't know!"

"Well, I do know. I know this is just a political hatchet job, Dean."

That seemed to give him pause. His nostrils flared like they did when he didn't get his way, and he folded his arms. A sure sign he was giving in.

Then he sat down at his desk. "Fine," he said, attending to something on his computer.

And that was that.

Annabelle left, then slunk back to her office feeling like all eyes were drilling her with suspicion and condescension, and that German word that always tripped her up.

Schadenfreude. That's it! That.

None of which she wanted or needed. So she grabbed her

purse and left for home. It was late, the sun had set, and she longed for jazz.

Arriving home, she pulled one of her daddy's old records, put it on her turntable, and positioned the needle to the second track. "Blue in Green" by Miles Davis, from *Kind of Blue*. Seemed appropriate, given what she was feeling after the day that had kicked her in the patootie from here to Sunday.

She kicked off her pumps and slumped down hard in a hand-me-down leather chair and just closed her eyes. Just let Davis's dreamy trumpet vibe take her away.

A matter of justice...

Annabelle smirked, shaking her head with eyes closed.

Most days, she believed that was her profession's calling card.

Others...

Not so much.

But good ol' Miles might be able to change her mind.

"Let justice roll down like waters," the Good Book says.

Exactly.

She'd drink to that.

She wanted to, too, with a bottle of sauv blanc awaiting in her fridge.

Annabelle stood and started for it when her phone squawked for her attention. She snatched it and followed through with her pursuit.

Then stopped cold.

Dean Lawlor.

"Can't a girl drink in peace..."

She huffed and almost put it to voicemail, but thought better of stiff-arming her boss after what had just gone down.

Reaching her fridge, she opened it, snatched the wine bottle then a glass, twisted off the cap and started pouring. Then she answered Dean's call.

Before she could offer a greeting, he asked where she was in a rush that bordered on panicked.

"Home, why?" she replied, throwing back a tart mouthful of white wine.

"I need you back at the office," he barked.

She laughed, taking her wine back to the leather chair. "No way, partner. I've got my shoes off and feet up on my couch for the night."

"I'm serious. I need all hands on deck tonight."

No way was this happening!

"Dean..." she moaned with complaint, plopping down and taking a sip. "I'm positively poopskied. Can't this wait until—"

"Now, Annabelle!" he yelled with interruption.

She straightened, not liking his tone, which was unlike him. Sure, he could be a real pain in the patootie, but he never yelled at her. Raised his voice, like he had back at the farm...but not like this.

She hesitated, taking another sip, then asked, "Why?"

A breath, a beat.

Then: "There's a problem with the O'Donnell case."

Chapter Thirty-One

I got out of the clink, for the second time, just as the sun had set. All I wanted was a drink. Nothing simple after what the last twenty-four hours had brought. Something snooty, in fact, was what was in order.

Scotch whisky. Macallan, neat.

I still had a bottle from my last major civil trial when I took an asbestos case on spec taking on Uncle Sam. A military base was full of the stuff. Still, after all of these years knowing the effects on lungs. Which led to a whole bunch of folks with mesothelioma. And a payout that had carried us along for a while.

Which bought me the bottle with about a quarter left at the bottom after the rest of the judgment had dried up.

It wasn't a 25 year, but not a 12 year either. Eighteen had been a good year during its release, aged in select Sherry oak casks from Spain, with dried fruits, spice, orange and woodsmoke heavy on the palate and a full-bodied feel in the mouth that lingered. Real smooth, real elegant, and a super aromatic finish. It's all I wanted when I stumbled back home.

Johnny P had other plans. Because my best bud had other plans. As in Max Blade plans.

When Lizzy and Reggie dropped me off at home, our intrepid defense attorney working her magic for us both, Max was waiting for me with the Golden Nugget, as he called his gold Plymouth Breeze from two decades ago. In the back were Johnny and Peter Daniel Young, the resident Baptist pastor. Didn't think I'd get along with the guy when we first met, but we had formed a friendship over pints at Max's Place.

Max had rounded up my pals and insisted on a night on the countryside. Said it would do me some good, get my head on straight, push all my cares out of sight and out of mind kicking back with the fellas and some brewskis. Said Johnny had picked up a 24-pack of PBR with my name on it—well, with my name on six of the cans, the others being evenly divided between Max, Johnny, and Peter. That was Max for you.

I tried getting out of it, saying I was beat and needed a night of sleep to get my head on straight, but he wasn't hearing anything of it. Literally picked me up by my legs and wouldn't let me down until I agreed to the "bro-napping" as he called it.

Now I was riding shotgun in the stuffy beige cabin toward destiny, barking at Max to slow down as he barreled down a dirt road that gave me flashbacks to the night before.

"Seriously, Max," I bellowed again against the din of air whooshing past the car from my open window. "Slow down before you kill us all. Or kill your car."

"Naw, there ain't no worry about the Golden Nugget. Been with me for a pair of decades and never let me down." Max gave the steering wheel a pat, then scowled. "Although, not sure I can say the same for Daimler Chrysler sending their ol' Plymouth brand out to pasture way back when."

"I'm with Gideon, kid," Johnny said. "This thing's gotta have one foot six feet under. How many miles does it got?"

"Just crested two-hundo-thousand miles a few months ago and still goin' strong!"

"Oy vey…"

Had to agree. I ran a nervous hand through my hair, staring outside. Tried not to picture my life flashing before my eyes metaphorically as it did literally.

Max slowed, the brakes throwing up a squawk that put an exclamation point on the metaphorical life-flashing.

"Now, granted," Max went on as he turned down a darkened, tree-lined road, "nearly every part has been replaced a time or three over the years. About the only thing left untouched is the engine. Still purrs like the kitty cat she was when I first drove her off the lot. And actually, alotta firsts in this car, yessiree."

"Eww!" I groaned. "Please spare us the details, Max."

"Yeah, keep it G," Johnny said, "for the kid in the back."

"Hey, I'm no kid," Peter protested.

Max laughed. "Bah! You're practically a teenybopper. What're you, like twenty?"

"Thirty-two!"

"There you go!"

Max rolled down his window, the wind whipping his overgrown blond hair while he popped in a CD and cranked the volume. Angsty electrics and *rat-a-tat-tats* of the snare opened up "Born to Be Wild." Soon we were following Steppenwolf's advice: our motor was runnin' and we were headin' down a county road, crusin' toward Lord only knew where.

I smirked. "Lovely taste in music."

"Hey, don't you dare knock the tunage!"

"Why don't you watch it!"

Max veered into the other lane for dramatic effect. When a pickup going the other way blared a livid warning and flashed its brights at us, the driver shouting some not-nice-words as we passed.

"Don't worry, fellas. Max Blade's got it all under control."

"That's what I'm afraid of..." I moaned.

He jerked the wheel, which set us off yelling our own not-nice-words. Max apologized before turning off onto another side road overgrown with grass and weeds. I worried Max would get the dang Golden Nugget stuck in the muck, but he plowed onward toward a field.

"We're here!" Max announced, then put the Golden Nugget into park and shut her down.

"Where's here?" Peter asked.

"Trouble," I said, climbing out.

A triple-wire fence with barbs ran along the north end, one side of it nearby collapsed from a downed wood post. A clear sky and full moon above actually made me thankful Max had dragged me out here. Heads of lettuce were arrayed in neat rows on both sides keeping us company as a symphony of crickets and tree frogs serenaded us, vegetation and cow manure and hay wafting all around.

"You got the case of PBR at the ready, Johnny?" asked Max.

"Sure do, kid" he said, kicking his door closed and holding up the 24-pack.

Max took the case from him and led the charge over the downed fence and through the lettuce up to a hillside that over-looked the farm.

We all settled on the soft grass, and Max handed out our cans.

I opened mine with a soft crack, a head of white foam rising but resting just at the lip, the golden pilsner glistening in the moonlight and looking mighty fine after the week from hell. Cheap thing, but it was right for the night.

Throwing back a swig, I *ahh*ed. Wasn't one to spring for such watered-down slop, but with a car of friends toasting to life out in the middle of a moonlit field, surrounded by the sounds of nature and smell of midsummer, with woodsmoke and cut grass and the faint tang of farm soil—well, the hipster beer of my youth was just about what I needed to help me kick back and leave all my troubles back in Mill Creek waiting for me when the sun rose next.

"Mind if I join?" someone voiced, coming up to my right.

I turned and gestured. "Peter! Of course. Sit, sit!"

Peter Daniel Young had taken over for the Rev a few years ago, pastoring Mill Creek Junction Baptist. Not the normal sort I'd hang out with for my night out of jail, the second time around. But he was a good guy. Not at all what I'd expected of a man of the cloth.

Peter smacked his lips after his first sip, then put a hand on my shoulder and leaned in. "Real sorry about your mother, Gideon. Real sorry."

I smiled and nodded. "Thanks. Appreciate it."

"For what it's worth, I understand a little of what you're going through."

That was surprising. "Your mother was killed?"

He finished a swig of beer and shook his head. "My brother died a few years back."

"Really?" asked Max.

"Sorry to hear that," I said. "I didn't know."

"How?"

Peter hesitated, then answered, "A drug overdose. And it might have been on purpose. It was sort of a confusing time."

Max whistled, giving his head a shake and for once not offering some quip.

"So, I understand a bit of what you're going through. The

suddenness of death stealing into your world—wrecking your family like that. Not entirely. Can't imagine my mother passing, especially in that sort of way. But, yeah, I empathize. And I'm so sorry, Gideon."

I smiled and nodded again, not knowing what to say.

The four of us just sat there, sipping from our cans as the night played all around us—the chattering and screeching sounds, the quiet rustles and gentle breeze, the scents of summer, warm and fecund.

Peter broke the silence: "You know, a professor of mine from seminary, Dr. Greg Morris, has said that being a Christian means embracing the fact that life sucks until Jesus returns."

"That'll preach," Johnny said.

"Amen to that!" Max agreed.

Had to agree with both.

Peter turned to me, adding, "Life can be so hard. Life can be so unfair. Life can be such a struggle. And you know what—it's OK to say so. It's perfectly fine to say, 'This sucks!' That your mom dying stinks to high heaven. Yeah, we tell ourselves that she's in a better place. And I'm sure she is, from what you've shared about her faith in Jesus, and all."

I didn't know what to say, emotion threatening to take over with all this talk. I just sat in silence and drank.

Peter took a swig and continued, "Still, this sucks because death sucks. It sucks she died. It sucks the way she died. And that's because death isn't the way it's supposed to be."

As much as I wasn't interested in an emotional pep talk, something about what Peter said resonated. Taking another swig myself, I nodded for him to continue.

He did: "God never intended for us to die. Death stole itself into our world. But here's the thing: That's not the end of the Story! Death isn't the end of your mother's story either.

God has promised your mother eternal life—his unearned gift of salvation for her faith in Jesus. He's also promised never to leave us or forsake us, that he will never give us more than we can bear. God is strong for us. He can be trusted, and that is super hopeful! Even when our mother or brother dies."

"*Oo-weee!*" Max exclaimed. "Preacherman's getting his preach on!"

Peter reddened, chuckling and draining his beer.

"Yeah, kid," Johnny said, smiling, "you're not going to stage one of those Protestant altar calls are you? Try and convert these old Catholic bones?"

He laughed and waved his arms. "No no no! And I'll stop. Just thought I'd share that. From one man to another who has lost someone close to him."

I nodded and smiled. "Thanks. Appreciate it."

Max smiled and then held up his can and offered a toast: "*La Hay-em.*"

Peter cracked a smile, then stifled a giggle.

Max took a swig and swallowed. "What's so funny?"

"*L'Chaim,*" I said with the scrape of my throat.

"Isn't that what I said?"

I laughed, shaking my head, but I left alone his brutish mangling of Hebrew. Instead, I joined him, raising my can, the white label and blue-and-red ribbon popping in the night with a special brilliance shining in the moon's silverlight.

"To life," I said, throwing back the lager and throwing up another *ahh*.

Not bad for cheep beer. Clean and fresh.

"To life," Max said, raising his half-drained can.

"To small-town America," agreed Peter, can raised.

"God bless the U S of A," I echoed, slurping back the rest of Milwaukee's finest and tossing the can to the grass with a clunk.

Another minute, and another few swigs, and the fellas added to what I assumed was going to be a growing pile by the end of the night.

The four of us cracked open another round of cans, the nighttime fauna serenading us while we drank in silence. A commodity in short supply in all of our lives, I'd imagine.

"So question for you, Gideon," Peter said.

"Shoot," I said, taking a swig.

"So the law, huh?"

I laughed. "The law."

"Tell me—" He paused to take a swig "why'd you do it?"

I suddenly stiffened and furrowed my brow.

"Yeah, brotha from anotha motha," Max said. "What he asked."

Now my frown turned into a scowl. Were they asking what it sounded like?

I couldn't believe they were asking me *thee* question that was on everyone's mind—most of all Annabelle's, I'm sure.

I stammered, "What do you mean, why'd I do it?"

Suddenly, Peter's eyes flared wide, as if he understood what he was asking.

Now he stammered, "No no no—"

"Because I didn't kill my mother!"

Max laughed, then slugged my arm. "No, dingleberry! The *law*, right?"

"Ouch!" I complained, then slugged him back.

"I think what Peter means is," Johnny said, "why did you become a lawyer, right kid?"

Peter swallowed back a gulp of lager. "Right. Your own personal practice. Defending the...well, the accused."

"Ahh, that." I drained my can and reached for another PBR. "Same as anyone else. The money."

Max snorted a laugh. "Yeah, right. Last I heard, your lights were still off thanks to bounced checks."

"Confirmed, kid," Johnny said, another beer in hand. "It's hot as a pre-Vatican II monastery in that joint!"

I took another swig, running through my answer.

Then dove in.

Time to bring more people into my past.

Chapter Thirty-Two

Throwing back a swig, I had this instant feeling of deja vu. The last, and first, time I had shared some of my story was in a similar situation. Sort of. There was beer, sure, but the setting was far different, as was the company.

Annabelle Kirkland.

She had been the first person I'd ever told my family story to. It's what had first gotten the ball rolling in our relationship, me initially eying her with skepticism when she had thrown me a similar question. After all, she was the Mill Creek Junction APA. My enemy. So opening myself up in that way, being that vulnerable...I wasn't sure I could trust her.

But I did, wondering whether it would build a bridge I could use down the road. Whether in a case she was trying or something deeper. Boy, did it ever!

Now look at things...

I frowned, taking another swig and readying to take the plunge.

When a rabid bark, followed closely by a hissing, screeching animal flared from behind.

Sending all of us scampering to our feet and spinning around for a sight of the feral fight—and for cover.

Max stumbled on tripping twinkle toes, losing his beer in a cussing, clumsy bundle.

Peter fell backward over Max, losing his own beer all over Max's head—who started up a cussing retort.

Johnny tripped over Max's feet, sending his own can of PBR head over heels—and dousing his face.

I was the only one who managed to keep my cool—until I saw Max soaked in Milwaukee's finest lager. Which sent me doubling over in laughter at the sight, him all soaked and the boys all jumbled up together.

"Laugh it up fuzzball!" Max complained, shoving Peter off from him and scampering out from under Johnny. "Would you get off of me?"

The boys gladly complied, crawling to find another resting spot far from Max, still a mumbling, cussing mess.

I just laughed, looking out across the field for our original offenders, then behind in a grove of trees and shrubs. Saw nothing but silver-tinged lettuce and a mile of carefree, night-time enjoyment.

Max barked, "Shut yer yapper, pop a squat, and spill yer tea, would ya, Gideon?"

"Better than spilling my beer, I suppose," I said with a grin.

"I don't know, kid," Johnny said. "Max looks like he would welcome another PBR shower."

"Don't you mean *golden* shower?"

"Why you—" Max lunged for me, but I dodged his grasp, the poor fella actually somersaulting down our grassy knoll.

And sending us boys back into stitches.

After recovering, and snatching the last few cans of PBR, Max barked back at me again to get on with it.

Cracking open my can, a head of foam spilling out this time, I slurped it up and got to it.

"You asked why I got into law," I said, "my private defense practice."

Peter nodded, taking a swig of his own.

"Well that reason goes way back."

"How far back?" he asked.

"Childhood back."

He gestured with his can for me to continue.

Another slurp of PBR and I did: "So get this. One day, my dad and I are driving into Mill Creek Junction. Just got off I-96 and made the turn onto the long state route leading to Main Street when the reds and blues start flashing."

Peter laughed. "A police officer?"

"That's right."

"Yeah, my daddy got pulled over a time or two coming and leaving Grand Rapids. I remember one time, I was ten or eleven, my older brother was twelve and younger brother six or so, when we had just pulled off the highway to home and the local sheriff pulled my old man over. Told us to shut up and let him do all the talking. I was scared out of my wits! How old were you?"

"About the same age. Maybe less. But..."

"But what?"

"This wasn't like when your dad got pulled over."

Peter shifted toward me. I took a swig of PBR. Could see Johnny and Max glance at one another, probably guessing what it was about.

I continued, "So Dad pulls over. The cop gets out and starts crunching across the gravel. This was before the state route saw pavement. And it was one of those West Michigan scorchers. Sun high and sky cloudless. Lake Michigan receding after a dry spell that spelled doom for the celery and onions wilting at the edge of town."

I took another large mouthful of beer, draining it and nodding to Max for another. He came up with the last can and passed it off. Boy, was I grateful.

"So what happened?" Peter asked, leaning in with interest.

Oh, brother—you don't know what's coming.

Cracking open the can, I threw back a swig and answered, "What happened was, Dad kept his hands on the steering wheel and told me not to say a word. Not to move."

"OK...then what?"

"Then the cop reaches my dad's door. He'd already had the window rolled down, since it was one of those summer afternoons. And when the cop reached it, he startled."

"Startled?"

"Yeah. Startled. There was this double skip to the cop's boots on the bone-dry gravel that gave it away. A skip and a hop. Skip, hop."

I threw back another swig and swallowed hard, the fresh wheatiness sliding down with a pleasurable crispness that lubricated the road ahead. Made telling the tale all the easier.

"Then his hand went to his sidearm."

Peter frowned. "What, his gun?"

I nodded, and he drained his drink and crumpled the can, face furrowed now with confusion.

"Why the weapon? Wasn't it just a simple traffic stop?"

Max and Johnny chuckled knowingly. I just grinned and shook my head.

Simple traffic stop. Yes, but...No, not really.

I went with, "That's right. The guy put his hand on the holster of his sidearm, then unclipped the flap holding it in place. I can still remember that slight unsnapping. Sounded like the brass button on my jeans."

Another swig. More fuel to get me through.

"Anyway, so yeah, he's getting ready—"

"For what? He pulled your old man over for speeding and now he's reaching for his gun?"

Peter sounded like he was getting mad on behalf of my father, no doubt lubricated by the same PBR that kept me going.

"He pulled his weapon for what came next," I said.

I took a breath, then another swig.

"What came next?" Peter asked, almost in a whisper, leaning in closer.

Another breath, then I dove in: "The officer took a step back, that bone-dry gravel throwing up a wicked crunch again, before raising his weapon and pointing it at Dad. Then he ordered him out."

"What the hell?" he said, then startled. "I mean—uh, heck?"

"So preacherman does have a pottymouth!" Max said, laughing and socking him in the arm.

Peter threw my empty can at him—which sent Max launching one of his own, then Johnny joining in. Before I knew it, we were having a PBR can fight, the leftovers of warm, stale beer, mixed with our backwash, slinging against our clothes and hair, even our faces.

It was the sort of teenagery night me and Max and Sam and Ross would've had back in the day, just four kids sneaking out to Farmer Jed's grassy knoll with a case of alcoholic contraband, jawing it up and horsing around.

"Alright, alright," Johnny said, putting out his hands, "I think we've had enough fun for one night."

"Spoil sport..." Max complained.

"You were saying?" He threw you're-done eyes at Max before glancing my way.

"I believe pastorman said what the hell," Max retorted, grinning at Peter.

Peter laughed. "Yeah yeah yeah. I suppose after six of these, my mouth is liable to get PG."

Johnny pointed at me now. "Gideon, you've got the floor again."

"So Dad whispered a few words to me," I went on, "then popped the lock to his door, eased it open on creaking hinges, and stepped out onto that bone-dry shoulder, his polished black leather shoes clacking against the road."

All of it was coming at me in technicolor, high-definition precision. The sights and sounds and details still crisply sitting in the synapses of my brain and dredged to the surface by my trusty hippocampus.

Peter whistled and shook his head. "What did you do? What were you...feeling?"

I laughed, my hippocampus throwing up a fresh detail from that memory that might have been embarrassing to share in mixed company. Not these guys. They were safe.

"I wet myself, if that tells you anything." I left it there and threw back another swig, then another, draining the can.

Crumpling it up, I tossed it to the pile, then took a breath and continued: "Anyway, so Dad stepped out, and before he knew it, he was on the ground, his forehead smacking into the gravel road."

I clapped my hands together with a *smack!* Then again: *SMACK!*

Sending all three fellas jumping and Max complaining. I didn't apologize.

The copper certainly hadn't.

"And then the cop said—"

My tongue stumbled over itself, choking on the words and the memory, righteous indignation welling from my belly.

Whether from the memory itself or its retelling or goaded by PBR, I wasn't sure. Either way, what came next wasn't pretty.

And it was hella hard...

"Don't even think about moving, the cop said," I went on, "Because no way no Junction judge will give two snots if a nappy coon takes one to the back of the head."

Took a beat for it to fully register, to fully sink in, the sort of racist rant from this part of the Midwest that still held tight to small-town living.

Then it did.

Peter gasped, eyes wide and mouth opened.

"My God..." He clenched his jaw and narrowed his eyes before resting a hand on my shoulder, those eyes actually filling with a glistening emotion that was sort of touching.

We sat that way for a while, in silence and stillness. In recognition of the racism that still lingered in Mill Creek's shadows.

Finally, Peter removed his hand and batted at his eyes, then he cleared his throat. "I didn't know your parents were African American. Certainly didn't know about that racial incident with the cops. And I'm sorry that's part of your story—part of your dad's story."

"It's also part of *my* story," I mumbled, straightening and looking off toward Mill Creek Junction, its soft glow in the darkness of the clear August summer the reminder, the *fuel*, for the road ahead when all of this nonsense was through.

"You asked why I was in this. *That's* why. To defend people like my dad from people like that cop. And also, I suppose, to still defend my parent's honor after dealing with so much injustice."

I glanced at him and smiled. "As you can see, I'm adopted."

He laughed. "I gathered that."

"Parents are descendants of black slaves, actually."

"With a name like O'Donnell? Isn't that Irish?"

"True, but their...well, Dad's slave owners were Irish, and Ma's ancestors came from the same stock. And actually, apparently my adoptive parents have Liberian ancestry. Brought on slave ships over from West Africa. Which sort of makes me Liberian, with a side of Irish slave owners thrown into the mix, on top of whatever my birth mother was."

Max snorted. "God bless 'Merica."

Peter nodded. "What about your birth side of your story?"

I shrugged. "Don't know. Mama—err, my birth mom left me at a Junction fire station over forty years ago. But I do know that Ma's parents were social justice warriors, before that was a meme."

"Really?" Johnny said now. "I didn't know that."

Max asked, "What, like marching with Doc King?"

I smiled. Doc King. That was Max for you.

"No. But they did march on Selma," I replied. "Man, the stories grammy told from back in their days in the Deep South, bussing down to Alabama from Baltimore that March of '65 to join the protests against Jim Crow laws..."

I stared off across the field, lost in that memory, holding it close and tight.

Memories from the oral history of my family, when the police hosed down Gramps and Grammy crossing the bridge, then let loose the German shepherds that had maimed Grammy's right cheek and tore off Gramps's left thumb. Being adopted into a black family off the stoop of a Junction fire station, with skin whiter than Lake Michigan sand, meant I'd confronted America's original sin, the buying and selling of black bodies for profit and the ongoing injustices of keeping those bodies underfoot, far faster than any of my white peers.

Couldn't not confront it with the stories I heard from Gramps and Grammy.

Thing about it was, they had been the first to start slipping into dementia, which had been devastating to know their stories and experiences would fade away from memory into the ether of broken neural synapses.

It had also made me thankful—*grateful* I'd been adopted into that heritage and given the O'Donnell name that had survived generations from the original slave-owning Irish merchant from Baltimore. Made me who I was. Gave me the vision for my life and all I fought for with my law practice, fighting for—

A grunting engine jolted me from my memories, then jolted all of us from the ground. It was so sudden through the silence of the night, so out of place.

Max was to his feet first. "What was that?"

"*Where* was that?" Johnny added, rising on weak knees himself.

I helped him stand, searching for the intrusion into our night of silent bro bonding.

"Are those four-wheelers?" Peter asked, looking off toward that grove of trees where the ferrel fight had been.

I followed his gaze, hands on my hips—discerning, intuiting, wondering what the heck that sound was.

Johnny said, "Sounds more like a souped-up tractor than four-wheelers."

"At this late hour?" I wondered.

"Only one thing to do," Max said.

He started off, motioning for us to follow.

We did, the four of us stumbling down the hill and through rows of lettuce. We raced inside the grove of trees, pushing branches aside and dodging pricker bushes. White lights cast their glow through haunting branches up ahead. I worried they would expose us, but figured the treeline did enough to cover us from whoever was beyond the grove. Which looked like several of those souped-up tractors now.

Five or six of them, in fact. And more than tractors. Earth movers doing their earth-moving thing beneath bright white lights raised high, powered by clunky, grumbly generators at the perimeter.

Johnny asked, "What the heck is going on over there?"

I said, "They're freakin' tearing up Farmer Jed's crops!"

"No, not crops," Peter said. "Soil."

He was right. There wasn't a vegetable in sight. No onions or celery, no corn or any of those lettuce heads arrayed around our grassy perch.

"For what reason?" I asked, confused.

Max said, "There has been some gossip..."

I turned to him. "What gossip?"

"'Parently, someone's bought Farmer Warner out."

"What?"

"Something about a new housing development or strip mall or something or other."

"No..." I shook my head in disbelief.

"That's the rumor anyway."

"Who?" asked Peter.

"Some city boys from out east."

"Detroit?" Johnny said.

"Nope. New York or something. Some Pisces, Perseus–"

"Wait, did you say Perseus?"

I spun toward Max, shocked at what I was hearing. Same for Johnny, the two of us moving closer to the man, and Max backing up with his face twisted in confusion.

He said, "Yeah, what of it?"

I pressed, "Could you have heard Perses instead?"

He snapped his fingers and pointed at me. "That."

Johnny sort of got in his face now, asking, "As in Perses Global Financial Group?"

Max took a step back, glancing at me. "Maybe. Why? That mean something to you?"

My private eye turned to me. "This is too weird for words."

I nodded, saying nothing.

"Your mother's trailer park is bought out by the same outfit that scooped up your father's senior care center. Now they've bought up Jed's farm?"

I looked at him and frowned. "That's a lot of property in one town."

Johnny grunted. "Sure does add up to a helluva lot of property. Probably not all of it, either."

"What's not all of it?"

His answer was intercepted by my phone blaring a ring.

I pulled it out, stomach sinking at who was calling.

Annabelle. Worst timing ever.

Really wasn't in the mood to chit-chat after the revelation—not to mention her arguing for my incarceration.

But...

I figured I should answer it. She was my girlfriend, after all. At least, I thought she was—hoped she was.

"Uhh, hey, Annie," I stammered.

Max raised a brow and snickered, mouthing *Annie?*

I shooed him away and waited for her reply.

The beats ticked by, and I thought I had lost her with the spotty rural reception. Nope. Five-bars strong.

I asked, "Annabelle, you still there?"

Throat clearing and a breath.

"I'm here, Gideon."

"Is...Is everything alright?"

A beat, another breath, a sigh.

Then: "There's been a...development."

"Development?"

"In your mother's case."

I looked up, finding Johnny looking at me with what-happened eyes.

"What development?" I questioned, putting up a just-a-moment finger.

Johnny came nearer, asking, "What's going on?"

"There's been a development," I told him.

"What sort of development?"

I put the phone on speaker, asking, "What's happened, Annabelle?"

"You should come down to Junction PD," she replied.

"I'm not going anywhere without my lawyers."

"I thought *you* were your lawyer!" There was that sigh again, then a breath before another beat. "Just...Just get down here, alright? And bring Reggie and Lizzy."

"Annie, what's going—"

"We're having a hard time identifying whether she—whether the body is your mother, that's why."

She ended the call, and ended our bro night.

Sending me scrambling for the Golden Nugget.

Chapter Thirty-Three

We're having a hard time identifying whether she— whether the body is your mother...

The revelation sent me scrambling out of the woods and sprinting to Max's car. Max shouted after me to "Hold up!" above the din of grunting, grumbling earthmovers, but I pressed on. I'd barely ended the phone call with Annabelle and bolted for a way to her, knowing exactly what she meant.

If Junction PD didn't know whether the body was Ma, then maybe it wasn't.

Which meant maybe she wasn't dead.

Maybe she was still alive!

The possibility was too remarkable to be true. And yet it made perfect sense. Sort of. The stash of documents stuffed away in her apartment—accounting documents that any accountant like Ma would have been able to decipher and find meaning in—certainly pointed to her being actively engaged in some sort of...what? Investigation, hunt, conspiracy?

Didn't know. Didn't understand it all. And it didn't matter. Not now.

All that did was getting to the station to make sense of the revelation bomb Annabelle had dropped.

"Hold up!" Max called after me again, joined by Johnny with the same.

Emerging from the forest, I slowed my sprint but kept going, my foot snagging on a lettuce head and nearly sending me tumbling to the soft dirt. I recovered and kept up my pace, the world alive with possibility, with hope, the insects and tree frogs and cawing crows and hooting owls almost cheering me on as I neared Max's car.

Now I was panting, but it felt good, my lungs burning with purpose as I raced to find out whether Ma was still alive.

The thought slowed my pace.

Because if she was alive...

Now I really slowed, a coldness spreading through me even as I had sweated through my shirt, face hot and slick, the taste of salt on my tongue joined by an even heavier taste of pennies from the adrenaline dump.

Because if Ma were alive, it meant that body they'd found wasn't *her* body—and, well, that meant it was some other black woman's body.

Which meant someone else had died. Then had been dumped in her room.

The thought soured my stomach and actually sent it clenching from the painful realization. Was thrilled with the news that Ma might not be the dead body discovered in her room. But I wanted to puke.

I didn't, but now I wondered who it was who had been killed—murdered, instead of Ma.

And who it was who had put her in Ma's apartment.

Which flared up a whole number of other questions:

Where was Ma? Was she still alive? Had she been kidnapped? Who would have done such a thing? Why would they have done such a thing? And why was this other woman killed instead of Ma? If she had fallen into a conspiracy, discovered something, found something after investigating something—well, then why wasn't she killed for it?

The questions roiled through me with a wicked boil as I picked up my pace across the field.

Approaching the downed fence, I slowed again, panting for breath and feeling my heart in my head. I swallowed, heaved a stabilizing breath, then climbed over the fence and hustled to the car. The pounding footfalls of three men through soft soil, joined by struggling breaths and cussing complaints, quickly followed.

"Did I hear your chickadee right, Hoss?" asked Max, coming from behind with the same panting breath. "That your mama's body may not be your mama's body?"

Johnny said, "Yeah, kid, please tell me my old ears heard wrong."

I leaned back against Max's passenger side door, still trying to catch my breath. Swallowing, I answered, "You heard right. Annabelle said something about them having a hard time identifying whether the body they found in Ma's apartment was, well, my mother."

"What does this mean?" Peter asked.

Max laughed. "Yeah, what, did your mama come back from the dead, all zombie apocalypse like?"

Johnny smacked him upside the head, which I sort of appreciated. Not at all the time to be making jokes.

He said, "What it means is this whole sorry sack of nonsense might have just taken a massive turn."

I suddenly felt all six eyes fixed on me, looking for answers, looking for direction. I had none. All I knew was that Johnny was right on the money.

Massive turn was right.

Maybe.

Possibly?

I reached back into my childhood faith and snatched a line for stability.

Lord Jesus Christ, Son of God...let it be so!

"Just—" I bent over to catch my breath, heaving a lungful of air and trying not to get my hopes up for a possibility I prayed to God Almighty above was an actual probability. "We need to get back to town."

"Saddle up, partner!" Max darted around to the driver's side and rapped the roof of his car, throwing me a finger gun. "Me and the Golden Nugget's gotcha covered, brochacho."

Then he climbed in and I followed, Johnny and Peter scrambling into the back seat. Max brought his Plymouth to life, and as he backed out of the field, I sent up a slew of prayers.

Prayed we wouldn't get stuck. Prayed we wouldn't blow a tire, that we wouldn't spin out or hit a deer or any number of other things that could derail us getting to Junction PD to see what the heck Annabelle had found. Mostly, I just prayed the hopeful possibility that Ma was alive was really, truly a probability.

I hoped the Almighty was feeling extra generous with his providential helping hand.

The drive was quiet and fast, Max pushing the limit of both the Junction posted speed as well as his bucket of bolts. On the way, I texted Reggie and Lizzy to meet me at the station. Didn't say much, other than what Annabelle had said:

There's been a development in the case and I need my lawyers to meet me at Junction PD.

What?

Ma's body may not be her body.

Say waaa?

Oh my heck!

Just meet me at the station.

Yessiree.

Roger.

God must have been looking down with love on me that night, because we made it back to Mill Creek without incident, rolling into town the whole way rocking out to Bon Jovi's "Livin' on a Prayer." It was next in the lineup on Max's mixtape.

Seemed appropriate. And smacked of providential intervention.

When we arrived, Max squawked his way into a visitor parking spot, and I leaped out before he threw his car into *PARK*. Annabelle was waiting for me at the entrance to the station, wearing a look I couldn't quite read.

It was a cross between bewildered and freaked, confusion and dumbfounded disbelief—even fear.

Her line came roaring back: *We're having a hard time identifying whether she—whether the body is your mother...*

What did that even mean? Is it what brought that look about her?

I was about to find out...

"Hey, Gideon," she said, offering a smile and a wave.

I stuffed my hands in my pockets, uncertain how to move

forward—literally slowing down, but also figuratively. It had been days since we'd had a conversation outside a courtroom. And with the tension between us, the two of us on opposing sides, her prosecuting me...I flat didn't know how to move forward with her—flat didn't know whether we could or would.

"Hey, yourself," I managed. "Thanks for the call."

Annabelle smiled, looking oh-so fine in dark denim and a tight white blouse, sleeves rolled to her elbows, ginger hair looking brilliant under the moonlight, falling just past her shoulders, lips glistening a bright red. A warm evening breeze gusted past, flaring up the scents of lavender and jasmine with a hint of sandalwood. Her scent, Miss Dior. She always looked fine and put together, but I imagined she had done herself up for me.

There was a moment when she took a hesitant step forward, and that waving hand began reaching for me, with an instinct that could only come from lovers. It passed when her eyes darted over my shoulder, and in pounded my Three Amigos.

"What's this about Florence O'Donnell's body and its identification?" Johnny said, getting right to the point with laser focus. Ever my faithful, trusty private eye, he was.

Annabelle stiffened, withdrawing her hands to her sides. "That's right. There's been a development. Come along. Chief Roller and Dean are waiting, along with the medical examiner."

She turned away and strode inside. I regretted missing my chance to take her hand, grasp it and squeeze it, but quickly followed after her inside the station.

Max and Peter stayed put, but I brought Johnny along for the ride. I'd need all the help I could get figuring out this "development" as Annabelle had put it.

The fluorescent lights were a particularly sickly white this time of day, the night amplifying their horridness and bringing strain to my eyes. As well as a twist to my gut at the memory of walking through these halls toward booking earlier in the week. In fact, we passed that same station, bunches of officers leaning back in their chairs with chipped blue coffee mugs suddenly straightening on our approach—and eyeing me with suspicion.

I ignored them, striding after her toward the rear where the medical examiner's office was. Had half a mind to toss some wise-ass remark as I passed for the hell they'd put me through. Last thing I wanted, or needed, was to get into a pissing match with the boys in blue, so I left it alone.

Reggie and Lizzy were already waiting outside the door when we arrived. They asked what this was about, but Annabelle just told them they would find out inside. She didn't wait for an objection, shoving through a heavy steel door meant to keep out intruders from messing with official Junction PD business, and evidence.

I'd been inside this room a few times with clients. Always felt depressed by the feel of it, with its mint green tiles covering the floor and walls, the six square steel freezer doors anchored at the side, with a matching steel table polished to a shiny sheen at the center, instruments reflecting the same and dutifully arranged on a white cloth draped across another matching side table. Then there was the smell of it: bleach and antiseptic mixed with the trace tang of body fluids and a briny, meaty smell.

It was also cold, chilled really, no doubt meant to stabilize the evidence. Bright white lights shone from above, with Chief Roller and Dean talking quietly in the corner with Wayne Talbert sitting at a computer. The man stood on our arrival, a tall, pale man with thick black glasses and a shock of black hair that didn't age, even after turning sixty last year. But they weren't the only ones waiting.

A figure, lying under a white sheet, on that polished steel table. Didn't even have to guess who that was.

Or, actually, apparently I might, given the development.

Lord Jesus Christ, Son of God, may it be so...

I was surprised at my reaching back into my childhood faith like that. Supposed it made sense, seeking God given the stress I was under and all.

It also felt right. Maybe because it had been right for Ma. And with this development, after her death and all that had gone down—it sort of made me feel more connected to her.

That could wait, though, the heavenly. I had more earthly things in mind.

Like what the heck was going on!

"What's this about?" I asked, getting to it.

Wayne Talbert led the charge: "We have been unable to locate your mother's dental records."

"Okay..."

"And she had neither finger prints nor DNA on file with the State."

"Okay..." I said again, confused.

"And, well, we need to make a positive identification of the body in order to move forward with our investigation."

"Hold on, Sparky," Reggie said, interjecting and offering a chuckle.

The man stiffened and eyed him through thick, black glasses shoved against his round face. "And you are?"

"Mr. O'Donnell's attorney. You do realize my client is the one being implicated in this woman's murder, right?"

Wayne crossed his arms. "But he's next of kin. We need him to ID the body."

"And ID himself right into handing the PA exculpatory evidence!"

I put out a staying hand, understanding what Reggie was doing, mainly protecting me. I also understood the medical examiner's position.

"Why?" I simply asked.

Wayne glanced to his right, where Chief Roller and Dean Lawlor had sidled up beside him.

Chief Roller did the talking: "We're uncertain of the woman's identity."

"Why?" I asked again, trying to get an answer I wasn't getting.

"Certain—well, certain features aren't lining up with what we had expected."

Irritation flashed hot up my neck and bloomed in my face. What the heck did that mean?

I asked, "Do you have the original autopsy report?"

Annabelle nodded. "Sure. Why do you—"

"Just give it to me!"

Didn't mean to snap at her like that, but I was getting irritated at all the coyness.

Wayne handed off a copy, and I got to work flipping through the dang thing as I had before. An addition caught my attention. A bright yellow piece of paper, paper-clipped at the back. An amended toxicology report. I held it, my hand trembling as I read:

IV. Toxicology (Amended)

Preliminary Results: No alcohol or common illicit drugs were detected.

Final Results: Elevated levels of oxycodone were detected in the blood, the concentration of which was approximately 0.38 mg/L. This is within the associated range leading to respiratory suppression and drug fatality for non-tolerance developed individuals.

This is the only substances of note found in the toxicological analysis.

Elevated oxycodone level present in the blood suggests the possibility of opioid toxicity, which is potentially fatal in individuals without a high tolerance for the drug, especially for elderly individuals.

V. Conclusion (Amended)

Cause of Death: Gunshot wound to the head.

Contributing Factors: Elevated levels of oxycodone consistent with a potentially fatal overdose.

The manner of death was still ruled a homicide by gunshot to the head and listed as the cause. Except for an addition—

I held up the report, disbelieving my eyes: "What's this?"

Wayne squinted and leaned forward. "Ahh, yes. My emendation in light of toxicological analysis."

"It says here *'the gunshot wound was the direct cause of death, with opioid toxicity potentially contributing to the overall fatality, particularly if the victim was incapacitated by the drug at the time of the shooting.'* You're saying Ma was poisoned?"

"Nope. I've analyzed she had used oxy—"

"Ma is no drug user!" I shouted.

Wayne huffed a sigh. "It is what it is. The science does not lie."

Reggie said, "Which suggests she could have been deliberately incapacitated."

"Did you note an injection site?" asked Lizzy.

Wayne's eyes darted toward Chief Roller and Dean

Lawlor, then replied, "I'm planning to make a second assessment of the deceased."

"I'll take that as a nopety nope."

This was unreal. I returned to the report, flipping back through it from the start and returning to what I had reviewed before and wondering what it was I was supposed to be looking—

Something stopped my flipping.

Cold. For a second time.

A page I hadn't recalled before. Probably because I had just glazed over it, not able—willing?—to face the facts of Ma's murder.

But this...

Thoracic Cavity:

Heart: 250 grams, normal size and configuration for a female. No significant pathology.

Lungs: Both show no signs of embolism or pneumonia. Significant anthracosis noted, consistent with age, environmental exposure, and a prolonged history of tar and carbon monoxide inhalation consistent with habitual tobacco use.

Abdominal Cavity:

Liver: 1,300 grams, no nodularity. Mild fatty infiltration consistent with age and severe sclerosis associated with heavy drinking.

Gastrointestinal Tract: No signs of obstruction, perforation, or—

I didn't read any further. I'd seen all I needed to see.

And flat couldn't believe my eyes...

"There it is," I muttered, the truth of the matter registering, but only barely.

Could it be true? Her lungs, her liver...

The truth of it all sank in, deep, starting with confusion but soon blooming into clarity—into hope!

"There what is?" asked Annabelle.

Lawlor added, "Did you see something in the report?"

I smiled, wide. "You bet I did! It's right here."

I jammed a finger onto the page. "It's all right here. In describing her lungs, it says a *'history of tar and carbon monoxide inhalation consistent with habitual tobacco use'* and then with her liver *'severe sclerosis associated with heavy drinking.'"*

"What of it?"

"She never smoked or drank a day in her life!"

I returned to the report, dumbfounded and also feeling foolish I hadn't seen this earlier. Had just skipped over this part entirely, believing that the person Junction PD had found in Ma's bed had been my mother. Except—

I closed my eyes and heaved a breath, the earlier coldness of adrenaline replaced by warm relief, confirmed by a recollection.

The wisdom teeth!

I turned to the medical examiner: "Wayne, your report indicated the victim had their wisdom teeth."

He crossed his arms and nodded.

"My mother had hers removed a few decades ago."

Wayne hummed and rubbed his chin, shaking his head.

"What does that mean?" asked Lawlor.

"It means—" Emotion—joy!—seized my throat and flooded my eyes. I couldn't finish the truth of what I had read, what it meant for Ma.

What it meant for *me*.

Johnny put a hand on my shoulder and gave it a squeeze. He finished my thought for me: "It means she's still out there."

Lawlor turned to the gurney, frowning. "So this victim..."

He trailed off. Annabelle finished for him: "Isn't Florence O'Donnell!"

I looked up, trying to agree but only choked back emotion. I did manage a smile, and met Annabelle's own eyes flooding with the same.

She stifled back a giddy laugh before lunging for me and throwing her arms around my neck.

"I knew it wasn't you! I just knew it wasn't you..."

"*'For this son of mine was dead and is alive again,'*" Johnny said, echoing that same giddy glee with a disbelieving chuckle. "*'He was lost and is found!' And they began to celebrate.'*"

I instantly recognized what he was quoting. The Parable of the Lost Son, from the Good Book. Ma's favorite of Jesus' stories. Could only grin and laugh with Annabelle's and Johnny's same giddy glee.

Ma was alive—she just had to be!

I wanted to freakin' dance a jig and shout it from the rooftops! Instead, I just held Annabelle, who returned the favor with a comforting strength I had missed.

What happened next was a blur, my head swirling with the implications that the body I had thought was my mothers wasn't, not being able to fully wrap my mind around the fact Ma could actually be alive—probably, *hopefully*—after days missing from Dreamscape Manor.

A sudden ping of rage began to wind its way through me, a dark cloud threatening my joy. Not at being fingered for Ma's murder. No, at the sheer incompetence of Mill Creek Junction PD and the prosecuting attorney's office for missing this before.

I swallowed back the cloud, refusing to let bitterness snatch my bliss.

That would come later.

Boy, would it ever...

All that mattered now was one thing.

"Find her," I said, glaring at Tweedle Dumb and Tweedle Dumber.

Chief Roller stiffened, Lawlor shifting at his side. Then they both nodded and left.

Ma was out there. Somewhere. And I wasn't going to leave her rescue to chance.

Or to Mill Creek Junction PD.

So—

I spun to Johnny with the same plea: "Find her..."

My voice cracked. Johnny nodded and left. Then Annabelle was at my side.

I prayed. Again. For the third time in as many hours.

Lord Jesus Christ, Son of God...find her!

Then turned to Chief Roller: "Can I get this blasted anchor off my ankle now?"

Chapter Thirty-Four

Last night's revelation had been a nuclear bomb dropped out of nowhere. Almost like what I imagined it was like in Nagasaki and Hiroshima when our American boys dropped Fat Man and Little Boy.

Like them, I had been going about life. Albeit, under the intense watchful, suspicious eye of committing a heinous crime. That wasn't even touching on the fact I'd gotten back to living after the grim news my mother had died as a result of said heinous crime. But I had. Had reconciled myself to Ma's death, her murder, and to the fight ahead to prove my innocence.

Then *BOOM!*

Eighty years ago, the world those Japanese had known had been incinerated in an instant, consuming them (literally) and blowing apart the tiny slice of their universe, their lives— spreading the fallout far and wide.

The fallout was just starting in the world I had known.

First up was mine! Knowing that Ma could be alive, was probably alive, had flooded me with a mixture of relief and disbelief, joy and confusion, bliss and anger. It went without saying, but my relief and joy and bliss came from the possibility that Ma was still alive. Disbelief and confusion and anger simmered from the fact I had not a damn clue what had happened to her.

For days, I had resigned myself to the horrifying realization that she had been killed—murdered, in her own bed, and under the watchful eyes of Dreamscape Manor. That wasn't even touching on the equally horrifying accusation that I was the one who had pulled the trigger.

Now Junction PD and the prosecuting attorney's office brought this bombshell revelation that they were having a hard time identifying the body as Ma's—that the body they had been refrigerating could be someone else?

Flat did not compute.

For Dean Lawlor's part, he'd apologized for jumping to the conclusion that I had killed my mother—complete with arrest and arraignment and the impending prosecution. I didn't say much to that. How could I? What could I say? Mostly just nodded while my mind spun out all sorts of scenarios about what had really gone down.

Chief Roller wasn't so conciliatory, mostly because Jamie Ramos wasn't.

It had been her investigation. She had been the one responsible for custodial and review, to gather the evidence and put the pieces together, making the connections that had led to my arrest and arraignment and the impending prosecution. And she was still the pain she'd been from the start.

While acknowledging the forensics report indicated the victim may not be my mother, she also insisted it was too soon to draw such conclusions. Said she could have been smoking and drinking without me knowing for years. Apparently that had been the case with her own grandmother, the woman dying at seventy from lung cancer after relying on cigarettes to cope with her ornery *abuelo*. She also insisted the incomplete phys-ical records that could give her clarity on the matter—the missing dental and blood records—didn't allow her to rule out the body was hers, given the fact her face had been blown off.

Despite her misgivings, Chief Roller organized a town-wide manhunt for Ma, coordinating with the county sheriff's department and commissioning every one of Junction PD's finest to search for her.

None of this was satisfactory. I wanted answers. Wanted revenge, dammit! Against whoever had kidnapped my mother. Against those who had accused me of killing her.

All I could do was wait. But wait I would not do. So I did two things.

First, I'd sent Johnny on a mission to find Ma. He was the only one I trusted to find her. The only one I trusted with her life—literally, maybe even saving it. He threw cold water on that prospect, gently suggesting the chances of her still being alive were slim, given the so-called "seventy-two hour rule" for kidnappings had passed long ago.

After this threshold, not only did the danger level grow for victims with each passing hour, the kidnappers wanting to cut bait and dispose of the evidence of the crime (the victim them-selves and their body). The more time that passed after those first three days, the fewer "bread crumbs" there were to follow to the victim. Johnny had worked a few cases for rich families on both Michigan coasts, and in both cases (successfully, he added), it was the first forty-eight hours that had been the most critical. He'd been able to follow up on leads that had come into a special phone line he'd set up. After that length of time, people's memories started to fade, so he was able to jog the memories of those witnesses who had been the last contacts of the victim in those early hours.

It had now been days since Ma was last seen.

But Johnny swore he'd work his magic to follow what leads they had, follow up with Sammy and Kelsey at Dreamscape, arm-twist Brock Sheldon into coughing up video surveillance, barge into every business and home if he had to in order to find Ma.

I was sure grateful for my partner, my friend. But I knew Johnny wasn't all that was needed.

Searching for Ma was only part of the investigation, as far as I was concerned. Because there was a part of me that still wasn't convinced the body under that medical examiner's sheet wasn't her. Mill Creek Junction PD had assumed the body in Ma's apartment at Dreamscape Manor was a deceased Florence O'Donnell. Why wouldn't they otherwise? A black woman, matching my mother's description was found murdered in a locked room. Made sense. Occam's razor sure came into play with this case: the simplest explanation for a body in a locked apartment would belong to the owner.

In this case, my mother.

Except the features of the deceased had been disfigured enough by the exit wound through the face that Junction PD couldn't make an easy positive identification. That took extra legwork. Blood samples of DNA and normally dental records. Presumably some of that dental work had been destroyed in the blast, but enough of it remained to note the wisdom teeth in the medical examiner's report, which I'd noted and was still odd to me. They had also had trouble locating those records, with some apparent mix up or down system or some other nonsense getting in the way. And without fingerprint and DNA data stored in some database, their options for a positive ID had narrowed.

Again, none of which stopped Junction PD from assuming the victim was Florence O'Donnell from the start because the room was monitored and secured by a passcode lock. So we're back to Occam's razor: the simplest explanation is usually the right answer. A dead black woman, in an apartment belonging to a black woman named Florence O'Donnell, equaled naming the victim as such.

Granted, that locked room wasn't a *secure* room, with lots of people having access to it—the senior care center staff, *me*. Which the police had jumped to at some point, and I wanted to know why. We hadn't gotten the full discovery file yet, but the list of items included an entry and exit log, with me entering and exiting, along with a recording. I wanted to know what they knew, what evidence had led them to assume I had killed my mother.

It all bothered me, and I needed answers.

So while Junction PD and Johnny Pope scoured Mill Creek and the surrounding area, I set up a little playdate with Jamie Ramos and Dean Lawlor in the early hours of the next day, along with my pals Reggie and Lizzy.

After the initial reveal, we had all left just after midnight. I'd laid tossing in bed for hours and needed answers. So I'd dragged my lawyers and Mill Creek Junction's legal knuckle-heads back to the station for those answers.

I had them first walk me through the evidence again. Everything they recovered from the crime scene, in all of its gut-wrenching detail. Then the medical examiner's report, all of which was review, but it helped to get the lay of the land. The most surprising part came with the ballistic report. They hadn't recovered the bullet, so they couldn't be sure it matched the gun recovered from my chimney, but the analyst suggested it was a match to the bullet wound, caliber-wise at least.

Then I came to what I was dreading.

I said, "I was told there was a recording of a conversation I had with my mother."

"*Así es,*" Ramos said, nodding. "Dreamscape Manor keeps

limited records of recordings for every room. And I understand that you had a conversation with the victim."

"Hold the phone," Lizzy said, shifting in her chair. "This isn't a custodial interview."

"Of course not. He isn't in custody. It is a voluntary conversation."

"Then let us stipulate," Reggie cut in, "that Gideon still reserves his rights as an accused person, and he admits to nothing, vociferously denying the charges."

"Granted," Lawlor said. "But as of this morning, we have put those charges on hold, pending the investigation."

That was news to me. And blessed news, causing me to take a deep, relieved breath. When I did, I noticed a fresh flush had flashed across Detective Ramos's face. She shoved a piece of gum into her mouth and narrowed her eyes, not looking Dean's way. Clearly, they were not on the same page.

"*Está bien,*" she said, leaning back and crossing her legs, clicking a pen and snapping her gum. She also withdrew her phone and set it on the table. "Let's have a listen, shall we?"

Ramos played an audio file of the last conversation I'd had with Ma. A coldness flooded me the instant I heard her voice:

> *Hi, sugar! I didn't know you were coming by.*
> *Hey, Ma. I was in the neighborhood. Thought*
>   *I'd drop in.*
> *Glad you did! The girls and me were just about*
>   *to start up a game of canasta. Nancy is*
>   *down for the count with some stomach*
>   *thing. So we're down a player. You can be*
>   *our fourth wheel and play with—*
> *No, Ma, listen. I can't stay long.*

What a surreal feeling, hearing myself like that. Ma like

that. She loved canasta. Played a mean game, too. Now I'd wished I would have stayed. But it was all business for me. Always.

What's eatin' ya, sugar?

There was an audible sigh, then a delay. I could feel Lawlor's and Ramos's eyes on me, knowing what came next. It did:

> *What is this I'm hearing about you wanting to*
> *pull out?*
> *Of what?*
> *Ma, come on. Don't mess.*
> *So that's what this is about? You just happened*
> *to be in the neighborhood, huh? No ma'am*
> *and no sir!*
> *Yes, that's what this is about! Is it true? That*
> *you're pulling from the suit?*
> *Where'dya hear about it?*
> *From your neighbor.*
> *It was Karen wasn't it, or maybe Janet? The pair*
> *of them together are nothing but busybodies!*
> *Ma...*
> *I'll be living' large, sugar. I'ma 'bout to have a*
> *major payday settling with HappyLiving, I*
> *just know it!*
> *Ma, listen—*
> *No ma'am and no sir, Gideon. My mind is*
> *made up.*
> *So it's true then?*
> *It's true.*
> *No way I'll let you stop the suit.*

There ain't no swayin' me.
Ma, you will pay for your decision and you will
suffer for it. I'll see to it.

"That's not right..." I mumbled, a hotness flushing away that earlier coldness.

Ramos asked, "Are you suggesting this isn't you on this recording?"

"It's...It's not me. Well, it is but—"

"Party's over," Lizzy said. "I think we're done here."

"No. It's alright."

"Gideon, let's take a break," Reggie added. "This interview is over."

"I'm fine. It's the recording!"

"Answer me this, *por favor*," Ramos said. "Isn't it true that you would have assumed ownership of your mother's property in the event of her death?"

I shifted. "Well, yes—"

"And also the right to vote to continue your lawsuit against HappyLiving Estates, returning that vote to a majority of backers?"

I went to answer when my legal instincts kicked in.

And that question surfaced a piece to this puzzle.

Holy cow...

The motivation. Or the appearance of one.

Which I hadn't seen until now.

Because the fact of it was true, what the detective was alluding to: If Ma died, I inherited not only her property but her class representative status—allowing me to keep the lawsuit alive. Clear motivation, or the appearance of it.

This doesn't look good, Gideon Paul...

A chill swept through me at another thought connected to this realization: I'd been framed.

Except—

Except if that body wasn't Ma's, then it also meant she had been caught up in something, or taken out in some way.

For some reason.

What the heck was going on?

"Isn't that right?" Ramos pressed.

Reggie leaped to his feet, Lizzy right with him.

He said, "Now we really are done here."

"No no no," I answered the detective, waving my hands before pointing at her phone. "*That* isn't right."

"What are you talking about?" asked Lawlor.

"The problem is it isn't right! The recording, it isn't true, don't you see?"

I lunged forward against the table, propping my arms against the side and raising them, my mouth open with a plea and eyes wide—and no doubt looking wild.

I must have looked crazed. So I heaved a breath and blinked, closed my mouth and swallowed, then leaned back into my chair. Without a sigh or huff, without a further comment.

"No...*No veo*. I don't see," Ramos said, glancing at Lawlor.

"So, what are you saying?" Lawlor asked again. "The recording is fake?"

"Like, what is being the word? Like, a deep fake?"

I straightened, leaning forward again. "You might be onto something there."

"Are you being serious?" Ramos sneered.

"Seriously. The tech on mimicking voices, even people on video—there have been leaps and bounds in the way software has advanced with creating fake imitations of people."

"Gideon..." Reggie said, voice sounding caution.

"Seriously! Some software just requires a few minutes of audio to create a replica of someone's voice. I read just the other day about a racist audio clip of a poor Detroit principal that went viral thanks to some free generative AI tool used by nasty students."

Ramos scoffed. "That's a stretch. And convenient..."

I sighed. "No, I'm telling you the truth, dammit! This conversation, a version of it happened—"

"Gideon..." Reggie cautioned again, putting out a staying hand.

"No, let me finish!"

Understood he was just protecting me from saying anything self-incriminatory, but I needed to think this through.

I said, "I did not say I wouldn't let her stop the suit. And no way did I say she'd *pay* for her decision!"

"But that's what we heard," Ramos replied.

"I know what we heard. That's not what I said."

"When?"

"When I stopped by Ma's apartment!" I was getting worked up, I could feel it. I could almost see myself as they did. But I had to explain. "Look, what I said was that there would be a day she regretted her decision."

"Okay..." Lawlor said now, shifting and frowning and looking like he thought I was high.

"And this whole bit about her suffering wasn't about her. I had made the case that her decision would make *others* suffer."

"Okay..."

Silence filled the room. I had to imagine there was a mixture of pity and scorn at my suggestion. Soon, Ramos filled it.

"Well, we'll certainly consider this in our investigation."

I clenched back a retort. Instead, I offered a curt "Fine" before standing and leaving, Reggie and Lizzy close behind.

When we left the station, the sun was just starting to rise over a hot and steamy Mill Creek Junction. Looked like rain had passed through, and might still roil the area. Thick, heavy charcoal clouds piled high on the eastern side of town were painted a foreboding crimson, orangey hue. The red morning sky was flashing a gigantic warning about the day. Except I would make of it what I willed, not letting fate decide the road ahead.

I reached my car and just stood outside, taking a breath and going over that recording again, my mind mush trying to recall the exact conversation but knowing, sure as hell, it hadn't gone down the way it sounded.

I needed coffee. More than that, I needed sleep. And a stiff drink. All three would have to wait until this blasted case was solved.

Which might hinge on the other thing that had been bothering me that seemed to grow in significance since a few days ago. One that was almost as frightening as the fact Ma really hadn't been murdered but had instead been kidnapped.

When Lizzy and Reggie arrived, I shoved off from my car and started pacing. I said, "Remember those files we looked through?"

Lizzy answered, "You mean that stash of papers the size of James Patterson's latest yarn stuffed up in a vent above your mother's bed?"

Reggie added, "The ones fingered by Junction PD as stolen property?"

I nodded. "Right. The one that had a sales contract, with a bunch of numbers—"

"And names," Lizzy said.

"Right. And names. Remember that it indicated Perses Global Financial Group had bought out CareBridge Senior Living Oasis?"

"Sure, but what are you suggesting?"

Reggie snorted a chuckle. "That Perses took out your mother?"

Didn't appreciate the doubt, but I let it go.

"Not took out," I said. "Kidnapped."

"Say *waaa?*"

"That makes no sense!" Lizzy said.

"It does if she knew something." The picture was sharpening into clarity now. "And found something."

"She got nosey, you mean?"

I nodded. "And stuck her nose in something that could expose PGFG. Bring them down. Stand in the way of... something."

"Why not just kill her?" asked Reggie.

I didn't have an answer for that.

"Good question."

"And besides, your mama had dementia, right?" Lizzy questioned. "A cognitive disorder that would surely put up all sorts of roadblocks in her lead role as Jessica Fletcher."

"Nice *Murder, She Wrote* reference," Reggie quipped.

"I do what I can to keep it light."

Had to smile at that. And nod.

Except that brought up another thing. Something that was too crazy to contemplate. A possibility that was too insane to even wish was a probability.

But that also fit in line with where this whole crazy week had gone.

"What are you thinking, Gideon?" asked Lizzy.

A glance, a breath, a beat.

Then: "I'm thinking..."

Another breath, another beat, now running it all through my head to make sure I wasn't the crazy one.

"I'm thinking that—"

"Your mama didn't have dementia," Reggie said with interruption, "like I'd suggested a few days ago."

Completing the thought I could barely bring myself to voice—let alone think.

Lizzy gasped. "So he was right?"

I shook my head. "I don't know. But I know someone who might."

At least, I hoped so...

Chapter Thirty-Five

"We're here to see the good professor," I announced.

A short, pudgy woman sat at a receptionist desk outside my old roommate's office, hair grey and swept into a bun that meant business, hunched over a book.

She broke off a piece of chocolate chip cookie and popped it into her mouth, turning the page without looking up or acknowledging us. Then she peered at me over a set of narrow raven glasses, black with up-swept corners, resting on the bridge of her nose, one eye twitching with suspicion between Reggie and me, then to Lizzy.

"Do you have an appointment?" she asked.

"No, but he's an old college roommate of mine. Just stopping by to say hello."

She regarded me above those black glasses of hers and popped another piece of cookie in her mouth, a flare of bittersweet chocolate and vanilla floating from her munching mouth.

"Dr. Dolph is a busy man," she said, returning to her book.

I replied, "It won't take long. We have some business we need to discuss."

"What business?"

I suppressed a frown. Nosy little thing.

"A *private* business matter," I simply said.

Her face sagged, but she hefted herself from her perch and waddled to the door, holding up her hand and instructing us to wait at a distance from the entrance while she announced us to the man I hoped could help us get closer to solving this mystery.

Scott Dolph. An old buddy from Wayne State University who had actually grown up in Mill Creek Junction. We had roamed in different circles back then as teenagers. Me with the jocks, having been a star quarterback and decent point guard, and him more into the debate team and theater. It wasn't until our sophomore year of college that we became friends, bonding over our shared frustration with statistics. We became roommates the next year, and I even stood up at his wedding the next after he married his high school sweetheart, a kind woman who was a nurse at Mercy General.

He and I parted ways and grew apart when I fled West Michigan to Washington, DC, for law school. After getting his Master of Arts in psychology, and then a doctor of psychology, Scott had returned home to care for his old hometown, eventually landing a teaching gig at Mill Creek Junction Community College. I figured, if there was anyone who could tell us about Ma, whether my instincts were right, it was Doc Dolph.

His office was on the third floor of the School of Social Sciences and History, with a hallway of walnut hardwood floors and walls painted moss, lit by yellow lighting in sconces—not the dreadful fluorescent lighting typical of colleges. Plenty of my friends had attended the school, and my father had encouraged me to go here before I went across state to Wayne State and then fled West Michigan to Georgetown Law.

When most people thought of a local community college, they expected a boring, unadorned campus on unwanted property next to the highway, filled with cinder-block eyesores passing for academia teaching tech-school basics for small-town teenagers without any ambition or prospects for life beyond Midwest onion fields and factories. That wasn't MCJCC in the slightest. It rivaled anything I'd seen while living on the East Coast. Almost like a mini Princeton University, it was, even Georgetown University, my alma mater.

"Boy, does this bring back the memories..." Reggie said, glancing down the hallway.

Lizzy said, "That's right. You went here, didn't you?"

"Yes ma'am. Thanks to Kip Walker, the school's founder."

"Really?"

"Dude wrote a large check to a trust fund to pave the way for any Junction high school graduate to get their college education paid for."

"Get out of here!" she said, glancing around.

"Only stipulation was they needed to maintain a 3.0 GPA and stay out of jail."

"Not bad requirements. And a generous offer."

"Sure was."

I added, "Lots of Mill Creek youth have become doctors and accountants thanks to this place, even tradesmen like mechanics and builders."

"Wait, you didn't attend here, did you?" Lizzy asked me.

I glanced at Reggie then looked away. "No, I didn't..."

"Gideon was too good for us Mill Creek folk." Reggie laughed and jabbed me in the arm.

Lizzy asked, "What did you study, Reggie?"

"Poli sci, baby."

"Figures."

"What's that supposed to mean?"

"Yeah, what's that supposed to mean?" I said. "I was a political science major myself."

"Need I say more?"

Reggie and I just looked at one another, shaking our heads without understanding.

The woman returned and said Scott would see us now. I thanked her, and she smiled curtly before waddling back to her desk.

Through the open door was a familiar bald man my age, just over forty, with a golden tan in a crisp black suit looking out into the hallway, brightening when he saw me.

"Giddy!" Scott said, grinning.

I strode inside, ignoring Lizzy's *"Giddy?"* question from behind and Reggie's snickering at the college nickname.

We embraced, sharing a few moments of catch-up. Which was sort of sad, knowing we lived in the same area and hadn't really seen much of one another. He had reached out through the WeShare social media platform a few times to get drinks. But with him having a family, two active twin teenage boys and a younger daughter, and his teaching gig on top of his counseling practice, and then my own legal practice and being wrapped up in my work, there just wasn't time. At least, that's what I had told myself. Now I felt foolish seeking his help after all these years and promised myself I would reach back out for those drinks after this was through.

Sitting behind a generous wood desk in a well-appointed office, Scott motioned us to sit in padded chairs.

The office was orderly, no piles of books or folders spilling papers strewn about, not like my messy space—which had led to plenty of fights about me picking up after myself and Scott being too much of a neat freak. Smelled familiar too, juniper and cedar, the piney, earthy scents of a burning candle that was common in our dorm room. He was nothing if not a man of routine. A chipped mug half drained of coffee was perched on his desk, bearing the familiar green and gold of Wayne State University. Go Warriors!

I went to sit when I noticed something on his desk. A silver pen, the initials PGFG etched on its side.

As in Perses Global Financial Group?

Scott said, "Sally said you have some sort of business to discuss?"

I nodded. "That's right. It's about my mother."

His face fell, and he shook his head. "I was devastated to hear about her death in the news. And then about Junction PD fingering you for—well, it all. What a bunch of malarkey!"

"That's the thing we came to talk about."

Without going into too much of the investigation, I explained the recent discoveries and questions surrounding the body discovered in her apartment.

"That's nutso," Scott said, leaning back. "What do the police think about it all?"

"They're not saying much, but there's a manhunt now for her, and it will be announced soon for the public's help in the matter. We're here, Reggie and Lizzy and me—" I gestured to my partners "—to ask about something related to the investigation. Something you have experience with."

"Sure, but how can I help?"

"Well, the reason Ma was at Dreamscape Manor was because I had thought she had dementia and needed extra care."

He straightened, furrowing his brow. "Thought?"

I shifted, glancing at Reggie and Lizzy who each nodded me onward.

"That's right. Now...I'm not so sure."

I explained what we had found stuffed away inside the vent in her room. The packet of papers, with spreadsheets and ledgers, names and numbers, all things an accountant might be interested in.

"An accountant like your mother..." Scott leaned back in his chair and stared off.

Reggie added, "We have been leaning toward the theory that she was on some sort of mission."

"Mission?"

"Gathering the documents," Lizzy said, "those specific ones, in that way, and then squirreling them away—well, it just seems all too deliberate."

"Too purposeful."

"So we're wondering," I went on, "whether you could answer a lingering question for us."

"And what's that?" asked Scott.

"You're a—I don't know how you put it, but a brain psychiatrist, right?"

He smiled. "A cognitive psychologist, but yes, that's right. I deal with matters of the brain."

Reggie leaned in. "A psychologist who deals with matters of dementia?"

Scott folded his arms, glancing at his watch before regarding him then turning his attention back to me.

"Love the pop-over reunion and all," he said, "but can we cut to the chase? I've got a class to teach soon."

I shifted, nodding. "Here's the deal. We're wondering if it is possible for someone to fake dementia."

His arms dropped, and he cocked his head. "You serious?"

"Dead serious."

"You think your mother faked having dementia?"

"It's the only explanation for what we found, what we think she was doing at Dreamscape."

"I understand you're pressed for time, doctor," Lizzy said, "and so are we. So, as you said, maybe we can cut to the chase? In your expert medical opinion, could Florence O'Donnell have faked having a cognitive disorder?"

"Toward what end?" Scott asked, pinching his face in confusion.

Reggie replied, "Not sure exactly, other than getting into Dreamscape to gather those documents Lizzy mentioned."

I leaned in: "So, what of it, Scott? Could my mother have faked her dementia?"

Now Scott laughed. "You can't be serious! Besides, I couldn't medically know that."

"But is it possible?"

He shifted, frowning. "Detecting something of that magnitude would require careful observation and a comprehensive understanding of the patient. A combination of clinical expertise and detailed, consistent assessment—that's how you differentiate between genuine dementia and faked symptoms. Which I can't offer."

Reggie said, "We understand, doctor. How about you ballpark it for us?"

I nodded. "Right. What sorts of things would such a trained professional look for?

Scott hesitated, then replied, "First of all, genuine memory loss is usually unpredictable. If someone constantly forgets certain things, and only those certain things, but then they recall other things, it might be a sign of faking it."

"Like always forgetting their keys, but never forgetting where they parked their car?"

"That's a good one."

"She did fixate on forgetting what she ate, breakfast or dinner. But then she would talk your ear off about the upcoming election, the candidates and their positions, why one is less of a scoundrel than the other."

Scott leaned back and hummed. "Selective forgetfulness, especially with consistent themes, is certainly a giveaway. I would also consider whether she over-acted her symptoms."

"What do you mean by that?" asked Lizzy.

"Such as repeatedly forgetting the names of close family members, and in a sort of overtly, overly dramatic way."

I said, "She did seem to have trouble forgetting Dad's name."

He grunted, rolling his eyes. "Now that right there is suspicious."

"Why? Isn't forgetfulness a sure sign of dementia."

"Yes, but often not intimate partners, such as a spouse."

That was troublesome...

"And watch for stressful situations. People who are genuinely suffering from dementia become more confused and agitated under stress. But a person who shows a calmness and composure during stressful situations or sudden changes, it might indicate they are faking it."

"Sudden changes..." I said. "What, like a new environment?"

"Exactly. How was she when she started living at Dreamscape Manor?"

"Fine. Actually, she seemed to love it. She especially loved the canasta tournaments and crossword puzzle challenges."

Scott hummed, bringing a hand to his chin. "Now that is suspicious."

"How so?" asked Reggie.

"Typically, someone who could still perform complex tasks and solve problems like a crossword puzzle or card games, something that would become difficult during the middle stage of the disease, well, that definitely might be a sign they were not genuinely experiencing dementia."

I said, "I just thought it was a way for her to try and keep her brain sharp. Was proud of her for her sticktoitiveness, for overcoming the mental bug, as she called it."

Scott asked, "What about inappropriate emotional reactions?"

"Like what?"

"Flying off the handle when someone makes a mistake on her restaurant order, for instance."

Reggie chuckled. "Don't we all?"

I shook my head. "Ma was always in control of her emotions. Still is."

Scott frowned. "Well, at any rate, it's the latter symptoms you should be concerned with. A significant difficulty with walking, sitting up, even swallowing. Does she have any difficulty with these, or is there an inconsistent display of these symptoms?"

"She does grab for my arm when we take walks, and slouches forward or braces herself to sit straight. But swallowing...never an issue. Not even dressing herself."

"What about lucidity? In later stages, it is brief and rare."

I said nothing, considering this angle. I had always been waiting for the confusion to settle over her. Sure, she would stare off, not engage at times. At others, she would be talking gibberish, usually things that went on at the manor. But most of the time she just seemed to snap out of it whenever I visited. Even the nurses talked about her extended periods of clarity.

"What about this," Scott continued. "Does she ever talk about her condition?"

I laughed, then cleared my throat at the awkward outburst. I replied, "She talks about it all the time. How she hates her decline. How her parents had caught the mental bug."

"Why is that a problem, doc?" asked Lizzy.

"Well, most people who are genuinely suffering through dementia are unaware of the full extent of their condition."

"But the question remains," Reggie said. "Is faking dementia possible?"

Scott smirked. "Theoretically. But malingering, which such a feat is known by, would be an extremely challenging undertaking to convincingly pull off."

"But possible."

"Replicating the complex and varied symptoms of this condition over time—I cannot imagine how one would do it."

"Why not?" I asked.

"Because people with dementia suffer through a range of cognitive, behavioral, and physical experiences that progress and fluctuate in specific ways, which can't be easily imitated, especially consistently."

"But possible?"

Scott answered, "Florence would've had to have had detailed knowledge of the disease, especially the ways symptoms manifest and fluctuate."

Reggie said, "She had a husband who suffered through it. Isn't that right, Gideon?"

I nodded. "And the motivation could be strong enough too, right?"

Scott said, "Well, sure. I can imagine a number of motives for someone to fake dementia. Financial gain, avoidance of responsibilities—"

I shook my head. "None of that is my mother."

"Don't be too certain..."

"I'm serious! She has always taken responsibility for her life. The hardest working person I've ever known. She's also financially set, for life. With her pension and Dad's, they don't need money."

"Be that as it may, with the legal consequences, including fraud, and the damage to personal relationships—I can't imagine it. Then I go back to what it would take to pull off. The acting, the knowledge."

I pressed, "Which she could have learned from her husband."

Reggie added, "And I can't imagine most caregivers at a joint like Dreamscape would have paid too careful attention to the symptoms."

Scott said, "These places are often understaffed. So perhaps she could have pulled the wool over their overworked eyes. But keeping up the deception over time would be extraordinarily difficult. Besides, I would refer back to her original tests at the start of her journey to make a determination."

"What tests?" I asked.

"Look at her neuropsychological testing, which can often reveal inconsistencies. Performing too poorly on a cognitive test for her dementia stage and worse on easier tasks than on more difficult ones would be a sure sign of faking it."

"She never took such tests."

He stiffened, eyes widening. "She never underwent testing?"

I shook my head, a mixture of confusion and hope rising.

"What does that mean," Reggie asked, "that she didn't have a test?"

Scott answered, "Testing is normally part of the diagnostic protocol."

He turned to me. "Why didn't she get tested?"

I shrugged. "With Dad's dementia, and the signs in her actions and mind echoing what he'd gone through, she suggested it was time to go to Dreamscape."

"Wait, she suggested it?"

"Right. She said she could feel the mental bug coming on,

as she called dementia, and then when I started noticing the patterns in her, I began exploring options."

Scott sat back. "Well, there you go."

"There what go?" asked Lizzy.

"I suppose I stand corrected. There is a chance she could have been faking her condition, given that dynamic. Of course, that's an exceedingly surface, non-clinical diagnosis."

Reggie added, "But you're saying there's a chance?"

"There's a chance." He looked off in thought. "In fact, I'd say a better-than-not chance."

There was that hope again, rising and actually causing me to stand. Ma faked her way into Dreamscape for a reason, on purpose. And I bet those documents spelled it out.

I thanked him for his help and went to leave when I said, "By the way, what's that pen about?"

I pointed at the one I'd seen earlier.

Scott frowned. "Oh, that. Apparently they're our new owners."

I flashed Reggie wide eyes.

"Owners?" he asked.

"Some finance firm bought us out. They promise bluer skies, but I had already liked my horizons, thank you very much!"

"Oh my heck..." Lizzy muttered.

Damn straight. I had to get ahold of Johnny.

And find Ma...

Chapter Thirty-Six

Sometimes life comes at you with a left hook that lays you out on your back side. There are other times when it dribbles down from the heavens with a splat of bird crap on your eyeglasses—right before the pigeon careens out of your blind spot made all the worse by the high-noon sun, comin' at ya bright and comin' at ya at a blinding angle right before the dang beach bum claws those eyeglasses clear off your face, right before peckin' your eyeballs clear out of your sockets.

More often than not, life comes at you like a two-by-four; sometimes a Mack truck. When it does, Johnny Pope's your guy.

Sure, he charged a steep price. A pretty penny, as the kids used to say. But it was more than worth it. Mostly because the Lord Almighty had providentially arranged the set pieces of his life to give him the special skills that lent themselves to just those kinds of situations.

Case in point: his number being drawn and his backside being shipped off to Nam.

On top of his stint in the communication's unit translating

commie pinko into English, reconnaissance and special operations had been a strong suit of his during his gig with Uncle Sam. After he'd left the priesthood he had defaulted to the hidden talent.

The East Coast was his first stop, setting up shop in the Big Apple and hopscotching down to DC and farther south to Atlanta. But a bad card played by a former client that got him wrapped up with the Italian mob sent him packing south. As in, Deep South.

Ever since childhood, he'd had a particular gift with numbers that made him adept at playing poker, particularly counting cards. Given his entanglements with the Italian mafia, Vegas was out of the question, so he tried his hand at riverboat casinos, making out like a bandit. Until the Dixie Mafia started poking around his games, which got the New Orleans crime family involved when he roamed farther south. Before either of them got too comfortable with the prospect of severing limbs and cutting off fingers and toes, he cut bait a second time heading back home to Mill Creek Junction.

All that to say, Johnny had gotten comfortable with the underbelly of society. Supposed getting mixed up with mafias of all sorts will do that to a guy. But it was the cases he'd taken, the murders that went unsolved for rich families wanting justice, the kidnapped kids sold into sex rings that law enforcement let slip through the cracks, the missing persons who got mixed up with the wrong drug gang—all of those investigations had hammered and honed his appetite for the fallout of human depravity—

Leading to a drive to take matters into his own hands.

Johnny was a firm believer that vengeance was the Lord Almighty's. Yet he also shared the same opinion of the prophet Micah, who waxed eloquent about the nature of what is good, what the Lord Almighty requires of us: *'to do justice and to love kindness and to walk humbly with your God.'*

And he served that justice at the raw end of a Colt M1911. With kindness (for the victims) and a dollop of humility, of course.

Which was why he had been roaming every inch of Mill Creek Junction the past half a day after Gideon O'Donnell's life had been set ablaze with a can of gasoline and a blowtorch by the revelation that his mother could very well still be alive.

Johnny was Gideon's guy, and there wasn't anything he wouldn't do for him. No stone he'd leave unturned to help him find his mama. Except he had come up empty, his well of options were running dry, and he needed help.

So he turned to the only source that had proven faithful over the years.

Johnny slipped his arm back inside his Ford pickup and took a drag on his Camel, a habit he hadn't been able to kick since Nam. Yet another gift from Uncle Sam that kept on giving after contracting hepatitis from shared razor blades out in the field. He took a drag, the stick glowing at the end and a tail of smoke spinning up into the midsummer breeze.

There was a pleasant bite to the August air. Cool and not as humid. A rainstorm had passed through earlier that morning, some lingering clouds still spitting. He enjoyed the change of weather, along with the calm pause to his frantic early hour search.

He also enjoyed another pleasurable drag on his cigarette before carrying on with his search.

The Turkish blend fell heavy on his tongue with a mildly spicy sweetness that focused his mind on a prayer for the moment. Not from his Catholic priest playbook; this one was much more ancient. As in Jewish ancient, an assurance of protection and guidance from Psalm 121:

Hostile Takeover

I lift up my eyes to the hills—
from where will my help come?
My help comes from the Lord,
who made heaven and earth.

Johnny took another drag, closing his eyes and letting the smoke linger while he finished the last stanza:

The Lord will keep you from all evil;
he will keep your life.
The Lord will keep
your going out and your coming in
from this time on and forevermore.

Blowing the smoke, he flicked his butt out his window then stepped out of his truck, extinguishing the habit beneath his boot in the parking lot of one spot he had a hunch was as good a spot as any to squirrel away a missing person.

Burt's Auto Parts.

He had investigated a fire that had consumed the joint a bit ago, the charred remains like some field after a napalm bombing raid still smelling of smoke and burned wood and melted plastics.

It had been a good-sized warehouse, painted forest green on the sides stretching back half a football field with a few windows that looked like they were still standing. Brown brick faced out toward another main drag off the far end of Main Street where a bunch of big-box retail outlets sat. Not the big corporate types, but some locally owned joints. Meyer's General, Happy Day Inn, The Green Thumb, and the like.

The arched roof, normally covered in bird crap, had collapsed in on itself. Looked like someone had taken a fist to one of those old-school Jiffy Pop popcorn plumes, tearing a hole clear through. A part of one side had collapsed inward, as well, leaving the joint a complete DOA loss.

Johnny's investigation had concluded it had been torched for the insurance money. Or, as some muckety-muck lawyers had charged, for insurance fraud. The owner had been teetering on bankruptcy, and he used it to help Gideon sow the seeds of reasonable doubt in another case that Gerald Peterson was wrapped up in before he'd killed his wife—

Allegedly, that is.

He'd been accused of torching the place as payback for Burt getting in the sack with his missus, but he'd used eyewitness testimony of a disgruntled employee to help Gideon argue that Burt had burned down his business and made it look like an accident.

At any rate, the place had been abandoned ever since, and the whole area had gone to pot. Just the type of place someone might hide a body.

Living or dead.

About the only lead he had after roaming Mill Creek all day. The other one had been that cotton pickin' log Dreamscape kept of Janes and John entering residents' rooms—which went mysteriously missing.

Of course it did.

Johnny came up first to the front doors. Still locked solid, without a trace of forced entry. Wouldn't peg a perp to have gone in that way anyhow, but you never knew.

He continued around to the side, glancing back toward his truck but finding no one interested in what he was doing. He edged around the corner and walked the length of one wall still standing strong, despite the collapsed roof and other walls still hanging on by a miracle.

Weeds clawed at his thighs as he walked its length, sidestepping rotting boards and crumbling cinder blocks, scanning the few windows that lined the wall and perimeter for anything amiss, anything indicating forced entry—anything indicating there was anyone inside.

Nothing, all around.

Same for the back. A rusted steel emergency exit door was sealed shut. No lock or knob on its face. Which meant no one could have gotten inside through the back.

Johnny continued around to the other side, where he was met by a wall with a serious case of palsy. It was cracked clear in the middle, where it had collapsed, the cinder-block edges like puzzle pieces. It was wicked dark inside. What little light did find its way through didn't indicate anything close to life. Shelves, formerly stocked with auto parts, were bare. Not even a sleeping bag and tent or clump of cardboard boxes indicated a hobo was holed up inside. He kept going, nearing the front and finding another pair of windows that were completely intact. Not a scratch or scrape or crack on 'em.

Finishing, he made his way back to the front, the rainy leftovers having died down to a mist. A weird fog stretched its tendrils across the pavement as clouds gave way to sun.

What a bust.

Climbing back into his Ford, Johnny noticed a car approaching from down the street. A sedan, unknown make and model. He worried it was headed his way. Maybe he had been right about the abandoned building.

He slunk down in his seat and held his breath—

It slowly worked its way down from the end of the turn until it passed. Then turned into another abandoned building across the street.

Graceland Memorial, the funeral home attached to a private cemetery on the outskirts of Mill Creek Junction.

Last time he was in there he'd been on an investigation from hell—literally, a demonic force possessing some dude who had staged a massive social media influence campaign through WeShare to cause a horrifying surge in suicides. The place had been abandoned ever since.

Or so he thought.

A heavy haze had settled on the abandoned road, the sunrise alighting like a fiery nimbus, the hot humidity a wet blanket on the summer morning quickly cresting toward noon. Insects and tree frogs and a barking dog up the street was the soundtrack for the moment.

Red brake lights flared up as the mystery sedan parked along the brick building. He just sat still—discerning, intuiting, wondering what was going on, and who was doing the goings on.

Opening and closing doors brought confirmation.

He flat couldn't believe what his eyes were seeing.

Who his eyes were seeing.

A pair, who looked frighteningly familiar hustling to the entrance. Except...no, they couldn't be.

"Mother Mary and Joseph—"

The interruptive shrill of his phone cut him off.

Thought he'd put the dang thing on silence, but he muted it real quick while glancing at its face.

Gideon. No doubt checking in on his progress.

The pair fiddled with the door, the one man glancing around while his partner worked to get them inside.

But why? And why here?

Unless there was something inside that they needed.

Or someone...

It hit him.

A memory, from a few days ago. Following the Three Amigos—or rather, the Three Comrades, those three Russian-speaking guests of Mill Creek—all over the Junction in his F-150.

Eventually to Graceland Memorial.

Along with Warner Farms, Mill Creek Community College. Heck, even City Hall had been on their tour! Along with Dreamscape Manor itself, Fred Myers General Store, the J-Max prison, Smiles Dentistry—

"Dentist..."

Was that why Florence's dental records had mysteriously disappeared? Had Perses Global Financial bought up the practice, then destroyed that evidence?

Were they buying up Mill Creek, wholesale?

Johnny's phone continued buzzing as he ran it all through his head. The call almost went to voicemail, but he answered it in time.

"Gideon, I think I've found your mother," he said, disbelieving the words that came from his mouth—while also liking their taste. They felt right, felt true—and wickedly wrong.

Had a hunch he had in fact found Florence. Still—

Flat did not compute what had happened, and who had taken her. And why...

"What? Where?" Gideon asked in a rush.

"At Graceland Memorial."

The pair slipped inside the front door and disappeared.

"Graceland Memorial? That doesn't make any sense. Did you get a look at who—"

"Just hold tight, Gideon. I may have an answer real soon."

Johnny ended the call and made another, to Junction PD. Finishing, he climbed out of his truck, snatching his fedora and Colt M1911, along with an extra magazine of .45s that he slipped in his front pocket. His pistol held eight rounds, which may not be enough for this rodeo, given who he spotted slipping inside.

Settling the hat on his head, he held the weapon fast at his side and strode toward his target. It felt solid and cool in his hand from resting on his passenger's seat, a reassuring heaviness for what might turn real ugly real quick.

The street was abandoned, sitting north of the tracks at an end of town that had seen better days. A quick glance up and down the road spotted no one and no thing, not a car or stray dog in sight.

Good. No need to worry about Nosy Nancys getting in the way.

The door was in sight now, and he prayed a go-to prayer he had often recited at the start of an investigation. Not often it spun out into a full-on confrontation with a pair of perps, and he figured now was as good a time as any to petition the Lord Almighty for a helping hand.

This time, Johnny looked to Rome instead of Jerusalem for his words:

> *Everlasting God, you have ordained and*
> *constituted in a wonderful order the*
> *ministries of angels and mortals: Merci-*
> *fully grant that, as your holy angels always*
> *serve and worship you in heaven, so by*
> *your appointment they may help and*
> *defend us here on earth; through Jesus*
> *Christ our Lord, who lives and reigns with*
> *you and the Holy Spirit, one God, for ever*
> *and ever.*

Coming up to the door, he crossed himself and grasped the steel handle to gain entry.

It didn't budge.

And he didn't have time.

So he aimed for the lock and fired a round, then another. The bullets splintered and ricocheted into the handle. A strong kick to the wounded dog standing guard sent it sailing to the cracked pavement with a clatter.

Wasted no time hustling inside the dark hallway.

A faint red light from an *EXIT* sign above blanketed the space filled with the tang of formaldehyde and bleach, joined by the fresh electric smell of a summer thunderstorm barreling across Farmer Jed's Junction fields.

Hallway was far too narrow for Johnny's liking. Wasn't one to feel the threat of claustrophobia, but the walls pressed in something fierce, exacerbated by the dim lighting and mercilessly hot quarters—compounded by the thrill of the chase and the adrenaline keeping every one of his senses on high alert.

A faint yellow glow was thrown from an open door at the end, joined by voices.

Foreign. Definitely Russian.

He crept through the corridor, tightening his grip on the Colt at his side. Didn't take long before he came up to a modest room at the end, about the size of a garage.

Expected a vast array of refrigerators. The kind that kept loved ones safe and sound until it was time for burial. Maybe an embalming table, some gurneys for transportation and other wares of the funeral trade. Coffins, caskets, cremation jars.

Instead, what he saw flat stopped him in his tracks.

And sent a coldness flooding him that compensated for the stifling heat.

A black woman resting on top of a hospital bed.

The spitting image of Florence O'Donnell.

She was sedated, by the looks of it. IVs were strung out from her arms attached to bags. Wires spiraled from her, going this way and that into monitors, waves and numbers keeping track of Lord only knew what, the faint chirps of indicators and the *chi-cuh* of a breathing machine floating toward him.

Standing around her, back to him, were two people.

He'd found her. And her kidnappers.
A man and woman. Confirmed and recognized.
But weren't at all who he had expected.
Made sense, running the numbers through his head.
Still—
Time to end this nightmare.
For good.

Chapter Thirty-Seven

I raced through Main Street the best I could through Mill Creek's business district, honking at slow-pokes and passing them when I could, slow stopping through stop signs and red lights without a care for the law, or others, I supposed.

Dumb, sure. But with word on Ma, her being found and alive—possibly, *hopefully!*—the only care I had, the only thought I had, was getting to Ma.

Lord Jesus Christ, Son of God, she better be alright...

Graceland Memorial was on the far end of town, opposite of the community college. Hadn't even worried about taking Reggie or Lizzy along for the ride. They told me to go and said they'd meet me there.

So go I did, racing like a crazy person. Given yet another turn in this wicked nightmare, I couldn't care less about anything except for—

The blaring grunt of a dump truck, then the actual turning front end of a dump truck sent me slamming on the brakes. It also snapped me out of my self-centered *Fast and Furious* bit role. I'd get there when I got there. Which was almost there.

Letting him finish his turn, and swallowing the single-finger salute and not-nice-words he threw my way, I completed my slide through the stop sign, took a breath, and paced myself for the north end of town.

Another seven minutes, I was pulling into the abandoned lot of the funeral home. A sedan sat parked along the side of the brick building, the front door wide open. Johnny was nowhere to be found, although I spotted his truck parked across the street at Burt's Auto Parts store.

Barely put my own Audi into park when I leaped out toward that open entrance—

Just as a faint *pop-pop* echoed toward me.

Was that gunfire?

Another *pop-pop* jolted my lizard brain into self-preservation gear, sending me scrambling back inside my car after I remembered something I'd heard from a survival show.

Run away from gunfire. Run toward a knife.

Or was it run toward a knife and run away from gunfire?

Hell, I didn't know!

And really, did it matter? Johnny had said he was sure he'd found where Ma had been held. At Graceland Memorial. After some car had pulled up to the joint and a pair exited and went into the building. Never did get an identification who, but I had a good sense of who it was, given the crazy connections Dreamscape had to that private equity firm, Perses Global.

No doubt in my mind it was the Asian pair Johnny said he'd seen in Millie's on Main. The same ones I had seen at Max's Place flanking that Cindy Crawford lookalike jawing it up with Mayor Goodall.

The thought sent me scrambling back out of my car and

bolting across the cracked black top into the darkened maw of the funeral home's open door.

Gunfire be damned.

A long corridor stretched before me, far darker than outside, sending my eyes into a course-correcting fit. It was blood red, which felt appropriate. The stuffiness compared to the cooler outside morning sent me heaving a stabilizing breath, bleach and antiseptics and other funeral home scents turning my stomach.

Voices flared from the end, pulling me through the hallway on uncertain feet that wanted to run away from certain danger but also run toward the promise of Ma's salvation.

"Ma?" I called out. "Is that you?"

Dumb, sure. Probably. Didn't care one bit.

"Gideon, back here!"

It was Johnny. His beckoning voice from a room lit a golden yellow flooded me with an encouraging ping of adrenaline. And hope, that what I'd been praying for had been given to me.

Lord Jesus Christ, Son of God, let it be so...

Stumbling down the corridor, I came up quick to the end. It opened into a modest room that looked about what you'd expect for a funeral home.

Except for one thing.

A hospital bed.

Resting peacefully was a woman in a blue nightgown wearing pink slippers.

"Ma..." I said on a disbelieving breath.

Relieved emotion sprang to my eyes—with joy! What Johnny had quoted instantly sprang to mind: *'For this son of mine was dead and is alive again; he was lost and is found!' And they began to celebrate.'*

My mother...found. Alive!

Time to celebrate was right—

Movement snagged for my attention, jerking me back to the moment.

First at my left, where Johnny Pope was holding his trusty Colt pistol, aiming for the opposite wall. I looked in that direction, stage right.

The sight stopped me cold.

What I saw—*who* I saw did not compute.

Yet there they were.

Sammy and Kelsey.

Ma's caretakers from Dreamscape Manor.

My breath caught in my chest, and it felt like even my heartbeat snagged on the revelation, tumbling down a well of confusion that made not a lick of sense.

Yet also made perfect sense.

They had direct access to Ma, complete with the passcode to get inside and the plausible story that would cover them from police scrutiny. Cover them doing—whatever the heck they were doing with Ma!

And yet—

"You bastards!" I screamed, the rage that echoed back surprising me as much as those two.

Gripping his Colt tight, Johnny said, "Guessing Sammy ain't your real name, is it, kid?"

The tall man with red hair held out his long, lanky arms. At first, it looked like a plea of surrender. Then I realized it was for a fight.

Kelsey was next to him, her auburn hair tied into a pony-tail. Ma had relied on that woman to bathe her, help her change clothes, and go to the bathroom. She looked like she was bracing for the same fight.

Both were unarmed, which I thought odd. Although, perhaps the good Lord above was looking down with love.

Supposed these sorts of scenarios weren't like bargain-bin Kindle or WeFlix thrillers.

"You…" the man I knew as Sammy said, Slavic accent suddenly heavy. *"Kak vy nashli nas?"*

Johnny smirked. "How did I find you? By the grace and mercy of God. And your stupidity."

Sammy literally growled. Kelsey stepped forward, eyes narrowed and reaching for her pocket.

To which Johnny now waved his Colt with intent.

"Not so fast, honey. The jig is up. Whatever you've got going on here—I'm here to put a stop to it." He nodded my way. "We both are."

"You can't stop it now," the woman said in a similar Russian accent, laughing. "No one can."

Sammy snorted a similar laugh, grinning widely. *"Da.* It is already being in motion. All of it."

My head filled with confusion, even as it felt faint from the combo of the stifling heat and noxious antiseptic and formaldehyde smells—the sight of Ma lying on that bed, a sedated prisoner!

Didn't have a clue what those two were talking about.

"The sale of Dreamscape," Johnny asked. "To Perses Global Financial Group. Same for HappyLiving, I reckon. And everything else in Mill Creek Junction, apparently. Except she discovered something that would have scuttled the deal, all of them, ain't that right?"

Apparently my private eye had the clue I didn't, putting the pieces together. Which is why I paid him the big bucks.

The pair said nothing. What was left unsaid was crystal clear to me: Perses had wanted Ma out of the way.

"Why didn't you kill her?" he asked.

Good question. One I couldn't ask. Couldn't even think to

ask. Couldn't think of anything, my brain a puddle of mush hyped up on the adrenaline coursing through me.

"We are not killers," Sammy said.

Now Johnny laughed. "Oh, really? Might want to tell that to the poor woman whose face was blown to bits at Dreamscape Manor!"

"She was already being dead."

"How? Who?"

Kelsey answered, "Some *zhenshchina* who died at woman's shelter in city west of here."

"Grand Rapids?" I asked in disbelief.

Johnny mumbled, "From one of PGFG's recent buys?"

"*Da*. The woman had died of drug overdose."

It clicked. The oxycontin found in that woman lying in Junction PD's morgue!

Johnny asked, "So, what, you used her body as a double?"

The woman said nothing, going silent.

My head swam with the revelation. A frightening thought surfaced.

I said, "And stuffed the murder weapon down my chimney?"

One end of her mouth rose, and she crossed her arms. Whether in satisfaction or surprise I'd connected the dots, it wasn't clear. What was, was that Ma's caretakers had framed me.

And almost gotten away with it.

"What are you going to do?" asked Sammy.

Johnny replied, "I'm going to take you two jokers with me, that's what."

"You must be having a joke!" Kelsey said.

He raised his Colt, leveling it with his waist and motioning with it to communicate his clear intentions.

"Consider this a citizen's arrest," he went on. "Now, step away from Florence."

Sammy raised his fists and growled. "I have better idea."

Johnny snorted. "Really, kid? What's that?"

"We fight like men. *Chelovek protiv cheloveka!*"

Now he smirked. "So that's the way this is gonna play out. Some *mano-y-mano* fistfight?"

Sammy growled again, spitting to the side and bending in for a street fight-style encounter I wasn't ready for.

Johnny shook his head. "Thanks for the invitation, kid, but I'm gonna take a hard pass on that one."

Then he shot him in the kneecap. Just once.

It's all it took to bring the brute down.

Like Goliath, with that one stone, right between the eyes.

The man screamed out in agony before clutching his leg. Blood gushed from the wound between his fingers, and—again, like Goliath of Gath—down the man went in a cussing fit.

Kelsey was a different story.

She lunged for Johnny with a feral fierceness he didn't see coming. Nearly popped off a shot, but he held fast.

I worried he would hit Ma, who was still and unconscious, completely oblivious to what was going on around her.

A flash of light glinted in the darkness.

A blade. Sharp and swiping and nearly slicing Johnny's nose off!

Then again.

And now a cry of pain.

Kelsey had sliced through his trench coat, a long, clean cut oozing crimson across his upper arm. Sending my P.I. tumbling back into a cart of equipment. Instruments and supplies, bottles and boxes, clattered to the floor as he fell.

And snapped me into activation.

I lunged for her, a yawping roar escaping me.

We connected, in an instant.

The suddenness of my attack threw her, and I managed to wrench a hand around her wrist holding the knife.

"*Nyet!*" she shouted, then growled something else that sounded like she was cussing up a storm.

I held fast, whipping her around, away from Ma who was just sleeping away on that bed without an ounce of awareness.

Kelsey struggled, a wicked, feral cat that wouldn't give up without a fight. And, really, more like a lioness, her strength surprising, her resolve scrappy and self-preserving.

She jerked the knife down, then again, her arm almost wriggling from my grip and brushing against my hip—nearly connecting with my abdomen and spilling my guts.

I tightened my grip, then did something unexpected.

In a single motion, I wrenched her arm toward her stomach, slipped a foot behind her ankle, and put my full weight against her.

Sending both of us tumbling to the floor.

Me on top.

Her on the bottom.

And a soft, sinking feeling beneath me, with the weapon's grip jabbing into my gut.

I winced and scrambled off from her, raising my fists to prepare for a defense.

She looked stunned, her eyes wide and mouth wider, gasping for breath. Gurgling really.

That's when I saw it.

The blade had sunk into the middle of her chest, at the base of her ribcage. Looked like it was protruding from her diaphragm, the handle bouncing up and down with each struggling breath.

I stepped back, watching her reach for air—taking some

satisfaction she was drowning in her own blood after what she had pulled.

Didn't take long before she went still.

Dead. Just like that.

Sammy groaned, clutching his shattered knee. I paid him no mind. Didn't even worry about Johnny, who was easing from the floor with a firm hand pressed against his upper arm.

All that mattered was Ma.

Johnny nodded toward her, grunting, "Go on, kid. Check on your mother."

I darted to her, not having a clue what to do, how to help.

"Ma!" I screamed. "You alright?"

She didn't wake.

All I could do was offer some words of reassurance as I slipped out my phone and dialed 911.

"You're found. You're safe. You're alright. Please be alright!"

Lord Almighty, let her be alright...

No sooner had I said those words did Junction PD show up, barreling into the joint with guns drawn and shouting at us to show our hands, acting all heroic, like they'd saved the day. Then Chief Roller arrived, followed by Jamie Ramos and several EMT nurses or doctors or specialists or whoever they were called. Even Reggie and Lizzy muscled their way inside.

They managed to bring Ma back to consciousness, waking her with some syringe of something. Then they got to work checking her over and hooking her up to an IV to get fluids rolling.

Ramos said she wanted to debrief her. I told her to "Go to hell!" Reggie's cooler head prevailed, taking over as her attorney and saying we'd make her available as soon as she was ready to speak. Which, as far as I was concerned, was sometime next kiss-my-backside after the way that woman had bungled this whole thing from the start.

Those EMT guys and gals spent a good hour with her, checking vitals and pumping her with fluids and antibiotics and vitamins—as well as Narcan. Apparently, Ma had been sedated with the same OxyContin that had killed that other woman serving as her double. They had tried to take her to Mercy General, but Ma no-sired-and-no-ma'amed them into giving up the fight and settling on a promise to go to the emergency room. Instead, we decamped to our office back in town.

Reggie drove as Ma and me rode in the back. I just held her, and she just rested against my arm, silent and still. But alive.

Lord Jesus Christ, Son of God, thank you she's alive...

Didn't take long before we were parked and heading upstairs to the law offices of *O'Donnell, Seward, and Wilson.* Thank the good Lord above our air was back on, same for the lights. It was cool and not all that humid, that musty basement smell gone, replaced by paper and toner and burnt coffee, the smells of my practice.

I helped Ma inside and down to my office. She didn't say much, and I was surprised she didn't finger-wag how messy it was. Lizzy and Johnny helped clear my couch of files, and Reggie fetched some water while I helped Ma lie down. Returning, Reggie handed off a cold glass to me, and I held it to Ma's lips. She drank it dry.

"Thank you, sugar," she said, voice raspy and weak and not at all sounding like my mother.

A fresh wave of emotion roiled through me, and I thought I might break, then and there. I swallowed it back and held it together. I needed to for her sake, because there was lots still to get through.

As much as I wanted her to rest, to sleep the next week

away, there was an active investigation underway. Not only with Mill Creek Junction PD and Dean Lawlor's prosecuting attorney's office, but with me.

I wanted answers, because I wanted revenge.

The Good Book might caution *'Vengeance is mine; I will repay, says the Lord,'* but I've also been told the good Lord helps those who help themselves. Yeah, sure, that was Ben Franklin instead of Saint Paul, but I was a firm believer in the mutual cooperation of the Almighty and humanity enacting justice on earth as it is in heaven.

Especially when one's mama was thought to have been murdered—by you!—before being found as kidnapped and left for dead.

So I took my mother's hand, leaned in, and got to work.

"What happened, Ma?" I asked, gentle but insistent.

She scoffed. "I was taken, that's what!"

"But how?"

"I'm not sure. One minute I was gettin' my Jessica Fletcher on, snatching the last piece of the Dreamscape puzzle."

"Knew I liked this one!" Lizzy said, grinning.

I pressed, "Then what happened?"

"Then, well, the rest is fuzzy," Ma replied. "There was a rustlin' and a shufflin', then a pinprick at my neck. Next thing I knew it was lights out and I woke up to you all!"

Rage flashed livid through me. Part of me was glad Kelsey had died with a knife thrust to her chest!

"We have reason to believe," Johnny said, "you were targeted."

She said nothing, eyes casting down.

"And we have a good reason why," I said, taking her hand. She looked at me, and I continued, "What were you doing with those documents?"

There was a look in her eyes. Not of denial or deflection,

like she would try and get out of what was plain. Rather, a twinkle in those pools of dark brown I had known since childhood. Not a lie, not something she was hiding.

A truth.

I wasn't sure I was ready to hear it.

She plowed forward anyway, telling her story.

Chapter Thirty-Eight

Florence O'Donnell was a proud woman who had lived two lifetimes over. What she had seen, what she had endured, because of her ancestry, was enough for one lifetime.

Then she had to up and get wrapped up in a global conspiracy of epic proportions! All because Herb got the mental bug.

Damn d'mencha. For more reasons than the one that took the love of her life. The other was that it had almost taken hers. The hundreds more was for all those others Perses had destroyed. Which was fitting.

Because in her research, she had stumbled upon a golden nugget of factoid truth: in Greek mythology, Perses was the Titan god of destruction.

Boy, had that group of vultures destroyed more than just the lives they were entrusted to care for. They'd destroyed entire industries. And I'd aimed to put a stop to it.

Still would. But first, story time.

Clearing her throat, Florence began:

I EASED MY ESCALADE TO THE SQUAWK BOX ANCHORED TO the driver's side in front of a wrought-iron gate that meant business. One of those large double-door security measures I had only seen from Keeping Up with the Kardashians, my guilty pleasure since making the transition to single life. Or, well, single-living life. Anyhoo, now those double-doors were part of my weekly routine, me rolling up to the tune of "Root Down," one of Herb's fave Jimmy Smith tunes, a rollicking, vibey song that opened with a bit of bass before rolling into a rat-a-tatting intro and a electric guitar solo that handed off the mic to that Hammond organ I'd fallen for all those years ago.

Alice Coltrane was more my style, sticking with the sisterhood of the traveling pantsuits, before that was a thing. Much more preferred the queen of jazz to her king husband John Coltrane than Jimmy Smith, her Wurlitzer organ something to sing about. But Herb was a true rhythm-n-blues soul to my more New Agey fusion jazz tastes. Which was why I'd listened to "Root Down" on repeat for the fifty-minute drive from the cornfields of Mill Creek to the lakeshore Herb had always longed to live on. He'd gotten his wish in a way I'da never wish on my worst enemy.

I rolled down my window to announce my arrival—

And got a slobbering kiss of Poseidon's nasty-nasty spraying me in the face! The frigid breath of rainwater whirlin' and twirlin' from the storm done ruined my makeup and hair, soaking the front of my silver silk gown—right down to my bosom!

Had to have looked like the north end of a southbound bear, which made me want to cuss and ask the Lawd Almighty for forgiveness after the fact. But God don't like ugly, especially cussing ugly. And neither did Herb, so I kept my trapper shut and got to my business.

"Florence O'Donnell to see Herb O'Donnell," I shouted, then promptly rolled my window back up nice and tight.

Could hear the intercom crackle to life and some Gigolo Joe ask for my name again as a clap of thunder rumbled overhead. Which meant I had to roll down my window again. And get a face full of nasty nasty again. Ruining my makeup and hair. Again!

Do I look like boo boo the fool?

No ma'am and no sir. I cracked it enough to offer a second helping of my announcement, then goosed the caddy a pinch, letting my horn do most of the talking instead of repeating myself a third time.

He got the message. A beat later, the gate swung open, and I scooted through toward destiny.

It was after noon now, but you wouldn't know it. Dark and foreboding it was, the February sun angled at the south struggling for a hearing through thick shelf clouds layered like navy and violet macaroons, a whole mess of 'em just stacked one on top of the other rolling up on shore. That's how Herb would've described it, anyway, his favorite dessert always finding their way into this or that metaphor. Or was it simile? Could never get that one right. Herb could, when he was well.

The cuckoo's nest loomed large beyond the gate. Sort of felt bad these past years thinking of Herb's d'mencha resort as Jack Nicholson's own sad story. But the dang thing looked like that same red brick monstrosity. Gave me the heebie-jeebie creepies, it did! Then there was the other part of it.

Lake Michigan.

I always hated the lakeshore. Not to be confused with the seashore, no ma'am and no sir! I knew the difference, and they were a world of difference.

Perhaps my special sort of snoot was to be expected. I was a Jersey girl, after all. Naw, not Palisades Park or Edgewater. Much too bougie for my black blood. I'm talking Trenton, which might as well be a borough of Philly, given it butts against the City of Brotherly Love. Or hate, depending on what side of the tracks you lived on.

Regardless, I knew what real beaches were. The sorts my family hit up several times each summer. With piers and Ferris wheels, with elephant ears fried and dusted in sugar and spice, and big teddy bears a man's man would win for his girl after swinging a twenty-pound sledge hammer on a high striker while proving his manhood.

Not these sorts of Midwest imitations. No ma'am and no sir! None of those piers and Ferris wheels in these parts. Definitely no elephant ears and certainly no high strikers or brawny fellas flexing what God gave 'em.

For Herb, my other half, who I always considered my better half—for him, this was how he'd wanted to go. Perched in a room overlooking Lake Michigan, marveling at the setting sun inflaming the horizon, waiting for Old Man Winter to work his magic spinning up a magical winter wonderland of solid ice sheets stacked high and proud or set the waters seething and spitting something fierce.

Speaking of which...

Today was a special kind of nasty. A bitter, biting rain lashed livid and angry against the windshield as I parked. It was the sort of weather that hurt your face and your feelings, like getting a good mama smack across the face at getting too mouthy.

Now I really worried about my silk dress with the way the rain was sheeting, that I'd turn a few heads with my wet bosom.

All that mattered, though, was getting inside to see my hubby boo boo with my box of chocolates. Dark chocolate-

covered cherries drowning in cordial sauce that would curl Herb's toes!

I shut down the caddy, snatched Herb's box of chocolates and my umbrella from behind the passenger's seat, wrapped a pink shawl over my shoulders then went for broke—darting out into the storm as thunder clapped overhead, racing through double doors that whooshed open.

"Oo-wee, if the creek don't rise and the Lawd Almighty wills it..." Got that backwards, but it seemed to fit the way the day had turned.

Couldn't wait to see my man! Fifty years...what an accomplishment.

Just hoped he was lucid enough to remember I was his wife!

My first stop was Trevor at the check-in counter. I tossed the beanpole in white a friendly howdy-do and asked for my main squeeze.

Signing in, I made some small talk about our anniversary, giving the box of chocolates a jiggle, and about how the Lawd Almighty was raining down the funk. He agreed and rang for Herb's nurse to find my husband.

A few huhs and that's funnies and I'll let her knows and Trevor ended the call.

He announced. "Looks like your main squeeze is missing, Mrs. O'Donnell."

"What the what? Missing?"

"Well, not missing missing." Trevor laughed. "Just misplaced, that's all. We've been a bit understaffed lately, and Caitlyn hasn't checked on him in a while it sounds."

"Really..."

"Nothing to worry about!" Trevor quickly added. "She's just had lots of other residents to attend to. She said he's around here somewhere, and she'll search for him in a jiff after her round is finished."

"How long will that be?"

A shrug, a clearing of his throat, a "dunno" before telling me I was free to find my husband myself.

You bet your skinny white backside I'm free to find my husband myself!

I offered a thank you and strode off through the dark wood-lined atrium into the main fellowship hall in search of my man.

The wet wood smell that had saturated the joint seemed especially pungent today, joined by wet dog and wet newspapers and—well, wet! To be expected, I supposed, but I hoped it didn't put a damper on our day. An excitement bubbled up now as I entered the vast hall where residents played mean games of gin rummy and canasta, or gathered for weekly watercolor and oil painting lessons, even for ballroom dancing. Never cared for that, but Herb did, so I joined him anyhow. In fact, I had a little surprise in my bosom special for tonight.

A candle light dinner in his room with...that's right: ballroom dancing! Well, dancing dancing, in his room. His nurse, Miss Caitlyn, had arranged for the special dose of anniversary love. And I couldn't wait to surprise him!

So I shuffled faster, clickety-clacking across the hardwood in hot pink stilettos that made my dress scream even louder.

Grinning from ear to ear, I strode into the main gathering hall searching for Herb, box of chocolates in hand. The gentle kiss of chocolate and peanut butter replaced the wet wood and musty basement smell now, riding on a warmth that felt cozy coming in from the rain. Baking cookies, the staff getting ready for midafternoon tea and coffee time, I reckoned. Soft conversations and laughter floated toward me from tables arranged around the vast space vaulted two stories with a bay of windows overlooking Lake Michigan.

A flash of white flickered like my daddy's Kodak 35mm camera. With a crash vibrating through the vast sitting room where the residents busied themselves. Windows, floor to ceiling, peered out onto the seething lake, the well-manicured lawn and gardens, their green grass and multi-colored flowers, all obscured by rain sheeting down the glass.

Herb would be agitated, I just knew it! Would ruin the whole day. Not that he minded the thunder or the rain or the lightning. He minded the view. Or rather, would mind there wasn't one!

So I shuffled as best my sexagenarian legs could take me on those pink stilettos.

I went from table to table, but no hubby boo boo. Caught sight of Herb's roommate, Lawrence, sitting in his wheelchair, balloon in one hand, a glass of sweet tea in the other wrapped by a folded paper towel that had soaked through with perspiration. I went to offer a hidey-ho when—

I caught the oddest sight.

His hands were stained an orangey color. Like he'd plumb slaughtered a chicken!

The one hand clutching the balloon was stained a sickly orangey red. Looked like blood.

Odd...

I leaned in for a look-see—

When glass smacked against glass from behind!

I gasped and spun and clutched a hand against my chest. A wicked, hissing breath of frigid air sent a door that led outside bucking something fierce.

Had to admit, I let loose a cuss that would make my ladies Bible study gals blush with opened-mouth surprise. But oh my heck did that surprise send me sailing from my skin!

And also skittering to secure the door since nobody but nobody who was on the clock seemed to be around. How a door could be left unsecured like that—with all these residents, with their conditions, with this storm raging!

Had half a mind to chew out the director, but I still had a mission.

Finding Herb.

I kept on clickety-clacking through the hall, searching high and low for my hubby boo boo.

Still no Herb. Must be at lunch.

I left the hall and clattered back across the scuffed hardwood floors into the dining room. Coffee and cheesy eggs and bacon still hung heavy from the morning, joined by something tomatoey and grilled cheesy. Probably just that: grilled cheese and tomato soup. Herb's fave! Surely he'd be around here somewhere.

Except—

Clickety-clacking through the dining hall, I went from wood table to wood table, all stained a nice honey brown and lined neatly in four rows, six to a row with the same number of sturdy padded chairs on either side. A few stragglers finished tiny bowls of tomato soup and chomped into burned grilled cheese sandwiches. The service sure had done and gone downhill since Herb had started.

She recalled handmade sandwiches to order for lunch, with carved meats and fresh steamed veggies, all made to order and prepared in portions that serviced each table. Now they were lucky to get golden grilled cheese sandwiches instead of the hockey pucks she saw the last remaining retired folks gnawing into.

And no Herb.

More of those windows overlooked Lake Michigan, a dock jutting out from shore overwhelmed by crashing waves and now looking like a popsicle. In fact...

I squinted and craned for a better look-see.

Yup, just what I feared.

Snow.

No ma'am and no sir would I want to stay much longer if

the drive home to Mill Creek Junction was going to be a frigid mess of sloppy, slushy snow! But we had dinner plans, and Herb was missing. I needed to find him. Stat!

Only place I could think of was his room. Looking at the time, I supposed that made sense, the day cresting toward midafternoon when he took his quarterly nap. So I beelined it for room 2341, in the second wing, down the third hallway toward the lakeside. He loved that room, sharing it with Lawrence, the pair getting along well for too old coots losing their marbles.

Reaching the door, I punched in the key code at the lock, a special open-sesame for caregivers, then gave a knock and opened the door.

A stuffy, stinky heat heavy with body order smacked me upside the head! Without a trace of Herb. Instead, I found Fido lying where I expected my hubby boo boo. That's right, Fido. As in the Shih Tzu I had gotten him to keep him company. He was an avid Civil War buff, particularly obsessed with good ol' Honest Abe. He'd pestered me for a short-haired golden something or other, like President Lincoln had had. For years, I'd said no, on account of allergies and the size of the thing and cleaning up its doodoo.

Too bad it took him getting the mental bug for me to finally relent. Not one to moan about the past. What's done and dusted way back when is in the way-back-when, and all that jazz. But denying Herb a companion while he was still lucid...

That still kept me up at night.

I shook away the thought and hustled to the thermostat. "What the hot Hades is going on..."

Would've dropped my dentures had I had 'em at the sight I saw.

"Eighty degrees?" I exclaimed.

No way would Herb have stood for that temp! I could barely convince the man to heat our double-wide to sixty-eight. Said to *put on more layers if I was too cold. Was one of those on-again-off-again arguments he and I would have.*

So what the what was that about?

I turned it down to a more comfy seventy and huffed a cuss Herb and the Lawd Almighty himself would surely finger-wag. Didn't care. All I did was finding my husband.

And on our wedding anniversary!

Maybe I missed him back in the fellowship hall. Like two ships passing in the night, me going one way and him going another. It was nearing that tea and cookie break. Herb was never one to miss his coffee and cookies. Something we shared, actually, the two of us with our cups o' joe.

So off I went, taking Fido with me this time and hustling back to the fellowship hall.

"Where are you, Herb?"

The faint echo of a scream suddenly flared, down the hall. Then another, followed by shouts of confusion—and was that fear?

"What the what?"

I hustled faster, reaching the vast room to find a huddled bunch of folks in sweaters and skirts. A real crowd had gathered at the far end down by the wall of glass streaked by rainwater, muttering and pointing out the window.

No, not the window.

Out the door. The same one I'd shut that had been flapping in the breeze earlier.

What the what?

I beelined it for the group, sure as the nose on my face that Herb would be among the gawkers.

Herb and I had taken many walks out that door and onto the soft grass. He always went barefoot. Said he loved the feel of the blades against his toes. I'da always complained, not being the nature-loving type. But he insisted, and persisted, and I relented, slipping off my stilettos and giggling like a school girl as we romped across the lawn and down into the sand, sinking our toes into powder dry—

"Sweet baby Jesus Lawd Almighty!" I gasped as I reached the door.

Then threw it open again, the glass door swinging open with a livid smack!

There was a body.

On the lawn!

Chapter Thirty-Nine

I gasped and cussed again, not giving a lick this time.

Could hardly see anything from that distance. What I could see was a man black and stiff and dressed in lime green jammies. Hair was short, down to within a half inch of the scalp. And those jammies looked soaked through, and actually frozen.

Looking way too familiar...

"Herb?" I screamed.

Then dashed out into the pouring rain, the sheeting, frigid water actually hurting my face far more than my feelings. The rain had frozen now, turning to sleet that felt like bullets pelting my face and bare arms.

What came next surely made up for it.

As I approached, my stilettos sinking into the wet ground with a squishy suck, I saw something lying on the ground a foot away. A large tree branch, broken and jagged and covered in something at one end, dark and shimmery in the dim light.

I knew, then and there, what was a possibility was surely a probability.

Still...I had to check. Had to make sure.

But I couldn't.

Couldn't take another trembling step from the fear of the moment and the frigid cold. Wanted to ask if it was Herb, if it was him, pleading with him to tell me that he was alright.

Four men rushed past instead, shouts of alarm and screams all around.

Which sent me rushing forward. Didn't get far.

Strong hands grabbed me, from behind.

I screamed, then spun around to face the threat.

It was Roland, one of Herb's attendants.

"It's alright, Mrs. O'Donnell. I gotchu."

Roland Richardson was like the younger brother Herb had never had, a few decades younger but kind and good and care-takery.

He had grabbed me by the shoulders, yanking me back. Now he pushed around to my front and held me firm, not letting me past.

"Let me go, Roland," I screamed. "I need to see for myself!"

Not that I could see much anyhow through the four atten-dants hunched over the body in the wet, freezing grass.

God was raining down the funk something fierce now, a mixture of rain and frozen ice shards, confirmed by a rowdy rumble of thunder that shook my shawl loose.

"Let them do their thing, Mrs. O'Donnell," Roland pleaded.

I did, but I didn't like it.

Time crawled, one minute stretching into the next as the men worked on—well, whoever it was. I lost all sense of things. My world was crumbling before my eyes, my vision clouded by rainwater and my trembling cold body.

Finally, one of the men in white lumbered over, a short, squat fella, knees muddied and stained green, what little black hair he had struggled for a hearing on a mostly bald head matted to the side, rainwater seeping down his forehead past downcast eyes and dripping off a knobby nose into a frowning, well-groomed comb mustache that spelled nothing good.

He approached, head held low and eyes not connecting with mine.

"We did all—" a hitch in Squat Fella's throat intercepted the verdict.

They did all they could. That's what he was fixin' to tell me. All they could to revive Herb.

Who knew how long he had been out there. I wanted to remember him warm and cuddly and alive.

Not—

Now a hitch in my own throat intercepted the possibility that was a probability of anyone spending the night outside, face-down in the grass, in the middle of a lakeshore midwinter rainstorm surviving.

Herb had always loved the lakeshore. Dipping his toes in Lake Michigan, skipping rocks across the waves, sending a line out into its churning depths for lake perch.

Now I had another reason to hate it.

How could this have happened?

No way in hot Hades would I let this go unchecked.

And unpunished.

Time to get to work.

About the only thing that had grounded him these past few years was that lake, seething beyond that beach, the whitecaps especially angry that afternoon beneath engorged storm clouds, dark with fury and spittin' angry.

I understood completely.

A spiderwebby streak of purply lightning lanced through the heavens before a clap of thunder rattled the brittle panes of old mansion glass a few yards from where Herb had been found. God sure was raining down the funk now, the mid-winter rain-

storm getting its sleet and hail on now. White pebbles scattered across the hibernating grass, covering Herb's place of last repose.

Good riddance.

I turned away, purpose and mission driving me to take matters into my own hands. Because if there's anything my people have learned, it's that the police weren't ever around when you needed 'em, and always around when you didn't.

Oh, they had turned up and made a show of things, stringing their yellow DO NOT CROSS tape around this tree and that tree, right after they zipped up Herb in a black rubber bag and loaded him up on a yellow gurney and wheeled him off the grass and through the fellowship hall and into an awaiting ambulance to take him away to the medical examiner. Some large, brawny man with a comb-over and comb mustache names Sergeant Crenshaw assured me they would do all they could to get to the bottom of what had happened.

Except I already knew what had happened.

Because I had seen the large log resting next to where Herb had laid, the end bloody and jagged and looking like it had connected with the back of his head! About the size of a broom handle and as thick as a man's forearm. Would've done some real damage against a skull, cracking it and rendering him unconscious—killing him even.

So, no ma'am and no sir. I knew exactly what had happened.

Someone had killed my Herb.

Whether intentionally or on accident, through someone whacking Herb upside the head or from sheer negligence, a d'mencha addled man wandering outside in the dead of winter and getting felled by a raging storm—none of it mattered. What did was who was responsible for it all. And I aimed to find out while the police played tiddlywinks.

I'd shed enough tears till my eyes ran dry and throat ran raw. Herb didn't need my sorrow. He needed justice.

Which I aimed to give—sealed, signed, delivered.

First stop: Caitlyn, his nurse.

So I slipped out from the fellowship hall, where all the investigative hubbub was going down. No one noticed, the residents having been sent back to their rooms and the staff securing the rest of the building. No doubt making sure no other d'mencha patient wandered outside and wound up dead!

When I arrived at room 2341, Caitlyn was inside—sitting on his bed! Back to me with Fido in her lap, a hand stroking his lonely head.

Anger welled within. At her being where she didn't belong. At her incompetence!

Had half a mind to march inside and give her a piece of my Jersey girl mind. My anger waned when I realized she was crying. Sobbing, her eyes puffy and running over, lip quivering and muttering something I couldn't hear.

Taking a breath, then a beat, I went to step inside to get my answers when I heard a psst echo down the hall.

I spun back toward where I'd come.

When a head poked out of a room, and a jutting arm motioned for me to skedaddle their way.

What the what?

I'd really wanted to speak to Caitlyn, but she didn't look like she was in any mood or condition to have a chit-chat with the victim's freshly crowned widow.

So off I skedaddled, looking back over my shoulder to make sure I was in the clear. I cringed at the clickety-clacking of my stilettos echoing through the hallway, but it didn't take long before I'd rounded the bend into a darkened, vacant room—

And the door slammed shut behind me!

I screamed.

Someone shushed me. Then the lights flashed bright.

And Roland Richardson, one of his attendants, was putting a finger up to his mouth to reiterate his command.

"You scared me half to death!"

"Sorry, Mrs. O'Donnell. I didn't know what else to do. Knew you'd be coming round looking to have a talk with Caitlyn, and I wanted to catch you before you did."

"Darn right I came around looking to have a talk with Caitlyn! She let my husband wander outside in a bleepin' thunderstorm!"

"I understand you're angry, hurting, but it wasn't her fault."

"Then whose fault was it!" I yelled, instantly regretting the outburst.

Roland shrank, which was quite the feat, given he towered over me at six-foot-something, all neck and major cannons for arms.

"I'm sorry for your loss," he said softly. "I loved Herb. Loved him like he was my uncle."

Emotion clenched my throat and sprang to my eyes. I batted it away and swallowed. Not now. Mourning would come later.

I managed, "Do you know how this might've happened?"

"Stuff like this has been happening a lot lately."

"What, people dying on your lawn?"

"No! I mean mishaps. The wrong medication being given. People falling getting to the bathroom when they should've had help. Doors being unlocked and people wandering off campus. Crazy crap like that that's almost cost us our license a time or twelve."

That was surprising. "How? CareBridge was such a well-oiled machine. It's why Gideon and I jumped at the chance to put Herb here, under your care."

Roland ran a frustrated hand across his bald head. "All I know is that ever since we were bought out, we've been terribly understaffed thanks to budget cuts."

I smirked. "Yeah, I noticed in the dining hall. Those grilled cheese sandwiches looked like hockey pucks! Your chefs must've gotten pink slips."

"That ain't the half of it! Nurses used to manage five rooms, ten residents. Now it's an entire floor! And us attendants would support them, doing the heavy lifting and moving and watching out for problems. Now we got an entire wing to manage!"

The revelation irritated me, angered me even. But none of this was getting me closer to what happened—and who might have happened it.

"And..." Roland went on before his sentence died.

"And what?" I pressed.

He frowned. "Now, I shouldn't be saying this. Patient confidentiality and all..."

"Spill the tea, Roland!"

"Well, the other night, I overheard an argument between Herb and Lawrence."

"A roommate spat?"

He nodded. "About owing him money from some card game."

"What, like gambling?"

"And apparently quite a lot of money. Threatened to do some real damage to him if he didn't pay up."

"Damage? What sort?"

"Caitlyn and I heard the threats but brushed them off as crazy talk. No disrespect, ma'am, knowing your own husband's...condition."

I waved him off, considering the revelation.

"You're saying Lawrence threatened to...what, clobber him? Upside the head?"

Roland nodded again, saying nothing.

But saying everything that needed to be said.

Which made not a lick of sense! I couldn't wrap my mind

around the turn. The two had been best buds since being paired up. And Lawrence, threatening violence in this way...it was so out of character for him! Sure he was cranky as a cat in heat, but he was always so mild-mannered. Knew the mental bug could make people do cray-cray—

I gasped.

And remembered.

"Those hands..."

"Hands, Mrs. O'Donnell?"

I said nothing, recalling those hands!

Lawrence's. Stained some sort of orange or—blood red!

"Thanks, Roland. Gotta jet!"

And I did, the man protesting, but I paid him no mind. All that mattered was those hands.

Which I found right where I left 'em. Back in the fellowship hall after leaving Roland in my clickety-clacking dust. Still holding that balloon.

I grabbed his hand. He protested. Expected a sticky feel to the hand but all I got was a softness from light labor. He tried yanking it back; I wouldn't let him. Instead, I eased down, bringing it close to my face for a look-see. And, to be honest, a smell-see. Working in a hospital most of my life, even in accounting, I got to know the tangy, metalicy scent of blood.

"Unhand me, young lady!"

Young lady. Had to smile at that.

"Not just yet, Lawrence..."

Coming in for a closer smell, I sensed neither and really didn't sense anything beyond lotion and soap. And coming in for a closer view, the thicker crimson I expected was more an orangey stain.

Agatha joined me, Herb's gin rummy playing buddy. I hated to ask, but I did anyway. Knowing what I knew, the dustup that had happened between Lawrence and Herb, the words that were exchanged—the threat...

I just had to ask: "Does that look like blood to you?"

"No, dear," Agatha answered, not even waiting a beat. "That's just Lawrence getting careless with the watercolors. He painted a beautiful sunset over Lake Michigan last night. Really captured the horizon, all crimson and whatnot. Look, it's hanging up at the back."

I followed her pointer. Sure enough. There was the painting. And not a bad one at that. Yet I still had questions.

"Well, where were you last night?" I questioned Lawrence.

He jerked a thumb Agatha's direction. "With her."

I turned to her. "With you?"

Agatha blushed, saying nothing.

"All night?"

Now she shrugged. "A woman has needs. Even at my age."

"I see..."

I let go of his hand now, happy to have checked off a lead but also disappointed in not getting an answer. I had more work to do. Time to go straight to the top of this sorry joint.

I left Lawrence and his paint-stained hands and marched over to the headmaster over CareBridge.

Doctor Murdoch, the third, as he introduced himself when I barged through past his perky blond secretary, motioned for me to sit in an oversized leather chair. He sat in another, then reached for a silver tea set ready for use on a glass coffee table.

The office was spacious and tastefully decorated, walls lined with bookcases and a large desk sitting before a bay of windows. Murdoch was a trim man in a blue pinstripe suit with an emerald bowtie. Pouring himself some tea, he conveyed his condolences for my loss.

Stuff your condolences in a sack, I wanted to say. But didn't. Instead, I went fishing.

"What happened, Mr. Murdoch?"

He smiled, saying nothing.

"Tea, Mrs. O'Donnell?"

"Florence is fine. And no."

"Very well, Florence."

He leaned back and raised his pinkie as he sipped from a white tea cup, closing his eyes and taking a breath before completing the ritual.

Which I interrupted: "Mr. Murdoch."

He startled, snapping his eyes open.

"No pun intended, but: spill the tea, wouldya? What happened?"

Murdoch set down the tea cup with a clatter.

"Happened?" he asked, as if dumber than dirt.

"To. My. Husband," I said with emphasis.

He waved a hand and crossed a leg. "He wandered out into the cold. What else? An unfortunate accident that breaks our heart."

I narrowed my eyes. Breaks your heart, my backside!

"How could that have happened?" I pressed.

"I suppose someone left the door unlocked. Although, we do allow residents to roam freely. You understand, don't you? Because you signed the contract stipulating the free-range philosophy we employ at CareBridge."

That sure raised my hackles. Signed the contract?

I took a breath, asking, "But where was the staff? Why weren't they supervising Herb? Roland said you've been terribly understaffed the past several months. Something about budget cuts?"

A blink, then a flinching of the eyes, stage right before snatching back that tea cup and taking a sip.

He didn't like that one bit.

So I didn't let up the gas: "And what is this about some outside entity buying you up?"

Now he choked. Which, truth be told, did my pea pickin' heart real right.

Murdoch excused himself and coughed some more, turning a shade of white before an irritated crimson.

He finally recovered and said, "I can't speak to that, you understand. Confidentiality and all. But as far as we're concerned, what happened to Herb O'Donnell is a most unfortunate incident that has never in all the years this institution has been in existence ever happened before. He stepped outside, of his own accord, and—"

"Died. Was murdered, even."

"Now I take issue with that characterization! Yes, he passed. But he was not murdered."

"How do you know? He was whacked upside the head!"

"I have it on good authority that the detective investigating is ruling it an accident."

That took me aback. Hadn't heard that. And I didn't know what to say.

"So there's nothing more you can do?" I pressed further: "Nothing you will do?"

He flashed a pained grin, teeth hidden behind thin lips. "I really am sorry for your loss, Mrs. O'Donnell."

Dr. Murdoch stood and motioned for the door. I hesitated, wanting—more, dang it! More empathy and sympathy. More answers.

Wanting my hubby boo boo back!

But I knew it was a useless effort at all of the above.

So stood I did, and out I walked.

Into the night after a day from hot Hades.

Chapter Forty

Wasn't long before I awoke with a start. Arms flailing, eyes darting about a darkened room, forgetting where I was.

The faint scent of cigarettes baked into the walls and carpet reminded me.

A cheapie motel down the road from CareBridge. After giving up my interrogations, and also being gently told I should let the police do their job, I crashed for the night in a Motel 66, hopping mad the police seemed to be dragging their feet and feeling like everybody was giving me the runaround. A full day had passed by and still no answers, no suspects who I could finger to blame for Herb's death.

His—

I couldn't bear the word, couldn't breathe the word.

A phone call on my cell intercepted it. It was a 231 area code, so a local number. I answered.

"Is this Florence O'Donnell?" a woman with a Hispanic accent asked.

"Yes, it is."

"Hello, Mrs. O'Donnell. My name is Detective Olivia Ortega, with the Muskegon Police Department."

My heart both sank and soared. Sank, because the police calling meant they'd found something about Herb's death. Soared, because that meant answers."

I managed an "Alright" which led to the detective asking if I would be able to come into the station. Which sent all the hairs on my arms standing at spidey-sense attention. Almost hung up, then and there, and rang up Gideon for legal help. Instead, I asked if I needed a lawyer.

The detective replied, "You are not a suspect, Mrs. O'Donnell, but you may certainly bring one if you would like."

Before I could hem and haw, she said there was a development thanks to the medical examiner's report that shed light on Herb's death, that we can discuss the findings if I could come down to the station.

Now my stomach sank beneath the mattress. Death? Why not murder? What had they found?

Answers, that's what. And that's what I'd been searching for the past day.

So I said I'd be there within the hour and set about getting ready for those answers.

The drive was cold and short, ten minutes that stretched into twenty thanks to piles of lake effect snow that wrecked the area. Drive was sort of nice, winding along the shoreline until the road jutted off into the city. The lake wasn't frozen, not like you would think it would be in the dead of a Midwest winter. Lake Michigan's waters were too warm for freezing.

A pier was frozen over, though, one Herb and I would walk together during the summertime. It was his pier, from what felt like ages ago now. The two of us had walked it umpteen times, salted pretzels doused by mustard in one hand and soda pop in the other (me, Coke; Herb, Dr Pepper). Herb had taken Gideon fishing off that pier for a decade, father and son bonding over their shared love of the lake.

Now all that was left of those memories were the jagged slabs of frozen water piled high along the shoreline giving me a flashback of yesterday, seeing Herb all stiff and frozen and—

The word dead hung heavy.

So I cranked a local gospel station on the radio and raced toward destiny.

The police station looked like any other station you'd imagine. One level, functional cinder block monstrosity painted brown, fluorescent lights inside giving me a wicked headache, with boys and girls in blue huddled in the hallways nursing cups of coffee.

One of those young boys helped me to a conference room when I introduced myself at the front desk. Asked if I wanted anything, coffee or water. I opted for water, feeling dehydrated from my investigative workout.

A few minutes later, Sergeant Crenshaw from yesterday returned with a bottle of Dasani, joined by a Hispanic woman in a crisp navy suit who introduced herself as Detective Ortega, the woman on the phone.

We exchanged pleasantries, her asking how I was doing and me asking her to get to it.

She smiled and did: "The medical examiner concludes that your husband was hit in the head—"

"See, I told ya'll! Someone killed my Herb!"

Ortega put up a hand. "Please, let me continue."

I huffed a sigh and crossed my arms, nodding for her to continue.

"What hit his head was a flying piece of debris."

My arms fell. What the what?

"I can confirm the piece of wood we found lying next to your husband was from a nearby tree. It must have cracked off from

the storm, and it matches the description of what we found lying next to Herb, the blood a match."

"Okaaaaay..."

"But that isn't what killed him. Ultimately, he died of hypothermia. Simple as that."

"No ma'am and no sir! My Herb is dead. My husband is dead—of fifty years yesterday! Ain't nothing simple 'bout that."

The detective shifted, throwing a glance at Sergeant Crenshaw before she answered.

He answered for her: "You're right. We apologize for the insensitive wording of the conclusion to our investigation."

"I apologize," Ortega corrected, "for my wording. What I meant to say was that your husband passed in the night from the frigid conditions, having been knocked unconscious by the piece of wood, leaving that gash in the back of his head and knocking him out cold. Then, well, the real cold took over and..."

She trailed off, leaving the obvious unsaid.

And he died.

I asked, "You're saying it was an act of God? All of it? Getting hit in the head, dying face down, after wandering outside in the dead of night, freezing to death—"

My tongue stumbled over itself as my throat constricted with emotion. It was quickly joined by my eyes flooding with the same.

"It appears that way," the sergeant said.

This wasn't adding up. No ma'am and no sir!

"What about CareBridge?" I asked, rage replacing sorrow.

"What about them?" Detective Ortega replied.

"Aren't they the ones ultimately responsible for his death?"

She looked at Sergeant Crenshaw again before replying, "I don't' understand your meaning."

"My meaning is, they freakin' left him unattended! I was

born at night but not last night. No way no one is responsible for Herb's death."

Sergeant Crenshaw replied, "I understand your frustration—"

I laughed with interruption. "No ma'am and no sir. You ain't begun to understand my frustration. Arrest somebody!"

"Unfortunately, that's not a matter for law enforcement."

"What the what? Why the bleepity-bleep not?"

"We can't arrest a corporation for negligence."

"What about the nurse who left him unattended? The head honcho who understaffed the blasted joint?"

Detective Ortega stepped back into the ring: "We're continuing to examine the evidence, to look at all possible angles on this to see whether a crime has been committed, and then explore possibly arresting and indicting anyone who might have been criminally liable for your husband's death."

I crossed my arms in a huff. "Don't let your mouth write a check your backside can't cash, sweetie..."

Sergeant Crenshaw said, "If I can be frank with you, ma'am, your best option is to litigate this in civil court. You certainly have a case for negligence, even negligent homicide."

"What do you mean?"

"Obviously I'm not a lawyer, and this isn't legal advice, but CareBridge itself, and its parent corporation, could be liable for damages for wrongful death. Civil proceedings in civil court could offer you a way to seek a level of compensation you can't get criminally, for your emotional distress and whatnot."

"Level of compensation? You mean financial compensation, don't you? Jeffersons and Benjamins?"

He nodded, saying nothing.

"Again, we're sorry we can't do anything more criminally, at least as it stands. Litigating his death in civil court is your best option at this point."

Oh, I'll litigate. Damn straight I'll litigate them into Timbuktu.

And I knew just who would take my case.

Done with those two, I stood, snatching that bottle of water I hadn't touched. I would take it on the road to hell if I had to.

Sergeant Crenshaw followed, joined by Detective Ortega.

"I'll see myself out," I said. "And I'll do what you won't do."

"What's that?" asked Crenshaw.

"Get justice."

"Except justice was fleeting in these parts," Ma said, closing her eyes and giving her head a shake.

Some of this was familiar to me from when Dad had died, especially with what came next. But all this drama, and the horrifying details described this way—I had no idea. But it did give me an idea. One that made sense of the past week. And the past year since Ma went to Dreamscape Manor.

"You got bupkis, didn't you?" Lizzy asked Ma, leaning forward and literally sitting on the edge of her seat.

Reggie snorted a laugh. "That's right."

I frowned, shaking my head.

Ma replied, "Oh, my boy worked his lawyerly magic the next few weeks. Didn't ya, Gideon?"

I nodded. "Did I ever. Threatened litigation and a public relations nightmare for CareBridge."

"Did it go anywhere?" Johnny wondered.

"'Round and 'round he went," Ma replied, "until finally reaching a settlement."

"Smart move," Reggie said. "But two million, right?"

I frowned at what my dad's death had been worth.

"Seems low," Johnny said.

"Gideon, what were you thinking?" Lizzy said.

"They had us by the balls," I exclaimed, "that's what I was thinking!"

"How? They were negligent!"

"A classic case of negligent manslaughter," Reggie added.

Ma said, "I didn't get all the legal wranglings. I was just happy CareBridge, and its parent company Perses Global Financial, had to fess up, and pay up. And Herb got justice. Sort of."

She frowned and leaned back, sighing and closing her eyes.

She suddenly looked old, frail, tired. Like a washcloth that had been wrung dry, with nothing left.

"You said Perses Global Financial," Reggie said. "Did you know at the time who was responsible for your husband's negligent death?"

"Not until afterward. That's when—well. It was at...what's it called?" She turned to me. "Settling?"

I nodded. "Settlement. The two million was split between two entities. And get this, I recall the woman who settled the deal for Perses, I imagine their counsel—she was that tall blond woman with a mole just above her upper lip."

"Cindy Crawford?" Johnny exclaimed, straightening.

"Dollars to donuts it was her."

"Get out of here..."

"That's deep," Reggie said. "That connection back then to that case. The one to this one."

"So we think," Johnny corrected.

"I want to go back to something," Lizzy said. "You said the money was split."

Ma nodded. "That's right. Between the Dementia Society of America and the Van Andel Institute."

That silenced the room.

"I hadn't wanted a red cent of that lecherous company's

money. Herb and I had done well enough for ourselves. Besides, *'Freely ye have received, freely give'* and *'God loves a cheerful giver.'* That's Scripture."

Smiles rose on both Reggie's and Lizzy's faces. Could tell they were touched. Impressed, even. I was just flat proud.

"I wasn't no Judas. I wouldn't stand for blood money. Neither would Herb. So instead, I bought a Potter's Field and put it to good use, sending half to a national dementia research foundation and the other half to a local research institution over in Grand Rapids."

"Both worthy causes, Mrs. O'Donnell," Johnny said.

Ma smirked. "That's what that Cindy Crawford lookalike had said. Right before she tied my hands."

She huffed a muttering complaint and crossed her arms. Understood completely.

"What do you mean?" asked Lizzy.

I shifted, almost embarrassed. "She had to sign a nondisclosure agreement."

Ma huffed again. "On top of an agreement absolving them of liability. Did I get that right?"

I nodded.

"Pretty standard," Reggie said.

"Couldn't sue no more. Couldn't blow the lid off their corruption. Couldn't whistleblow, or whatever it is."

"Why not?" Johnny asked.

I replied, "Because there was no actual proof of wrongdoing."

Ma huffed another sigh. "No proof of wrong—"

"At that point, it was just a string of facts and a series of unfortunate events. Remember what I said then, Ma? It could have taken years and lots of money to prove anything close to the sort of negligent disregard that would lead to a compelling judgment. The settlement was the best we could hope for."

"Still stank to high heaven..."

Felt real bad about it then, knowing how torn up Ma had been about the financial arrangement, the non-admission, the nondisclosure. But I still felt now what I felt then.

I explained, "You know we settled because CareBridge and its deep-pocketed parent company would have used every legal maneuver and trick in the playbook to stall and bleed us dry, even with that two million you gave away. I know it doesn't feel that way—doesn't feel like it now, given what happened. But justice was served at the time. Figured we could feel good about that."

Ma frowned but nodded. "I wasn't so sure at the time. Wondered whether justice was served. Sure, all that money would do wonders for d'mencha research. I just wanted more. For me."

She paused, looking my way, adding: "For my husband, Herb."

Something in me broke at hearing that, knowing how Dad had died like that, and what it had done to her.

"But the Lawd Almighty says that vengeance is his. And yet, *'Thus says the Lord: Act with justice and righteousness and deliver from the hand of the oppressor anyone who has been robbed.'* I was robbed of my husband! My Herb was robbed of life. And I wanted to act with justice."

I nodded with understanding. I'd wanted that too. Just knew it wouldn't happen. Except Ma seemed to know better.

Reggie clued into what I had sensed: "And you did, didn't you? You acted against Perses."

One end of Ma's mouth inched upward with knowing revelation.

Which struck me that my professor buddy had gotten it wrong. Ma had tricked us all. Must have, putting on some sort of show. Because clearly she hadn't lost her wits! Not one single brain cell. She was the only one who had her wits about her, especially when it came to the fight for justice. How she did it, how she pulled it off...now that was a mystery worthy of a full-priced Kindle thriller!

They just kept coming and coming...

"Go on, Ma," I said. "What's the rest of the story?"

Chapter Forty-One

Ma did go on: "Gideon had said he'd make sure that woman lived up to the terms—"

"And I did," I interrupted. "CareBridge hired more staff. Safety reports went down. They got their act together. I checked."

"Regardless, when I left that day, after signing away my justice, I couldn't shake a verbal worm that had burrowed down something fierce inside my noggin."

"What sort of worm?" asked Lizzy.

"Something he'd said...I just couldn't let go of it."

That was surprising.

"By *he* you mean me?" I asked.

Ma nodded. "Gideon, you said, '*If we ever get proof Care-Bridge was knowingly negligent and acting with reckless disregard for the safety of its patients—well, then we might have a case.*'"

I didn't remember saying all that, but it sounded like something I'd say. More a throwaway comment to a client to make them feel at ease for taking a settlement than anything else. As far as I was concerned, there was no point in pursuing a civil suit that would tie me and Ma up in litigation for years with no guarantee of a civil judgment.

She continued, "I couldn't help but feel there was more to do."

One end of my mouth curled upward. Pride suddenly welled, along with a dose of shame. She did what I should have done. What I basically refused to do, seeking the easy out.

She fought.

Now I smiled knowingly. "And you did, didn't you?"

Johnny leaned in. "You found proof of wrongdoing?"

"That CareBridge, Perses Global Financial," Lizzy said, "had acted with knowing negligence and reckless disregard for the safety of its patients?"

"Yes sir and yes ma'am!" Ma said with a laugh.

"The package..." I whispered.

"Shoved up in that vent," Reggie added.

Ma nodded, saying nothing but saying everything.

She'd done it.

And it almost cost her her life.

"Why don't we start from the beginning," Johnny said, taking over. I was grateful for him putting on his investigator's hat for me.

Because I suddenly felt dog tired. Bone weary, really, my muscles aching from the whiplash of the week, from the fight with some commie pinko, as Johnny would say. I was in pretty good shape, running and lifting weights each day, but that chick was fierce. And I was sore from it all, on top of just flat emotionally drained and my head spinning from Ma's turn.

"When Herb died," Ma started, "I had this fight in me to carry on. To do more. But what could I do? I was a simple accountant. A bean counter. I had no power. No fancy levers I could pull to bend the universe toward justice, riffing off from Doc King."

Had to smile at that. Dad hadn't much cared for Martin Luther King Jr., believing his commitment to the social gospel placed too much emphasis on the social and justice side of the equation, with man's gumption and ingenuity changing the world, and not enough on the gospel side of things, with God's eternal gift of salvation in Christ the means and method of transforming the madness into godly goodness. While a committed Christian, and committed to the gospel, Ma wondered why it couldn't be both, where God partnered with people in his movement of rescue and re-creation.

I returned my attention to Ma, who described the moment it all changed: "Perses Global Financial Group showed up on a memorandum one morning."

"Huh?" I said.

"Boy, how many times do I gotsta say that if you can *'Huh?'* me, you can hear me!"

Johnny chuckled. "She's got ya there, kid."

"Yeah yeah yeah," I complained.

"Anyhoo, I'm at Mercy General," Ma went on, "and a memo comes across my desk to open up our books to these muckety-mucks flying in from London."

"To Perses?" Lizzy said.

"Right as rain."

"But an organization like Mercy General would only open up their books if they were being bought out."

"Now you're catching on, sweetie. Perses was making a play to buy our Junction hospital, and I was assigned to walk them through our financials."

"To open up your books," Reggie confirmed.

"PGFG was doing their due diligence," I said, the picture drawing into focus.

Ma replied, "I worked with them hand over fist to appraise the business. Thing about it was, in the course of my work, I got a peek into their own portfolio. Lo and behold, buying things was their business model."

"What, like other hospitals, healthcare facilities like CareBridge?"

"Hospitals, dental clinics, entire subdivisions, you name it. Including assisted living healthcare facilities like CareBridge—and another local joint in their crosshairs that was still in process but almost buttoned up."

Didn't have to say who, but I did anyway: "Dreamscape Manor."

She heaved a breath and nodded, settling back and crossing her arms in a huff.

That sent a hushed ripple of understanding through the group. It also clicked something into place, recognition dawning on another piece to the puzzle that had bothered me.

So: "And HappyLiving?"

Ma's mouth clamped shut, and she cast her eyes to the floor, offering a slight nod.

"Is that why you wanted to pull out of the suit?"

Now her face twisted up, a mixture of anger and sadness. "I was hopping mad at that buyout, mostly what it meant for my neighbors. But once I started working my magic after what I'd discovered about those Perses vultures, I didn't want to poke the bear. I needed to lay low, not ruffle feathers. You understand?"

I nodded. "You figured settling, giving in to Perses, would take the heat off you, and the target."

"I'm sorry, Gideon!" Ma's eyes flooded with emotion, and she sniffed it back.

I leaned in and embraced her, reassuring her I understood, even though I didn't quite get it, not yet.

Johnny asked what I wanted to: "What did you mean by work your magic?"

Ma dabbed her eyes and continued, "Well, I was already fit to be tied when I saw those PGFG vultures making a play for my hospital after what they'd done to CareBridge, to Herb. And when I saw them making the same play for Dreamscalpel —I mean Dreamscape, I started hatching a plan to get in on the inside."

Johnny snorted a laugh. "Dreamscalpel. Nice."

"And true! They done carved up the lives of the people entrusted to them. Which I saw firsthand the minute I arrived."

"Just so I understand," Reggie said, "so we're all on the same page and got the lay of the land, as your attorneys and all—"

"Tell the truth, shame the devil," Ma said. "Just spit it out, wouldya?"

He stifled a smile and nodded. "You posed as a dementia patient, is that right?"

"That's right."

"And you used that as a cover to put your accounting know-how to work."

"Yup."

"But why?" asked Lizzy, almost in a whisper. As if both intrigued and in aww.

Ma smirked. "Because I ain't no boo boo the fool, that's why! Figured if they caused my Herb's death, then they caused others."

Johnny *ahh*ed, then asked, "The names?"

"All fellow residents who died thanks to their neglect."

"Those were a lot of names."

"There were a lot of deaths."

Reggie shook his head. "All attributed to Perses Global?"

"I got the receipts, sugar. All of them."

Lizzy asked, "Is that what all those ledgers were, those spreadsheets were about, the numbers?"

It hit me before she responded. "The numbers…Were those payouts?"

Ma grinned. "You was born at night but not last night, Gideon. Always was a sharp one! That's right."

"Those were big amounts."

"Million-dollar payouts," Lizzy said, "like you had gotten?"

She nodded, her smile fading.

"What I want to know," Johnny said, "is how you pulled it all off."

That smile returned, and she shrugged her shoulders. "I'm good."

He laughed. "I gathered that, but it'll be important for the providence of the evidence."

I nodded. "I agree, Ma. You are good. But I also agree with Johnny. How'd you do it?"

"Well, like I said, and as you gathered, I opossumed it up! Not that I was dead, but sure played the part of a brain-dead d'mencha lady. When I was invited into the main office to help around the place with simple tasks, things Dreamscalpel liked to do to keep the resident's engaged, although I'd always thought it felt more like free slave labor than anything."

Ma huffed and shook her head.

"Anyhoo, I did my little tasks and helped myself to their computers when they weren't looking. Went rooting around their books for anything that looked shady. What you found stuffed up in my apartment was the fruits of my labor."

Johnny said, "Which are now in police custody."

She turned to me. "What the what?"

I frowned, raking a frustrated hand through my hair.

"He's right. The police confiscated it as stolen goods. We did get some pictures, though, which could be useful."

Johnny nodded. "Definitely useful. Hopefully enough to get an investigation rolling."

"This changes things..." Reggie said, a smile growing.

"Sure does!" Lizzy said, the same smile spreading.

"What do you mean?" I asked. "What changes?"

"The Whistleblower Protection Act and the Sarbanes-Oxley Act."

"Huh?"

Johnny chuckled. "Ahh, I see where you're going with this?"

"How am I the only one not in the know?"

Ma smacked me; I yelped. "Should've hired them two!"

Now I frowned. "Thanks, Ma..."

Reggie laughed. "Seriously, both acts of Congress protect people who report illegal activities or violations, even if they have signed an NDA, and with proof."

"Sarbanes-Oxley, especially," Johnny added, "which those sausage makers in Congress managed to muscle through after those morons bankrupted Enron. It gives whistleblowers protection who report corporate fraud."

"Look at you," Lizzy said, "all Johnny on the spot."

She winked; he frowned. "As if I haven't heard that one before, honey."

Reggie added, "These laws can render NDAs unenforceable when they are attempts at preventing such reporting."

Lizzy said, "And that's not even addressing the biggest elephant in the room that any judge would give his left nut to render null and void."

"Colorful," Johnny said.

Ma laughed. "I like this one. She's spicy."

"I do what I can," Lizzy said.

I agreed with Ma, and I also understood where Lizzy was going, which started getting my lawyerly juices flowing. I was itching for a fight, itching to get vengeance for Ma. And this was the way.

Johnny turned to me and hooked a thumb toward Lizzy. "What's this elephant she's talking about?"

I replied, "If the entity that benefits from an NDA engages in subsequent harmful actions, the agreement can be voided."

Lizzy said, "Especially, if they are illegal or violate public policy. Courts may also consider retaliatory actions as a reason to void a nondisclosure agreement."

Johnny whistled, then snorted a chuckle. "I'd say kidnapping and murder are right up there with illegal and retaliatory acts!"

Reggie said, "Not to throw shade and cold water on y'all, but we're missing another elephant."

I inhaled a disappointed breath, knowing what he meant.

"Proof," I said, slumping back.

"What do you mean by *proof?*" Johnny said. "I shot that Gen Z numbskull in the kneecap! And you killed the other one, Gideon."

"That's not agist at all..." Lizzy said.

Couldn't help but stuff a smile at both Johnny's cranky old-man routine and Lizzy, who was herself at the very top of the Gen Z spectrum, having graduated from law school at twenty-four. Regardless, Johnny was right.

I said, "Reg is right. We don't have proof those two were hired by Perses."

Lizzy scoffed. "Sure we do! They were there. That Blake Sheldon guy took us to them. Introed them to us as her caregivers."

"But they were employed by Dreamscape Manor."

"Same diff!"

"I'm not sure...there are lots of moving parts to this. And if we want to nail Perses, we've got to get the law right."

"Whistleblower statutes," Johnny said, "would definitely work in our favor. She's got documented proof."

"*Stolen* proof," I reminded him.

Lizzy nodded. "Unlawfully obtaining evidence is frowned upon, even in whistleblower suits."

"What about immunity?" asked Johnny.

"From criminal prosecution, maybe, but then there is the civil side of things. PGFG could go after her civilly, for hacking into their systems."

Ma gasped, actually clutching her chest. "Hacking? Lawd Almighty have mercy..." She trailed off, going silent, then looked at me. "Maybe now you can understand why I had to put a pause on the suit. Didn't want to ruin what I'd started."

I understood what she meant. "You didn't want to blow your cover."

She nodded, face falling.

I turned to Reggie. "What do you think?"

"I don't know, Gideon," he said lowly, above a whisper, leaning back and looking at the ceiling.

"Don't know what?"

"This feels bigger. Feels bigger than this. Than *us*."

Lizzy nodded. "Bigger than Mill Creek Junction, even."

"With far bigger stakes than this case. This senior living center, even."

"As in national stakes."

"Global stakes!"

"Hold on," I said, putting up a staying hand. "What do you mean by stakes?"

Reggie said, "Look at the roadmap, partner."

"Mill Creek's map!" exclaimed Lizzy.

"You picking up what I'm putting down, sister?"

"Totes."

She raised a fist; he bumped it.

Johnny groaned. "How about you two spell it out for this Boomer, would ya?"

"And this one!" Ma said.

"OK, Boomers, here's the deal," Lizzy said. "You've got CareBridge, from a few years ago, getting bought out by Perses Global Financial Group, right before it scoops up Dreamscape Manor, which you found out about, Florence."

Reggie nodded. "Then PGFG makes a play for HappyLiving."

"And don't forget Farmer Jed's land," Johnny added.

"Bingo! I'd forgotten about that."

"And MCJCC..." I said, growing disturbed now at the roadmap.

Johnny turned to me. "Come again?"

"That's right. There was a pen with those PGFG initials. My professor friend said they were buying them out."

He shook his head. "Confirms my suspicions the Junction itself is up for sale."

I smirked. "Wouldn't be surprised if it was with the way I saw Mayor Goodall and Cindy Crawford yakking it up at Max's Place."

"I'd wager Fred Myers General Store, the J-Max prison, and Smiles Dentistry are on that list too."

"Say *waaa?*" Reggie said.

Lizzy jerked a thumb his way. "What he said. How do you know this?"

Johnny waved a dismissive hand. "Doesn't matter. What does is what it all means."

"I'll tell ya what it means," Ma said. "What it means is, a whole helluva lot of people's lives are at stake!"

She was right. And her bald-faced, plain-spoken way about her shut us up.

It *was* about people's lives. All those names she'd found.

The good folks of HappyLiving, their ability to have a home. My friend and his students. Hell, maybe even Mill Creek Junction itself.

"One question," Reggie said. "What do we do about it?"

"Not the right one," Lizzy said. "Can we stop it?"

He grunted a nod, joined by Johnny. Even Ma got in on the action, which she'd been in the thick of from the start, starting the fight and looking like she was itching to keep at it.

Which got me thinking.

"Actually..." I said, trailing off as a crazy idea started coming together. Then again, maybe it wasn't so crazy after all.

"Actually, what?" Johnny said.

I replied, "Actually, I think we might."

"How?" asked Ma.

"An old buddy from law school who..."

I trailed off, reddening from embarrassment as much as from the memory of the way I'd left things.

"Who..." Reggie said, leaning in with cough-it-up eyes.

I straightened. "I'm not sure he'll want to see me."

"Why not?" Ma asked. "My life is on the line, son! And a whole heckuva lot more are."

"Well..."

Lizzy smirked. "You're killing us, smalls!"

"Your mama's right, Gideon," Reggie said. "Lots of lives are on the line. So what's the plan—*your* plan?"

I felt foolish now. For the reason.

But Ma was right. So was Reggie.

So I stood. "Johnny, care for a trip to DC?"

Chapter Forty-Two

I winced as thunder rumbled overhead from engorged storm clouds, an unrelenting onslaught making me more nervous than I already was. Flying halfway across the country to make an appeal for help to a former friend had set me on edge, after all that I had already been through. Last thing I needed was a mad dash through a deluge.

Never liked storms, especially driving in them. More so as an Uber passenger at the mercy of a college kid with baggy shorts and a wife beater and Caribbean braids jamming out to Bob Marley. Not that I had anything against Bob Marley, but knowing DC had legalized weed on top of the bro vibe set my heart ratcheting.

Johnny and I were stuffed in the backseat of a Kia something with a dicey air conditioner and a grumbly, mumbly muffler sloshing our way up Constitution Avenue toward the Capitol Building. Darkness had settled thick and heavy, those engorged storm clouds compounded by the sun cresting toward the horizon. Ornate street lights glowed a hazy yellow through the rain, joined by shifting red-yellow-green traffic lights, bright and piercing.

Soon, a view emerged through the whipping wiper blades far more penetrating: the Capitol Dome, a golden orange glow lighting the way. Almost like the shining city on the hill metaphor Ronald Reagan had used to implore American excellence and world-wide inspiration. Who himself borrowed it from both the Puritan minister John Winthrop and Jesus.

Now...not so much.

I wasn't much the political sort, at least not any more, though I still had my convictions. That was my buddy Jayce Robinson's domain. I was more of a history buff, appreciating Winston Churchill's wisdom: *"Those that fail to learn from history are doomed to repeat it."* A variation of which the good British Prime Minister probably swiped from the Spanish philosopher George Santayana, given how much of a history buff he himself was.

My old Georgetown Law buddy was far more interested in the march of history than studying it. Which really cashed out as the march of progress, what lay ahead. Or, rather, the *myth* of progress, strangled by the tyranny of the present, our fascination with the new, the progressive. Yeah, he'd rooted it in his faith, but Jayce believed redemption was just a legislative tweak away. Not me, by a long shot. There was nothing worse than hearing *"I'm from the government, and I'm here to help."*

We'd gone round and round over plenty of pints back in the day at The Front Page bar, a local haunt for young politicos like him who were long on ambition and short on wisdom. It's what got us into this mess in the first place, us parting ways those years ago. There'd been a couple of times I'd intended to reconnect. To repent, really, of letting my own politics get in the way of our friendship. He was far more gracious and adept at handling disagreement than I was. Probably why he went into politics after law school while I'd been slumming it as a small-town defense attorney.

Just hoped he was interested in reconnecting.

Johnny had called in a chit from some rich muckety-muck he helped with a divorce investigation to borrow his jet for a chartered flight to the nation's capital. The goal was to reconnect with my friend and work a political solution that would turn the screws on Perses Global Financial Group. Didn't know how that would look exactly, how that would work. All I knew was that I needed to save the Junction from the clutches of this financial vulture.

Ma wanted them to pay for what they had done to Dad, wanted accountability, which I understood. I wanted the same, knowing my piss-poor legal work hadn't brought the justice and vengeance Dad deserved, regardless of the legal complications such a case meant. I just hoped there was a political solution where a legal one was hard to come by. If there was anyone who could bring that about, it was Jayce. But I wasn't banking on it, so I had a contingency plan.

While we were zooming through the stratosphere, Reggie and Lizzy were working the Junction courts to bring Dreamscape Manor, and their benefactor, to heel. After contacting Annabelle and giving her the lowdown on all that Ma had done, they marched into Dean Lawlor's office to offer up the whole story in the hopes that they would bring a criminal case against PGFG.

It was a risky move, exposing Ma to civil liability. But we banked on the fact that public sentiment, on top of judicial deference, would be in her favor. It was still risky. Annabelle assured me she would fight tooth and nail to protect my mom, to make sure Dean didn't pivot to protecting his political ass, but I knew better. If what I saw held true, that Perses was cozying up to Mayor Goodall, and they were making a play for Mill Creek Junction assets, its businesses and homes, for the government itself—well, then there would surely be political hell to pay. And Dean was a survivor, along with Goodall, so there was a chance they'd be out for self-preservation blood.

With Ma in Mill Creek's crosshairs.

It was odd, but I'd resigned myself to the good Lord above keeping her in his good graces, under his providential protection. It was all I could do while pursuing this other lead. That pivot to my childhood faith had been a theme this past week. An unexpected one.

We had arrived in just under two hours to the soggy swamp I'd long thought should be drained of more than just its water. But that was for another day. What mattered now was our arrival at the Russell Senate Office Building and our drop-in visit to Senator Mark DeWitt's office to see his chief of staff.

Thankfully, the rain had let up some when Kid Rock dropped us off at the marble stairs leading to doors of solid oak and glass. Metal detectors greeted us, along with three stern-faced Capitol police officers, who looked both suspicious of our arrival and bored.

A fresh-faced recruit ordered us to put our keys and wallet in a small grey Tupperware-looking bucket before sending them through an airport-style x-ray machine. Johnny and I complied, then we walked through the detector, one by one. I made it through unscathed; Johnny, not so much. Said an old Nam injury set those things off all the time. Something about a bullet in his leg the field docs couldn't remove.

An older officer grunted a command for Johnny to stretch out his arms. The man wanded him while I waited in a rotunda that looked about what I expected Senate office buildings to look like. White marble columns soared to three floors, with a simple cream ceiling decorated by hunter green squares and lined by gilt, a skylight straight above looking menacing. Large windows anchored the perimeter on each floor, with wide hallways branching off to the Senate offices.

After Johnny got the all clear, we hustled down the hallway at the left toward Senator DeWitt's office on the first floor, our stiff shoes echoing with a clatter and my private eye muttering complaints from said stiff shoes.

The corridor was dark, with plain, cream walls lit by sconce lights glowing yellow. Halfway down was our destination. A Kansas flag stood proud outside a closed door stained a dark mahogany. I worried we were too late.

Trying the knob, it opened into a spacious square painted the color of corn. White marble floors were covered with a navy woven rug, large *KANSAS* letters greeting us in gold along with the state's seal of rolling green hills and a purple mountain. A sunflower design was anchored at the far end between two mahogany desks, where a young blond woman in a pencil black skirt and white blouse had just shut down her computer and looked like she was leaving.

I made for the interception before she could shoo us away for the evening.

"Excuse me," I said, the woman spinning toward us and scowling. "We need to see Jayce Robinson."

The scowl deepened. "Uh, it's late."

"I know—" I sort of fake glanced at my watch before smiling and laughing "—sorry, but we just flew in."

The woman set down her purse and looked at something at her desk before shaking her head.

"And you are?" she asked without looking up.

"O'Donnell. Gideon O'Donnell."

"Sorry. Jayce doesn't have any appointments by that name."

I swallowed back a rise of irritation. We didn't have time for this.

"I need to see him. I'm an old friend, from Georgetown Law." I stepped forward, opening my hands. "Please. It's important."

She took in a breath, held it, glanced over my shoulder at Johnny, then huffed it out and picked up a black receptionist phone, pressing some numbers without a word.

I glanced behind at Johnny, who just shrugged.

The woman gave my name, paused a beat, *uh-huh*ed and *OK*ed with a skeptical eye trained my way, then set the handset back into place.

"You can have a seat. Jayce will be out in a few minutes."

I thanked her. She left out the front office door, apparently done for the day.

Johnny and I sat on a crimson loveseat that looked about as old as the Senate itself. A few minutes later, another mahogany door across from us opened, and out stepped a face I hadn't seen since law school.

Jayce was trimmer than I had seen him last, more athletic. Dark hair was as coiffed as I remembered, wearing a navy suit, white shirt, and his trademark bowtie, this one lime green with baby blue polka dots. I expected him to come bearing a scowl and a grudge. Instead, his face opened up when he saw me, so did his arms.

"Geep!" Jayce exclaimed, a chuckle flaring as I stood. Right before he bare-hugged me.

Relief flooded me as we embraced.

"Geep?" Johnny questioned.

I explained, "As in G P. My initials for Gideon Paul."

He ushered us into the adjoining offices, the two of us catching up on six years of life as we walked through rooms of plain, white walls. Fluorescent lights shined down on wood desks and similarly fresh-faced congressional staffers as the receptionist, dutifully clacking away at computers. After passing through three of these disappointing expressions of American legislative power, we entered something entirely different.

The room was twice the size as the receptionist room. The size of my modest craftsman's footprint back in Mill Creek Junction, the walls were a calming indigo, ceiling vaulted high and painted the same yellow as the cornfield on the State of Kansas seal, with several lamps lighting the room a soft yellow. A large wood desk commanded the center of the right wall overlooking a courtyard darkened by the storm, piled high with stacks of thick binders stuffed with paper and sticky notes, with books scattered about and a closed laptop.

Jayce ushered us to a grouping of black leather couches and chairs near an unused fireplace. He went to a cabinet and pulled out a bottle, holding it out with a grin.

"Care for some Wild Turkey?"

I raised an eyebrow. "Booze at the office?"

"How do you think we get anything done around here?"

Johnny chuckled. "You're my kind of guy."

He brought the bottle and three crystal tumblers over to a coffee table, settled next to me on the couch and poured Johnny his drink.

As he poured, I gestured at the door. "Those staffers out there—look a little young for Senate work."

Jayce handed off Johnny's drink and started mine.

"Actually, you'd be surprised. Average age on the Hill is twenty-seven."

"*Twenty-seven?*" Johnny and I exclaimed together.

Jayce laughed, finishing the pour and moving to his own drink.

I whistled. "And here I thought the place was overrun by a

bunch of octogenarians with Caesar complexes. Instead, Congress is run by twenty-year-olds!"

Johnny snorted a laugh. "Explains the capital crazy, that's for sure."

"You have no idea," Jayce said, raising his drink and making an unexpected toast: "To lost friends united."

Regret replaced that earlier relief.

I quickly raised my glass. "To lost friends."

And threw back half the Wild Turkey. The rich bourbon slid smooth into my empty stomach, vanilla and orange peel filling my head.

Johnny said, "Gideon, here, says you both knew each other back in the day. Law school, right, Georgetown?"

Jayce nodded. "We *did* know each other. Isn't that right, Geep?"

I flushed hot shame, shifting and taking a short sip.

Johnny threw back a swig. "I sense a story in there somewhere."

Jayce laughed. "Is there ever!"

Without looking to me for confirmation, he threw back a swig of his own and dove in, ever the storyteller.

"So get this. Several years ago, during one presidential election—what, wasn't it six years ago now?"

I nodded, saying nothing.

"Six years ago, we had these three candidates running for president. Robert Santos and Amos Young, on the Democrat and Republican tickets respectively."

"Right," Johnny said. "And that Matthew Reed guy, the third-party candidate."

"The *Evangelical* third-party candidate," Jayce corrected. "Which Gideon didn't particularly like."

"Why not?" asked Johnny.

I threw back a swig and answered, "Because I was afraid he'd set up some theocratic government, that's why!"

Jayce slapped my back and laughed. "Unlike *your* guy who actually wanted to set up a theocratic American state!"

Johnny gasped and turned to me. "You backed the Amos Young horse?"

I shrugged. "I liked his slogan."

"America's Moment, America's Mandate? And you were worried about a Christian nationalist taking the stage?"

I finished my bourbon and sank into my chair.

Jayce just laughed.

"For real?" Johnny questioned with a mocking chuckle. "The guy who was busted for conspiring to actually setup a theocratic government, the Mormon Church, and usher in their end times golden age?"

"Alright, alright, Johnny. I get it."

He laughed again and drained the rest of his whiskey.

Jayce said, "We had some pretty heated debates over several pints leading up to the election. And we had a sort of falling out after that, didn't we, Gideon?"

He drained his drink and started pouring another, without looking at me.

I took a breath, then a beat, then got to the chase—well, my chase, before the real one.

"I was a jerk, what can I say?" I slid my tumbler over to him as he finished his pour. The glass clinked his, and he looked up. "Actually, what I can say is, I'm sorry."

Jayce didn't look at me. Just filled my tumbler then snatched his and settled back, taking a sip.

I took mine and turned to him. "I'm serious. I was a royal jerk."

"Yeah, you were..." One end of his mouth curled upward.

"I know, I know! I'm sorry for putting politics ahead of our friendship. I've learned my lesson. Haven't voted since."

Now he laughed. "The Republic thanks you for that!"

"Yeah yeah yeah," I said, taking a sip and starting to feel the alcohol now.

"So what's this about, you coming all this way to DC?" Jayce took another sip and set his glass down. "Surely it wasn't to apologize, though it was a dang good reason to make the trip."

I set my glass down as well and settled back, looking at Johnny, who nodded me onward.

"I've got a case I'm working on back home."

"What sort of case?"

"My mother's actually."

He frowned. "What happened?"

I filled him in on the details, covering everything from the initial shock of what I thought was her death, and my accusation of her murder, to her rescue.

Jayce shook his head. "Thank Christ for protecting her."

"There's something we discovered in the course of the investigation that we need your help with."

That seemed to set him off kilter, my old buddy tilting his head before leaning back and focusing on me with unblinking eyes.

"How can I help?" was all he said.

"Well, I don't know how to say this, but Ma discovered something that led to her kidnapping."

"Uh, say what?"

"I know it sounds crazy, but she was kidnapped because she discovered a cover-up. Some bad dealings by some bad people and a wicked bad private equity firm."

Now Jayce straightened, eyes widening and head jutting forward with interest.

"Private equity, you say?"

I nodded.

"Who?"

Johnny answered. "Perses Global Financial Group."

Jayce glanced at him, and his face fell. His eyes narrowed, and something like hatred flashed in his blue eyes. Had never seen that before.

"Tell me more," he said.

Chapter Forty-Three

I started from the beginning, with the story Ma had told about when Dad died, how the payout, the cover-up, had motivated her to seek justice. The opportunity came when she worked with Perses on the hospital acquisition, and they had to open up their books and she got a glimpse into the underbelly of the beast.

"By God's providence..." Jayce muttered, looking riveted by the story. "If that detail had not fallen into place, I imagine the justice she was seeking from those vultures would have slipped through her fingers."

I nodded, thinking there was some truth to that.

"If you thought that was providential, then you'll be bowled over by what happened next."

I explained how in the course of the due diligence, she had caught a glimpse of PGFG's own books, seeing how they had bought Dreamscape Manor, as they had CareBridge. That's when she got to work, putting a plan in place to dig deeper into the accounting at the senior living center, by putting her book-keeping know-how to work. It's also when she saw the Happy-Living buyout, and all it meant for her neighbors, which made her even more determined to turn the screws on Perses.

"A real Deborah, your mother is," he said, laughing and shaking his head in disbelief. "What a lioness!"

Johnny grunted a nod. "The Old Testament judge who set Israel right when no man was found worthy of Yahweh's righteous justice. That pretty much describes the Florence O'Donnell I've known over the years."

I smiled with pride, throwing back the rest of my bourbon and marveling at what Ma had pulled off.

Almost.

That's what brought me to Capitol Hill, to my old buddy. Given what I saw in his eyes when I mentioned PGFG, I had a hunch there was something about this he might be able to help with.

"So that's why we're here," I said. "I want justice for Ma."

Johnny nodded. "Make those vultures, as you put it, pay for their crimes."

"Can you help us, Jayce? Surely there's some political—something, *anything* that could fix things, make Perses pay."

He startled at that last plea, settling back with his drink but not taking any more sips. Just sat, still and staring off above my head, to the fireplace or the bookcases or the wall behind.

Then: "Do you remember why I had wanted to work on Capitol Hill after law school?"

I shook my head. I hadn't.

"Not the most lucrative of choices as a civil servant with six-figures of school debt."

I smiled. "Neither is small-town lawyering the most lucrative of choices with six-figures of the same."

"Suppose not! But I know something about that, because of where I was from."

"Manhattan, right?"

Johnny brightened. "You a Yankees fan?"

Jayce laughed, one of his mouthy belly laughs. "Closest thing we got to a baseball team is the Royals, and they're across state lines."

He looked at me, brow furrowed in confusion.

I explained, "The other Manhattan, Johnny. As in Kansas."

"About a twentieth the size of the New York borough."

Johnny *ahh*ed. "So, small-town Kansas."

"Farm-town Kansas!" He smiled proudly. "Generations of Robinsons have had a strong foothold in agriculture."

"What did you grow?"

"Corn, wheat, soybeans. You name it, we grew it."

That smile faded, and now he took a drink.

"That is," Jayce went on, "until a London private equity firm pressured dozens of our Manhattan area farmers to sell their land for some fancy new deal."

Got the reference instantly.

"Perses Global Financial Group," I said.

"For the deal to work," Jayce went on, "they needed one contiguous 45,000 acre plot of land, with a dozen or so smaller farms banding together to make it work. Except for one hold out."

I nodded knowingly. "Your father."

"Said the only way those Brits across the pond would get the deed to his land was if they wrenched it from his cold, dead fingers."

A beat, a swig, a breath, another swig.

"It was a vicious time. A dangerous time. We lost friends. Lost our church community. Even lost our dog."

"Dog?" Johnny said.

Jayce waved a dismissive hand. "Too gruesome to get into."

Another swig, then a huffing sigh.

"Eventually Daddy gave in, and he lost his whole livelihood. His whole reason for living. Sure, he got a check that set him up for life, but to what end? He hated himself for selling out, and he spiraled. Drank until his liver gave out and he was six-feet under."

I didn't know what to say. Knew his father had passed young, but Jayce hadn't talked about the details. How tragic.

Jayce continued, "That's when I got interested in politics. It's also when I got interested in private equity, and in the long line of American icons they've gutted like my daddy's farm."

He started naming a bunch of familiar companies: clothing stores like J. Crew and Aeropostale; the beloved kids store Toys 'R Us; Payless Shoe Store and Radioshack; Gymboree and Shopko.

I asked, "All bought out by Perses Global Financial Group?"

"No. Other like-minded private equity vultures. They're vampires, sucking dead or dying companies for what little financial blood they've got left to feed their greed."

Johnny snorted a chuckle. "Tell us how you really feel, kid!"

"Housing is the perfect example," Jayce continued, ignoring him.

"Housing?"

"Especially mobile home parks."

The private equity plot thickened, given the class action suit that had been put on hold.

I leaned in with interest. "Tell me more."

Jayce held the Wild Turkey bottle up and gestured toward our tumblers. I probably shouldn't have, but I nodded him onward.

As he poured, he explained, "It's sort of remarkable,

because an industry built to make money targets the poorest of home owners with their schemes, making even those homes increasingly unattainable in a country already burdened by a massive affordable housing shortage."

Finishing, Jayce refilled his tumbler and settled back.

He continued, "Historically, mobile homes were great deals that offered alternatives to the increasingly unaffordable housing market. Especially now, with the way interest rates have skyrocketed, and how the median housing price is basically unaffordable to the average worker in most of the country, on top of the massive shortage in housing—given all this, mobile homes used to offer families a chance to own property. In the past, you could buy a used unit for as little as ten grand. For most lower-middle-class homeowners, it was a solid investment and housing choice."

"What changed?" I wondered.

"Do you really need to ask?"

"Private equity," Johnny said.

"There was a time," Jayce said, leaning back, "when family businesses ran most of the industry. But in the last decade, these massive investment firms came in and changed it all, spending billions buying up mobile home parks."

I said, "Which led to rising costs for residents, I'm guessing."

"The average price of a mobile home has increased 35 percent, to more than sixty-one grand."

"Doesn't seem all that profitable," Johnny said.

I nodded. "Why would some New York or London outfit pay any attention to some Midwest trailer park?"

Jayce replied, "They make total sense for private equity! These guys get a steady cash flow with little responsibility, which is the playbook. They don't have to deal with all the upkeep of the houses themselves, unlike apartments. Cut the grass, keep the roads plowed and repaired. That's about it. Even then, those upkeep costs are pushed onto residents with fees and rate increases. They're not even responsible for the utilities."

"That's exactly what was going on with HappyLiving!" I exclaimed, my voice fueled by rage and a bit of Wild Turkey.

"What happened?" asked Jayce.

I explained my lawsuit, the one Ma had championed before pulling out of fear of exposing her other plot against Perses.

"Didn't know who when it all went down," I said, "but Perses Global Financial Group bought it for over $150 million. Existing residents already paid for their own utilities and property taxes. Then these new fees for all that upkeep you mentioned came rolling in, and rents skyrocketed by a double-digit percentage, the largest increase in the park's fifty-two-year history. That's not even touching on the rates for new residents, where lot rents were going for $1,400—a forty-percent increase! All of which made it harder for existing owners to sell if they wanted out, gutting the equity in their homes."

Jayce swept a hand. "None of that's surprising."

"They paid two fees. First was the mortgage on the property they owned, which was the home itself. The second was for renting the lot. But by messing with the one, they screwed up the other."

Jayce frowned, shaking his head. "Reminds me of another story I heard from our state. Another private equity firm bought out a similar mobile home park, only to sell it down the road for north of $250 million. They inflated the value by jacking up the fees and lot rentals, the residents basically trapped, like you said about those renters in your suit. Made a killing on both the front and back ends."

Johnny said, "And on the backs of those poor renters."

"ManorCare is another prime example of private equity at work."

"What's that?" I asked.

Johnny said, "Sounds like some nursing home."

Jayce nodded. "It's a chain of facilities bought out by the same firm that bought out that Kansas trailer park."

"Also sounds like PGFG!" I said.

"Well, if Perses is anything like this outfit, instead of investing in the company, they bought up their real estate and then forced the facilities to rent back their property. Manor-Care was obligated to pay nearly half a billion dollars a year in rent to occupy the buildings it was already using—along with property insurance, building upkeep, and property taxes."

Johnny asked, "So, what, they double dipped?"

"Exactly. They owned and rented the property to the same entity, resulting in millions of dollars on top of millions more in fees ManorCare was forced to pay for the privilege of being owned by the firm."

"How is that legal?"

"It shouldn't be!" Jayce said, throwing back a swig. "Yet, with our current laws the way they are, it is. And the nursing home side of the business suffered for it. It led to hundreds of layoffs and other cost-cutting programs that affected patient care. As you can imagine, health code violations soared. Remarkably, despite all this cost cutting and selling their property to the private equity vulture, the company was in debt to the tune of ten million."

"What? That's crazy!" I said, throwing back a swig myself.

"What's crazier, is that the burden of this debt that had piled up was the sole responsibility of ManorCare, not their private equity owner. The nursing home owed it, not the firm, which owned the property. Eventually, the company went bankrupt and was sold for a mega profit. It was a smart business decision, though. Gotta give that to them."

I asked, "Why, when they went bankrupt?"

Jayce shook his head. "Not the private equity firm. The nursing home. Buying them up is an obvious play for these outfits."

"Why is that?"

"The simple fact is they have a ton of cash flow. Nothing more reliable than the kind of money that comes from government sources like Medicare. They also have physical assets, buildings and equipment, that can be sold for profit. Except they ignore their core service."

I snorted a laugh. "What, like actually caring for their patients?"

"Not just patient care, but *human* care. Better care comes from well-trained caregivers who spend time with residents. Private equity firms disregarded both of these basic elements. These vultures slash the number of staffing hours at nursing homes left and right."

Johnny said, "That can't be good for care."

"Of course not!" Jayce exclaimed. "These poor people injure themselves, they soil themselves, they develop bedsores. Unaddressed, these are all deadly serious. These firms also rely less on registered nurses and more on lower-skilled workers, requiring only a one-year certificate. They also rely much more on drugs to make patients docile, which are nothing more than crutches for staffing issues."

All of this rang of CareBridge with my father...

"What can be done about it all then?" I asked.

Jayce slid back in his chair with a sigh, cradling his almost-empty tumbler.

"Nothing," he said, shaking his head.

"I don't buy that."

"It's true."

"Why's that?" asked Johnny.

Jayce shrugged. "Lots of reasons. Often when inspectors do flag issues the homes can challenge them, so it goes into a black hole. Then state regulators themselves are scared stiff to call them what they are, violations that harm residents, even when those harms are obvious and lead to death."

I asked, "Why are regulators so scared?"

"Because when a nursing home does receive sufficient harm deficiencies and is shut down, guess who takes over?"

"Let me take a wild guess," Johnny said with a smirk. "Uncle Sam?"

"Bingo. They fall into the hands of state governments, then they're the ones who have to manage the facility. As you can imagine, this is an expensive and difficult proposition."

"Don't have much incentive to go hard on the facilities then, do they?"

"Bingo. That's not even addressing the biggest elephant in the room."

"What's that?" I asked.

He oinked like a pig and waved his arms around.

Johnny and I just looked at one another.

Jayce replied, "Pork, and all the lobbying money that makes the sausage! There are two things in the world you never want to see made, fellas. Sausage and legislation. Last year alone, the main lobbying group for nursing homes gave twenty million in federal contributions and spent almost a billion dollars lobbying state and local governments around the country."

I said, "In other words, the government isn't that interested in forcing regulation and change."

Johnny added, "Can't imagine with that much cabbage on the line politicians would want to pick a fight with these big companies."

Jayce nodded. "Which puts all nursing home residents at risk, especially residents of private equity-owned homes, where mortal danger is a possibility. At the end of the day, given this reluctance to regulate, protecting residents is left in the hands of people like you, Gideon. Even then, there's no point."

That was surprising. "Why not? What if we sue them?"

He laughed. "Good luck! I know of a similar case, where a woman lost her husband to negligent disregard, that took several years of litigation for a jury to finally hear about the nursing home's fraudulent practices. The suit exposed all sorts of other such cases. Other deaths."

"Really? What was the verdict?"

"Guilty, with almost half a billion in damages."

"That's great! Like I said, we'll sue Perses."

"Not so fast."

"Why not?"

"Because a year after the trial, the district judge vacated the jury's decision with a *judgment as a matter of law* decision."

"What's that?" asked Johnny.

I explained, "Basically, a conclusion that the plaintiff failed to show the losses were material or that the nursing home acted with sufficient knowledge that what it was doing was wrong."

"Gotta love our justice system. No offense."

"I'm with you."

"The worst of it," Jayce continued, "was that the judge also found that the management company wasn't shown to be liable for the actions of the individual homes."

That was surprising. I said, "You're saying the private equity owners were insulated from the actions of the individual homes."

Johnny added, "Even after people suffered, died?"

Jayce nodded. "Exactly! Eventually, most of the jury's verdict against the company was reinstated by an appellate court. But that was only after a decade after filing the complaint in the first place! You can probably guess what happened next."

I shook my head and frowned, definitely knowing what had happened next.

I replied, "The nursing home declared bankruptcy."

Jayce made a finger gun. "Bingo. The private equity-controlled corporation was able to discharge almost all of the damages the plaintiff had won. In the end, they settled with the Department of Justice for just four million in damages, with only a quarter going to the plaintiff and the rest getting eaten by the government in fines."

"Mother Mary and Joseph—" Johnny cut off his curse.

I muttered one of my own and downed my Wild Turkey.

"So after a decade," Jayce went on, "she got a million dollars for the loss."

"What's the fix?" asked Johnny. "How do we make it stop?"

"The short answer is that regulators must be made accountable to residents themselves, not the organization controlling nursing homes."

"People who have been harmed at these places," I said, "they need their day in court!"

"I agree, and so does my boss, actually."

"The senator you work for?"

"He has legislation drafted and ready to go."

"What does it say?"

"For one, he wants to require nursing homes to meet minimum staffing requirements and to disclose who owns them. There's a repeal of their liability shields and arbitration agreements, requiring the courts to litigate liability suits. It establishes a special office of the Attorney General to investigate private equity malfeasance."

"Sounds reasonable," Johnny said.

I asked, "Why hasn't it moved forward?"

"For all the reasons I explained earlier. You think money makes the world go 'round? Nope. Money throws cement into the gears and entrenches people."

"Lobbyists," I said with a sneer.

"You'd think with all that corporate greed these firms would be tight-fisted penny pinchers, not wanting to part with their Benjamins. Nope! Money flows from their hands to Hill coffers by the billions."

"Let me get this straight," Johnny said. "Instead, of caring about their workers and customers, the businesses they run and services they provide, they issue cutbacks and lay people off to save money—then, what, they turn around and give it away to politicians?"

I said, "Sounds like institutionalized money laundering!"

Jayce grunted a nod. "Bingo..."

I leaned in, having heard enough. I was ready to make the offer I'd come to make.

"What if you had proof?"

"Proof?"

"Documents, with names and numbers that show what one private equity firm did when it took over a nursing home."

"You have those?"

"Basically."

Jayce leaned forward, a twinkle in his eyes and one end of his mouth curling upward. Might have been the Wild Turkey, but I'd seen that look before.

The look of a man smelling red meat.

"Then here's what we're going to do," he said.

Then laid out a plan.

I listened, for what felt like an hour, not saying a word and not quite sure I liked Jayce's suggestions. There were risks, for

Ma. And, honestly, for my class action case. By the end, we'd gamed out a plan that might just work.

By the good grace of God. Which led me to do what I'd found myself doing more times than I'd done the past twenty years in half as many days.

Prayed.

Lord Jesus Christ, Son of God...this better work!

Chapter Forty-Four

Time seemed to turn, on a dime. Before I knew it, the hot, sticky mid-August West Michigan had given way to falling reds and yellows and oranges. And before long, the white stuff was flying and piling, carrying me and my team into the new year.

Through the fall and Christmas season, most nights were spent burning the midnight oil in my living room. The embers of a waning fire warmed me and filled the space with woodsmoke while I worked to execute on the next phase of things, a half-drained bottle of a mouthy Malbec steeling me with the soft tang of blackberry complemented by the softness of vanilla and sweet tobacco and fueling me for the job ahead.

Which, for six months, had been plowing the hard ground of two parallel tracks we hoped would shut down Perses Global Financial Group for good.

The first track was my original one: the class action against HappyLiving. We were back in business, and it was proceeding on course. I had completed the deposition of the CEO and learned nothing that I hadn't already known about the basic plans PGFG had for the park and residents, their rents and fees rising astronomically.

The one thing that had surfaced during the legal interrogation was a passing comment on PGFG's larger Mill Creek Junction play that niggled in the back of my lizard brain. Something I had sent my trusty private eye, Johnny Pope, chasing down. Could be nothing, might be something. With the way August had gone, I didn't want to take any chances. He was supposed to have checked in by now, given we were headed to trial later in the morning to make good on my class action promise to restrain Perses and save Ma and her neighbors.

The other track was the diciest, and frankly scariest. For it had put Ma directly in the crosshairs of Perses and in direct legal jeopardy. Jayce Robinson had barreled forward with a plan to bring accountability and regulatory oversight for Perses and similar private equity firms that would also strengthen consumer and worker protections.

The legislation was classic Jayce, his Christian faith compelling him to give voice to his worldview convictions that wealth and money should serve the greater civic good, not merely line the pockets of fat-cat CEOs and pad the balance sheets of Wall Street hot stocks and retirement portfolios. It also happened to align with his boss, Senator DeWitt, who had been part of the vanguard of a new populism that had overtaken the Republican party. Reagan's Grand Old Party, and grand old bargain, was a thing of the past on the other side of NAFTA's hollowing out of the Rust Belt, from which DeWitt was originally from, and the Great Recession and coronacrazy nonsense that had ravaged families' savings and financial stability.

I didn't pay too much attention to the politics of it all. All that mattered to me was Ma, and the legalities of breaking her confidentiality agreement with Perses Global Financial Group.

Because part of the plan Jayce had hatched after dusting off his boss's legislation was leveraging the power of the bully pulpit. As chairman of the powerful Senate Committee on Health, Education, Labor and Pensions, he was in a unique position to expose PGFG for the reckless, greedy vultures they were.

And Ma had played a starring role.

At the start of the new legislative session, she had appeared before a HELP committee hearing to lay out everything she had witnessed—and found. Her testimony was moving. Her evidence was damning. It had riveted the Hill, and the papers. Everything from *The Washington Post* to *The New York Times*, *Time Magazine* to *Newsweek* had covered her incendiary revelations.

Things had moved quickly after that, with the promise of a political solution to a civic one that had eluded Western capitalism for a generation. Wasn't sure how it would all shake out, or if it would, given the political dynamics. Again, didn't pay attention to any of that nonsense. My focus was elsewhere.

Defending Ma against any fallout and plowing ahead with our game plan to save HappyLiving residents.

I was finishing a gulp of fresh, hot coffee and readying to put the final touches on that plan when my door flew open—and Reggie and Lizzy strode inside with clear purpose.

"It's happening!" Reggie said in a rush. "Where's your remote?"

He started rifling through stacks of papers, shoving aside empty fast food bags, darting about my office.

I stood. "What's happening?"

"The bill," was all Lizzy said.

"Bill?"

"From Senator DeWitt."

"Your buddy Jayce Robinson called me a bit ago with the good—" Reggie planted his hands on his hips and shook his head. "This place is a pigsty, Gideon! How you get any work done in here is a mystery of mysteries. And where's that dang remote?"

I frowned, opening my top desk drawer and withdrawing a black plastic candy bar-size device.

"Looking for this?" I said, holding it up.

Reggie smiled and snatched it from my hand, then zapped my TV to life and searched for C-SPAN.

"So it's happening then?" I asked, a mixture of disbelief and anticipation snatching my breath now.

"It's happening."

Reggie had taken point as lead counsel for Ma on that front of things. Given his political science background and particular knowledge of the legislative branch, I thought he was best suited to counsel Ma and defend her, but also work with Jayce to hatch our plan.

Which, apparently, was coming home to roost.

C-SPAN was on location at the Capitol Building, and it offered an establishing shot of the Senate Chamber. A hundred small wooden desks were neatly arranged across its regal navy carpet in the half-oval room, walls a plain cream that bordered on golden punctuated by dark marble pillars. It was calm, serene, and oddly empty. I had always assumed the place was packed and busy, men and women huddled and conspiring, speaking and speechifying. Not today, and maybe not most days. A woman commanded the heights of the chamber's dais in the vice president's chair at a massive mahogany desk, an indigo curtain draped behind. She wasn't the only person ready to legislate.

Down below was Senator DeWitt, who had taken to the floor of the stately chamber, standing hunched over his personal desk that had to be at least a century old and had changed countless hands over the nation's two centuries and a half. Straightening, he held a few printed pages and adjusted a microphone resting in his charcoal suit breast pocket before speaking.

"Madam President," he started, "Today, I rise to introduce before the American people a piece of legislation that is long overdue—the Private Equity Accountability and Corporate Enforcement Act."

Took a beat, but then I got it.

PEACE Act. Nice.

"For too long, private equity firms have operated in the shadows of American corporate and consumer power, evading accountability for impacting and upending the American economy and communities. This bill is meant to finally take deliberate, decisive steps to rein in these unchecked powers that have bloomed into outsized influence over American consumers and workers, ensuring these corporations act as responsible, productive members of society and are held responsible when their actions cause consequential damage in the lives of ordinary citizens.

"Private equity firms are the single greatest driving force in our modern economy now, employing nearly ten percent of American workers and generating a twentieth of our gross domestic product. From healthcare to manufacturing, retail to housing, even banking and government—their influence stretches across America, and their control is unchecked. Current laws make it difficult to enforce civil and criminal accountability for faulty or dangerous products and services. What's more, hardworking American men and women have lost countless jobs thanks to faceless boardrooms making decisions that best serve their bottom line. This cannot continue."

Senator DeWitt paused to turn the page and take a sip of water. I wondered what this new turn of things might mean for Ma, given her participation in this political turn.

"Last fall, as chairman of the Health, Education, Labor and Pensions committee, I arranged to introduce testimony before my committee by a brave woman who had firsthand knowledge of the chilling effects of private equity on the real lives of real people."

I clamped a hand on Ma's shoulder, pride rising on a head of joyous emotion. This was it. No way to hide now. Oddly, any anxious dread I'd had about Ma's liability had sieved to nothing but nothing, and a sort of peace that surpassed any understanding filled me.

Ma flinched under my grip, and I loosened it into a show of reassuring solidarity. She put a hand on mine, eyes fixed on the flatscreen.

"Florence O'Donnell," the senator went on, "with the help of my staff, offered a whistleblower account as someone who lost a husband to the negligence of corporate cutbacks that plague nursing homes, as well as documents outlining the financial scheming that went into covering up those fatalities. I, in coordination with the Department of Justice, provided her immunity from prosecution for her testimony. She was a brave citizen who came forward to offer a chilling account of reckless disregard for the quality of care in nursing homes bought out and hollowed out by Perses Global Financial Group."

Senator DeWitt turned another page and adjusted spectacles perched on his nose. He was a slight, short man in an ill-fitting suit who didn't at all strike me as a person of power. Yet there he was, laying down the smack on these vultures.

He said, "The Private Equity Accountability and Corporate Enforcement Act will make it clear to the likes of Perses and other such firms that they are responsible for what they do. Legal loopholes and tricks to circumvent liability will end. Private equity firms will be wholly responsible for the harm their companies cause consumers. Bailing through bankruptcy will end. Hiding behind complex ownership structures to evade responsibility will end. Every firm at the top of the ownership pyramid will be held accountable by the courts and rule of law. With the PEACE Act, consumers will win again."

Reggie laughed and clapped his hands. "There it is! The money line."

Lizzy smirked. "Sounds like shades of that orange-haired politician, but it works."

Couldn't help but smile at that line. It's one my buddy Jayce had trumpeted throughout the entire process. *Make consumers win again!* had been his mantra, and his fingerprints were all over this piece and legislation. I was sure grateful for my friend. Not only for his handiwork, but for his care in giving Ma a platform to air her story and shed light on the fraudulent, negligent practices of one private equity firm.

"Closing liability escapist loopholes is only one part of the problem, however. This bill also protects American jobs to ensure our communities do not shoulder the burdensome consequences of reckless private equity practices. The Department of Labor will be empowered to review offshoring and outsourcing of American jobs. A new provision, called the WorkShield Stability Fund, will provide retraining and job placement services when these firms ship jobs overseas."

Another page turn, another sip of water.

"This bill also establishes a new Office of Private Equity Oversight within the Department of Justice. It will monitor compliance and enforce penalties for violations. Significant fines and forced divestitures will accompany failure to meet enhanced disclosure requirements for their structures, investments, and financial health—ensuring transparency and accountability."

No way would Perses Global Financial Group stand for this. There'd be political hell to pay, that's for sure.

I glanced down at Ma.

Maybe even legal...

"Madam President, this legislation will benefit the American public. Holding these firms accountable will protect consumers from defective products and fraudulent practices. Ensuring American jobs stay put on American soil will support a stable economy and robust communities. Increasing transparency will foster fair markets that serve our public needs, not just the wealthy few."

"Damn straight," Reggie muttered.

"I'd vote for him," I said. "Even though he's from Kansas."

"Hey, I'm from Kansas!" Lizzy complained.

"Need I say more?"

She smacked my shoulder; I yelped.

Senator DeWitt said, "This bill is about fairness, accountability, and justice. It is about standing up for the rights of consumers and workers to ensure our economy works for everyone. I urge my colleagues to take a stand together for the American people by supporting this legislation. For too long, unaccountable corporate entities have gotten away with skirting the law and evading accountability. Let's make consumers win again. For this reason, Madam President, I move for unanimous consent to adopt the PEACE Act, Senate Bill 527, into law."

"Say *waaa?*"

There was a commotion in the chamber that signaled uncertainty.

"What's the problem?" I asked Reggie.

Ma turned to him as well. "What's this unanimous consent business?"

Mouth wide and eyes wider, he swallowed and replied, "Unanimous consent is almost always used for non-controversial bills and procedural matters, for simple resolutions and senses of the Senate, and whatnot."

"What is it?"

"It's a way to pass bills without a vote. For Senator DeWitt to push for a UC agreement, for this bill...my my my. That's ballsy!"

"Why's that?" asked Lizzy.

Reggie explained, "Because if one senator objects to the request, it's nixed. Unanimous consent is basically asking the entire Senate to give the green-light without debate or added amendments. And with the nature of this legislation, with its regulations and liabilities, concerns about judicial overreach, the strong ties senators would have to the financial sector—no way is this happening without debate and a vicious fight."

The room fell silent, holding its collective breath.

The Senate seemed to fall into the same expectant rhythm, winding down to a hush as the president pro tempore asked if there was any objection. Time slowed. It seemed to stand still. Coughs and whispers were thrown up from the Senate Chamber. But crucially, no one objected.

Yet.

Four and five seconds ticked into the teens.

Then, miraculously, there was heard a familiar sound. One I'd gotten more times than I could count from Mill Creek Junction Superior Court.

Wood against wood.

And that was that.

There were a few cheers and claps from the well of the Senate Chamber, with some of the pols glad-handing and back-slapping one another—chief among them Senator DeWitt. Thought I caught a glimpse of Jayce Robinson at the back of the chamber, standing and clapping in a crisp navy suit, complemented by a bright yellow bow tie.

I turned to Reggie: "What just happened?"

He eased his head my way, whispering, "It passed."

Said nothing more, looking as shocked as I felt.

"Passed?"

"Passed."

"Like, law-of-the-land passed?"

A breath, deep and long, then a beat.

Then the wide grin I'd come to know and love.

"Hella to the yeah!" he cried, clapping his hands together before opening his arms wide and bear-hugging me.

Lizzy threw up a screech of delight before joining in. Then another pair of arms reached around from behind and gave me some familiar love.

Mama love.

We were laughing and crying and cheering. Before I knew it, we were jumping up and down and doing some dance that Reggie and Mama seemed far more dialed into than Lizzy or I were familiar with.

"We did it!" Reggie finally said, coming out of a groove before heaving a breath and exhaling. "We did it..."

"Not we." I turned to Ma. "*You* did it."

She bowed her head and offered a weak smile, chuckling and sitting, averting my proud eyes.

"Suppose so" was all she replied.

Lizzy scoffed. "Suppose so? Uh, nopety nope!"

"Excuse me, young lady?"

I laughed. "Lizzy's right, Ma! Sitting before that committee, sharing your story about Dad, about what you had learned sleuthing around Dreamscape Manor the way you did, all incognito as you did—"

"Which I saw right through, bee-tee-dubs," Reggie added, crossing his arms and nodding.

I swatted him away. "Anyway, what you found, what you did—and what you *risked*..."

Trailing off, I considered the legal jeopardy she'd put herself through. It was no small thing to renege on a settlement agreement. Especially to renege on a nondisclosure agreement. We were certain she had a good case to make for such a breach of contract, with plenty of cause and legal outs.

Except—

Except Perses Global Financial Group had yet to mount a reply.

Which was flat worrisome.

No telling what they would do.

And when...

"You're a regular Jessica Fletcher, Mrs. O!" Lizzy exclaimed.

Had to smile at that, leaving my worries behind for just a moment.

Reggie said, "Guarantee you this is just the beginning."

I glanced down at my watch, surprised by the time. He was right; it was. And the next phase of things was set to begin shortly.

"Another few hours till trial starts," I announced, turning off the television. "You ready for what comes next, Ma?"

Her face fell, getting real serious, before she nodded and stood.

I was about to take her arm and leave when the front office door thudded open, an echoey interruption that sent visions of Junction PD storming inside ready to make an arrest skating through me.

I popped my head out for a look.

It was Johnny Pope. Hustling toward us and holding up a file folder.

Wearing a face I flat couldn't read.

Chapter Forty-Five

I didn't waste any time, rushing to intercept him. Knowing what I had sent him to do—who I had sent him to interrogate.

Lord Jesus Christ, Son of God, please let it be good news...

"Please tell me you've got good news."

He stopped short, dipping his head and shaking his head.

My heart seized in my chest and disappointment snatched my breath. My stomach did one of those plummeting-to-the-floor maneuvers you read about in bargain-bin Kindle books that actually pretty much feels close to that.

That was it, then. They had no leverage.

Ma was screwed.

Not only with this trial, our case against Perses Global Financial Group through our injunctive relief barring Happy-Living from raising rates and honoring original contract terms despite the change of ownership. That was one thing, and not the real thing I cared about. What would really screw Ma over was what PGFG did with her dicey legal situation on the other side of the Senate hearing—and on the other side of the Senate bill that promised to make them and their cronies hopping mad.

"What's the matter, sugar?" Ma said, coming up behind.

Her voice sent my shoulders slumping toward the floor along with my stomach. Looking to the scuffed hardwood in search of an answer, Johnny offered one for me.

"Nothing, Florence."

I snapped my head up, furrowing my brow with confusion. When it dawned.

In the light of Johnny's grinning, laughing face beneath his black fedora.

"Gotcha, kid!"

Now I frowned, wanting to snatch that hat from his bald head and smack him with it. Instead, I huffed a sigh as he carried on. Hated when he did that, teasing me when he knew darn well I wasn't in the mood, especially with Ma's life on the line.

Johnny carried on like that, laughing as he withdrew a manila envelope from his back behind his trench coat. It was thin and sealed shut, but I guessed it was exactly what I wanted. After another throaty, mocking chuckle, Johnny slapped the envelope against my chest.

"It's all right here, kid!" he said.

I snatched it and tore through the flap, pulling out a bundle of papers that seemed to be the theme of my life the past half a year.

"Whatcha got?" asked Lizzy.

"Proof," Johnny replied.

"What proof?" pressed Reggie. "What's he talking about, Gideon?"

Holding up a finger I ignored my partners and started flipping through the papers, recognizing what Johnny had brought me.

I simply said "Bank statements" as I scanned the lines of transactions and flipped through the pages.

"For who?" asked Reggie.

Johnny said, "Not who. What."

"Huh?"

Lizzy said, "Spell it out for us, Sherlock."

He smirked. "I'm more a Sam Spade sort of fella myself than the kooky Brit."

"Yeah, you do have more of *The Maltese Falcon* vibe about you than *The Hound of the Baskervilles*."

"What's that supposed to—"

Reggie cleared his throat. "Can we focus, please? What the heck did you find?"

"He's right," Lizzy said. "Spill the tea, JP."

"What are all of these recurring expenses?" I asked before Johnny could answer. "They're sporadic, but the amount is consistent."

"What you're holding there, what you're wondering about, those expenses and whatnot—" He pointed, adding "that's what I found."

"Whose are they, and do I want to know how you got a hold of these?"

"It's all on the up and up. I contacted a buddy of mine. Wanted to know if he'd heard of any shady business with any members of the Mill Creek Junction City Council."

I raised a brow. "A buddy?"

"What buddy?" asked Lizzy.

Johnny said, "Not what. Where."

"Where?"

"Where."

I huffed a sigh. "This is getting old, JP. We're expected at trial soon."

He nodded. "The IRS."

Reggie whistled. "Them big-dog guns!"

"Indeed."

"And what did this buddy say?"

A beat, a breath, a grin. "Someone connected to Junction City Hall was indeed being investigated for tax fraud."

"Say *waaa*?"

"Oh my heck!" Lizzy agreed. "How did you know about that?"

Johnny shrugged. "Didn't. But during Gideon's Happy-Living deposition of Gage Strauss, the CEO mentioned that the buyout from Perses had the full backing of the City Council."

"And when I pressed him on it," I added, "he let it slip that it was a unanimous recommendation championed by the city council with the mayor's backing."

Reggie said, "So these are kickbacks to Mayor Goodall?"

Johnny shook his head, jerking a thumb my way. "An old client's."

Took a beat to register his meaning.

Then it did.

I couldn't voice a response, I was so thrown.

Lizzy huffed a reply for me. "Gerald Peterson."

Just shook my head at that. Had wondered whether there was a current of corruption jolting this Perses deal into action. Figured it was Mayor Goodall himself, with his election on the line. Not that HappyLiving would boost his numbers, but the way Perses Global Financial Group was investing in our small town, I figured he was somehow in on it all.

Now I knew that corruption wound its way back to my own handiwork.

Johnny said, "But it was more than the HappyLiving play, wasn't it, Gideon?"

I nodded. "Strauss had said they had a vision for a private

equity public, where the market efficiencies of capitalism ran every aspect of public life."

Reggie smirked. "And let me guess, Mill Creek Junction was their sandbox?"

"That's right."

"Damn vultures," Lizzy cursed, which wasn't like her.

I said, "Strauss said there was someone on the inside of the Goodall administration who had greased the skids to make it all go smoothly."

"A fixer," Johnny added. "That's how he'd described it."

"I wondered if there was some sort of corruption at work in the broader play Perses had in mind for the Junction, so I sent Johnny to find out."

Reggie turned to him. "And did you?"

Johnny pointed to those bank statements. "A series of payments made by an off-shore shell company to Gerald Peterson."

"Connected to Perses?"

"You're talking a quid pro quo," Lizzy said.

"With Peterson at the center of a laundering scheme to exchange cash for the votes needed to make their play for our town to go through."

Johnny replied, "That's what my buddy and the IRS suspects."

Just shook my head at that. Same for Reggie and Lizzy, the pair going silent. Even Ma sat still with disbelief.

"There's more," he went on. "Which you may want to sit down for, kid."

He gave me a look that flared up one of those staticy reactions across my skin.

I stood still, asking, "What more, Johnny?"

"My buddy tells me the IRS had a cooperating witness that was helping them and the Department of Justice build a corruption and tax evasion case against him and most of the Junction City Council. She had all the receipts and was ready to go public"

"She?" Lizzy said, brow furrowed. Johnny just nodded.

I muttered a "Whoa" at the thickening plot, our small town being embroiled in a corruption scheme that would make East Coast mobsters blush.

Except—

I said, "You look like there's more to the story, Johnny."

He shifted. "Here's the thing, and this is where it gets deep. Their cooperating witness was eighty-sixed about a year ago."

"Murdered?"

"That's their theory. Never proven, but she died suddenly, under mysterious circumstances."

"Did they give you a name?"

He nodded. "Penelope Peterson."

Took a beat to register his meaning. Then it did.

With Reggie throwing up his standard "Say *waaa?*" reply, followed by Lizzy's own "Oh my heck!" rejoinder.

For my part, I just shook my head, disbelieving the turn—and the connection. My gut tightened. Twisted, really, with the realization that I had gotten Gerald Peterson off. Had a hunch he'd done it. Didn't want to believe it, my eyes fixed on the dough a not guilty verdict would bring the firm. I do remember one thing, though.

That look in his eyes, during trial, when I suggested we plea. His reaction, those eyes...I knew he'd done it.

Reggie said, "You mean to tell me that joker actually did kill his wife?"

"Might have," Johnny said with emphasis. "But there was a good reason for him to do the job. Not that there's any reason to off someone, but you get my drift."

"Why?"

Lizzy said, "Seems clear to me."

I nodded, putting it all together. "Gerald found out his wife was ratting him out. That he was taking unreported kickbacks from Perses—" I returned to those bank statements, shaking my head. "To the tune of several hundred thousands of dollars."

Johnny said, "Yeah, but here's where it gets dicey. The thing about it is, Peterson didn't pocket the money."

"Say *waaa?*" Reggie exclaimed.

"I've got the figures all worked out on a spreadsheet at the back, but the long and short of the number crunching is that the money that went into Peterson's bank came out at various times, in various ways. It all adds up, perfectly."

"Like a pass-through entity?" asked Lizzy.

Reggie shook his head. "Money laundering entity, more like it."

Johnny pointed a finger at him. "That."

Lizzy said, "You're saying money came in only to come back out again."

"To the penny."

"All accounted for?"

"All accounted for. And not just to the council members, where that exchange dried up before the HappyLiving play."

I said, "You're saying the trail of initial monetary exchanges ended, what early last year, then picked up again?"

Johnny nodded. "That's right."

"Who did the money go to, then?" Reggie said, before quickly adding "And don't go into this not whom but where nonsense!"

He smirked and replied, "I was able to trace a series of recent payments to a pair."

"A pair?"

"Of what?" added Lizzy.

"Of knuckleheads, that's what."

"Don't you mean that's *who*?"

Johnny was being far too coy for Johnny Pope. In between that revelation and wondering what he was getting at—the answer dawned with a jolting bolt of understanding, flooding me with a coldness that also boiled my blood.

I stepped forward and said lowly, "Sammy and Kelsey."

He just crossed his arms and nodded.

"Hold up!" Reggie said, putting up a hand. "You're saying Councilman Peterson paid the two knuckleheads who kidnapped Gideon's mama?"

"Working theory is he was the conduit between Perses Global and Mayor Goodall. The one who made the connections between the private equity firm and the city council and all the businesses they'd snatched up the past year."

"How?" I asked.

"Apparently, Cindy Crawford and Gerald Peterson were having an affair. Knew each other in a former life when the councilman worked on Wall Street before settling back in his childhood home. The rest is history."

Reggie ahhed. "So Perses needed a backdoor."

"A launderer," Lizzy corrected. "Like you'd suggested."

"Someone to pass the scratch to grease the skids on their buying frenzy."

Johnny said, "Which Florence O'Donnell was about to mess up by going public with her discoveries of fraud and negligence."

Perses had indeed bankrolled mama's kidnapping. And the man I'd defended, had set free, had aided and abetted their crime...

I muttered, "Which makes this case a whole other thing."

"What thing?" asked Johnny.

"Don't you see? This is no longer a simple contract dispute.

It's a conspiracy to defraud not only the residents of HappyLiving, but—"

"Mill Creek Junction itself!"

"Bingo."

The room fell silent at the revelation.

And no doubt the implications.

Lizzy interrupted it: "What's our play, then?"

Reggie added, "Yeah, Gideon, what are you thinking?"

I said nothing, unsure.

One thing I did know was that I needed Gerald Peterson to testify to what he had done.

My wrist barked for my attention. Not a sound, just a subconscious tingle.

Dang. Running late.

Stuffing the papers back inside, I held up the envelope. "This is great, Johnny. We have to run, but I need you to do one more thing."

He nodded. "You got it, kid."

I told him what I wanted. He wasn't sure he could pull it off, but promised to try. I prayed he could.

Because Mama's life depended on it.

Chapter Forty-Six

I led the charge hustling down Main Street to Courthouse Road for our rendezvous with Perses Global Financial Group, where our civil case against the private equity firm was set to start. Except the way it started wasn't the way I had ever imagined it going.

No longer was this a simple contractual matter. Like I'd said back at the farm: this case was a whole other thing. Something I was beginning to see I could use to our advantage in litigating my class action on behalf of Ma and the HappyLiving residents, which was also about protecting her and Mill Creek Junction from these vultures.

The air was crisp with a bite to it, the frigid wind gusting from behind flaring brewed coffee and baking cinnamon rolls. My stomach rumbled in revolt, angry I hadn't taken Ma's childhood advice that breakfast was the most important meal of the day. Who had time for breakfast when the fate of your mama was hanging in the balance?

Or apparently an entire town...

Didn't take long before we were bounding up the limestone

stairs pockmarked by weather and lawyerly wear. It hit me that the last time I'd climbed these stairs I was wearing an orange jumpsuit and barking at Tracy Nolland for accusing me of murdering my mother. I said a quick prayer of thanksgiving for the good Lord getting me out of that mess—and prayed he was in as generous of a getting-out mood this morning.

Familiar chandeliers glowing yellow in the dim rotunda vestibule lit the way inside. No bright sunlight today, thick snow clouds blotting it out and threatening to unleash Old Man Winter's fury later in the day. One by one, my team and I checked through the metal detectors, then hustled across a familiar patchwork of red-and-blue tiles with whorls of green and gold on toward destiny.

Glancing above, I caught a glimpse of Lady Justice swimming high above in a white cloud accented by pinks and golds, swarmed by cherubic guardians. The celestial image sparked a memory from church Sunday school. A saying from the Book of Proverbs, actually: *'The king's heart is a stream of water in the hand of the Lord; he turns it wherever he will.'*

I just prayed he steered the judge's heart our way that day.

Bringing the funk down on Perses Global Financial Group.

The private equity firm had waived their right to a jury trial, taking their defense straight to a Mill Creek Junction judge. In this case, that was Judge Staggs, just my luck. I thought it was an odd strategy, but probably carried far less risk submitting to the whims of small-town men and women who might have felt they were defending the honor of their townsfolk on top of ruling on matters of justice for Ma.

With such a waiver request both parties were required to agree to it. Neither party could unilaterally waive the right to a jury trial without the consent of the other party. We had gone back and forth whether or not to agree to the tactic. Reggie and Lizzy made convincing cases for both agreeing and rejecting the waiver. Since I was first chairing the trial, I'd agreed to their request, believing our best bet was to hope for a directed verdict from the judge himself at just the right juncture of the trial.

We'd see whether that bet would pay off in due time.

Heavy wood doors stood open leading inside the stately chamber. Our clattering echoed throughout the vast chamber of dark wood and matching polished floors. Past several rows of stiff wood pews stood a magisterial dais where Judge Staggs would take up his perch behind a similar dark wood desk.

Generous tables of the same sat down below just past a wood waist-high bar. Ours at the right near the jury box stood empty. The one to the left was already filled, a heavy presence of dark wool suits filling four chairs, with the row behind filled to similar capacity. Clearly a show of force from the defendants meant to—

Something caught my attention as I neared.

And stopped me in my tracks, cold.

From disbelief.

It was Cindy Crawford. The woman I had seen at Max's Place jawing it up with Mayor Goodall. Who Johnny had seen at Millie's on Main with two Asian bouncers jawing it up in Russian.

And I had faced down a few years ago at the settlement conference, where I had sold my parents for a cool two mill.

I swallowed, hard, my tongue stumbling over a throat that had gone dry.

She stood out from her pack of male counterparts, all wearing black suits with white shirts and crimson ties. Hers was a dark brown pantsuit, an uncommon color for lawyers, but it worked. Classic and conservative, conveying confidence and authority, groundedness and approachability. She paired it with a blush pink blouse and a simple chunky gold necklace, matched by an oversized gold Rolex watch. Definitely London money, which she wore well.

Her blond hair fell across her shoulders and looked radiant in the light as she turned toward me while I entered through the bar. She said nothing, except for one end of her mouth curling upward. She threw me a wink before returning to a leather portfolio. And was that a kiss, her crimson mouth puckering just so?

I slipped into the first chair of our table, then slipped a hand into my pocket. I clenched the classic Meisterstück LeGrand Montblanc pen my father had gifted me for a dose of stability. Adrenaline skated through me now, ratcheting up my ticker a notch and sending my lungs searching for an extra breath.

I was embarrassed she could elevate my anxiety, but this was unexpected. And yet—

Yet it was also welcomed. I would do what I hadn't been able to do the last time we met.

Make Perses pay.

I heard a gasp from behind, then a scurrying clatter of steps before Ma slipped beside me and clenched a hand on my arm.

"Isn't that the woman who robbed me blind?" she whispered in a rush.

Now my gut twisted with regret before it sank.

"I believe so," I answered. "But we've got a solid case. And I guarantee we'll win, Ma."

She eased her grip before taking a deep breath and sighing with a nod.

Soon, the benches behind us were filled with the other class members, and the hour I'd been waiting for over a year arrived.

"All rise," Silvia announced, the court clerk. "The court is now in session, the Honorable Judge Stanley Staggs presiding."

We did, me and Ma, Reggie and Lizzy at her right. Then

Cindy Crawford and her cronies at our left. Took everything within me not to glance her way, but I didn't. Wouldn't even acknowledge her.

Clerk Silvia continued, "The matter before the court is Florence O'Donnell, on behalf of herself and all other members similarly situated, versus Perses Global Financial Group. Case Number 81624."

A sudden lancing slice of sunlight pierced into the vast, stately chamber through stained glass windows. It fell just right on Lady Justice perched behind the bench. I almost took it as a sign, but didn't want to press my luck.

Bodies shifted in the rows behind on stiff shoes clattering beneath waiting for what came next. I understood the anticipation.

I couldn't wait to pace a rut in front of the judge's box to make my case. Definitely couldn't wait to spring to object to whatever nonsense that weaselly Cindy Crawford raised. Mostly, I just couldn't wait to fight for justice. For Mill Creek and the HappyLiving residents. For Ma—

By getting that other weasel to the stand who had made it all happen in the first place.

Lemon polish hung heavy again, as before, waiting for Judge Staggs to make his entrance. I kept one hand in my pocket, clenched on my Montblanc pen, its weight and solidness, grounding, reassuring. The other I rested on my open legal pad that also carried a few printed pages of remarks, the paper's softness steadying me and readying me for the fight ahead.

I kept my eyes trained on the massive solid walnut crow's nest where the judge would perch himself soon enough. I had argued a few hundred cases before that bench over the years. Mostly small, minor offenses. Sometimes big-time ones, the criminal kind that got blowhards like Gerald Peterson off, scot free.

This would be entirely different.

I wasn't just arguing for Ma's sake and for the sake of the class. Not entirely, not really. Because Reggie had nailed it: This was bigger than just the HappyLiving case. It was a conspiracy to defraud and subjugate an entire town.

My town.

And it was crucial I get the chance to make the case. Which my trusty private eye was in the process of securing. Or so I hoped.

I glanced behind, hoping to see him settled at the back with two thumbs up.

Nothing but the class members sitting behind.

A whooshing sound, followed by the trailing thud of a door, yanked my attention to stage right.

"Goodie, both parties are present." Judge Staggs bounded out from his chamber and into the courtroom.

With his entrance, the wheels of justice began turning.

"Good morning, Your Honor," I said. "Gideon Paul O'Donnell, representing the plaintiff class, with Florence O'Donnell as the class representative."

"Yes, it is being a good morning, Your Honor," the woman at my left said, a singsongy, almost mocking tone to her I didn't care for. "Sonya Kuperov, representing the defending party, Perses Global Financial Group."

That sure yanked my attention from the judge. And snapped my head toward the Russia's Next Top Model. Sure carried with it a Cynthia Crawford ring to her name. Suppose I wasn't too off the mark.

She brushed a stray lock of golden hair back behind her ear, turning her head toward me, but not fully. Almost as if to acknowledge my gaze—or gawking, as was the case.

I quickly returned my attention to Judge Staggs, who sent us back to our seats. He launched into a lengthy opening speech, addressing court decorum, preliminary matters, and the trial's schedule—which began with our opening statements.

With me up to bat.

Rising, I buttoned my jacket, looked down at Ma and smiled, then over to Reggie and Lizzy before taking a parting glance behind—eyeing the class members, yes, but searching for someone else.

Johnny Pope.

He was due back before my opening statement with word, either way, about the thing I'd sent him to do.

And secure.

Because without it—without him...

I wasn't sure about the rest of the case.

Creaking benches and coughing onlookers narrowed my attention back to the moment at hand, sending me slipping my right hand into my pocket and gripping my Montblanc for stability. I was going to need it for the road ahead.

"Your Honor," I began, "the case I bring before you is one about systemic negligence and a remarkable breach of trust on the part of HappyLiving Estates, which later became part of the portfolio of equity investments by Perses Global Financial Group. HappyLiving had originally entered into contracts with hundreds of Mill Creek Junction residents in good faith—"

I paused, sweeping my hand toward Ma but keeping my eyes fixed on Judge Staggs, adding: "—including Ms. Florence O'Donnell. She, along with the other members of the class, were offered promises of stable rents, rising equity, and a sustainable middle-class life. HappyLiving reneged on the promises, breaching not only their contractual relationship, but also their trust and goodwill with the good people of Mill Creek Junction. Over the course of this trial, we will not only prove such a breach, but also a deliberate engagement in fraud that engendered real harm for every member of this class."

Another pause, and now a breath. Deep and contemplative.

And stalling.

Because I had to know whether the next thing—my next *words*—would hold water.

I reached for a glass still full of water, a tremble overtaking my hand at the anticipation, when—

The courtroom door opened with a substantial whoosh on cranky hinges, creating a window for us all to take a collective breath and pause. I followed its lead and took my own breath and pause—hoping and praying someone had entered rather than exited, and that the entering someone was a friend.

Anticipation skated through me at who I saw standing at the back, cold and searching.

It was Johnny, returned from my errand.

Better late than never.

He slipped into a row at the back and settled in, his eyes connecting with mine and readying to give me the yay or nay.

The thumbs up or down.

My do or die.

There was no thumb.

Instead, Johnny tipped his hat to me. Our sign.

Which gave me the green light to do the next thing.

Loud throat clearing from the bench yanked me back to the judge.

And set into motion the next stage of things I prayed to the good Lord above I could pull off.

I continued, "Breach of contract and fraud for class members is merely the tip of the iceberg, however, Your Honor. For the real tragedy of Perses's designs against my clients had more than *them* in mind."

A breath, a beat.

Then the hammer: "We are amending our complaint to include the charge of civil conspiracy to defraud Mill Creek Junction."

Predictably, Sonya Kuperov was on her feet objecting.

"This is an outrage!" she said.

"You have proof of this-this?" asked Judge Staggs.

Wasn't sure exactly. But Johnny always came through.

So I said, "We will prove to the court our claim."

Then I took my seat, easing a held breath.

The judge settled and nodded toward the defense, inviting her to offer opening remarks. Perses's general counsel wasted no time.

"Your Honor," Sonya Kuperov started, voice firm and commanding and driving, "Perses Global Financial Group has at its heart the operational value of integrity and transparency. Across all of our properties, we have always operated in full compliance and transparency with our contractual obligations to our clients and stakeholders. I can see the plaintiff is already planning to inflate the harm supposedly rendered against their clients—our residents," she added, bowing toward the judge and gesturing toward our side of the aisle.

Her Russian accent started coming through clearer now the more worked up she became: "They will be trying to paint a picture of a heartless company full of fat-cat executives engaged in a campaign of deception. However, I am assuring you that the facts of the matter will be showing that these are exaggerated claims designed to inflame. What's more, they are wholly, fundamentally unfounded—"

She stopped short, turning from the judge to me and looking me squarely in the eyes.

"Including the ridiculous emendation to the suit of civil conspiracy. I am seeing the counsel—"

Loud throat clearing from the bench for the second time

that day actually startled Sonya, throwing her off her game and snapping her head toward the judge with wide, uncertain eyes.

Judge Staggs said, "How about you try addressing me-me, counsel, instead of the plaintiff's attorney?"

He wiggled his fingers in front of his eyes when he said this, sending hot embarrassment spreading across her face.

Had to laugh at that. Didn't, except on the inside, but...go Judge Staggs!

Sonya Kuperov shifted and continued, "Right. At any rate, we will prove we acted within the bounds of the law upon our purchase of HappyLiving, and will look forward to your wise, timely judgment in our favor, Your Honor."

She sat, stiff and straight at the edge of her seat, clearly ready to go. If she was fuming, she didn't show it. But I knew my amendment to the suit, designed to throw her as much as strengthen our case, would have lit a fire in her. If it were me and I'd been blinded by that, on top of the charge that would have left me open to major liability danger, I would have been spitting mad, ready to go to the mat to wage war.

Conspiracy was a heavy charge. More so when it involved a government at some level, a town like Mill Creek Junction or another state entity. Monetary penalties would be the least of Perses Global Financial Group's worries. Disgorgement of profits and restitution to victims would definitely be on the table, resulting in possibly billions in compensatory damages on top of the punitive ones. Given the hand I was about to play, the corporate officers themselves could face criminal prosecution and decades in prison.

For my part, the stakes were as high. Arguing civil conspiracy claims carried a high bar for a winning judgment, requiring rock-solid evidence and skillful strategy. The fact Junction city actors were involved added another layer of complexity to it, with the state action doctrine and qualified immunity issues layered into likely RICO claims and the False Claims Act—both possibly (and probably) getting the Mitten State's attorney general involved as a plaintiff, even taking over my case.

So, yeah, lots at stake.

Which is why I needed Johnny to come through.

Another glance across my shoulder

Don't fail me now, JP...

Wasting no time, the judge addressed me: "Are you ready, counsel-sel?"

I nodded. "Yes, sir."

"Goodie! How about you call your first witness and let us get the show on the road."

Easing in a deep breath, I stood.

Here we go...

Chapter Forty-Seven

I stood, buttoning my jacket before slipping my hand in my right pocket and clenching my Montblanc again.

This was it.

My moment to do what I'd failed to secure for Ma those years ago—what I'd failed to claim for Dad.

Justice.

No way would I let it slip through our fingers this go around.

So I looked at Judge Staggs and made my announcement, one I knew would be unexpected.

"I call Florence O'Donnell to the stand."

There was a muttering whisper at my left as Ma joined me. I smiled, figuring Perses would have expected me to call Gage Strauss to the stand first, trying to nail his backside to the wall by drilling into the contract dispute. I figured right.

But had other plans.

Ma shuffled out from behind the table as I stood in the aisle, then I gestured for her to make her way to the front next to Judge Staggs.

She took careful steps with glassy care, my strong mother looking older today. The past year had taken a toll, especially after the kidnapping, the trauma and drugs having messed with her system. But she was a fighter. That she was standing in the well-used Junction witness box to stare down the Perses vultures was proof positive.

"Raise your right hand," the bailiff instructed. Ma complied. "Do you solemnly swear to tell the truth, the whole truth, and nothing but the truth?"

Ma nodded. "So help me God."

Judge Staggs leaned over. "You have to say, Yes."

"Yes," she quickly complied.

He smiled and said Ma could sit. She did. Then the judge instructed me to begin my questioning.

Taking another steadying breath, I walked toward Ma.

Readying to give the most important performance in the most important case of my life.

I walked her through the perfunctory, preliminary questions to establish her name and her relationship to the suit as a resident of HappyLiving Estates. She covered when she and Dad had moved in and how long she had been a resident, with some stories thrown into the mix to make the dry case more personal, jerk some tears and warm some hearts. Mostly for Judge Staggs's sake.

After establishing those facts of the suit giving her standing, I offered into evidence our first item: the contract itself. I went over its main terms, whether she recognized the original contract she had signed a property lease with HappyLiving (she and Dad had). Asked her to explain what it stipulated (she did). I also made it a point to hit home what she understood those terms to mean, especially its outlining of rent and other fees. I wanted to establish a baseline meeting-of-the-minds for the contract, a foundation to contract law for the agreement to be valid and enforceable.

She did and offered testimony we had gone over to put into evidence the finer points of the contract. None of which was in dispute, except for the continuation of the contract part of it. The sticking point with this suit from the get-go was always an unfortunate aspect to the suit thanks to the previous mom-and-pop owners that didn't plan for the future—and which residents couldn't have foreseen either. The contract carried a typical assignment clause, transferring the leases to new owners. However, it carried a vague change of control clause that seemed to allow for an acquiring business to terminate the contract or renegotiate the terms with an acquisition.

Since no one could have imagined the mobile home park changing hands, the residential neighborhood a staple of Mill Creek Junction for two generations, no one paid it any mind. It was a pain in my backside, that's for sure. I also didn't care for it at that moment, care for litigating it.

What I did sat in a manila folder on the plaintiff's table.

Which I went to retrieve now.

I threw a glance at the defense, and a slight grin. For Sonya Kuperov's part, she just sat scribbling on a legal pad while her phalanx of legal cronies and Gage Strauss himself stared ahead.

Until I made a show of snatching the folder.

Which drew their attention.

Including Comrade Kuperov's.

I tightened my jaw and strode toward Ma, holding up the folder and readying for the next line of questioning.

"Ms. O'Donnell, you worked for Mercy General, is that correct?"

"You know I did, Gideon," she replied.

Had to smile at that. A few others scattered about the courtroom joined with a smattering of laughter.

"Right, but the court does not." That got another round of chuckles.

She reddened some and nodded. "That is correct."

"As an accountant?"

"Right."

"Objection, Your Honor," Sonya Kuperov sounded, right on cue. "Relevance?"

I addressed Judge Staggs: "Laying foundation, Your Honor."

"For what?"

Judge Staggs hummed and nodded. "I must agree-ree. What is the relevance of bringing this information into a contract dispute?"

"Goes to a pattern of fraud—as well as the civil conspiracy charge that is connected to our class action seeking injunctive relief."

"You have got to be kidding me..." Kuperov muttered.

Judge Staggs sat back and stuck his pointer between his two front teeth, taking a breath, and a bite, with a few beats thrown in.

He overruled her, interested in the line of questioning—for now. Warned me not to drift, giving me a short leash.

I eased out a breath I hadn't known I was holding, relieved to have made it this far. Wasn't done yet, by a long shot. But this got us in the door and moving toward the finish line.

I continued, "In your role, you happened to work on an accounting project during the hospital's acquisition, isn't that right?"

"That's right, sugar," Ma replied.

Now I felt myself reddening, but I let the personalism go.

"Who was the acquiring party?"

"Perses Global Financial Group."

"I must be objecting again, Your Honor," Sonya returned—again, on cue. "What is the relevance to this suit?"

"I'm getting there, Your Honor," I replied.

"Do it quickly-lee..." Judge Staggs warned.

He overruled her and gestured for me to continue. Knew my leash was running out. I would have to hustle to my point.

"What did you discover?"

She heaved a deep breath and cast narrowed eyes toward the defense.

"I *discovered* you vultures had gone on a buying spree!"

"Objection, Your Honor," Sonya sounded, understandably.

"Sustained," Judge Staggs ruled, turning to Ma. "Please refrain from addressing the defense—and calling them vultures-tures."

Thought I caught a suppressed grin at the characterization, which did my heart glad.

I asked, "You discovered they had bought up several other properties, correct?"

"Correct," Ma replied.

"Including CareBridge Senior Living Oasis?"

"Right as rain."

"Which you sued?"

Sonya was to her feet now, the chair scraping across the floor.

"Objection! This matter has been settled out of court, with a non-disclosure agreement preventing public comment."

Now the judge frowned, turning to Ma. "Is this true-true?"

I intervened: "There was a settlement, Your Honor. I brokered it. However, she has come forward as a whistleblower seeking legally provided protection that—"

"Not in civil court!" Kuperov was quick to interject.

"That's at His Honor's discretion," I snapped back.

Judge Staggs waved a hand and sat back, taking a breath

before ruling. "For now, refrain from speaking about this previous incident, Ms. O'Donnell."

"But she wishes to violate—"

"Sustained," he interrupted, rapping his gavel. "Move along."

I did: "Ms. O'Donnell, do you recognize this document?"

She nodded. "I do."

"Your Honor, I offer Plaintiff's Exhibit 2 into evidence."

Kuperov barked, "Objection, Your Honor. Lacks foundation."

"Getting there," I replied, handing off to her a duplicate package to the one I offered Judge Staggs.

She took the copies as he overruled her, snatching his packet for a look-see. I held my breath, praying they held up, because this packet wasn't of the originals, which were in some Junction PD evidence cupboard. These were copies of the photos I'd snapped in Reggie's car.

So, yeah, it was a gamble...

"You discovered these while a resident of Dreamscape Manor, correct?"

Ma nodded. "That's right."

"You were assigned tasks for spending money in the main office, isn't that right?"

"Correct."

A breath, a beat.

Now for the tricky part, which I rhetorically massaged a bit: "And you stumbled across these documents during the course of your employment."

"Objection, Your Honor." Sonya Kuperov was on her feet again, one hand clutching those documents. "This is stolen property!"

"It is evidence of a conspiracy to defraud the public," I countered. "An exception to the exclusionary rule allows for good faith acts and whistleblowers, both of which my client falls well within."

Kuperov scoffed, stomping a foot and waving that hand clutching those documents now.

"Even then, I further object on the grounds we cannot authenticate these documents!"

I turned to her, then spun back to Judge Staggs. "Your Honor, as an officer of the court, I can confirm they are authentic."

He leaned in, brow raised with curiosity. "How so-so?"

I slipped my hand into my pocket for my Montblanc. Then took in a breath, then a beat.

Then: "Because I'm the one who took the photos of the originals."

That drew a raucous round of whispers and murmurs from behind.

Judge Staggs rapped his gavel, instructing the court to order.

Sonya Kuperov kept at her objecting: "Your Honor, these are copies of images of spreadsheets!"

I quickly moved to intercept the valid objection: "Judge, the United States Senate entered these same documents into the official record during a committee hearing uncovering the very same conspiracy to defraud the good people of Mill Creek Junction that is in question—" I turned to Kuperov "—and on trial. I'd wager that if they were good enough for the legislative branch, they should be good enough for Your Honor's courtroom."

Knew that didn't matter, whether the bar for evidentiary admission was low enough to allow these copies of copies into evidence for the purpose of the Senate hearing. All that did was whether Judge Staggs would allow them in his court.

The man leaned back and looked up, taking a beat to make a split-second decision that could help or kill the case.

And my quest for justice...

A breath, another agonizing beat.

Then: "I'll allow them."

I huffed that breath in a show of surprise. Sonya Kuperov set sail a bout of hot air herself.

She said cooly, "I am wishing to reassert my strenuous objection and note it for the record to preserve it on appeal, Your Honor."

"Noted," he said curtly. "Proceed, counsel."

I did, getting to it: "These images were from a series of original documents you took, correct?"

Ma nodded. "Right. I squirreled them away up in the air vent in my apartment at Dreamscape Manor—which you found."

Expected an objection, but received none. I plowed forward, walking her through the high points of how she had come across them—working in the office as help, stumbling across the documents on the computer, realizing what she had discovered, printing and keeping them safe to offer a public good as a good-faith whistleblower. All of which exposed her to major liability, but we'd cross that road later.

Time to get to what mattered now.

I asked, "What do these documents show?"

"Names of former residents who died under suspicious circumstances."

"Objection, Your Honor! Not only does the plaintiff lack personal knowledge and assume facts not in evidence, but the testimony is inflammatory and defamatory!"

Judge Staggs put out a hand and nodded, sustaining the objection and telling me to move the line of questioning along.

"You discovered several monetary payments were made to the relatives of these deceased residents, correct?"

Ma replied, "Correct."

"How many?"

"Don't you mean how much, sugar?"

I smiled, answering, "First, how many residents?"

"A hundred fifty-eight. That I could find…"

"Seems like a lot of incidents."

"And that was just in one year! With an important correlation."

"Correlation?" I asked, shaking my head.

"It's as Roland described." She turned to Judge Staggs. "He was my husband's caretaker. He told me—"

"Objection, hearsay," Kuperov complained.

"Sustained," the judge replied.

"Just tell me what you found," I instructed Ma.

She explained, "The fewer nurses and staff Dreamscape employed and scheduled, the more incidents there were. Just like Roland told me was going on at—"

Kuperov interrupted, "Objection, Your Honor. Again, *hearsay*, and this testimony calls for an opinion."

"An *expert* opinion," I retorted. "The numbers don't lie!"

Judge Staggs overruled the objection and I pressed: "So when Perses cut staff, patients suffered."

"Objection!" defense counsel exclaimed.

"Sustained," the judge replied.

"That's correct," Ma answered anyway before I withdrew the statement and moved on.

"How much money were families compensated?"

"At least three hundred-and-sixteen-million buckeroos. Two million per resident. Same as me."

I let that settle in the room. It did, hard.

Now for the kill.

I took a step, then another. "But payments weren't all the numbers you discovered, were they?"

Ma regarded the defense table, drawing a mama scowl I'd come to know and fear from time to time.

"No ma'am and no sir."

I drew her attention to one particular page from the evidence I'd submitted and asked her to explain it.

"It's an incident report. One of a slew of them I'd found buried in a black hole. Except the FRI numbers didn't add up to a hill of beans!"

"FRI?"

"Facility Reported Incidents. It's what these outfits must document and file when there's an adverse event with one of the patients." She cast a wicked gaze at the defense table. "I became an expert in these things when my Herb passed from negligence—"

Sonya Kuperov hissed an "Objection, Your Honor, calls for a legal conclusion," which Judge Staggs sustained and I moved on.

I asked, "Why didn't the FRI numbers add up?"

Ma smirked. "What they submitted to the government was only a quarter of the actual amounts of accidents and incidents up in that place."

"A cover-up, you're saying?"

"Objection!" Sonya predictably exclaimed. "Argumentative. Not to mention defamatory."

I threw up my hands, saying, "Withdrawn," then spun back toward my chair.

Flashing her a grin and nodding before turning back to the judge, ending my line of questioning. Ma had done exactly what I needed her to do, introducing the evidence and explaining how it revealed a systemic history of fraud and abuse.

"That will be all, Your Honor."

"You're right, son," Ma said from the witness chair in a final jab. "It *was* a cover-up."

Sonya hissed another objection, and the judge issued another sustaining ruling before offering a gentle admonishment.

Now for the hard part.

I returned to my seat. Ma went to stand when Judge Staggs gestured toward Sonya Kuperov and said it was her witness. She eased back into her chair, glancing at me.

I gave her a reassuring smile, sending up a prayer that the good Lord would steady her.

Then said one for me.

Chapter Forty-Eight

Sonya Kuperov stood and strode toward my mother, arms at her sides.

I retrieved my Montblanc, resting a hand on my legal pad while clenching the pen next to it, heart lurching forward and hammering in my head now, lungs beginning to search for breath and tongue heavy with a metallic tang as adrenaline skated through me with anticipation.

Perses's counsel didn't waste any time with her cross examination: "Your husband passed away at one of Perses Global Financial Group's senior care facilities, isn't that right, Ms. O'Donnell?"

Ma shifted. "That's right."

"CareBridge Senior Living Oasis."

"Yes."

"The medical examiner determined that blunt force trauma to the head from a fallen tree limb, compounded by hypothermia, had been the cause of death, isn't that right?"

She shifted, frowning. "So he said."

"After he wandered outside into the mid-winter evening?"

"No ma'am and no sir! He died from your *negligence* after you failed to keep an eye on my husband with d'mencha and—"

"Objection, Your Honor," Kuperov interrupted.

"Ms. O'Donnell," Judge Staggs interjected, "as I said, you are not to comment on legal findings, like negligence. Just answer the questions you are asked. Yes or no answers only-lee, please. No editorializing."

"But I *was* answering the question!" she protested. "And it's true!"

Had to smile at that.

He cleared his throat. "Let me be the judge of that. After all, it is my first name."

Staggs chuckled before letting it die in a show of self-conscious embarrassment. He gestured for Kuperov to proceed.

She said, "As I was saying, Ms. O'Donnell, your husband walked out into a frigid, rainy night and tragically passed away, isn't that right?"

Ma flashed crimson, and she merely replied with a curt nod.

Judge Staggs instructed her to answer yes or no, and Ma replied in the affirmative.

Kuperov stepped toward the witness box, resting a hand on the railing. "How did that make you feel?"

I stood and said, "Objection, Your Honor. Her feelings aren't relevant to this case."

"Goes to motive," she replied.

Judge Staggs hesitated, then nodded. "I'll allow it."

"Your Honor!" I exclaimed.

"I'll allow it-it," he reiterated, voice rising.

I frowned and sat, locking eyes with Ma.

Kuperov stepped in front of my field of vision, saying, "Do you need the question repeated?"

Ma replied, "No, I remember it just fine, thank you very

much. As to how it made me feel, I felt cheated! Robbed of my Herb."

"Angry? Like you wanted revenge?"

"You betch your sweet bippy I did!"

Not good Gideon Paul...

I was to my feet in an instant: "Objection, Your Honor. She's badgering my witness."

Kuperov spun to me. "No, I am questioning *your* witness."

"By suggesting she had hatched some revenge plot?"

"Just because you don't like her answer doesn't give you cause to object!"

"Alright-right you two-two," Judge Staggs stuttered, reining us in with the rapping of his gavel.

Then the unexpected: "Overruled."

"Are you kidding me?" I blurted.

Staggs jutted his head out toward me, eyes wide like a beetle. "You heard me-me. Overruled, counsel. Now sit *down!*"

I hesitated, but relented, slumping in my chair.

Sonya Kuperov continued, "Did you want revenge, Ms. O'Donnell?"

For Ma's part, she took a breath before shifting and taking a moment. Thank the Lord...

"Nope. Justice," she replied.

Kuperov laughed. "Is that why you faked your dementia and stole yourself into Dreamscape Manor?"

I gasped, stealing Ma's line: What the what?

"All to hack into our system, steal our private and privileged work product, in order to manufacture a story and frame us for some concocted storyline—"

"Objection, Your Honor!" I finally interrupted, recovering from the surprising turn.

"You're the fraud, isn't that right, Ms. O'Donnell?"

I pounded a fist into my legal pad. "This is an outrageous accusation, Staggs!"

"*Excuse* me-me?" the judge roared, whipping his outstretched gavel toward me.

I caught myself, far too late, addressing His Honor in that way.

I swallowed—back my rage as much as my pride—then apologized. Before I could renew my objection, he dismissed me and instructed defense counsel to dial it back and ask a question.

So she did: "Is it true you came to Dreamscape Manor under the false pretense of having dementia?"

How the heck she knew that...*could* know that—I flat didn't have a clue. Maybe Sammy and Kelsey had figured it out? Would make the most sense. The pair were awaiting trial, no doubt represented by lawyers tied to Perses.

Regardless of the how—the *what* was flat bad news.

Because now Ma was the one with conspiratorial designs. With intention behind her actions. Premeditation. Would throw serious shade on our public-good defense for her whistle-blowing...

"Answer the question, Ms. O'Donnell," Judge Staggs instructed.

She looked at me, mouth wide and eyes wider, searching for direction.

I gave it, nodding her onward with a frown. Should have seen this coming, and prepared her for it.

"Yes, that is true," Ma said softly.

"What was that?" Sonya said, cupping a hand to her ear for dramatic effect.

I wanted to puke, and object, but didn't, knowing I was on the ropes.

She cleared her throat and affirmed her answer more loudly.

"So you lied on your application?" Kuperov said. "The *contract* you signed with Dreamscape Manor—" She turned to me now, one end of her mouth curling upward with an addition: "With your son as a co-signing conservator, in fact..."

The revelation was more a statement of fact than a question. One that sent a ping of anxious dread blooming in my stomach.

"Yes," Ma answered.

"Which means you made false claims in your lease agreement, isn't that right?"

"I suppose so."

"With the intent to come to Dreamscape Manor and hack into our systems and steal our informational property and defraud—"

"I did not hack into anything!" Ma protested with interruption.

Sonya crossed her arms. "But you did access our secure property, did you not?"

"I was *given* access!"

"Not to those files, though, right?"

Ma huffed a sigh, agreeing she hadn't been given that access.

"Truth is, you don't know what you downloaded."

"I know numbers when I see 'em," Ma insisted. "And yours don't add up to a hill of beans!"

"Move to strike, Your Honor."

Judge Staggs took a beat to consider her objection, but shook his head.

"I'll allow it. Ms. O'Donnell has testified she has a professional background as an accountant, making her testimony expert testimony before this court."

"Your Honor...I must—"

"Next question," he snapped back.

Had to smile at that. Go Judge Staggs!

Sonya Kuperov let her arms drop and said she had no further questions before slinking back to her seat. She had done her job, and her damage, painting Ma as the perpetrator of a conspiracy to defraud Perses. It wasn't even in dispute she had taken the documents. But now the motive and intent was out there, something Judge Staggs would have to contend with in his ruling.

"Goodie! Your redirect, counsel," the judge instructed me.

I replied, "We're done with this witness, Your Honor."

Nothing more to add or take away, and I didn't want to give defense counsel any more opportunity to redirect herself.

Judge Staggs turned to Ma. "Very well, you are dismissed, Ms. O'Donnell."

She stood and carefully stepped out from the witness box. Looking defeated, with eyes cast to the floor, hands clenched at her waist. She returned to our table and slumped in her seat.

I took her hand and gave it a squeeze of solidarity, throwing her a reassuring smile.

"Call your next witness, counsel," the judge instructed.

Ma was the easiest play of the morning.

This next one could get dicey.

Spinning around, I motioned for Johnny to join me at our plaintiff's table. He hustled down the aisle, Judge Staggs clearing his throat as the seconds ticked by.

"Are we ready?" I asked in a rushing whisper.

"We're ready," Johnny reassured.

"Because we need this to be solid."

"It's solid."

"In the bag?"

"Tick-tock, tick-tock, counsel," Judge Staggs complained from the bench.

I turned toward him. "Apologies, Your Honor. Another few minutes?"

He rapped a pointer against his faded Seiko with a scowl. "How about another few *seconds*?"

I nodded and returned to Johnny with searching is-this-a-sure-thing eyes, whispering a *"Well?"* for reassurance.

Johnny threw up a thumbs-up and said our witness was ready, waiting in the lobby. I told him to play fetch.

Then readied my Hail Mary.

Johnny clattered down the aisle and the doors creaked open while whispers were exchanged at my left and behind and joined by a loud throat-clearing from the bench.

Standing, I announced, "The plaintiffs call Gerald Peterson to the stand."

A gasp, then a chorus of them, then the predictable.

"Objection, Your Honor!" Sonya Kuperov exclaimed.

I smirked. "Why? Because he's inconvenient?"

"Unfair surprise, that's why," she hissed.

"Approach-proach," Judge Staggs said, wiggling his fingers at us before motioning for us to come hither.

I explained, "We only just learned of his importance to our case recently."

"What a load of crock!" Sonya Kuperov retorted.

"It's true. You saw me with my private investigator."

Just thought of that one on the fly. A minor fib. One neither she nor the judge would know was true—or false.

Judge Staggs leaned in, jutting that oversized head of his with those buggish eyes toward me. He did not look amused.

"I don't like this, counsel. Not one bit-bit."

"I understand. I wouldn't have either." Figured a bit of self-identifying empathy would do some good. Along with: "I apologize, counsel. And, judge, I assure you the witness is relevant to the suit."

Kuperov scoffed. "Your Honor—"

Staggs put up a hand and said he would allow the witness, shooing us away and gaveling his ruling and the court back into motion.

Time for the big-time fireworks.

Chapter Forty-Nine

A commotion near the back of the chamber indicated the man had appeared.

There he was. Councilman Gerald Peterson. Black hair streaked by silver, all slicked and shining under the lights. Black suit crisp and fitted and expensive looking, wearing a starched white dress shirt and a traditional regimental tie, simple diagonal bars of red and blue divided by thin gold lines.

The man strode down the aisle amidst a refrain of hushed whispers and gasping cries and pointing fingers, Johnny trailing with a nodding grin. The bailiff ushered him to the witness chair, and he was sworn in.

I wasted no time: "Please state your name for the record."

"Gerald Edward Peterson."

"What is your occupation?"

"City councilman, for the town of Mill Creek Junction."

Before proceeding to the next question, I looked back to Johnny, extending a hand and a questioning look.

He retrieved from a briefcase a familiar manila envelope with a nod, handing it off to Reggie. That man deserved a raise!

I turned back to Peterson: "Can you identify something for me?"

I retrieved from my partner two paper-clipped bundles of papers, yellow highlighter racing across the pages in neat lines. I handed one off to Sonya Kuperov, who snatched it with a scowl, before handing the other to the bailiff, who handed it to Judge Staggs.

"Your Honor, I offer Plaintiff's Exhibit 3 into evidence."

Kuperov scoffed. "I thought you said you were just being made aware of this witness."

"I was."

She held up the papers. "Then what is this?"

I shrugged. "Evidence."

Loud throat-clearing drew our attention to the front. Where Judge Staggs sat frowning. "How about you address me-me instead of each other, hmm?"

She did, formally objecting. Which led to Judge Staggs asking us to approach him again before asking me what was going on.

I explained, "Exhibit 3 contains bank statements, which we just received this morning making us aware of this witness's connection to our amended civil conspiracy claim that also shows a pattern of fraud and corruption to bolster our original injunctive relief claim."

"Your Honor," Kuperov replied, "this is unfair surprise. Plain and simple."

"Come on! What part of 'we just received this morning' and 'were just made aware of this witness's connection'—"

"Don't lecture me!"

"Alright, alright-right," Judge Staggs bellowed, waving his

arms around and shooing us back from the bench. "I'll allow the exhibit and witness. Overruled, counsel."

For her part, Kuperov kept her mouth shut, but her clomping clickety-clacking said all she needed to say.

She was not a happy comrade.

I got to it, and got into it, straight away: "Do you know the defense, Gage Strauss?"

Peterson regarded the table where Sonya Kuperov and company were sitting.

Then replied, "I do."

"HappyLiving and Perses Global Financial Group, you're aware of them?"

"Yes."

"In what capacity."

"I helped broker a deal between HappyLiving and the City Council to allow for their sale to Perses."

I went for another question when a psst caught my attention. From behind.

Reggie held out a piece of paper and shook it with take-this eyes.

I hustled to him and snatched it.

There was a question I didn't get, along with an instruction about Junction lease agreements, but quickly asked before Judge Staggs got his Jockey's in a bunch.

"And why would they need their approval?"

"A provision in the zoning code of Mill Creek Junction, going back generations, requires a majority approval for such an acquisition. A regulatory thing or some small-town law."

That sparked another question: "Along with a change in lease agreements under such acquisitions?"

He nodded. "That's right. We, the City Council, approved the change in a closed-door session."

That sure got a rise out of the courtroom, which Staggs quickly tamped down with his gavel.

I stepped forward, going in for the kill. "Now, by brokered, you mean you were part of a quid-pro-quo bribery scheme involving the defense, acting as a financial conduit for payoffs that exchanged money for votes, isn't that right?"

No objection came. None could.

Peterson shifted. "That's right."

A flurry of whispered I-can't-believe-it gasps raced through the courtroom.

I continued, "How did this scheme come about?"

He pointed at Sonya Kuperov. "She approached me."

I followed his arm. "Let the record reflect Councilman Peterson identified defense counsel."

Her lily face was a rageful red now. But what could she do? Caught as red-handed as her face shown crimson.

"Now, Perses paid you a lot of money," I went on, "with the express instruction to pass along thousands of dollars through to City Council members."

"That's right," he replied.

"For not only HappyLiving, but also for several more properties all across Mill Creek Junction, isn't that right?"

"Yes."

"Junction staples, right—Dreamscape Manor and Smiles Dentistry, even Jed Warner's farmland?"

"Correct."

Another grumbly rise threaded its way through the courtroom. Junctioneers sure weren't happy with that revelation! Must've felt like they were bit players in a WeFlix legal thriller. I knew I sure did.

There was one more play here, one more detail to the story I needed to get into the record to bolster my storyline and fraud claim.

So I went for it: "And your wife found out about it, didn't she?"

Deer-in-headlights eyes flashed my way before seeking the judge for direction. Didn't know what he expected to find. Neither did Judge Staggs, who instructed him to answer the question.

Swallowing, he did: "That's right."

Now for the thing that would seal the deal.

"Then you killed her because of it."

A choking rasp gripped Peterson, the man's mouth opening and closing like the lake trout Dad and me had fished from Lake Michigan. No words came.

I stepped toward him, locking eyes with those deer eyes, putting up an interruptive hand then actually interrupting him before he replied.

"Let me remind you, Councilman, you're under oath."

"Objection, Your Honor, badgering," Kuperov sounded from behind.

I scoffed, turning toward her. "He's my witness! Who I also want to remind cannot be retried or convicted for previous crimes he's been acquitted from."

"Objection, argumentative!"

Judge Staggs didn't seem to know how to rule, his eyes snapping from Kuperov to me and back-and-forth again before overruling both objections and instructing me to get on with it.

I nodded, suppressing a smile—and giddy glee.

I'd laid this trap on purpose. It was risky, because while I technically wasn't his attorney any longer, there was grayness around whether my knowledge of his crime was privileged. And what I'd said was true: He could no longer be tried or convicted for the murder of his wife, given double jeopardy. Still...

Regardless, it flat didn't matter, not in the slightest. Not when Ma was concerned. And the question would strengthen the veracity of his testimony—that he went to such heinous lengths to conceal what he had been doing.

Acting as a conduit of kickbacks between Perses Global Financial Group and Mill Creek Junction City Council.

"Answer the question, Mr. Peterson," the judge instructed.

The man's face suddenly steeled itself. Jaw clenched tight, eyes narrowed, face raged crimson.

Until: "Yes. I did."

"Because she was going to blow the lid on your operation."

"Yes."

"That you had been the conduit for Perses's influence peddling scheme."

"Objection, Your Honor, argumentative," Kuperov barked.

"Overruled," Judge Staggs replied.

"Isn't that right?" I asked Peterson.

"Yes," was all he said again.

It hit me, in that moment, that my last case, the one on the wrong side of justice, would be what clinched a just verdict this go around. Flat didn't know what to think of that.

"Nothing further, Your Honor," I said, then returned to my chair.

Judge Staggs passed Peterson off to Sonya Kuperov for questioning. Took a beat for her to respond, but she said they had no questions. How could they? They were caught, red-handed.

Which led me back to my feet to do the last thing.

To make the final play.

"Your Honor, at this time we move for a directed verdict."

"*What?* This is preposterous!" Kuperov roared, bolting to her feet.

"It isn't. The evidence is overwhelming, compelling, totalizing—"

"Any more inflammatory words you'd like to throw into your word salad?"

"We have the right to make the request in light of this damning testimony. Your Honor, it's clear Perses breached their contract, aided and abetted by a bribery conspiracy at the highest levels of city government. We ask for injunctive relief, requiring HappyLiving to honor their original contracts."

"I agree," Judge Staggs said, without missing a beat.

It happened so fast I didn't know whether I'd heard him right.

So much so that I uttered an "Excuse me?" before the judge went on.

"I find there is sufficient cause for a breach of contract finding."

"Your Honor..." Sonya started—without being able to finish.

"I'm not finished, Ms. Kuperov," Judge Staggs snapped. "I also find sufficient cause for a finding of conspiracy to defraud—not only the residents of HappyLiving, but also Mill Creek Junction. Not only do I rule in favor of freezing rents at their contractual rates. I agree to their punitive claim, imposing the fine of $2 million per class member. Furthermore—"

Gasps and cheers and can-it-be-trues interrupted the judge!

He quickly gaveled and ordered the court to order. It did, after a minute.

"Furthermore, I am issuing a stay of any further real property acquisitions on the part of Perses Global Financial Group within Junction city limits and ordering a review of the legality of pending and previous purchases in light of evidence proffered by Councilman Peterson."

With the rap of his gavel, Judge Staggs proclaimed, "So ordered!"

And that was that.

I found myself sliding into my chair in a relieved slump, relieved but also flat drained. I'd pulled it off—*we'd* pulled it off, all of us, my team, my partners. Most of all, the one person who mattered most.

As the room continued its eruption, and those partners gripped my shoulders in shows of congratulatory celebration, I couldn't help but fill with pride at what Ma had accomplished. I also let my eyes fill with a dose of marveling emotion at the thought. Knew this wasn't the end of the road, that Perses would surely appeal, and there could be fallout for Ma. But for now, for this moment, I basked in what we had done.

Ma gripped my hand. Eyes filled with the same emotion even as her face beamed with—was that relief, joy, pride even?

"You did it, Gideon." She laughed with the same marvel and clenched my hand tighter. "You done did it, my boy..."

"No, Ma," I corrected, throat tightening. "*You* did."

"*We* did, then." She gave me don't-mess eyes, and I just smiled and nodded.

Johnny leaned in, a hand clenched on my shoulder. "Don't argue with her, kid."

I didn't. Learned years ago Mama was always right, always *in* the right. And now, for the first time in a long while, so was I.

I was on the right side of justice. In the right with my legal fights, fighting for a righteous cause instead of merely a not guilty verdict. I liked how I felt about that, about myself.

I planned on keeping it that way.

Epilogue
The Next Day

Fifty-two years.

That's what it would have been today. Eatin' and dancin'. Not drinkin' mind you. Florence and Herb had given up Grandpa's cough medicine decades ago, on account of both their mama's having had a bad run in with alcohol, in different ways.

But eat and dance—*oo-wee* they'da been slinging bites into their mouths and swinging their hips till the wee hours of the mornin'!

Instead, the woman in her black Sunday best and wide-brim lavender hat and her son, Gideon, and some of his friends, were gathered around her husband's grave, remembering the man and mourning his loss. But also celebrating his brand-spankin' new resurrection-life with his Lord and Savior, Jesus Christ—along with their win.

Gideon done did his daddy proud, and his mama! A win that was overshadowed by the anniversary of Herb's passin' and buryin', a real shame considering what he had pulled off in court for HappyLiving residents. But the boy had insisted and persisted with his suggestion that they visit Herb's grave on the anniversary of his death. Hadn't even realized it had been creepin' up on her, the day after trial, which was fitting.

The Lawd Almighty sure does work in mysterious ways.

So there they were, she and Gideon, Reginald and Elizabeth and the P.I.—the five of them standing around that cursed plot of soil as Lake Michigan rained the funk down on them in sheets of frigid disregard. The snow had really piled all around. The sight of all the white stuff instantly snapped her back to that moment two years ago.

Didn't have time to pay it any mind, because Gideon's friend, his private eye—he called him Johnny Pope—launched into a reception of a familiar psalm.

Psalm 23.

"The Lord is my shepherd," the former priest intoned, "I shall not want."

Which sparked a memory.

From when she had watched her Herb get lowered down into the belly of God's green earth.

"THE LORD IS MY SHEPHERD; I SHALL NOT WANT," THE REV intoned, our pastor from Mill Creek Junction Baptist, going on forty years now.

Dabbing my eyes, I smiled. 'Twas Herb's favorite psalm. Had it memorized, in fact, reciting it as a prayer before his feet touched the floor after waking from a night of sleep. Sometimes I'd hear him muttering those words. Awakened, actually, from a deep slumber too.

Herb had been an early riser. 'The early worm catches the fish!' he'd always say. Then I'd go, 'No, it's the early bird catches the worm! And besides, worms don't catch fish. Fishermen catch fish!' Then he'd go 'Same difference!' And I'd roll my eyes and huff a sigh, and turn over, reaching for some imprecatory prayer that would summon the Lawd Almighty to snatch his breath or send down a bolt of lightning to take him out.

Now that memory just made me sad. Especially calling down lightning on Herb.

"He maketh me to lie down in green pastures: he leadeth me beside the still waters."

Leadeth me beside the still waters...Now that was a strange irony, considering Herb had led himself to those cursed Lake Michigan waters that had froze his skinny backside stiff.

A tremor took over my lower lip at the thought.

"Surely goodness and mercy shall follow me all the days of my life: and I will dwell in the house of the Lord for ever. Amen," the Rev concluded.

"Amen," I mumbled, not sure about that last stanza.

Surely goodness and mercy shall follow me all the days of my life...

For real?

Where was the good in Herb's neglect? His murder?

Piss-poor gears threw up a chirping squeak, drawing my attention to that wretched jaw of blackness.

Which was eating Herb whole!

The pallbearers were lowering my husband down into the belly of the Lawd Almighty's green earth. Or rather, snow-covered earth, the white stuff whirlin' and twirlin' and pilin' to beat the band!

That final refrain clanged around inside my noggin again.

Surely goodness and mercy shall follow me all the days of my life...

A coldness swept through me at that line from that psalm clamoring for my attention. Not from the frigid wind that blew, all around, but from the frigid fright that needled my noggin!

I had been a believer my whole life. Born and bred, raised and baptized, then wedded and now awaiting the same blessed promise of eternal life as Herb. Today I wasn't sure I could muster up enough belief to carry me through.

Sure, justice prevailed, 'running down as waters, and righteousness as a mighty stream.' Could thank the prophet Amos for that daily bread crumb of divine promise.

If'n you call a check justice, a righteous judgment upon Perses Global Financial Group. Flat not sure about that one.

And yet—

And yet I know the Good Book has something else to say about it all: "'Vengeance is Mine, I will repay,' says the Lord."

Damn straight.

So while I mourn, while I rage at what that faceless equity firm took from me, I'd take comfort in what they've got coming.

"Amen," JP said, crossing himself.

Florence Gail O'Donnell grinned in the splash of winter sunlight slicing through the snowy onslaught. Not only because of the Scripture but because—*oo-wee!* did Perses get what they'd got coming or what?

Sniffing caught her attention, from her right.

It was Gideon, batting away emotion from his eyes. Which she smiled at. Never was one to shed a tear, that boy was. Stuffed his emotions down deep, he did. Had always wondered whether it was from some deep-seated, subconscious trauma from having been abandoned at the Mill Creek Junction fire station. Perhaps a wound marking his itty-bitty baby soul from his birth mama leaving him behind.

He recovered, and the party began to break up. But not before her son snagged JP for a chit-chat.

"How'd you do it?" Gideon asked his private eye. Who, she was not ashamed to admit (to herself, of course; Herb was dead and gone but Gideon woulda choked if'n he'd knew what she was thinking) that the bald Boomer was quite the looker.

The man looked at him, brow furrowed.

"How'd I do what?"

"Get Gerald Peterson to testify? Basically cop to multiple felonies?"

Now he laughed, shaking his head and looking off into the gray sky that had closed back up again. From the sun, not the snow.

He stood that way, for the longest time, a weak smile playing across his mouth.

Until: "Let's just say I found something far more painful from his past than testifying to what he'd done."

Gideon leaned back some, eyeing JP. Then he let it go. Must've figured it was best to let it alone.

"Besides," JP said, slapping Gideon on the back, "I promised him you'd represent him. Get the FBI or IRS or whatever to drop their charges with his cooperation in one of the largest corruption schemes to strike the Midwest!"

"Gee, thanks."

"I do what I can."

Had to smile at that. And she did. Florence Gail O'Donnell sure did like this cat.

And the others, all of them. Reginald Wilson, Elizabeth Seward. And, of course, Gideon Paul O'Donnell. They'd all done what she'd been praying for the past two years.

They'd gotten justice for her Herb.

Particularly the scruffy fella with the bald head...

Florence recalled a man about his height and weight and look about him coming to call on her while she was strapped to that gurney, drugged up and wires strung out from her like one of them old-school telephone poles.

Her knight in shining armor, come to rescue her from those two communists who'd snatched her in the dead of night.

She regarded the grave, the place where Herb lay resting.

Nope. No ma'am and no sir! She knew better.

He was resting at the feet of Jesus Christ himself.

Given that dynamic, Herb up in some other dimension, awaiting his resurrection, she figured he'd be good with the next thing.

Florence snatched JP's arm, slipping her's in his and asking him to take her home.

A glance at Gideon, which actually got a nod, and they were off.

Perhaps into the next chapter of her life.

Author's Note

Thanks for coming along for Gideon O'Donnell's ride. And quite the ride it was! As with most of my novels, I like to offer a bit of insight into the story, especially the factual aspects behind the story.

First up: the characters and series itself.

An insightful reader might find shades of another legal drama, at least in the characters, and the mavericky, bootstrapping-it nature of our hero, Gideon O'Donnell. He and his escapades were inspired by a childhood (and later adulthood) television show from the late-1990s I've rewatched several times: David E. Kelley's *The Practice*. Gideon O'Donnell is a nod to Bobby Donnell. Same for Reggie (Eugene) and Lizzy (Lindsay). Like this cast of characters, they were also renegade lawyers with their own sense of justice. The most obvious homage was a moment in Chapter 13, the monkey story, which was inspired by an episode that clearly stuck around inside my noggin. I changed some details, but its color still shaded my version.

Mill Creek Junction came about during (of all things) the

Great Pandemic. I had just turned forty two weeks into lockdown (yeah, that was a swell birthday!) and signed up for a short-story-a-week writing challenge. I'd been kicking around the idea of creating a fictional smallish town in West Michigan for several months, thinking it could be a fun way to tell the stories of real people living life while exploring faith, taking a page out of Stephen King's playbook with Castle Rock, Maine, and John Grisham's Clanton, Mississippi. Figured this was a good way to use all that time on my hands.

Thus was born my fictional small town.

Since then, I've written thirty-plus short stories so far, two previous novels from two separate series, and now this one. I plan to write many more stories in my favorite Midwest town.

Now to the heart of the story.

Most of the stories I tell are rooted in some form of realty. There's a larger theme to life going on beneath the story surface. Same for this one, which arose from a book I read in the summer of 2023, called *Plunder: Private Equity's Plan to Pillage America* (New York: PublicAffairs, 2023), by Brendan Ballou. It is a fascinating read on how one sector of the economy has managed to muscle its way into many facets of our economic life, and beyond.

Much of Chapter 43 is rooted in the facts of this book, especially the story about ManorCare (Chapter 4 of *Plunder*) the author recounted in a sad chapter on the state of nursing homes, inspiring Dreamscape Manor and CareBridge Oasis. HappyLiving Estates's actions that led to Gideon's class action lawsuit were likewise drawn from and inspired by Chapter 2 of *Plunder*, inspiring the details of Chapters 10 and 11.

Nursing homes and mobile homes are particularly meaningful to me: my early years were spent in the latter, my nonagenarian grandfather has been living in the other for years. Both experiences, I should add, are nothing like what this book describes. However, after reading *Plunder*, I wondered what they might have been like in the hands of private equity firms who seem to care more about wringing pennies from their conquests than caring for the people their investments are meant to serve.

In this story, I hoped to draw a stark contrast between Florence and Herb O'Donnell's frugality for the sake of using money to love their neighbor and Perses Global Financial Group's cutthroat capitalism for the sake of padding their bottom line. Yes, not all private equity firms (or mobile home parks and nursing homes, for that matter) are the sort of vultures Jayce Robinson describes. I do wonder, however, about these businesses: Why do they exist; what's their point? Is it to provide families jobs and income and solid a middle-class life, to facilitate thriving communities with middle-class amenities, to contribute in some way to economic stability and national progress? Or is their sole objective to make money, for themselves, their shareholders, their investors?

Sure, I'm probably oversimplifying and erecting a bit of a straw man with Perses. However, my fictional firm (which is named after the god of destruction) does reflect much of the operational nature exposed by Ballou in *Plunder*. And, again, what my characters endured, especially Florence and Mill Creek Junction, reflects what thousands have experienced thanks to these large financial firms.

I'm not suggesting making money, even a return on your investment, is evil. However, I do believe someone said something about our inability to serve both God and Money (Matthew 6:24). Dueling masters will force us to do wicked things, forsaking the Way of the One for the ways of the other, resulting in chaos, unlove, even death. Not a sermon, just a thought. One I hope was sparked by some of what my characters endured.

Author's Note

As for the legal and medical side of things—remember: this is fiction. I tried my writerly best, leveraging my (limited) legal experience working in politics and research gumshoeing to be as accurate as possible with the ways of Lady Justice and her handlers. I'll appreciate the grace and understanding if some of those procedures felt more like *Law & Order* (or, I suppose, *The Practice*) than the orderly unfolding of the law itself. Again: fiction!

Same for the cognitive behavior side of the story, which Doc Dolph did a bang-up job of explaining. His insights into how someone might fake the mental bug (as Florence O'Donnell called dementia) is accurate as far as it goes, as well as how one might detect such subterfuge. There have been cases when someone has (unethically) playacted cognitive decline in this way, and I thought it would make for an interesting way for Florence to avenge her husband's negligent death—the motive for the whole legal drama to begin with.

Thank you again, Dear Reader, for joining me on another adventure. I trust it was an entertaining ride, along with an insightful, inspiring one. Look for Gideon O'Donnell to tackle more impossible legal situations as a renegade small-town lawyer soon. I certainly look forward to seeing how he will use his newfound passion for fighting the good fight for justice.

One story at a time.

Explore More of Mill Creek Junction

Welcome to a new story world inspired by such fictional towns as John Grisham's Clanton, Mississippi, and Stephen King's Castle Rock, Maine.

Get to know this world one character, one setting, one event and situation at a time. You're sure to find some of your own story in theirs, while being entertained and inspired for the journey.

Visit www.millcreekjunction.com for more about the story world and a list of stories, following people living life and exploring faith.

Get Your Free Thriller

Building a relationship with my readers is one of my all-time favorite joys of writing! Once in a while I like to send out a newsletter with giveaways, free stories, pre-release content, updates on new books, and other bits on my stories.

Join my insider's group for updates, giveaways, and your free novel—a full-length action-adventure story in my *Order of Thaddeus* thriller series. Just tell me where to send it.

Follow this link to subscribe:
www.jabouma.com/free

Also by J. A. Bouma

Nobody should have to read bad religious fiction—whether it's cheesy plots with pat answers or misrepresentations of the Christian faith and the Bible. So J. A. Bouma tells compelling, propulsive stories that thrill as much as inspire, offering a dose of insight along the way.

Order of Thaddeus **Action-Adventure Thriller Series**

Holy Shroud • Book 1

The Thirteenth Apostle • Book 2

Hidden Covenant • Book 3

American God • Book 4

Grail of Power • Book 5

Templars Rising • Book 6

Rite of Darkness • Book 7

Gospel Zero • Book 8

The Emperor's Code • Book 9

Deadly Hope • Book 10

Fallen Ones • Book 11

The Eden Legacy • Book 12

End of Days • Book 13

Silas Grey Collection 1 (Books 1-3)

Silas Grey Collection 2 (Books 4-6)

Silas Grey Collection 3 (Books 7-9)

Backstories: Short Story Collection 1

Martyrs Bones: Short Story Collection 2

***Group X Cases* Supernatural Suspense Series**

Not of This World • Book 1

The Darkest Valley • Book 2

Against These Powers • Book 3

Deliver Us From Evil • Book 4

Luck Be the Ladies • Novelette

***End Times Chronicles* Sci-Fi Apocalyptic Series**

Apostasy Rising / Season 1, Episode 1

Apostasy Rising / Season 1, Episode 2

Apostasy Rising / Season 1, Episode 3

Apostasy Rising / Season 1, Episode 4

Apocalypse Rising / Season 2, Episode 1

Apocalypse Rising / Season 2, Episode 2

Apocalypse Rising / Season 2, Episode 3

Apocalypse Rising / Season 2, Episode 4

Antichrist Rising / Season 3, Episode 1

Antichrist Rising / Season 3, Episode 2

Antichrist Rising / Season 3, Episode 3

Antichrist Rising / Season 3, Episode 4

***Faith Reimagined* Spiritual Coming-of-Age Series**

A Reimagined Faith • Book 1

A Rediscovered Faith • Book 2

A Refined Faith • Book 3

Find all of my latest book releases at: www.jabouma.com

About the Author

J. A. Bouma believes nobody should have to read bad religious fiction—whether it's cheesy plots with pat answers or misrepresentations of the Christian faith and the Bible. So he wants to do something about it by telling compelling, propulsive stories that thrill as much as inspire, while offering a dose of insight along the way.

An award-nominated bestselling author of over sixty religious fiction and nonfiction books, he blends a love for ideas and adventure, exploration and discovery, thrill and thought. With graduate degrees in ministry and theology, and armed with a voracious appetite for most mainstream genres, he tells stories you'll read with abandon and recommend with pride—exploring the tension of faith and doubt, spirituality and culture, belief and practice, and the gritty drama that is our collective pilgrim story.

When not putting fingers to keyboard, he loves vintage jazz vinyl, a glass of Malbec, and an epic read—preferably together. He lives in Grand Rapids with his wife, two kiddos, and rambunctious boxer-pug-terrier.

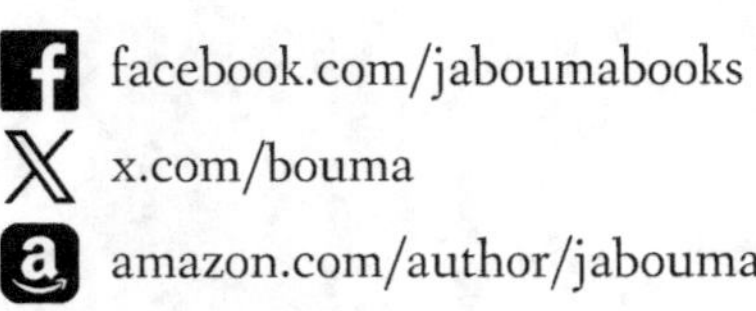

www.ingramcontent.com/pod-product-compliance
Lightning Source LLC
Chambersburg PA
CBHW070228200726
48293CB00005B/1527